A Bounty with Strings

Markus Matthews

Tellwell Talent
www.tellwell.ca

ISBN
978-0-2288-1914-1 (Hardcover)
978-0-2288-1912-7 (Paperback)
978-0-2288-1913-4 (eBook)

To my wife, Kathy:
Without her love, patience, and understanding,
this book wouldn't have been possible.

And to Sven, the pool boy,
who my wife assured me helped her immensely
during the writing of this book …
even though we don't own a pool.

Chapter 1

Friday, February 9

The wailing police sirens were closing on my current position and would be here in seconds. I looked around at the charred and blackened sidewalk, the thick dark smoke that was pouring out of the jagged hole in the red Canada Post mailbox, the smashed plateglass window of the Bank of Montreal, and the unconscious leprechaun suspended ten feet in the air beside me, and sighed. This day definitely hadn't gone as planned. The carnage around me looked like something out of a war-torn country, not something you'd expected to see in Hamilton, Ontario.

I reached for my wallet and gritted my teeth at the pain radiating from my right hip—getting hammered by a wooden Irish club also hadn't been part of the plan. On the upside, the leprechaun had been aiming for my nuts with his glossy black shillelagh, so taking it off the hip wasn't as bad as it could have been. Hell, judging by how badly the hip was stiffening up and bruising, if he had nailed me where he'd been aiming, he would have crippled me.

As I fished out my wallet, the dark-grey clouds that had been looming all day finally released the snow that everyone had been dreading. I flipped open my wallet so my Hero ID was clearly showing and lifted my hands in the air to look as benign as possible. I was probably being overly cautious—most Hamilton cops knew me—but with my luck, the first on the scene would be some keen, hyped-up rookie who didn't.

The crowd of onlookers were thankfully staying well back on the opposite sidewalk, gawking and snapping pictures with their phones. I was sure there would be a few new YouTube videos posted with the title "The Hamilton Hurricane Returns." It had been six years since I'd actively patrolled over the city as the Hamilton Hurricane, but I still had a lot of loyal fans. I was proud of the ten years I'd spent using my elemental Air and Lightning powers to protect Hamilton from superpowered villains, normal criminals, fires, and natural disasters, but being a hero didn't pay the bills. Now I was just Zack Stevens,

Bounty Hunter. I spent my days taking down monsters for money. (I'm not supposed to use the term "monsters," so technically, they should be "Enhanced Individuals" so as to not offend anyone.)

A black-and-white cruiser braked hard in front of me and slid a few inches on the grey-brown slush covering the road before coming to a stop. My day instantly got better at the sight of smiling dark-haired Sergeant Robert Quinn emerging from the cruiser. I waved at him and put my ID away.

Rob was one of the good guys and one of my closest friends. We were the same age at thirty-three years old, but that was one of the very few things we had in common. He was charismatic and outgoing and always seemed to find the brighter side of things. Me, not so much. Physically, he was a good three inches taller than me at his six-foot, one-inch height. I'd put him about ten pounds heavier than my 190 pounds, but thanks to serious cycling and a swimming routine, he was all muscle. He had the body of a Greek god, whereas I was more like the cook at a greasy Greek takeout place. The spandex costume I used to wear back in my Hamilton Hurricane days wouldn't be a good look for me now.

Rob's face mirrored his body. He had a chiseled chin, beaming smile, deep-brown eyes, and thick, glossy black hair that was always styled to perfection. His nose was a little crooked, though. It had been broken during his rookie days on the force and hadn't set quite right before it healed; that flaw actually worked for him, though, as it gave his face real character. My looks would be described as average and boring at best. I had dull-brown hair that had enough curl to it to stick out in an annoyingly random lopsided fashion, so I tended to keep it short to avoid that happening. I, too, had brown eyes, but rather than being the deep pools that Rob's were, mine were a lighter brown, common and unremarkable.

In short, Rob looked like he had stepped off the cover of *GQ*; I was more suited for the cover of something like *Accountants Quarterly*.

Normally, I would have hated someone that good-looking on general principle, but under those sickeningly good looks was a caring, funny, and all-around decent human being you couldn't help but like.

Rob closed the distance between us as his keen eyes surveyed the area. His gaze lingered on the big black mark on the sidewalk where the snow had been melted away, the smoldering mailbox I'd fired on, the shattered glass in front of the bank, and the unconscious ninja-attired leprechaun hanging in the air. He shook his head in amusement.

Rob stepped in front of me and said, "I'm guessing this takedown didn't go according to plan."

"It was going great until one of my fans yelled, 'Hey, look, it's the Hamilton Hurricane,' and completely killed the element of surprise I had going on."

He nodded and unclipped the radio from his vest, then called into dispatch to let them know what was going on. The distant sirens of a fire engine were getting closer. The wind shifted, and I got a nose full of burning paint and charred paper from the smoldering mailbox. I used my powers to push the smoke away from us.

After a bit more communication, he clipped the radio back to his vest and said, "SWAT will be here in less than ten minutes with a power blocker and spelled handcuffs. They will take him into custody. You okay holding him up there until then?"

I nodded; it only took the barest amount of my Air power to hold a four-foot faery in the air.

His eyes searched around for a moment, and he asked, "We had reports of a man in a black mask and an elderly woman indecently exposing themselves?"

Leprechauns are masters of illusion. After I'd caught this one, he had put on a display of his power. He'd conjured an image of me wearing only my black balaclava and nothing else. He embellished that image by expanding my waistline and adding an erect two-inch penis. He also cast the illusion of a nude, heavyset elderly woman and a sign with an arrow pointing at her that just read, "Mom." He then proceeded to have the two illusions fornicate like pigs on the slush-covered sidewalk.

I explained the leprechaun's illusion to Rob. He laughed and said, "You have to admit, that is a little funny."

"It was, but there were small children around."

Normally, the illusion would have amused me. I'd be man enough to admit he burned me pretty good with it, but the children in the crowd that had gathered and the horrified parents trying to cover their tender young eyes from the graphic display took the humor right out of it. I'd used my Lightning power to disrupt the illusion and then hit the leprechaun with a much more powerful blast. After a brief scream, the lightning knocked him out and stopped him from casting any more illusions.

"Yeah, that isn't right," Rob agreed. The smirk that danced across his face contradicted his words, though.

I knew this story would make the rounds down at the precinct, and I was sure Rob would bring this up and bust my balls about it at our monthly poker game with his cop friends.

As we talked, other officers roped off Main Street and Bay Street with bright-yellow plastic police tape that contrasted against the dull greys and browns of slush and churned-up city snow. It was just coming up on 5:00 p.m.; there were going to be a lot of unhappy commuters this evening due to this main artery being blocked.

Rob studied the small unconscious form hanging in the air. "I am assuming this is the Ghost Bandit who hit those banks in Mississauga, Oakville, and Burlington?"

"I think the fact that this leprechaun was decked out head to toe in black, carrying a large sack, and heading directly for the Bank of Montreal's main Hamilton branch is a pretty good clue. There are times I wonder how you haven't made detective yet."

"Smart-ass. What's the bounty on him?"

I smiled and said, "$25,000 US tax-free dollars, my friend."

Sergeant Quinn whistled. "There are times I think I am in the wrong career."

The snow began falling harder as the SWAT truck rolled up. Four guys and one girl in helmets and black Kevlar tactical gear with "Police" written across the front in bold white lettering hustled out of the back of it. Four of them headed directly to the immobilized fae. The one with sergeant's stripes veered off from the pack and headed for us. The short, stocky build and the arrogant strut told me it was SWAT Sergeant Tim Murdock leading the team. I sighed; this day kept getting better and better.

Murdock briefly looked at me like I was something bad he'd stepped in and then turned his attention to Rob. "What do we have here, Quinn?"

"Hey, Murdock, it seems the former Hamilton Hurricane caught the Ghost Bandit."

"Nice work, Zack. The Feds warned us he might be in our area. They didn't mention anything about rampaging mailboxes, but it looks like you dealt with that too." Murdock flashed a cocky grin.

I scratched my eyebrow with my middle finger in response.

He either didn't notice me flipping him the bird or chose to ignore it. "Lower him slowly, and the *professionals* can take it from here."

This was Murdock's main beef with me: He didn't like non-law-enforcement personnel playing in his sandbox. The fact that I knew more about and was better at dealing with threats from the Enhanced community just annoyed him even more. Pointing out his faults had become a hobby of mine. He was always making dumb mistakes due to his lack of knowledge about the Enhanced community, and today was no exception. I smiled as I spotted the ring of bright-silver paint on the magazine on the bottom of his slung MP5 submachine gun.

He noticed my glance at his weapon. "What?"

"Silver rounds?" I asked nonchalantly.

"Of course," answered Murdock. His tone of voice suggested I was an idiot.

"You may want to spend less time pumping iron and more time packing it. That isn't a vamp or a Were up there, so those silver rounds aren't going to be much use. That is a leprechaun, which is a member of the fae; iron-tipped rounds are the most effective option. Please, Murdock, read a Lore manual once in a while. It might actually save your ass."

Murdock went red at this—whether from anger or embarrassment I couldn't tell—but yelled the information over to his team. They all switched to the magazines with the dark-grey painted bands on them. He made a furious sweeping "down" motion at me with one finger and then stomped off to join his team.

Rob shook his head at me. "Do you really need to piss him off like that?"

"He is a meathead who needs to start using his brain more, or he is going to get his team killed."

I lowered the still-limp form of the leprechaun, and they slapped a power-blocking collar on him and cuffed him with silver spelled cuffs. The collar and cuffs were overkill; either one by itself stopped an Enhanced Individual from using their powers. On the other hand, when dealing with things that can tear a person in two without much effort, a little overkill isn't such a bad idea.

I took out my iPhone and snapped some pictures for my records. They hauled the leprechaun into the truck shortly after that.

Rob wrote up a claim ticket for me and told me that he would email the federal claim number when the Feds came and picked up our leprechaun friend.

I stepped forward to take the ticket from him and winced as my right hip protested the sudden movement. The hip was still functioning, and nothing was broken, but I would soon be looking at a nasty bruise, and it was going to stiffen up badly if I didn't do anything about it. I made a mental note to visit Marion, my healer friend, after this and get it fixed.

Rob spent the next forty-five minutes taking my statement and getting all the details down for his report. My hip throbbed the whole time, and I was getting anxious to go see the healer. "You need me for anything else?"

He shook his head. "Nah, everything is about wrapped up here. I'll call you if I missed anything. Thanks for catching this guy, and have a good one, eh?"

I was about to fly to Marion's when my iPhone played the "Mo Money, Mo Problems" ringtone I'd assigned to Darryl's number. Darryl was one of my more reliable street contacts. I pulled out my phone and answered it.

Darryl got straight to the point. "Zack, McMahon just walked into Club 73."

Bounty hunting was like the hero business in that it came in peaks and valleys. Sometimes, days or weeks could go by with nothing happening, and then everything seemed to happen at once.

"Is he going to be there for a while?" I asked.

"Looks like. He pulled a big wad of cash when he slipped the doorman some jack. I'm betting he is getting his drink on and meeting some ladies."

"Great. Thanks, Darryl. I'm on my way."

"Don't thank me, just pay me when you get the guy."

"Don't I always?" I countered.

"Yeah, man, you're always solid, but it never hurts to remind people sometimes, you know?"

I told him I wouldn't forget, then hung up. I really wanted to get my hip healed, but I had been trying to track down James McMahon for weeks. His bounty was set at a juicy $250,000 US. I used my Air power to lift me into the air and headed for Toronto.

Chapter 2

Friday, February 9

It was just past 6:30 p.m. as I flew out of Hamilton. The sun had set, and the snow had stopped for the moment. Below me were the nonstop snaking lines of white headlights and red brake lights of bumper-to-bumper traffic on the QEW Highway and the approaching 400-series highway.

Fun fact: I'm thirty-three years old and don't have a driver's license. When you can fly, why would you need one? I pitied the commuters below me slugging it out in stop-and-go traffic and figured it must truly suck to do that day after day.

I made it to Toronto in about twenty-five minutes; I could do it in twenty minutes, but this time of day, there was a lot of air traffic out of Pearson Airport, and hitting a Boeing 777 could really mess up your day. The wide berth around the airport added an extra five minutes to the trip, but I had no doubt that the commuters I flew over would think Hamilton to Toronto in twenty-five minutes would count as the world's greatest superpower.

As a proud Hamiltonian, I didn't have a lot of love for Toronto. Due to its size, the Ontario provincial government and even the federal government tended to kiss the city's ass while Hamilton got the shaft. A new government agency with lots of good-paying jobs? Let's put that in Toronto. A halfway house for dangerous offenders or a drug rehab clinic? Hey, Hamilton, enjoy!

Since I didn't have a lot of use for Toronto, I tended not to spend much time there; consequently, I didn't know my way around the city that well.

I hovered above the CN Tower and fished out my phone. "Siri, directions to Club 73."

"I could not find any places matching 'tub seventy-three.'"

I swear to Odin, Siri loved to annoy me. I took a deep breath and tried again.

Siri replied, "Getting directions to Cub Creek Park."

I spent the next minute cursing up a storm that would have made the most hardened sailor blush and implying that Siri's parentage was a cross between a defective toaster and a Microsoft Zune music player. My righteous anger obviously did some good—Siri finally got it right on the third try.

It turned out that Club 73 was only six blocks away. I turned and felt like an idiot when I immediately spotted the bright-neon-pink 73 sign. I smacked my head, let go another string of obscenities, and headed for the club.

I flew over the three-story club and cheered up when I faintly felt McMahon's presence. Elementals can sense other nearby elementals. My power was Air, and his was Earth, which was the opposite power of mine; being near someone with Earth powers set my teeth on edge and filled me with a feeling of wrongness.

I almost welcomed the feeling of wrongness from McMahon's presence, as I'd been tracking down this animal for three weeks without even a whiff of him until now. He'd been like a ghost. Even without the hefty $250,000 bounty, I wanted this guy off the streets. He'd left too many broken bodies and ruined lives in his wake and gave all elementals a bad name.

I touched down on the roof of a six-story building a few doors down from the club. Thankfully, there was a pristine one-inch layer of snow on it that hid the probable layers of bird crap underneath it.

A handful of pigeons cooed and roosted on the window ledges of the second floor of the building behind me. I hated pigeons; if you flew, pigeons were the speed bumps in your life. They were the dumbest birds on the planet—I swore they were always trying their best to fly into me. At least pigeons didn't fly much, unlike seagulls. Many a seagull had tried to end my life prematurely.

Without even really thinking about it, I fired a low-powered arc of lightning at the ledge and was rewarded with a chorus of surprised squawks and a cloud of feathers. The flock took off like there was a hawk in the area, and I grinned in satisfaction as they flew away. That was an abuse of my power. I could clearly hear my departed mother in my head, lecturing me about "always using our powers for good," but sometimes you just have to enjoy the little things.

I focused back on Club 73. I could barely sense the wrongness of McMahon's power, so I hoped that I was far enough away he wouldn't sense my power. The more powerful you were as an elemental, the farther away you could sense other elementals. I was betting I was more powerful than he was. If I wasn't, I'd probably die in this upcoming confrontation anyway.

As much as I wanted to take McMahon down, this wasn't a fight I was looking forward to. Earth elementals were tough deal with. They could transform themselves into a rock-covered form. That form was almost impenetrable. They also had the ability to cause small earthquakes, and they could manipulate the ground below your feet.

It was only just coming up on seven o'clock, and already the club was coming to life. Most dance clubs wouldn't get busy until at least nine, but Club 73 was the trendiest one in the city. I could hear the bass pumping all the way up to my sixth-story perch, and a small line was already forming at the door. The young, hip, and beautiful were currently freezing their asses off in line, looking to blow off steam on a Friday night. Some had winter coats on, but there were a few cheapskates trying to save a few bucks by not having to pay for the coat check. Some of the outfits showed off more skin than they covered, and in this type of weather, that was either insane or a good indication that they were already high or drunk.

I debated entering the club and apprehending McMahon, but decided that wouldn't be a great idea. A packed club with hundreds, if not thousands, of civilians inside was not the place to start an elemental duel. I could be patient; from my perch I had a great view of the back entrance to the club and the parking lot. I also had a decent enough view of the front that he couldn't leave without me seeing him. I would be able to sense him moving closer or farther from me. Earth elementals couldn't fly, so he had little chance of getting away.

My stomach growled, which distracted me from my throbbing hip for the moment. I couldn't do anything about the hip right then, but hunger was a problem I could fix. McMahon probably wasn't going anywhere soon, and there was a shawarma place down the street. That sounded pretty good, so I made a small side trip.

Ten minutes later, I was back at my post, enjoying steaming-hot spicy chicken in a pita heaped with garlic sauce. The last six years in the bounty hunting business had been good to me; I could now afford to eat decently and on a regular basis. I was still grateful for something relatively inexpensive like takeout shawarma. I shuddered as a flashback of weeks of nothing but Cup Noodles from my hero days came rushing back. I'd been so broke back then, that was all I could afford.

It was still early, and I figured I was in for quite a wait until McMahon came out of the club. I sighed and opened my iPhone and started reading *Lawson's Guide to Mythical Creatures, Volume Eight.* Most of the things in it were quite obscure, and my chances of running into a unicorn or something similar were slim to none, but knowing its weaknesses might save me from taking a horn to the chest. I'd spent the last twenty-plus years of my life studying the Enhanced community, and that knowledge had saved my life more times than I could count ...

I had just finished a fascinating section on medusae when the air shimmered in an odd way at the back of the rear parking lot. Four Enhanced Individuals appeared out of the shadows, which just made this job a whole lot more complicated.

Chapter 3

Friday, February 9

My first clue that the newcomers were Enhanced was the fact that the four people appeared out of thin air. My second clue was that their auras shone around them like beacons in the night. When I had come into my elemental powers in my early teens, I had also developed the ability to see the auras of Enhanced Individuals. The aura colors told me the type of powers they had, and the size of the aura told me the strength of their power.

The closest one was a vampire—the blood-red aura outlined in black was a dead giveaway.

This vampire was a smoking hottie and was dressed to go clubbing. The impressive four-inch heels she wore had thin black straps that crisscrossed each other along her feet and ankles like a Roman sandal. Black fishnet stockings showed off her long, lean legs leading up to a black mini, or maybe micro, skirt—I'd seen wristbands that covered more than that skirt. A mesh black crop top covered a black bra that pushed up her small, perky chest in interesting ways and showed off her flat, sculpted stomach. Her long, shiny dark-brown hair was tied back in a simple ponytail that kept the hair out of her attractive face. She was probably five foot nine, but her lithe form and the heels made her look taller. I guessed her age at about eighteen or nineteen, but it was always tricky to guess ages with vampires.

I chided myself for getting distracted by her beauty. Sure, she was stunning, but that didn't change the fact that there was a predator underneath those good looks.

The blonde girl just behind her had a vivid purple aura with an outline of red and black. The purple meant she was a Were, and the red meant a cat type of Were, but the black was something I'd never come across before. Purple, red, and gold signified a Werelion, and purple, red, and orange signified a Weretiger. I pondered the black part of the aura and guessed that it might mean Werepanther or Wereleopard.

The blonde Were was much shorter than the vampire. I had no idea what her physique was like, as the full-length puffy pink winter coat she wore came down to almost her ankles. Her shoulder-length blonde hair was down and obscured her face. Her stunning blue eyes, though, almost seemed to radiate in the darkness. She, too, looked about eighteen or nineteen, but Weres, like vampires, aged slowly.

Based on the size of their auras, the Were and the vampire were younger; they hadn't been Enhanced for any longer than twenty years. They had probably only been changed in the last couple of years. After being changed for more than a decade, vampires tended to move with an inhuman grace. Weres also carried this trait, but to a lesser extent. These two still moved like normal humans.

The two hanging back in the shadows had me more concerned and puzzled. The taller one in the shadows stood above the vampire by a good six inches. She had dark-blue skin, blue hair, and pointed ears. There was a tail peeking out from behind her back. Her aura was just a shimmery field that had no color; it blurred the air around her, giving me no clue as to what her abilities were.

The shorter one was probably the biggest surprise of the night; she looked no older than ten or eleven years old. My gut churned at the idea of someone that age being anywhere near a dangerous criminal like McMahon, but the girl did have an aura, which meant she was Enhanced and might not be as young as she seemed. A dotted red aura only covered her left side; the right side was clear of any auras, which puzzled me. If she had a dotted red outline all the way around her, she would be a Tank—someone who could take and dish out massive amounts of physical punishment.

The four of them were huddling up. I manipulated the air between us to listen in better.

The blonde Were said, "Liv, you go into the club and lure McMahon out to the parking lot. Once he is clear of the club, we'll all jump him."

The dark-haired vampire whined, "Why do I have to be the one to go in?"

The Were crossed her arms and went quiet for the count of five before replying, "Stella looks like she is ten and won't get into the club, and unless McMahon is a pedophile, she won't be able to lure him out. Blue can't do it for obvious reasons, and I need to change to be useful in this upcoming fight. Besides, you are better at flirting and are actually dressed for clubbing."

"Fine, but you better act quickly once I get out here. I don't want to touch that creep for any longer than I have to."

"We'll be ready," the blonde promised. "Just think about how much shopping you can do with your share of $250,000."

"Ooohhh, new shoes!" The vampire sounded so gleeful it was almost childlike. She raced to the door in a blur.

God, I hated vampire speed, but it was impressive that she could pull off that type of speed in four-inch heels.

Liv, the vampire, put the mental whammy on the doorman guarding the back entrance. The little voice in the back of my head couldn't resist thinking, *These are not the droids you are looking for, move along,* as the doorman opened the door to the club with a blank look on his face.

The four of them going after McMahon probably meant I was out of luck for the $250,000 bounty. I silently cursed up a storm. I debated flying down and asking to join their little party—$50,000 was better than nothing—but figured that the four of them probably wouldn't want to split it five ways, so I passed on that option.

I kicked around the idea of just calling it a night and flying home. My aching hip was strongly in favor of that idea.

In the end, I settled on just staying put and watching the upcoming show. There was a chance they would lose or McMahon would get away, and then I would get my shot at bringing him down and grabbing the bounty.

The blonde Were kicked off the running shoes she was wearing and handed them to Blue. She reached for the coat but stopped and glanced around nervously. She took a deep breath and then shrugged off the coat.

My jaw fell open, as I'd been expecting her to be wearing sweats under the coat and not be naked. Most Weres tended to wear clothing like sweatpants and such, as those were easy to get off so the Weres didn't ruin their clothes when changing forms. Seeing her naked also answered why she was so short: A chest that size had to have stunted her growth.

Almost immediately, she began trembling. Her nails grew into wicked-looking talons, and fangs appeared over her teeth. Her body contorted and changed before my eyes. The sharp cracking of bones and the wet sounds of muscles tearing echoed around the lot. The blonde's mouth and nose rapidly extended into the shape of a feline muzzle. Black fur sprouted and covered her pale nude form. Her spine and neck arched. She raised her head in a silent scream as her bones twisted and knitted under her skin. Having your body torn apart and reshaped like that couldn't be fun.

The change was over in less than fifteen seconds. A lethal-looking Werepanther in her upright form took the place of the curvy, attractive blonde girl. The Were stood well over six feet and probably weighed a good 300 pounds in this form. It always amazed me how they gained size and mass when they changed.

My opinion of her went up a few notches. Normally, young Weres took several minutes to fully change into their beast form, and they usually couldn't do the upright hybrid form for a couple of decades. The fact she had done this in fifteen seconds and pulled off the upright form meant she was either older than I thought she was or she'd been turned by a powerful alpha Were—the more powerful the vamp or Were sire was, the more powerful that vamp or Were would be.

Blue finished stuffing the knapsack with the Were's discarded jacket and tossed the pack behind her. There should have been a soft *thud* or some sort of noise, but it didn't make a sound. I couldn't see where it landed; it was like the pack just disappeared into thin air.

Blue pulled a wicked-looking sword out of a sheath on her back. It was similar in design to a Japanese katana but had a bit more curve than you'd expect. The two nasty-looking three-inch pointed hooks extending from the cross guard and angling toward the blade were also not something you would see on a katana. The gleaming blade looked deadly from here, and the confidence with which she held it made me want to keep my distance from her on my best day. She stepped back and hid in the shadows at the back of the lot.

A low growl rumbled in the night. At first, I thought it came from the Werepanther, but the growl had come from the little girl, Stella. Stella really did look like she was ten years old. She had long, braided brown pigtails and a plain but angelic-looking face. The white dress and black polished shoes with the high white socks looked like something out of *Little House on the Prairie*. The outfit was probably at least fifty years out of date; a normal ten-year-old girl wouldn't have been caught dead in it.

The air shimmered for a moment around her. In that instant, she was replaced by the most hideous-looking humanoid thing I had ever seen. This creature was now at least seven feet tall, muscle-bound, and probably weighed easily over 600 pounds. It had its hair in braids, too, but the braid on the right was only six inches long, and the braid on the left was probably three feet long. Everything about her body was out of whack. She had one large boob on the right and nothing on the left. Her

14

arms were like tree trunks, but one was a good six inches longer than the other. It was the same deal with her legs, which at least were closer in length, but the right one was much more muscular than the left.

Oddly enough, her clothes had grown to cover her new massive form. I wondered how that was even possible and figured the clothing had to have been spelled or something.

The creature's face was the hardest thing to look at. One eye was tiny and partially shut; the other was huge, bloodshot, and wide open. A large bulbous and wart-covered nose stuck out at an odd angle. The mouth was uneven: The left side drooped down, and the right side turned up in a distorted smile. The teeth were jagged and uneven in size and a mixed bag of white, yellow, and black in color.

To think that this thing and that sweet-looking little ten-year-old girl were one and the same was hard to believe. Her aura had flipped, too; the dotted red line was now on the right side of her body, and the left side now had a blank, empty aura.

I thought of the story of Dr. Jekyll and Mr. Hyde, and the split aura made more sense. It had been a potion that had caused the whole Dr. Jekyll and Mr. Hyde curse—what kind of monster would give a ten-year-old girl a potion like that?

The new creature radiated menace and power. I was grateful to be six stories up and well away from it. I tried to remember what Mom had said about Hyde creatures when she'd briefly covered them during my training as a teen. We hadn't spent much time on them, as they'd been extinct for close to a hundred years. This brought up another question: Had someone recreated Dr. Jekyll's infamous potion, or had someone found a lost one? The lesson came back to me that they were basically like Tanks in that they could dish out and take massive amounts of damage. What made them more dangerous than a Tank was that Hyde creatures had no fear and felt no pain. They kept coming at you until they were either unconscious or dead.

The Werepanther moved farther into the parking lot to get closer to the back door. She crouched down beside a BMW and went still. The Hyde lumbered closer to the club and hunched down beside a van a few cars down from the Werepanther. Her trying to hide behind the van was amusing and reminded me of a cat that "hid" under a bed but only put its front half under.

Other than the steady pumping of the bass from the club, it was strangely quiet. The minutes ticked by. A lowered, riced-out Honda

Civic with a giant wing on the back entered the parking lot, did a quick lap, and left, but not much else happened.

Things changed suddenly. The back door opened, and Liv walked out with the burly, tattooed form of James McMahon. When he exited the building, the slight background feeling of wrongness increased until I balled my hands into fists and clenched my teeth to deal with it.

McMahon must have felt it, too, because he stopped dead. Liv walked deeper into the parking lot before she realized that he was no longer with her.

He looked around warily and then focused his eyes on Liv as she turned back to see what was going on.

He growled, "Whatcha playing at, girlie?"

"Huh? I am just looking for a good time, but hey, if you aren't into it, that's cool. I'm sure there are more men inside who would like to play with me."

She walked back toward the club. He reached out and grabbed her arm as she passed him by.

"You ain't going anywhere—I'm all the man you need. We are going to get to know each other real good, understand?"

Liv nodded and then made her first mistake of night. "You will release my arm and go to sleep."

Liv trying to whammy McMahon was a terrible idea; elementals had a high resistance to mental compulsion.

He instantly rocked up and turned into his full golem-like form. He snapped her arm like a twig in the rock-like vice his hand had turned into. Liv screamed, and McMahon released her and then swatted her back toward the club with a vicious blow. The vampire flew back and hit the side of the club hard enough to dent the bricks and send a cloud of dust into the air. I cringed at the sickening sound of bones breaking on impact. Amazingly, it didn't knock her out, but she was extremely dazed.

The muscle-bound bouncer guarding the back door took one look at McMahon's monstrous rock form and wisely disappeared inside the club.

A deep growl echoed in the night. The Werepanther sprang out and landed on McMahon's back. She tried valiantly to rake his rock-covered hide with her claws, but they didn't leave a single scratch. McMahon reached back and grabbed her arm. He yanked her forward, and a loud *snap* filled the air. The Were squealed in pain. My shawarma tried to come back up at the gruesome sight of the bone of her forearm protruding from her black fur.

He tossed the heavily muscled Were a good twenty feet across the parking lot, and she became a hood ornament for a parked blue Subaru. The Subaru's alarm, as well as the alarm of the Porsche 911 parked beside it, wailed to life. The blaring noise of rapid honking echoed in the air as headlights flashed across the parking lot.

A flash of light pulled my attention to the area near the back entrance of the club. Blue stepped out of the shadows with the blade of her sword completely enflamed.

My mind reeled at this. She had been hiding at the very back of the lot, and now, out of nowhere, she appeared on the other side of the lot behind McMahon. She was either exceptionally fast, or she could teleport somehow. I leaned toward teleporting, as that would explain how they all had appeared out of nowhere earlier.

I stopped worrying about how she got there as she charged at McMahon's exposed back. The bright glow of the sword must have caught his attention, because a moment before her sword descended, he turned around and blocked it with his left arm. The glowing orange blade buried itself a good couple of inches into the dense stone covering of his arm.

That sword must have been something special to penetrate at all. I'd seen Earth elementals shrug off bullets like they were mosquitos.

McMahon released a low, rumbling roar of pain and swung out with a devastating right hook that connected with the center of Blue's chest. The dull, hard *thud* of the impact reached up to my sixth-story perch. She flew back ten feet and crashed headfirst to the pavement, where she lay in an unmoving heap—whether she was out cold or dead, I couldn't tell. Her sword hit the pavement with a *clang*, the fire on the blade instantly extinguished.

You would think that Earth elementals in rock form would be slow, judging by their size and makeup, but nothing is further from the truth. They can move quite quickly, as Blue unfortunately found out.

The Hyde creature roared as she stomped toward McMahon. He turned back around, and she slammed into McMahon, but neither went down. They started trading blows heavy enough to make the Tyson versus Holyfield fight seem like kittens playing.

The Werepanther extracted herself from the caved-in front of the Subaru. I was stunned that her arm had already healed back to normal; she looked to be heading back into the fight. I knew Weres had amazing healing abilities, but I hadn't known they were *that* good. I was a touch envious of that, especially when I thought back to all the money I'd spent over the years on healing my bumps and bruises. My hip throbbed again as if to punctuate that point.

The vampire clutched the wall and puked up blood. Though she was upright, she wouldn't be rejoining the fight anytime soon. Vampires healed quickly but usually had to feed to heal as quickly as the Werepanther had. The fact that she was conscious and standing after smacking that wall was a testament to vampire toughness; if a normal human had hit that wall, it would have killed them.

Blue hadn't moved, but her chest was slowly rising and falling. I didn't know how badly she was injured, but at least she was still alive.

Sirens were closing in the distance, but the cops wouldn't get involved. They would just cordon off the area until the federal Enhanced Individual Response Team (EIRT) got here.

The building I was perched on shook slightly. I looked down at the fight in time to see a great tear in the pavement below the Hyde creature's feet open up. She tumbled into the chasm, and the ground immediately started to seal itself up over her. The Hyde creature tried to jump free before the ground slammed shut, but only her head made it out. The rest of her body was trapped in the ground.

McMahon began moving toward the Hyde creature. He was about to kick her head like he was an NFL field-goal kicker going for the win from the thirty-four-yard line when I launched myself off the building. I worried that if that kick made contact, it would kill her.

The Werepanther beat me to it, pouncing on him mere feet before he reached Stella.

McMahon's responding attack was even more fierce than the first one. McMahon grabbed her arm and leg and crushed both in his hands. The Werepanther roared in pain, and then he tossed her into the air. She landed headfirst on the hood of a red Mazda 3, which, by the visual damage, wouldn't be driving anyone home this evening. The Werepanther didn't move this time. She stayed prone and lifeless. Weres could take an immense amount of damage and heal incredibly fast, but if you hit them in the head hard enough, it scrambled their brain functions and really messed up their healing abilities.

I landed a good twenty feet behind him, and McMahon immediately turned his attention to me. I used my Air power to lift him into the air.

I groaned at the effort it took to lift him even just ten feet. I prayed that he'd expended most of his power in the fight, or this was going to get ugly fast. I hit him with the highest dose of electricity I could manage. I was sweating and shaking as the seconds ticked by, but I kept pouring the lightning into him. It was now a contest between us on whose power would run out first.

C'mon, c'mon, change back, fucker, I thought as my reserves dwindled.

I almost wept with joy when I heard him scream in pain. The electricity slammed into his human form, and I instantly turned off the juice. Due to the sudden change in mass, his body shot straight up into the air, and I turned off the air pressure under him. At about sixty feet up, his momentum stopped. He hovered for a moment, then tumbled lifelessly back toward Earth.

When he was about twenty feet from the ground, I used the wind to slow his descent. At ten feet, I stopped him completely and held him suspended there. He didn't struggle. He didn't move. I glanced up at his limp form with a bit of concern, wondering if I'd killed him. He was slightly charred and smoking a bit, but he still seemed to be breathing. The nasty cut on his arm from Blue's blow when he'd been rocked up was bleeding, which was another sign he was alive. I kept him up in the air. If I let him down, he'd use the ground to recharge his powers.

Movement to my right caught my attention. Liv, the vampire, limped slowly over to Blue and checked on her, sighing in relief when she saw that Blue was still alive.

Liv eyed me warily but seemed to relax when she saw Mr. Crispy out cold and floating in the air. Her face fell, and I swear she said, "I guess no new shoes are in my future."

Chapter 4

Friday, February 9

Aminute later, a loud roar of anger shook the air. Stella exploded out from her earthen prison, and I was pelted by bits of pavement, dirt, and rock. The Hyde creature searched for a target for her anger, and her homicidal gaze fell on me. I gulped and hastily scrambled backward.

Liv yelled, "Stella, no! He is a friend. Help me with Blue!"

The creature stopped and turned at the sound of Blue's name. She lumbered over to Liv and her downed friend. I exhaled in relief. I was pretty sure I might have had a little bladder leakage. I was amazed at how gently Monster Stella picked Blue up. She cradled her limp form with the utmost care.

Liv looked around in a panic and cried, "Oh my God, where's Bree?"

Bree must have been the Werepanther. I called out, "Liv, she is over there, embedded in a red Mazda, but she is still breathing."

Liv looked at me in confusion and then looked over to where I was pointing. She dashed over to the downed Werepanther. With one of her stiletto heels broken, her gait was awkward and almost comical.

She had just finished extracting Bree from the Mazda when EIRT showed up. EIRT was part of the Royal Canadian Mounted Police (RCMP). They used to be called the Monster Response Team (MRT), but about eight years ago, governments around the world bowed to pressure from various rights groups, and the term *monster* was considered racist and derogatory. The term had been replaced by the politically correct term *Enhanced Individual*.

Some of these creatures could tear limbs off people like wings off a fly and eat people, but we were worried that we were hurting their feelings by calling them monsters? Really? I'm sure there were master vampires out there who had killed more people than humanity's worst serial killer could even dream about, and they shouldn't be called monsters?

The RCMP were federal-level law enforcement and Canada's version of the FBI. An EIRT unit usually consisted of five or six officers;

at least one or two of them were Enhanced Individuals. This team had one officer who was Enhanced; based on his aura, he was a mage.

All the officers except the mage had their MP5 submachine guns up and out and were scanning the parking lot for active threats. Based on their quick motions and the way their heads were moving around and rapidly searching, they were all keyed up and on alert.

One of them asked, "Hurricane, is that you?"

A huge and unmistakable blond-haired six-foot-five giant headed toward me, his weapon trained on me and the scene around me.

I said, "Bobby Knight, how's things?"

"Good. Is everything here under control?"

His eyes scanned the lot, and his weapon was still up and ready to fire.

I stayed perfectly still. "We are clear. The bad guy is down, and there are no active threats."

Bobby lowered his weapon and made a motion with his hand to the rest of his team. They pointed their weapons toward the ground.

He looked around the war zone that had once been a peaceful parking lot. "You want to tell me what's going on?"

I spent the next couple of minutes explaining about James McMahon and the girls' attempt to capture him. As soon as I mentioned McMahon's name, Bobby glanced up at the still-smoldering limp form in the air and smiled. McMahon had put a couple of Toronto cops in the hospital with life-threatening injuries—it didn't surprise me that Bobby recognized the name.

I spied an athletic-looking brunette in tactical gear approaching McMahon with a power-blocking neck collar and cuffs. I lowered him closer to the ground, and she slapped the collar and cuffs on him. I cut the Air power holding him up, and he plummeted the last few feet to the ground. He groaned as he bounced off the pavement with a satisfying *smack*. A couple of members of EIRT picked up him and hauled him off to the transport vehicle waiting at the end of the parking lot. I smiled to myself as they "accidently" dropped him twice on the way to the vehicle.

The next half hour was spent answering questions and filling out paperwork with EIRT; with a $250,000 bounty on the line, I wasn't going anywhere. It was funny how paperwork always took ten times longer to complete than the actual incident getting written up.

The EIRT kept their distance from Stella, who was still cradling Blue in her arms and growling whenever anyone got remotely near her. They also avoided Liv, who was tending to Bree; the hungry gleam in her eyes would have deterred anyone pretty quickly.

Once everything was wrapped up, Bobby pulled me aside and asked, "What should we do about them?"

The "them" in question referred to the four ladies. The Werepanther was still out cold, with Liv anxiously sitting beside her. Blue was being cradled by the Hyde creature, who had such a look of profound sadness on her ugly mug that I couldn't help but feel sorry for her. With their teleporter down, they probably had no way home. I doubted that they had any money on them to get a cab home or a room somewhere for the night.

I sighed to myself. My hip still throbbed, my power reserves were just about tapped out thanks to the fight, and all I wanted to do was go home and get some sleep, but I owed the ladies for at least softening McMahon up, and I had just scooped the bounty they had risked their lives for. The least I could do was get them to a healer and find a place for them to stay for the night.

I turned my attention back to Bobby, who was waiting for my answer. I spotted a Taser on his belt and smiled. "I will take care of them, but I need a favor first." When he lifted a questioning eyebrow at me, I explained, "The fight drained me, and I need a pick-me-up. Shoot me with your Taser, and I will take care of the ladies for you."

"You know that every time I discharge it, I have to fill out paperwork, right?"

I nodded. "Yeah, but how much paperwork and time will it take you to deal with four Enhanced Individuals who have no IDs, no money, and no way home?"

Bobby looked around the lot for a moment. "Good point. I will use this as a teaching moment, then—at least it will make the squad laugh." Bobby waved his team over and told them what he was going to do. He pulled the Taser and said, "Where do you want it?"

I turned my left side toward him. "In my left thigh."

He nodded, aimed, and fired.

I grimaced for a moment as the two barbed prongs buried themselves into my leg through my jeans, but the pain disappeared from my thoughts as the juice shot into my body. I moaned in pleasure as the electricity coursed through my body and my power levels rose rapidly.

Five seconds later, I had fully drained the cartridge, and it was over. I heard a "Wow," a "Holy shit," and a couple of laughs as I casually reached down and pulled the prongs from my legs like nothing had happened.

I handed Bobby the ends. "That hit the spot. Thanks. See you around, Bobby."

Bobby and his team wished me a good night and headed back to their SUV. I made a call to Marion, my healer in Hamilton, and asked for the name and address of a healer here in Toronto. She gave me the information and details on a Dr. Chapman and said she'd call ahead and let him know I was coming. I tossed the address into Google Maps on my phone and was pleased to find that it was only seven blocks away.

I wandered over to Liv. She had tossed her high heels and was sitting against the bumper of the crumpled Mazda in stocking-covered feet beside Bree's unconscious form. As a vampire, she wouldn't care about the cold.

"Hi, Liv. I'm Zack."

"It's *Olivia*. Only Bree can call me 'Liv.' "

"Fair enough. It looks like Bree and Blue could do with some healing. I have made some calls, and there is a healer nearby we can go to who will fix them up."

Olivia stared quietly at me as if sizing up either my offer or my potential as a meal. When the hairs on the back of my neck went up, I worried it might be the latter.

Olivia broke the silence with a sad look on her face. "We don't have any money for a healer."

"I'm paying."

She glanced down at the Werepanther, and a look of deep concern became etched across her face. "Okay. Do you have a car?"

I was puzzled by that. "No, but I can fly us over. It would be easier if Stella was in her smaller form. Do you think you can talk her back into it?"

"Fly? Really?" Olivia suddenly perked up with an excited grin.

I smiled at her enthusiasm and nodded.

Olivia carefully propped her friend up against the car, got to her feet, and said, "Watch Bree for me. I'll be right back."

Before I could answer, she had blurred off and reappeared by Stella. I shrugged and took a seat beside Bree, who was passed out cold but at least seemed to be breathing okay. I warily kept an eye on her and hoped Olivia would be back soon; the idea of sitting beside a Werepanther who might wake up disoriented and confused was making me a touch nervous.

Olivia was suddenly standing back in front of me, which startled me.

"Stella's changing back," she announced.

I got to my feet. "Can you lie down next to Bree and hold on to her?"

Olivia nodded and lowered herself to the ground, putting her arms around Bree. I focused and carefully used my Air powers to lift them both off the ground by a few feet, then walked over to Stella and Blue, with Olivia and Bree floating in tow behind me.

"This is so cool!" Olivia squealed as she glided through the air.

I reached Stella, who was standing and shivering in the cold beside Blue's inert form. She watched me like a mouse would a house cat and then eyed the hovering Olivia and Bree with curiosity.

"Hi, Stella. I'm Zack. I am going to fly all of you to a nearby healer and get help for Blue and Bree."

"Why would you do this for us?" Stella asked in a prim-and-proper English accent.

The accent caught me off guard, but it did seem to fit with her puritanical-looking dress. It dawned on me that her outfit was pristinely clean and intact, which was odd, considering she'd transformed into a creature at least four times her size, but I figured maybe that was just part of her powers and decided not to puzzle over it; it was getting late, and I had a feeling this night was going to be a long one.

"Well, I did just roll into a large bounty, and while you failed to capture McMahon, you at least softened him up a bit. In return, the least I can do is get everyone healed on my dime."

I got the sense that she would have preferred to decline my help, but she was shivering badly in the extreme cold and really didn't have any option but to accept. She nodded slowly.

"Can I get you to lie down and hold on to Blue?"

Stella looked like she was going to question this, but in the end, she just got on the ground. She wrapped her small arms tightly around Blue and watched me closely.

I used my Air powers to gently lift both of them and then moved Bree and Olivia closer. I grabbed Bree with my left hand.

I used the air currents to move Blue and Stella closer. I was about to grab on to Stella, but the look of sheer horror she gave me when

I started reaching for her immediately changed my mind. I rotated them around and grabbed on to Blue instead. A look of immense relief crossed Stella's features. I wasn't sure what her deal was, but I got the feeling that there were good reasons behind her fear.

I was about to take off but decided to reassure Stella and Olivia first. "The healer is only seven blocks away. This will be a short flight. If you are concerned, just close your eyes, and I promise it will be over before you know it."

Stella gave me unsure nod, and Olivia yelled, "Giddyup!" With that, I took off. Stella's loud whimper of fear was almost drowned out by Olivia screaming, "Wheeeeee!" as we shot into the air. I took us up about a hundred feet up and headed for the healer.

Olivia yelled out, "This is awesome!"

Stella had her eyes firmly shut; her knuckles were pure white as she gripped Blue. I was pretty sure Stella was also softly whispering the Lord's Prayer.

Chapter 5

Friday, February 9

I touched down in front of a thirty-story condo building that looked modern and well-kept.

We—well, Olivia, Stella, and I—walked up to the entrance; Blue and Bree floated behind us. I found Dr. Chapman's name on the directory and entered his code on the intercom. He didn't reply through the intercom, but the door buzzed loudly, and we were in. His unit was on the ground floor near the rear of the building. I knocked on the door, and an older, thin gentleman with a neatly trimmed gray beard and green hospital scrubs let us in. Based on the impressive-sized light-blue aura with the silver outline around it, this had to be Dr. Chapman.

I was surprised to find a fully decked-out medical facility, complete with a couple of surgical tables and a human nurse inside the apartment. I was impressed that the nurse didn't even bat an eye as I floated Blue and Bree onto the tables.

He held out his hand and said, "Marion called and said you were coming. You must be Zack. I'm Dr. Chapman."

I shook his hand. "I am Zack. The tall, dark woman here is Olivia, and the little girl is Stella. The patients on the table are Blue and Bree. I'm assuming you can guess which is which."

He smiled and nodded. "I don't mean to rude, but as I can sense that neither of the patients seem to be close to dying, can we discuss payment first?"

I knew he was a more powerful healer than Marion due to the size of his aura, but I was floored that he could diagnose everyone's injuries by just a glance. Marion needed to touch me to tell what was broken or damaged. At least Bree and Blue would be in capable hands.

He walked us over to a desk with a computer and payment terminal on it, then sat down behind it. Stella hopped onto one seat, and I sat in the other. Olivia had wandered over to Bree but seemed to be sniffing intently around the nurse, which concerned me.

The doctor cleared his throat. "The Werepanther has a broken arm and leg that have already started setting incorrectly; they will need to be reset. My larger concern is her concussion, but that, too, is treatable. The one you call Blue is a problem, though; she is an alien, so her entire genetic makeup is unknown to me. I am hesitant to treat her, as I'm afraid I could do more damage than good."

"Can you do anything for her?" I asked.

Stella was sitting beside me, but her body language suggested she was dying to get as far away from us as possible. She probably only stayed out of deep concern for her injured friends.

"I could bandage and splint any wounds or breaks, but even that is something I am not sure of—bandages will inhibit oxygen from getting to the wounds, which might slow down her natural healing process. She seems to be in some sort of self-induced healing trance at this moment. I would recommend letting her work through the process without my interference."

I turned to Stella. "Any thoughts?"

"In the years I have known her, Blue has usually managed to avoid damage due to her training and speed. She did break an arm once, but she just left it alone. In a few days, it fixed itself. The doctor's advice would be my recommendation as well."

I caught a low murmuring behind me, and the hairs on the back of my neck went up. I looked over my shoulder and saw Olivia gazing deeply into the nurse's eyes and speaking softly. She was about to feed off the nurse.

"Olivia!" I barked, and she flinched. She looked guilty as she glanced over at me. "Don't eat the help."

The nurse came back to her senses and immediately scrambled as far away from the hungry vampire as possible.

"Okay, to heal the Were fully, you are looking at $7,000." Doctor Chapman paused as if making sure that I could handle that fee. I nodded, and he continued. "The vampire has cracked ribs, a small fracture in her right arm, and a sprained knee. I can heal those for another $2,000. For $500, I can fix that nasty bruise on your hip."

"Do you have bags of plasma here?"

He nodded.

I asked, "How much per bag?"

"They normally aren't for sale, but I see where you are going with this. I can sell them for $200 each. How many would you like?"

"Two, please, and I will take you up on the healing for myself."

I decided that blood would heal all Olivia's injuries, so spending $2,000 to get her fixed was a waste. Weres healed quickly on their own, too, but with the head injury, I wanted Bree to get professional help.

"Okay, that is a total of $7,900, plus HST. We accept all forms of payment." The doctor smiled pleasantly.

I almost giggled at the thought of a black-market clinic charging sales tax, but let it go.

I broke out my credit card and noticed Olivia slowing edging toward the nurse again. "Doc, you mind breaking out those plasma bags sooner rather than later?"

"Sally, grab two units of plasma and give them to Olivia, okay?" the doc ordered in a calm voice.

Sally looked puzzled until she looked at Olivia, who was now flashing her fangs. She quickly disappeared into the walk-in fridge to her right.

The doctor pulled out a credit card machine and handed it to me. I punched in my pin code as Sally reappeared and cautiously handed the two bags of blood to Olivia.

"Oh, juice boxes!" Olivia squealed with delight.

Olivia's attention was fully on the blood bags now—Sally, the walking snack, was forgotten. The bags had plastic tubes on them for hooking up to IV tubes, and Olivia put one bag down and used the tube like a straw, draining the bag.

"Cold," Olivia mumbled as she hungrily drank the blood.

The doc gave me a receipt for the credit card purchase and an invoice. "Let's get you done first, okay?"

I nodded.

He walked over to me and placed his hands on my hip. A soft blue glow surrounded his hands for a few seconds, then the area tingled, and the pain instantly disappeared. He removed his hands and gave me a nod before heading over to one of the large sinks and thoroughly washing his hands.

Stella looked worried and lost, so I suggested she go over and talk to Blue.

She raised a questioning eyebrow at me. It looked odd on her young features; that was an expression I was used to seeing from adults. I had no idea of Stella's real age, but the more I was around her, the more I doubted she was only ten.

"I read somewhere that people in comas can recover quicker hearing the voices of loved ones. Since Blue is in a healing trance, which is similar, I figured it was worth a shot. It can't hurt, at the very least."

She nodded, climbed off the chair, and walked away. She stood beside Blue and whispered in her ear.

A loud exclamation of surprise from Olivia startled everyone in the room. We all turned to look at her.

"Sorry. Brain freeze." Olivia sounded sheepish. She rubbed her head vigorously.

I stifled a laugh. "Olivia, why don't you come over here and sit down? Let the nice people fix Bree in peace."

She nodded, grabbed the other bag of blood, and took over the seat beside me that Stella had occupied earlier.

The doc and Sally secured Bree to the table with heavy duty restraints. I figured that was prudent in case she woke up as they were fixing her, but I wasn't sure how Olivia would feel about it. I decided to keep her distracted.

"How long have you been a vampire?" I tossed out.

Olivia took a long pull off the bag and eyed me as if debating whether to answer. After a few moments, she answered, "It was a year last month. I was nineteen when I was turned … Since we are sharing, are you really the Hurricane?"

"I was, but I have been retired from the hero game for the last six years. Why?"

"When Bree and I were kids, we were huge fans. We lived in Oakville. We snuck out that night you put down the zombie uprising. We saw you take down the necromancer controlling the walking dead. We were members of your fan club."

I remembered that night. It must have been close to nine years ago. The zombies hadn't been bad, but the necromancer had been a pain. He was immune to my electrical attacks and had spells to prevent me from changing the air around him, which meant I couldn't suffocate him until he passed out. Thankfully, the wooden platform he stood on wasn't immune to my attacks. I ended up blasting the platform, with him on it, about 10,000 feet into the air and then letting it fall. He'd come down around half a mile away and left a small crater in a mall parking lot. Once he'd died, all the zombies had collapsed like puppets with their strings cut. Normally, as a hero, you always tried for nonlethal takedowns, but necromancers were one of the exceptions to that rule. Every country on the planet had automatic death sentences for anyone practicing that dark art. They were too dangerous to let live.

I did the math in my head and figured Olivia and Bree would have been about eleven years old at the time. The thought of eleven-year-old girls around all those zombies and a necromancer brought on a shiver of fear. "What did your parents say about your little nighttime adventure?"

Olivia laughed. "We were caught sneaking back in, and the sleepover was canceled. We were both grounded for a week, but it was so worth it. You shooting that guy into the air like a rocket is one of the coolest things I have ever seen."

Olivia went back to her blood bag, and a loud slurping noise filled the room as she finished off the last drops. She tossed the bag in the garbage beside us and reached for the other bag. I noticed that all her bumps and bruises had disappeared and that she wasn't favoring her right side anymore.

"How did you and Bree get turned?"

Olivia went a little pale at this question; I worried I had hit a sore spot. A loud, sickening *crack* filled the air, and I looked over at the table with Bree on it. My stomach churned uneasily at the sound, and I was grateful I hadn't eaten in a while. The doctor had just rebroken Bree's leg and was currently setting it. Olivia and I watched as he splinted it in place. A soft blue glow surrounded his hands and Bree's fur-covered leg as he did his magic.

Olivia's voice pulled my attention back to her. She glanced quickly over at Stella and said, "I'm not supposed to talk about that night, but since you are paying to get Bree fixed and you are the Hurricane, I'll make an exception."

She took a long pull off her second bag of plasma and said, "Last year, Bree and I were contracted for one night to serve drinks and appetizers. Unfortunately, we ended up becoming the appetizers. The night started out great. We were in awe of the huge, beautiful estate where the event was being held. All the guests were super stylish and stunning." She paused and then, in an excited tone, added, "The shoes! Oh my God, so many of the women there were wearing shoes that I'd have killed for. We figured it must be some low-key celebrity or fashion industry gathering. We had to sign a nondisclosure agreement and everything. It turned out that it was the annual Master/Were Summit."

The shock on my face caused Olivia to pause in her story. The annual Master/Were Summit was a gathering where the masters from the vampire courts and the most powerful alpha Weres met to discuss their grievances and issues. The events themselves were always shrouded in secrecy. Each year, the location moved and was hosted by a different master. They were super-exclusive. It must have been Elizabeth's, the master of the English vampire court, turn, as Canada was part of her territory.

"Everything was going great until about midway through the evening," Olivia continued. "The sound of material tearing filled the large room, followed by a load roar that almost seemed to shake the entire house. In the middle of the guests, there was a huge Werepanther that started attacking one of the guests. I dumped my tray of food and ducked behind a couch and hid. More animal noises followed, and the room became filled with screams and the sounds of fighting."

Olivia took another sip of blood, then continued. "I wanted nothing more than to stay curled up behind that couch, but then I remembered Bree. I lifted my head up to take a quick peek for her and was stunned at the bloodbath the place had become. A badly wounded vampire suddenly appeared in front of me. Before I could even blink, he grabbed my ponytail and yanked me to my feet. He started going in for, you know, the kill. But then I screamed, and someone drove a wooden table leg through his chest. All that blood exploded onto to my face and into my mouth. But the guy wasn't even dead! He ended up drinking from me anyway—until he finally died."

Olivia shuddered for a moment and went quiet. I was staggered by her story, as the odds of her turning were nothing short of a miracle. For a human to become a vampire, there needed to be an exchange of blood. It had only been by sheer luck—or tragedy—that the vampire being impaled by the stake and splashing his blood into Olivia's mouth had made this happen. Even then, the odds of her turning were only about 5 percent. That low turn rate was probably the only reason the world wasn't swimming in vampires.

"I don't remember the first time I awoke after becoming a vampire. Bree told me that I had been so consumed by bloodlust that I'd tried to attack her, but Stella—in her Hyde form—had saved Bree. Blue got bags of blood, and they fed me the next time I awoke until the bloodlust receded and I was in control again."

"How did Stella and Blue become involved in all of this?"

"Blue, with her shadow-traveling ability, does contract work for the English vampire court. After everything went to hell at the summit,

Elizabeth had Blue and Stella clean up and cover up what had really happened. When they were going through the estate, they found Bree, and she was still alive. They rescued her, but she insisted that they look for me too. They found my body and brought it back to their place in London, so Bree could say goodbye. That was when I suddenly came back to life and tried to attack her."

So Blue was a shadow-traveler. That made more sense than a teleporter. Teleporters were limited by weight and distance; transporting herself and three others from London would have been impossible for a teleporter. Shadow-travelers didn't have those restrictions, though. All they needed was a shadow on each end, and they could travel between them instantly—it didn't matter how many people they brought along for the ride.

Shadow-travelers were rare. I certainly had never fought one.

The implications of Bree and Olivia having been at the Master/Were Summit came crashing home: Bree must have been attacked by the Werepanther that had started it all. That Were would have been one of the strongest Werepanthers on the planet if he had been attending the summit. That explained why Bree could do a hybrid transformation, despite only having been a Were for a little over a year. That also meant Olivia would have been turned by a master vampire.

"Do you know who turned you?" I asked.

"Henri of the French vampire court."

If I hadn't been sitting, that tidbit of information would have knocked me from my feet. Henri had been the oldest and most powerful vampire in Europe when he'd died last year. His death had caused a large stir among the public. At the time, the French vampire court had issued a press release stating that Henri had taken his own life. He had lived for over 1,200 years and had come to feel that he was no longer connected to the world as he once had been and so had decided to kill himself. This was a common problem for older vampires; the world was always changing, and some had problems changing with it.

I didn't follow the French vampire court that closely. They tended to be one of the more reclusive courts, so there wasn't a lot of information out there on them. After Henri's death, though, there was a period of mourning for one year. Last month, they issued a brief press announcement that Giselle Dupris was the new master of the French vampire court.

I didn't know anything about Giselle's history. If she wasn't in Henri's direct bloodline, Olivia might have a stronger claim to the throne than Giselle. The problem was that Olivia was too young and nowhere near powerful enough to defend that claim. If the French vampire court ever found out about this, things would get ugly fast.

Chapter 6

Friday, February 9

Agroggy "Where am I?" pulled our attention to Bree, who was now awake. She was still strapped to the table but was back in human form—a very naked human form.

"Bree!" cried Olivia.

She bolted out of her chair, blurred over to Bree's side, and hugged her. Olivia softly whispered something in Bree's ear; I assumed she was filling her in on the events of the evening.

Dr. Chapman and the nurse were washing their hands thoroughly in the sink. I got up and wandered over to them, trying to ignore the attractive nude blonde on the table; I seriously needed to get a social life—or at least one a monk wouldn't envy.

"Nice work, Doc. Is she 100 percent?"

He pulled some paper towels from the metal dispenser to dry his hands. "She should be fine. She will need food and sleep, but after both, she should be 100 percent again."

Bree's state of undress was another issue I needed to deal with—her clothes were currently in a knapsack in the shadow realm, and Blue was in a coma. They wouldn't be returning anytime soon.

"Doc, any chance you have an extra set of scrubs?"

He looked puzzled at my question, but when his gaze fell on Bree, a light went on. "Yeah. Sally, can you grab a set for Bree?"

Sally returned moments later with a set of scrubs. She placed them on the end of the table and quickly moved away from Olivia, who was undoing the straps holding Bree down.

Olivia got the restraints undone and helped her friend sit up. I tried to find a place to keep my eyes that wasn't Bree's exposed form. Out of the corner of my eye, I saw her nimbly hop off the table. Even though Olivia was hovering nearby to catch her, she didn't need the help. Bree got dressed quickly and walked over to me, studying me for a moment with her ice-blue eyes before saying, "Thank you for paying for my healing."

I shrugged. "Least I could do, given the circumstances."

She nodded. "Thank you again. We won't take up more of your time." She turned to Olivia and said, "Liv, grab Blue, and let's get going." Based on her take-charge attitude, it was obvious that she had alpha blood in her veins and that she was the leader of this group.

Olivia grabbed Blue off the table like she was lifting a baby—carefully but without much effort.

Stella wandered over to Bree and said quietly, "Bree, just where are we supposed to go? We have no money, and with Blue out of commission, we can't travel home. It is freezing out there."

Bree crossed her arms and set her jaw. Through clenched teeth she said, "We'll figure something out."

Stella looked like she was going to argue but kept silent and lowered her head, heading for the door behind Bree. Olivia was the last in the group. She awkwardly waved at me with Blue in her arms and disappeared through the door moments later.

I mentally sighed to myself—I knew I was going to regret this—but after thanking the good doctor for his help, I chased after them. I caught up to them in the hallway. "Bree, wait!"

She took another couple of steps before reluctantly stopping and turning to face me.

I pulled off the balaclava I'd been wearing to hide my identity all night. Bree's eyes widened a bit in surprise at me revealing my true identity. "Bree, I know we don't know each other very well, but I can't in good conscience let you go out there. It is one o'clock in the morning, and you still need sleep and food to fully recover. I know Weres run hot, but a couple of hours out in that weather and even *you* will be feeling it, especially in your weakened condition. I know Olivia doesn't feel the cold, but what about Stella and Blue? Will they?"

She didn't answer, but the concern that popped up on her face told me the answer.

"I thought so. I have a large house back in Hamilton near a twenty-four-hour grocery store that I can grab food from. I can fly us all back there, and then you ladies can eat and rest in peace. I have contacts in Hamilton who can get plasma for Olivia. What do you say?"

After a moment, her shoulders slumped, and she gave me a small, defeated nod.

"Great. I only ask that when you leave, you all keep my real name and my home address to yourselves, okay?"

"Of course," answered Bree. Stella and Olivia nodded in agreement.

I handed the balaclava to Stella, who was standing next to me; she stepped back but then cautiously took it from me. I unzipped the spring jacket I was wearing and held it out to her as well.

"What are you doing?" She eyed the jacket like it was on fire.

"The flight to Hamilton is twenty-five minutes, and it is colder up there than on the ground. Please wear them—they will help a bit. I'd suggest holding on to Bree and leeching her warmth too."

"I couldn't—don't you need them?" Stella looked concerned.

"I have a touch of elemental Ice power that makes me almost immune to cold; I only wear the balaclava to hide my identity, and the jacket has pockets for my phone and stuff."

Stella nodded and took the jacket from me. She stepped back again and put on the hood and jacket. It certainly didn't match her quaint, dated outfit, but winning fashion awards wasn't the goal.

We exited the building, and a large gust of wind kicked up. Stella and Bree both gasped at the cold temperature. Bree picked Stella up, and I took hold of Bree's and Olivia's arms, then asked, "Ready?"

Olivia nodded excitedly, and Bree gave me one wary nod. Stella shuddered and buried her face against Bree as she nodded that she, too, was ready.

I lifted us off the ground, rising above the noise of the city and heading for home …

The flight was uneventful. We made it back to my house in about twenty minutes. Thankfully, there wasn't a lot of air traffic coming out of the airport this time of night—that allowed me to take a more direct route home, which was fantastic because by the time I touched down in my front yard, both Bree and Stella were shivering so violently with cold that I could hear their teeth chattering.

The girls followed me inside, and I turned off the house alarm. Stella took off the balaclava and my jacket and handed both back to me. Bree gave me a curious look as I immediately put them both back on.

"There is a twenty-four-hour grocery store nearby. I am going to get us some food. Feel free to grab a bath or shower while I'm gone if you want. My bedroom is the first room at the top of the stairs. The one beside it is my home office. The other two rooms up there are spares, so please use them as you see fit. You can raid my closet—I'm not sure if anything will fit any of you, but you are welcome to whatever you want. I have some pop or beer in the fridge. Help yourselves to whatever food is in the kitchen as well."

"You don't need to get food," Bree argued as her stomach rumbled loudly, suggesting otherwise. She blushed slightly at the noise.

I raised an eyebrow at her, and she nodded in surrender.

"Good. I will be back in less than thirty minutes. Don't answer the door, and don't talk to strangers while I'm gone," I teased.

Bree rolled her eyes, but Olivia retorted, "But strangers have the best candy!"

I laughed at her comment. I grabbed my reusable grocery bags from inside the one of the cabinets at the front door. I wasn't super environmentally friendly; it was just that the thin plastic bags the stores used tended to split, and dropping a can of peaches from 2,000 feet was a touch dangerous. With my luck, I would hit someone with a good lawyer and spend the next few years in court in a civil suit—so I used the cloth bags.

I left the girls and lifted off back into the night, making it to the grocery store in less than a couple of minutes and landing around back. I power-shopped and got everything I needed for that night and the next day in less than fifteen minutes, then paid for the food and was on my way.

I reentered the house and was greeted by Olivia coming downstairs wearing my Detroit Lions jersey—and nothing else. The jersey came down low enough to cover her lady bits, but not by much. If I hadn't already been a fan of the Lions, seeing Olivia like this would have converted me instantly.

She pulled the bottom hem of the jersey away from her body a little and said, "I hope you don't mind. I needed something to wear while my clothes were in the wash."

I smiled at her. "No. I said to help yourselves, and I meant it. Besides, you look better in it than I ever did."

She laughed at that, and her eyes twinkled with mischief. She seemed almost playful, which brought another concern to my mind. "Olivia, um, how long until you need to feed again?"

She shrugged. "I'm probably good until tomorrow night at least. Why?"

"Bloodlust is nothing to mess with. I was just concerned that you would be okay until I can connect with my contacts tomorrow and get you some supplies."

She smiled and picked up the heavy bags of groceries I had put down in the hall like they weighed nothing, heading for the kitchen. I followed her to find Stella seated at the table, having a cup of tea. Her hands were wrapped tightly around the cup as if to leech every drop of warmth from it. Since nobody had said that Blue was awake, the sound of water running upstairs meant Bree was probably grabbing a hot shower.

Olivia and I unpacked the groceries, and she longingly eyed the tenderloin I'd picked up. "God, I miss steak. Bree is going to be overjoyed; it's her favorite."

I went out on the back deck and fired up the gas barbeque. Barbequing in minus-fifteen-degree temperatures is a Canadian thing; as long as the barbeque isn't buried under a ton of snow, it is still barbeque season.

Half an hour later, I served up three plates of medium-rare beef tenderloin with Béarnaise and sides of baby potatoes and still-crisp sugar snap peas. I had made more than what was on the plates, so I put the extras on a platter in the center of the table, in case anyone wanted more.

We all dug in, except for Olivia. Bree, on a first bite of steak, let out a small moan of pleasure, and Stella seemed pleased with hers as well. It had been awhile since I'd cooked for anyone else, and I was pleased that I hadn't lost my touch.

Before I was even a quarter of the way through mine, Bree had already finished her fillet and was eyeing the two remaining ones like a lion eyeing a fat zebra with a limp. "Bree, help yourself to more."

"You sure?"

"This is more than enough food for me. Unlike some lucky people with hyper metabolisms, some of us have to watch our girlish figures." I winked at her.

She laughed at that, and Stella interjected, "I am struggling just to finish what is on my plate, so help yourself, Bree."

Bree's face lit up at Stella's words. She let out a little moan of pleasure as she scooped up the platter and emptied all of it onto her plate.

Olivia laughed. "You keep cooking like this for Bree, and she will have your babies!"

"Liv!" admonished Bree sternly, but then her face softened, and she added, "Well, maybe not bab*ies*, plural, but one *baby* would be acceptable for food this good."

We all laughed, but I started imagining Were babies with elemental Air powers, and I shuddered a bit, even though the rational part of me knew this wasn't possible: If Bree and I had a child together, it would either be a Were or an elemental—it couldn't inherit both powers.

After we finished, Stella excused herself, saying she was going to check on Blue and turn in for the night. We all wished her a good night.

I asked Olivia where she was going to sleep tomorrow; the spare bedrooms all had windows, and vampires and windows that let in sunlight didn't mix well.

Olivia smiled. "The cold cellar in your basement will work for what I need."

I yawned and decided it was time for bed. "I'm beat. I'm going to call it a night. I'm assuming you and Olivia are up until sunrise?"

Weres weren't nocturnal, except for the night of the full moon, but I figured that since Bree and Olivia were best friends, Bree probably spent her evenings awake and slept during the day to spend more time with Olivia.

Bree nodded. "Thank you for taking us in—and for the food."

"No problem. It is actually nice having other people in this big old house for a change, and it's fun to cook for a group. If you get bored, there is a TV in the living room that is internet-enabled and logged into my Netflix account. Good night."

The girls wished me a good night and chatted with each other as I left the room.

Chapter 7

Saturday, February 10

The next morning, I slept in until close to 11:00 a.m., which was something I rarely did. After a quick shower, I was ready for the day. I got dressed, hit my home office, and fired up my PC, then spent the next twenty minutes filling out the bounty claims on James McMahon and the leprechaun. Once I was finished, I made a call to my healer friend, Marion.

We exchanged pleasantries for a bit before Marion asked, "I'm guessing you're not calling to chitchat. What do you really need?"

"Do you have any contacts who can get donated blood?"

"That's an odd request. I'd ask why, but I get the feeling I'd be better off not knowing. Yeah, I can get it. How much do you need?"

"Six bags?" I tossed out, figuring that would get Olivia through at least a few days.

"It will take me a couple of hours. Stop by after three—and it will cost you."

"How much?"

The line was quiet for a moment before Marion said, "A thousand bucks for all six bags."

"Done. See you at three."

Marion said goodbye and hung up. I opened the safe in my office and grabbed $1,000 from the $10,000 I kept in there for emergencies. I paused as I looked at the stack of bills in there, as that much money was more than I had usually made in a year back in my hero days. I shook my head and stuffed the $1,000 in my pocket, then closed the safe.

It was coming up on noon, and I was getting hungry. The house was still quiet, but I figured if I started breakfast—brunch, now—that would wake people up. If you cook it, they will come.

I started cooking up bacon, sausage, scrambled eggs, hash browns, and pancakes and set the table for four, just in case Blue woke up. I wasn't sure what she ate, but I didn't want to be rude. I put out a large jug of orange juice, brewed a pot of coffee, and put all the condiments on the table.

I found myself smiling as the bacon sizzled in the pan and I flipped pancakes. I was enjoying cooking a large meal again. I used to cook when Rebecca and I were together. Rebecca and I had been high school sweethearts, and she had been the one serious relationship I'd had in my life. We had moved in together after she finished university. We broke up three years later. My erratic schedule and her worrying about me every time I went out on patrol became too much for her ...

As I continued cooking, movement upstairs meant at least one person was up and about.

A few minutes later, a sleepy-looking Bree, still in the scrubs from last night, wandered into the kitchen. "Something smells good."

Stella wandered in behind her. Bree poured herself a coffee, and Stella grabbed a tall glass of orange juice.

I added the last of the pancake mix to the pan. "Just about done! I will be serving up in a minute."

As we began eating, I asked Stella about Blue and was told there had been no change. I let the women know I had arranged blood for Olivia and would have to head out at three o'clock to get it, and then I asked if anyone needed anything while I was out.

Bree fessed up that she needed some clothes, a toothbrush, and other minor essentials. I kicked myself for not realizing that—I mean, the poor girl didn't even have shoes at this point. We made a list of things the ladies needed, and after loaning Bree a jacket and an ill-fitting pair of sneakers, the two of us made a quick trip to Walmart.

Once we returned home, I turned to Bree and asked, "I was going to hit my healer contact and pick up Olivia's, um, juice boxes. You want to come along?"

Bree seemed to consider it before she shook her head. "I'd like to, but the idea of underwear appeals more, which means I have a ton of laundry to do."

I nodded and left her to it.

On the way to Marion's, I had to make two emergency maneuvers to avoid birds that seemed to be determined to fly into me. I was grateful when I touched down safely on the roof of Marion's twenty-story apartment building. A few minutes later, I was knocking on her door.

I was surprised when a man answered instead of Marion. He had to be in his late sixties or early seventies, making him and Marion roughly the same age, and he had a long, scraggly gray beard and long silver hair that was tied back in a ponytail. The John-Lennon-style round reading glasses and the red bandana folded and tied around his forehead completed the hippie look. He was even wearing a tie-dye shirt and bellbottoms. I could just hear the '70s calling and asking for its style back. I had no doubt that he was a friend of Marion's.

"Is Marion in?" I asked.

Before the guy could answer, I heard Marion say, "Al, that is Zack. Let him in."

He opened the door and hurried me inside. After glancing out into the hall, he quickly closed the door.

Marion stood up from the couch, looking worried. Al seemed tense, as well, and I wondered what was up. Marion's apartment looked normal—like a '70s garage sale had exploded all over her living room—but that was normal for Marion. I was always amused at the sight of the bright-orange shag carpet and the strings of brightly colored beads instead of doors to her two bedrooms. The lava lamp, the Andy Warhol replica paintings hanging around the place, and the toy stuffed birds tucked into nooks and crannies were all part of Marion's style.

Al reached into the hemp bag he was carrying over his shoulder. He fished around for a moment before pulling something out. He cupped his hands together and held them out to me. "Hi, Zack. I'm Al. I'm a friend of Marion's. Peace and love be with you."

I took the business card and the smooth colorful rock he was holding. The business card had "Al Moon, Horticulturist" on it. Under that was written, "Peace and love be with you." The card also had a phone number, address, and email on it.

I caught a skunky smell lingering in the apartment that even the pungent incense candles burning in the background didn't cover and mentally changed "Horticulturist" to "Pot Dealer."

I thanked him for the gifts as I fished out my wallet and put his card in one of the pockets. I examined the rock. One side was painted light blue and had a hand-painted white peace sign on it; the other side had a colorful tie-dye pattern on it. The rock had some nice weight to it. It was about the same size as a credit card and was about a half-inch thick in the center. It narrowed at the edges and had smooth, rounded sides.

Al held out his hands, closed his eyes, and said, "I sense much stress in you. Whenever the stress gets to you, hold the peace rock and meditate on the universe; this will help you."

42

I nodded. Not knowing what else to do with the rock, I slipped it into the front pocket of my jeans.

Marion almost ran over to us. The first thing I always noticed about Marion was her blue eyes, as they were magnified by the large, thick, round glasses she always wore. I had never seen her wearing makeup, and her clothing was always colorful. Today, it was a tie-dyed long-sleeve shirt, faded bellbottom jeans with a large hand-drawn peace sign on the upper right leg, and open-toed sandals. Her long silver-gray hair was tied back in a ponytail and braided, but there were a few strands sticking out, refusing to conform with the rest of her hair.

I asked, "Everything okay?"

"Not sure. A couple of hours ago, I had two well-dressed church types, a man and a woman, at the door asking about you and if I knew you. I asked them why they were looking for you, but they told me it was 'church business' and were reluctant to go into details about 'God's work.' They asked if I had an address for you or had seen you recently. I told them I hadn't seen you in weeks and that you just came by here when you needed my services, so I didn't have your address either. They asked to come in, but I had a bad feeling about the two of them. I told them I was currently in the middle of helping a client—you know, to discourage them from entering—but the man stepped forward like he was going to barge in anyway. He stopped at the edge of my threshold, though. I think he sensed the wards protecting this place and backed off. The woman opened her purse and took out this business card." Marion handed me the card. "She held it out to me, but I said I couldn't help her and didn't want to get involved. She tucked the card into the gap in the doorframe and said to give it to you if I saw you, and then they both left. Once I heard the elevator ding, I grabbed the card and closed the door. The whole encounter freaked me out a bit, so I called Al over to keep me company."

The man being able to sense Marion's wards worried me. Wards were basically protection spells cast on a home or business; if the wards detected that a person intended harm to their owner, they would prevent that person from entering. Most magic users could cast ward spells. Like Marion, I had paid a wizard to have my own home warded.

If the man could sense Marion's wards, that meant he was Enhanced in some way. Elementals like myself had no way to sense wards, but many Enhanced Individuals such as vampires, fae, and magic users could sense wards.

I took the card from her. It read, "Our Lady of the Lord Ministries, Edith Baxter, Minister." The address was in Barrie, Ontario, which was north of Toronto and quite a drive from Hamilton. There was a cell number, main number, fax, and email on it. There was no website listed, which was odd. The email was weird, too—it was a G-mail address and not a custom domain. I tucked the card in my pocket, figuring I'd Google Edith and her church later and see what I could find.

"Any ideas what these people want from you?" asked Marion.

"Not a clue, but it is curious that they would come to you looking for me. Not a lot of people know about our relationship."

Marion's face erupted with anger, and she sputtered, "Damn it! I knew I should have sent you to Betty instead of Chapman."

"You think Dr. Chapman is the reason those people were sniffing around?" I asked, not sure what my visit to him the night before had to do with Marion's visitors earlier today. The only thing I could come up with was that he was one of the only people who knew about Marion and me, since Marion had referred me to him.

"The healing community is pretty tight. There are two types of healers out there: those who do it for the joy of providing healing to those in need and those who are in it for the money. Chapman is a good healer, but he is certainly in it for the money."

"You charge for your services. What is the difference?"

Marion laughed. "We all charge—we have to eat and pay bills, you know. But for some, money is more the driving force than healing. There have been rumors about Chapman providing patient information if the money was right and violating healer/patient privilege, but nothing has ever been proven."

My conversation with Olivia about her sire came back to me, and I suddenly had an "Oh shit" moment of my own. I also realized Chapman would have my real name from my credit card and would have known I was from Hamilton because of Marion's referral. My concern must have shown on my face, because Marion gave me a questioning look. I explained, "I can't talk about the details, but there were some things said last night in his office that, if they got back to the wrong parties, would bring a lot of unwanted interest in the women currently staying with me. Marion, I don't mean to be rude, but I think I need to get that blood and go."

She nodded and headed over to her old harvest-gold-colored fridge. I followed. I opened my reusable grocery bag, and she transferred the six bags of plasma into it. I fished out the $1,000 in cash from my pocket and handed it to her.

I went the door to her apartment and said, "Thanks. I'll talk to you later."

"Zack, be careful out there. If you need me, you know where to find me."

"You too. Nice meeting you, Al. Thanks again for the rock."

I opened the door and peered out cautiously, but the hallway was empty. I made it to the roof a few minutes later and made a beeline for home. On the flight home, while keeping my eyes peeled for kamikaze birds, I pondered how hard it would be for someone to find my house. I only used my cellphone and didn't have a landline, which meant looking up my phone number wouldn't yield my address. I'd bought the house under the numbered company I used to run my business with, so Googling my name shouldn't yield an address for me. And I didn't advertise, as the UN bounty website provided all the business I needed.

If Dr. Chapman was the one who had given the people information about Olivia, he had my credit card number. If they were connected enough, there were ways to turn that into an address for me, but the fact that they had stopped by Marion's place looking for me meant they probably didn't have those types of resources. On the other hand, I knew from bounty hunting that if someone wanted to find you bad enough, they would.

Chapter 8

Saturday, February 10

When I entered the kitchen, Bree was busy raiding my fridge. She was making herself a sandwich that could have fed a small country. I once again envied her rapid metabolism. I slipped around her and cleared some space in the fridge to stock it with Olivia's "juice boxes" (which was easier than thinking of them as bags of human blood).

I debated telling Bree about the churchgoers, but I let her enjoy her snack in peace and headed up to my office to do some Google kung fu.

I entered "Our Lady of the Lord Ministries," but none of the results matched a church or church group in Barrie. The search for "Edith Baxter" yielded nothing relevant, and neither did "Edith Baxter Barrie Ontario." The whole church thing must have been a front, and "Edith Baxter," an alias. That was nice to prove, but it didn't help me figure out what they wanted.

I studied the phone number on the card and kicked around calling them, which might give me an idea of what they were up to. It was tempting, but I held off at that moment. Instead, I shut off the computer and went to find Bree. Maybe the information on the card would ring a bell with her or Stella.

I grabbed a can of pop from the fridge and asked, "Bree, do you have a minute to talk?"

"Sure, what's up?"

As I sat down, the peace rock in my pocket shifted and was suddenly trying to compete for the same space my right nut was currently occupying. I winced in discomfort and reached down to adjust the rock to a more comfortable position.

Bree joined me at the table, and I handed her the card. She looked at the card with a blank expression on her face, which changed to one of confusion as she read it. Either she was a stunningly good actress, or she had no idea what this card was about.

She handed the card back to me. "You trying to convert me or something?"

I smiled and shook my head, then spent the next couple of minutes bringing her up to speed on Olivia telling me about how she and Bree had been turned, Marion's odd visitors, the fake name and fake church, and Marion's concerns about Dr. Chapman sharing confidential patient information.

Her expression instantly changed to one of alarm, and she asked, "You think Olivia's or my turning has something to do with these people?"

"I'm not sure, but the McMahon bounty was the only thing I have been working on recently. He is now in a federal holding facility, so the only thing I can think of that would attract this type of attention is your or Olivia's history."

Bree went quiet. After a moment, she said, "We will leave you once Olivia wakes up. I don't want to endanger you."

"Don't be ridiculous. You aren't going anywhere. Blue is still out of commission, and you have no money, which really limits where you can go. I've spent sixteen years in careers that aren't exactly low-risk; I can handle a little danger. The house has wards around it, and those people might not be able to even find this place. If they do find the place and manage to crack the wards, they'd still have to deal with me and your team."

By the look on her face, I could see she wasn't entirely convinced that staying here was right, so I took a deep breath and added, "Besides, it is partially my fault that Olivia is in this mess in the first place." Bree's face bunched up in confusion, and I explained. "In Dr. Chapman's office, if I hadn't bugged her about how you two had been turned, we wouldn't be in this mess."

Bree looked like she wanted to argue, but she sighed and said, "Thank you. If things do get too crazy, though, we will leave."

"Fair enough. For now, though, I am thinking about calling this 'Edith' and having a little chat with her."

Bree eyes widened, and she blurted out, "Are you nuts?"

"It is the quickest way to find out what they want, and it isn't like they can trace the call."

"You sure?"

I smiled. "Pretty sure. If they were that good, they would be here already. Look, maybe we'll get lucky and they'll get to the point, but even if they don't, at least knowing what they want gives us direction. Right now, we're just sitting in the dark and guessing."

Bree reluctantly nodded.

I picked up my iPhone and entered the number. After two rings, a strong female voice with an overblown rural Canadian accent answered. "Our Lady of the Lord Ministries." The accent didn't ring true to me.

"My name is Zack Stevens. I heard you are looking for me."

"Mr. Stevens, thank you for calling. We have an issue at our church that you might be able to help us with, and we are willing to pay for your services. Do you think we can meet to discuss this?"

"Edith" sounded overly happy.

"Edith, how about we cut through the shit and get down to what you really want, okay? I Googled you and your so-called church, and neither seems to exist."

The silence that followed lingered, but then the women said, "Very well, Zack. You are correct. My name is Lilith, and I am the leader of the drow Blood Dagger clan. We have been hired to retrieve the vampire you are harboring and return her to our employer. I am going to make you an offer you would do well to heed: Give us the vampire, and you may live."

Her earlier fake-friendly voice was gone. Lilith's voice, now sporting a slight French accent, dripped with menace.

"Tempting, but I have grown rather attached to my little fanged friend, which means you are going to have to sweeten the deal before I give her up."

Bree smothered a gasp and shot me a look like I was crazy. I smiled and held up a hand to silence her.

Lilith replied, "You dare barter with a drow? The offer to let you live was more than generous."

"Lilith, honey, don't get your panties in a bunch. I'm not looking for much: a couple of frozen-yogurt coupons, a buy-one-get-one-free Happy Meal coupon, and, of course, you letting me live, and we have a deal."

Bree's eyes went wide at my comment. She turned away to smother her laugh.

The line went quiet for a few seconds, and then Lilith exploded with rage on the other end. "You dare mock me? You will die slowly for that. I will tear out your still-beating heart from your chest and show it to you as you die. Know this: When the Blood Dagger clan takes a contract, we complete it—or die."

"I'll take option two then. Ridding this world of your evil kind is something that I will be happy to do. Take my advice: Go back to your employer and tell them the vampire isn't worth this effort. Beg to be let out of the contact, or I will end your clan."

"We will find you and the vampire, and you will die screaming," said Lilith. There was a loud *click* on the line, and it went dead.

"Well, that was rude," I said to Bree. "I wasn't finished deal-making."

"You are insane," said Bree. She shook her head while trying to hide her own grin.

"Probably, but now we know they want Olivia, and I have a pretty good idea of who hired them."

The smile on Bree's face instantly disappeared at Olivia's name. After a moment, she asked, "Who are they, and who hired them?"

I took a deep breath and explained. "They are dark elf mercenaries— or assassins, depending on the job. I think they want Olivia alive, but they are willing to settle for dead. They are probably getting a bonus for bringing her in alive ... undead? Lilith, their leader, has a French accent, and that makes me think Henri's successor sent them. If that successor isn't Henri's spawn, Olivia has a better claim to the throne than they do. They probably want Olivia alive to challenge her to a duel to the death. Beating her will bolster their claim to the throne."

Bree nodded. "I thought the dark fae were banned from Earth under penalty of death?"

"Yeah, they are supposed to be. That was one of the earliest resolutions passed by the UN after the atrocities the dark fae committed while serving the Nazis during World War II. They were hunted down, but various dark fae were taken in or hidden by vampire courts and other factions. The rest went underground. The bounties are still there, but few people bother to go looking for dark fae anymore. Generally, most of them keep their heads down and don't make trouble. They cast a glamour to disguise themselves to more easily blend in and look human."

Bree was quiet for a bit and then asked, "Are there ways to detect them?"

I swallowed my mouthful of Coke and said, "Of course! There are certain magic items that can see through glamour, and certain Enhanced Individuals can see their true forms."

"Can *you*?" she asked, getting to the heart of the matter.

I paused for a moment. I knew that light fae and dark fae had auras that I could see, but I had never discussed my ability to see auras with anyone but my departed mother. I reluctantly nodded.

"How?" Bree asked the question I was both expecting and dreading.

I silently argued with myself about whether to tell Bree. She must have sensed my reluctance, because she said, "Never mind. The *how* isn't important; as long as you can spot them, that is the main thing."

It impressed me that Bree was willing to take my word for it. She trusted me enough to just let it go.

I could already see the wheels turning in her mind about how to deal with this new threat. Despite her young age, it was obvious why Bree was the leader of this group I had taken in—she was bright and decisive, and something about her directness made me instinctively want to trust her.

I decided that if we were going to deal with this threat, I would *have* to trust her. "I see auras."

"Huh?"

"All people with Enhanced abilities have different-colored auras around them that tell me about their abilities. Your aura is purple, with red and black outlines. The purple tells me you are a Were, the red indicates a cat type of Were, and the black indicates a panther. You are the first Werepanther I have met, so the black threw me a little when I first saw you. Olivia's is blood-red with a black outline." I lowered my voice. "You are the only person alive that I have ever told about my aura-seeing ability."

Bree's eyes widened at the last part, and she said in a soft voice, "Thank you for sharing that. I swear no one will ever learn about it from me." She paused for a moment. "Zack, I have two questions about your ability, and then I will never bother you about it again. Do the auras tell you how powerful someone is, and have you seen a dark elf's aura before?"

I liked how Bree got to the heart of the matter with her questions. The dark elves were a threat to us, and she was trying to figure out how we could deal with them. It hit me that it was *we* who would deal with them and not *I*. I had been on my own so long that *we* was a new thing for me. I had three powerful allies in Bree, Olivia, and Stella, but I also didn't know a lot about them. It was time to change that. "Good questions. I will share those answers with you, but I also have a couple of questions about you and your abilities that I would like answered. Deal?"

Bree laughed and said, "A bit of you 'Show me yours, and I'll show you mine,' eh?"

Her comment brought a smile to my face. "Something like that, but if you want to play that game for real, I'm up for it." I gave her an exaggerated leer.

She rolled her eyes at me. "Let's just keep this verbal, okay?"

I laughed, held my hands up in mock surrender, and continued. "The size of an aura generally tells me how powerful someone is. You and Olivia have auras that radiate out about three inches, which is impressive for only being a little over a year old. Normally, they are less than an inch at that age. Three inches puts you both in the range of a normal fifteen-to-twenty-year-old Were or vampire."

She seemed a little surprised at this, and I moved on to her next question. "I have never seen a dark elf's aura, but I have seen a wood elf's aura, and I suspect they will be similar. The fae are all magic-based creatures, so their primary aura is rainbow-colored. Since there aren't a lot of fae among us, once I see rainbow auras, we will have found our drow."

The washing machine dinged, and Bree went to deal with her laundry, leaving me alone with my thoughts. As glib as I had been earlier with Lilith on the phone, I was concerned about taking on dark elves. They were ruthless and vicious. I had seen photos of villages and towns they had attacked during World War II. The mutilated state of their victims made me determined to never let them take me alive. On the upside, the bounties on them ranged from $10,000 to $20,000, and depending on how many there were, it would make a nice payday—assuming, of course, I survived the encounter ...

Bree joined me again a few minutes later and said, "You wanted to know about me and my abilities?"

I had a bunch of questions, but I took a moment to organize my thoughts. I asked, "How many Weres or vampires have you and Olivia been around since you've changed?"

"None. Most of this last year has been spent at Stella's secret underground laboratory."

I tensed at the second part of her statement. "Stella has a secret underground laboratory? Is she a mad scientist or something?"

Bree laughed and shook her head, "No, though she does tinker and invents some useful items on occasion." Her whole demeanor changed, and she added, "When the 'man' who adopted her died, she inherited it." She paused and added, "Since we were changed, we have spent most of our time in the lab. Liv or me would go out with Stella and Blue once a week to get groceries and blood for Olivia. In the last few months, Blue has taken us out hunting once a week in some isolated woods, but the club was our first real trip out in public since being changed."

By the way she had clenched her teeth and spat out the word 'man,' I knew there was a story there, but I sensed it was a heated issue for her and let it go. I got back on the topic of her being a Were. "You are an odd duck as far as Weres go. Your abilities and control are much more advanced than a yearling Were's should be. Also, most Weres need a pack for structure and support, but you have managed to go a whole year without a pack."

Bree thought for a moment. "You said I was probably turned by the most powerful of the Werepanther alphas. Wouldn't that explain my abilities and control? As for pack, Stella, Blue, and Olivia are my pack. I feel extremely protective of them; any type of threat to them gets me incredibly angry."

"The alpha blood would account for the abilities, but not the control—that is all *you*. I suspect you were an exceptionally strong-willed person before the change. I'm guessing in the absence of a real Were pack, you have adapted. Making your friends your pack would make sense. It will be interesting to see what happens if you meet other Weres—whether you will be drawn to them or feel a strong urge to join a pack. Do you need to be locked up during a full moon?"

"Not anymore. The first two full moons I did, but after that I was able to control the beast. I'm still forced to change into my beast form, but I am in control. I really have to watch myself near the full moon, though, as my temper ripples just below the surface. I end up walking a knife's edge from going into a violent rage, but I've managed to keep the anger in check and not kill or injure anyone yet."

Normally, learning that control was something a pack helped with. The fact that she had done it without a pack to teach her and had managed to tame her beast in just a couple of months was truly impressive. "During your fight with McMahon, you were able to change into a hybrid form, and that, too, is remarkable. It usually takes years, and some Weres never master that form. Given your progress with control and the hybrid form, have you ever attempted to try a partial transformation?"

Bree gave me a look that implied she had no idea what I was taking about, so I explained, "Only the strongest and most powerful Weres can transform partially. It is just changing one part of yourself into that Were form, like your hand or your eyes or your fangs."

"No, I haven't. I've never even thought about doing something like that."

A curious expression appeared on Bree's face. She held up her right hand and focused intently on it. After only moments, her fingers started lengthening into deadly claws. She gritted her teeth, and a light bit of sweat formed on her brow as the hand continued changing.

A few moments later, it was over. Her lovely human hand had been replaced by a dark-fur-covered hand with razor-sharp claws. Her eyes went wide as she examined her hand with a proud look on her face. "That is so cool!" she exclaimed.

"That is certainly a handy skill to have if you can't find a can opener, scissors, or knife when you need one. If you are still here in two days on garbage night, I will be making you cut up any boxes that need recycling."

"Cute," said Bree. She focused again on her hand, and the claws retracted, the fur receded, and her normal human-shaped hand was back. It had long nails, but these were much less deadly than the earlier ones.

I glanced over at the clock in the kitchen and saw that it was 4:30 p.m. I pondered what to do about dinner. With Bree tearing quickly through the food in the fridge, I needed to hit the grocery store—the last thing I wanted was a hungry Were in the house.

"Zack, how do you know so much about vampires, Weres, and the Enhanced community in general? I can't see Hamilton and southern Ontario being a hotbed of Enhanced Individual activity."

"My mother was an Air elemental, and when I was growing up, she had me read lore books and taught me about the supernatural world every free moment she had. Mom was relentless. There were quizzes, flashcards, and even games she made up to test me and help me learn. I hated it; I just wanted to be a normal kid and spend my time playing with other kids. It might be cliché, but she felt that knowledge was power. The more I knew about what a person's abilities and capabilities were, the more chance I had of survival. She used to grade me with either an A or a D."

"Pass or fail?" guessed Bree.

"Close. The A was for 'alive' and the D was for 'dead.' "

"You talk about her using the past tense," said Bree softly.

"She died from cancer when I was eighteen."

"I'm sorry. I shouldn't have asked," said Bree. She looked mortified.

"It's fine. It was a long time ago, and I have made peace with it. Mom did have a point: Knowledge *is* power. You and Olivia need more of it if you are both going to survive and flourish in this new world you've found yourselves in. You need to spend some time in a Were community. Olivia needs to spend time in a vampire one. They will teach you things that will help you. You also need to learn about the other Enhanced Individuals out there."

Bree arched an eyebrow at me. "Such as?"

I thought about the immense amount of monster lore I had learned over the years and figured I'd start with the basics. "How much do you know about the seven classes?"

She gave me a blank look.

I sighed. "In 1868, Charles Darwin published a book on Enhanced Individuals called *The Five Classes*. At that time, the book was confiscated by the British government and never made available to the public, due to a worldwide government agreement that the knowledge of monsters and others with extraordinary powers should be kept from the public to prevent mass panic. The book did make the rounds through various governments around the world, though, and was considered the ultimate guide to monsters and such."

Bree's expression turned angry at the term "monsters," and I held up my hand to forestall her reply before continuing. "I'm being historically accurate using the term 'monsters.' In 1868, no one used the term 'Enhanced Individuals.' "

She huffed and reluctantly nodded.

I continued. "The book broke all creatures with extraordinary powers into five classes. The first class was the God class; this contained gods, all their servants and avatars, and demons. The second class was the Magic class, which included mages and witches and elementals like me. The third class was the Fae, which ranged from tiny three-inch faeries to dragons. The fourth class was the Undead, which was fairly self-explanatory. The fifth class was the Beast class; Weres made up the biggest part, but it also included yeti, wendigos, and people with the ability to talk to or control animals. It is thought that the individuals in each of these classes have existed since the beginning of human history. In some cases, they may even predate human history."

I took a quick drink and continued. "After the Nazis exposed the Undead, Fae, and God classes to the world when they used them to try and hold on to their conquests, the worldwide ban suppressing the existence of these creatures was lifted. *The Five Classes* by Darwin was published and released to the world just after the war ended. In 1960, Darwin's work was updated through a UN mandate, and the Super class and the Alien/Unknown class were added—the new Super class exists because of the Hamburg Raid in July of 1944."

An expression of understanding lit up Bree's face, and she asked, "That was the raid by Allied commandos to stop the Nazis from opening a portal to Hell, right?"

I nodded and continued. "The Thule Society, working with the Nazi SS under Hitler's orders, was attempting to open a portal to Hell by tapping into a ley line. The Allied raiding party had mages, Weres, and light fae in their group, all of whom could shut the line down. They were almost too late—as they fought their way into the secret complex, the Nazis activated the portal. No one knows what actually happened, whether the portal failed or the raiding party was somehow successful, but there was a massive explosion, and both the complex and the line were completely destroyed.

"Never before in history had a ley line been destroyed. You unleash that much random magical energy, and you are going to have issues. To this day, the area fifty miles around the crater is a magical dead zone. Spells and magic items don't work. At the time, there was great fear and uncertainty about what the destruction of this line would bring, and the world collectively held its breath. Nothing seemed to happen until 1954, when reports started coming in about children hitting puberty and having amazing powers. These superkids had powers that had never been seen before: Some could fly, some were immensely strong or fast, some could make themselves smaller or larger, some could manipulate gravity, some could read minds, and some could move objects with their minds. There were a whole host of other weird and wonderful powers. With these new Enhanced Individuals, the Super class was born."

Bree pondered this for a moment. "When they covered this in school, I always wondered why anyone would want to open a portal to Hell?"

"Yeah, it sounds insane, but remember that by 1944, the war was going badly for the German army. They were getting pushed back on the Russian front, and Allied bombing raids were hampering their production abilities. The Nazis made a deal with the queen of the dark fae, and the dark fae joined the fight. Drow, orcs, trolls, ogres, and a host of other dangerous creatures spilled out across the Russian front and halted the Russian advance. The Allies drafted as many Enhanced Individuals as possible to counter this, including Weres and vampires, who had been hunted and killed on sight until they were recruited for the war effort. Any Were or vampire who joined got full rights as a citizen. This pushed the scales back to the Allies' favor, and the Russian army began to advance again.

"Adding the dark fae had helped the Nazis before, so they began looking for other powers to align with. A demon approached the Nazi high command and offered Hell's services, and a deal was struck: The Nazis would keep all the territory they had captured to date, and Hell's minions would keep whatever lands they captured themselves. The Nazis were desperate—it was inevitable that they would lose the war—and this deal would allow them to keep their gains and bring an end to the war they were losing. As long as the Fatherland was intact, I don't think they cared what happened to the rest of the world. They started work on opening a portal."

Bree went quiet, obviously taking in what I'd said, and I took a sip of pop. She frowned and asked, "The seven classes are a way to group similar Enhanced Individuals, but how are they any help in the real world?"

I smiled. "Let's take the dark elves who are hunting us as an example, okay?"

"Sure. They would be part of the Fae class, right?"

I nodded, and she continued. "But I don't see how knowing that helps us?"

"It tells us two things. First, dark elves, like any fae creatures, are magical. They have magical abilities. All of them can cast spells, though the spell levels vary from dark elf to dark elf. Some are capable of grander wizard-level spells, where others just use a bit of glamour and cast a few minor spells. The second thing it tells us is they don't like iron. Just the touch of it burns them, like silver does a Were."

"Does something need to be iron to kill them?"

I shook my head. "No, elves can be killed just like normal humans."

"Other than their magic, then, what makes them so dangerous?"

"They are fast and nimble, so hitting them is tricky. Also, the ones who aren't powerful magic users are usually expert archers or swordsmen."

"I thought you said they didn't like iron. How can they use a sword?"

"Their swords are made from silver."

Bree blanched.

"And are spelled to be unbreakable," I added. "While we are on the subject of their weapons, drow use poison on their swords and arrow tips. Even a minor hit can be fatal. I suspect that, for you, the poison probably won't be as big an issue, due to your healing ability."

Bree asked, "Which are more dangerous: the magic users or the bowmen and swordsmen?"

"Take out the magic users first," I instructed. "They will be casting fireballs, poison clouds, acid attacks, and lots of other nasty surprises. Their bowmen are top-notch, so keep moving and don't ever give them a stationary target. They should be your secondary targets after the magic users. Deal with the swordsmen last."

"Anything else I should know?"

I mentally went over all we'd discussed and finished with "Dark elves are vicious and cunning and will never show mercy. If you get one down, don't hesitate to finish them off—they will kill you without blinking. In a fight, get close and use your superior strength to beat them ..."

We chatted until after five o'clock, and Bree promised to share the information about dark elves with the others if they surfaced while I was out shopping. The dryer downstairs buzzed, and she got up to deal with it. I told her I was going grocery shopping and would be back shortly.

Chapter 9

Saturday, February 10

I was home thirty minutes later. When I dropped the food in the kitchen, I saw Stella at the table, talking to Bree. Both went silent when I walked in. I asked them if they would mind putting the food away and headed back out to grab dinner—it would have taken too long to cook at that point.

I stopped by the local rotisserie chicken restaurant and ordered two quarter-chicken dinners for Stella and myself, and a family pack consisting of a whole chicken, four orders of fries, a macaroni salad, coleslaw, and four buns and dipping sauces for Bree. I prayed that would be enough for her.

I entered the house and was greeted by an anxious-looking Bree. She took the bags of food off me without saying anything and disappeared toward the kitchen.

"Hey! The two quarter-chicken dinners are for me and Stella!" I yelled after her.

I almost bumped into Olivia as she came up from the basement looking sleepy and still wearing my Lions jersey. She perked up when she saw me, and I got a little nervous at the hungry gleam in her eyes. My worry turned to fear when she leaned closer and sniffed me. Her voice sounded low and dangerous when she said, "Oh, you smell good."

I accessed my powers on reflex as she moved closer, and I managed to squeak out, "Olivia, your juice boxes are in the fridge."

She stopped. "Oh! Juice boxes!" Her voice sounded overly perky. She blurred to the fridge.

I felt like I was in a twisted version of one of those Snickers commercials—Olivia certainly wasn't herself when she was hungry.

In the few seconds it took me to enter the kitchen properly, Olivia already had one of the bags of plasma out and was warming it up in the microwave.

I grabbed a beer from the fridge and joined the ladies at the table. I was impressed that my chicken was still waiting for me; I had been more than a little worried that Bree was going to eat it too.

Olivia wandered over to the table and sat down with us. She had a happy smile on her face as she drained her bag of plasma. It was amazing how she could transform from scary predator to perky in such a short amount of time.

I popped the plastic lid off my dinner and dug in. Bree was almost halfway through her whole chicken; the side she had finished was picked so clean the bones almost gleamed. Stella seemed to be enjoying her meal as well.

"Chicken is another meal I miss … Hey, maybe after dinner one of you could let me take a small nibble off you! Maybe after eating chicken, you'll taste more like chicken." Olivia looked around hopefully.

"Pass," I said as she looked at me.

Stella shook her head at Olivia. "You know that my blood isn't safe for you to drink."

God, did I enjoy hearing that perfect, crisp English accent when Stella talked. I also filed away the fact that the Hyde potion had made her blood unsuitable for vampires to drink.

Olivia's gaze settled on Bree, who looked up from her first empty box of fries and shook her head. "I let you feed off me those two times because they were emergencies; I'm not doing it again just because you miss chicken!"

Olivia gave everyone a playful pout but went back to her juice box and didn't seem overly concerned about not getting her own special version of a chicken dinner.

After dinner was over, Stella tried to excuse herself from the table. Bree stopped her. "Hold on, Stella. Zack found out this afternoon that we have a problem." Bree spent a couple of minutes filling Stella and Olivia in about all the relevant details of the drow hunting Olivia. She finished with "Now that you are aware, we need to discuss this and how to deal with it."

The table went quiet, and I asked, "The elephant in the room isn't the drow—they are just hired lackeys. The big questions are who sent them and why."

Stella answered, "Thanks to Blue's shadow-traveling abilities being in demand with the English vampire court, she and I have spent a good deal of time with them and have gotten to know Elizabeth quite well. If she wanted Olivia, she would just send her own vampire enforcers to pick Olivia up. This is Elizabeth's territory; she would not use drow to cause issues in her own backyard. This has to be the French vampire court. Olivia has a claim to the throne; therefore, she is valuable to Giselle—or Roman."

"Roman?" I prompted.

"After Henri died last year, Giselle and Roman vied for the throne. Giselle won, but Roman was not happy. He is still lurking in the background, seeing if she can hold on to it."

"Were Giselle or Roman spawned by Henri?" I asked.

"Henri had only been the master of France since 1796, when Sebastien, who was his master and sire, was killed during the French Revolution. Henri's only spawn, Ada, and another of Sebastien's spawn were killed with Sebastien, leaving Henri and Roman to vie for the throne. Henri was a lot older and more cunning than Roman, so he assumed the vacated master's throne. Giselle's sire was the one killed with Sebastien, but she is about the same age as Roman—both are about 600 years old, give or take a few decades."

I kicked around what Stella had said. "Then Olivia, as Henri's direct spawn, actually does have a stronger claim to the throne than either of them."

"She would if she were in any position to defend it, but at her age, she doesn't have the strength to fight either of them."

Olivia gave a little pout and playfully flexed her arms as if posing at a bodybuilder competition.

I ignored her and asked Stella, "Would sending drow be something Giselle would do, or could this be Roman making a play for the throne?"

Stella paused. The expression of intense concentration that appeared on her face seemed out of place on her young features. "Roman wouldn't be this subtle. He is more the old-school warrior type; if he wanted Olivia, he'd come out himself and get her. Sending drow to do her dirty work would be much more Giselle's style. She is more of a thinker and plotter. She ran the intelligence arm of the French court before taking the throne. Giselle still has not appointed anyone to that position, so she is still running intelligence, in addition to her duties as master. Giselle is easily the more dangerous of the two; there is a keen mind lurking behind her beautiful exterior. She is completely ruthless and deadly."

"How do you know so much about the French vampire court?" I asked.

"The English and French courts meet quarterly; they alternate the meetings between France and England each time. For the last few years, Elizabeth and Henri have paid Blue to do the transport, and I have gone with Blue each time. The vampires take pity on me because I look like a child—vampires have few rules or morals, but the one crime they all agree on is turning a child. Seeing me brings out their protective side, so they do their best to make me feel comfortable at these meetings. I have gotten to know some members of both courts quite well, and they were only too willing to share their histories with me."

Bree piped up. "Any chance that Elizabeth can intervene on our behalf to get Giselle to back off?"

Stella shook her head. "Elizabeth didn't know about you and Olivia, and if she has found out, she is probably quite unhappy with me for keeping this from her. I doubt she is in the mood to do any favors for me at this moment."

I shifted in my seat and got squared by that bloody peace rock again. I fished it out from my pocket, fully intending to toss the stupid thing in the garbage after this conversation. I ended up idly rolling its smoothness in my hand while I listened.

Stella turned her attention toward me. "What is your plan for dealing with the dark elves, should they find us?"

I shrugged. "I will deal with them if they find us. There are wards around the entire property they'll have to get through first, which means we won't be taken by surprise. If they do attack, I want you ladies to grab Blue and get out of here if the fight looks to be going badly for me."

"No way! We are in this together, and we'll fight with you," said Bree firmly.

"No, Bree. Zack is right," said Stella. Bree glared at her, which Stella ignored as she explained, "We haven't fought with Zack before. We might get in his way. He handled the Earth elemental successfully when all of us failed. If the drow breach the wards, they will have free access to the whole property. If we join him in the fight, one might get by us and kill Blue while she is helpless to defend herself. Also, remember that their target is Olivia. If she goes out and joins the fight, we could be making things easier for them. I don't like it, either, but we need to stay together and protect Blue and Olivia."

I could see that every fiber of Bree's being wanted to argue, but her shoulders slumped. She made a small nod at Stella. Her beast probably influenced her thinking—protecting her pack would be the beast's first instinct, even over the prospect of a good fight.

Stella got up from the table and said, "Now that is settled. I do not believe there is anything else to discuss, as we can do nothing but wait to see if the dark elves find us or not. I am going to make myself some tea and go keep Blue company."

"Movie time!" exclaimed Olivia, who bounced up from the table in excitement.

Bree started to get up, but I stopped her. "Bree, hang here for a moment. There are a couple of things I need to discuss with you."

She turned to Olivia. "Liv, go find a movie, and don't worry about waiting for me. I will join you when I'm done here with Zack."

Olivia disappeared into the living room, but Stella was still making her tea.

"Bree, if the drow attack, get out of here and find a Hamilton cop. Ask them to find Rob Quinn. Tell him I sent you, and he will make sure you are safe."

I could tell Bree wasn't happy with this, but she agreed.

Stella then left the kitchen with her steaming brew cradled in her hands, which was what I had been waiting for.

"Have I done something to upset Stella?" I asked Bree.

Bree looked confused for a moment, and then a look of understanding flashed across her face. "No, it isn't you. It's because you're a man. Stella was sexually abused for years by her adopted 'father.' She's uncomfortable around men in general."

Bree's statement hit me like a punch in the gut. I stammered out an apology for asking.

"You didn't know, and you weren't the one who did it," she replied. "You have nothing to apologize for."

"Is the scumbag in prison?" I asked.

"No, he has been dead for over 100 years now."

That statement rocked me more than her first one; Stella looked about ten years old, but Bree had just said that she was over 100 years old.

Bree laughed at my expression. "Yeah, our little Stella looks good for 137 years old, doesn't she?"

No wonder Stella seemed mature for her age! She was thirteen times as old as she looked. I'd suspected that she was older than ten, based on her bearing and demeanor, but I'd figured she was in her thirties—at most.

If I had thought it through, it should have been obvious that she was older than she appeared. The Hyde potion, as created by Dr.

Jekyll, first appeared in the late nineteenth century, and several Hyde creatures appeared in the next couple decades, but there hadn't been a new Hyde appearance since 1901. It was believed that the formula to the Hyde potion had been lost after that, so either Stella was from that time period, or she was the first new case in 116 years.

"Any chance you can tell me Stella's story?"

Bree pondered this for a moment and then said, "It is really Stella's story to tell, but she has never hidden it from us. After all you've done for us, I'm sure she would prefer you knew, rather than you thinking she had an issue with you. Stella values manners over almost everything."

Bree rolled her eyes at that last part and then said, "Stella was born in 1880 in the East End of London. She never knew her father, and her mother was a prostitute. Her mother died just after Stella's fourth birthday. She had no other known living relatives, so she ended up in an orphanage. The conditions in that place sounded awful. Stella said the kids there were always dirty and hungry, and their caretakers barely seemed to care if their charges lived or died. She hated that place.

"On her sixth birthday, a wealthy 'gentleman' named Sir Reginald Whitworth came by and adopted Stella. Stella ate her first full meal in over two years. Her face lit up when she described how glorious the food was." Bree paused, and with a humorless laugh then added, "It was funny hearing Stella talk about having a bath in clean water. On the rare times the kids got a bath at the orphanage, Stella ended up taking hers after a number of other kids had already taken theirs in the same water."

Bree turned somber. "The sexual abuse started on that first day, too, and happened just about every day after."

The thought of an innocent six-year-old being molested on a daily basis was almost too much for me; the thought of a molester giving his victim a Hyde potion didn't make any sense at all. "How does an upper-class English gentleman get access to a Hyde potion, and why would he be stupid enough to give Stella an alternate form that could tear him limb from limb?"

"Sir Reginald was a mad scientist. You are jumping ahead, but I must warn that the story gets worse as it goes on. You sure you want to hear this?" Bree looked concerned again.

I nodded, and she continued. "After a week of being at Sir Reginald's, Stella complained to one of her tutors about the abuse. The tutor didn't believe her, but when their lesson ended for the day, Sir Reginald killed the tutor with an acid gun. The tutor melted into a puddle of liquid right before Stella's eyes. Sir Reginald warned her that saying anything to anyone else would result in the same thing happening to them.

"This routine of Stella learning during the day while Sir Reginald worked in his secret underground laboratory and then him abusing her at night continued for three years. Stella was an exceptionally bright student, and by the time she was nine, she was already doing university-level studies. Sir Reginald loved that she was highly intelligent, and he brought in tutor after tutor to push her. What Sir Reginald didn't love was Stella was growing taller and becoming less childlike with every passing day. He became desperate to stop her from aging.

"He first approached the English vampire court, since he had provided them with his inventions for years, and asked one of the vampires to turn Stella. The vampire refused, since turning a child was one thing they will not do. The vampire told him that if he had asked Elizabeth for this, she would have killed him instantly.

"Sir Reginald turned his attention toward a different solution. Months later, he traded for the Hyde potion. The Hyde potion had a side effect that he desired: It slowed down the aging process. Sir Reginald strapped Stella down and injected her with the potion and then attached a power-blocking collar that he had designed to prevent her from changing into her Hyde form. The Hyde persona whispered to Stella that if she could get the collar off, it would kill Sir Reginald and they would be free. Stella spent all her free time trying to remove the collar. She injured herself a couple of times trying it, and that tipped Sir Reginald off to what she was up to."

I whistled and said, "Even with the collar, Sir Reginald was playing a dangerous game. If Stella ever got it off, he was a dead man."

Bree nodded and continued. "In response to Stella's attempts to break out of the collar, he invented a stasis chamber that kept whoever was inside it in suspended animation. That was where the real nightmare began. He would abuse Stella and then simply put her back in the chamber. Stella's life became one continuous rape after another, with only the occasional bath or meal to break things up. There were no more tutors, just his unwanted attentions nonstop.

"One day, he broke from this routine and removed her from the chamber to have dinner together to celebrate the new year. Stella was floored to find out that it was New Year's Eve 1900, not 1890. She had spent over ten years being pulled in and out of the stasis chamber.

From that point on, she made a point of asking the date each time she was pulled out of the chamber. The last day she saw Sir Reginald was March 21, 1903."

I was not ashamed to admit that my eyes welled up at this point. The idea of nonstop abuse for over a decade was monstrous and unimaginable. How did someone stay sane through that?

Bree continued. "Sir Reginald, by that time, was quite insane. He piloted a giant steam-powered robot of his own creation into London and threatened to destroy Buckingham Palace unless he was paid £1 million, but a group of English adventurers were in town and thwarted his plans. The robot was destroyed, and then the steam boilers were breached and literally cooked Sir Reginald to death in his cockpit."

Ouch, I thought, but then I smiled. If anyone deserved to be boiled alive, Sir Reginald would be at the top of that list.

"Unfortunately for Stella, no one else knew of the secret lab buried under London. She spent the next 108 years in the chamber, blissfully unaware of the passing time. Blue crashed into the chamber after escaping her home world through a portal that her father had built. Stella was freed from her prison and confronted by a strange blue alien who didn't speak any English. Blue didn't see Stella's small form as a threat, and she needed a guide in this strange new world she found herself in.

"Stella taught Blue English, and the two of them became friends. Blue used her sword to cut the power-blocking collar off Stella and helped Stella learn to control her Hyde form. After a few months, Stella had mastered her Hyde form and Blue's English was better. They both felt ready to leave the safety of the lab, so they traveled to the surface via Blue's shadow-traveling abilities. Stella found a newspaper and was shocked to read that it was 2011. Everyone she knew was dead, and she was overwhelmed at this new world, 'with its horseless carriages and flying machines,' as she put it." Bree smiled amusedly.

"They spent the next six months learning about their new world. Stella learned as much as she could through stealing newspapers and watching with Blue from the shadows. She decided she needed to talk to someone from this time. She had hoped that the vampire who had refused to turn her during her time with Sir Reginald was still alive, and she and Blue went to the English vampire court to track him down. The vampire had died during World War II, but she was granted an audience with Elizabeth.

"Elizabeth took pity on Stella and Blue and agreed to help them both adjust to the new world they found themselves in. It probably didn't hurt that Blue had shadow-traveling abilities either. The Chinese and Japanese vampire courts both had a shadow-traveler on staff, and this was something Elizabeth had envied for a while.

"Last year, Stella and Blue found us. We have all been living in Sir Reginald's secret underground lair ever since. Blue's travel fees from the English court covered the cost of buying blood for Olivia, but once the Food-O-Tron busted a few months ago, things got tight."

"What the heck is a 'Food-O-Tron'?" I asked.

Bree got a happy, faraway look on her face. "Sir Reginald would get wrapped up in inventing and would miss meals because he did not return to his house. He fixed that by inventing the Food-O-Tron. It's basically like one of replicator thingies from Star Wars."

The inner geek in me cringed at her mistake, and I corrected her. "Star Trek."

"Whatever. It's all the same crap."

Must contain nerd rage. Pretty lady doesn't realize the blasphemy she just spoke.

"Anyways, the Food-O-Tron had more than 100 recipes and drinks programmed into it. You just selected the number and pulled the lever, and a minute later, instant food … At least, that is what it used to do, until Blue and I broke it ordering the amazing oatmeal raisin cookies it made. We didn't do anything different than usual, but it made a crackling sound and a little smoke came out of it, and then nothing. Between the costs of blood and food, Blue's money was running out. That is why we came out to try and get that bounty," explained Bree.

"I'm assuming that the only way to reach this secret lair is via the shadows?"

Bree nodded.

"If Blue wakes up, you will be able to head back there? Olivia will be safe?"

"That's the plan. Now we just need Blue to wake up," said Bree with a sigh.

Chapter 10

Sunday, February 11

I awoke to the sound of a loud crow continuously cawing. In my haze, I wondered what the hell was going on. It eventually dawned on me that sound was the alarm for the wards; the wizard who had installed them was a bit of a nature freak.

I glanced over, and my bedside clock said it was 3:48 a.m. I scrambled from my bed and tripped on the sheets. My nude form hit the floor hard, but I got up and quickly dressed in the clothes I had left on the floor.

I almost bumped into Stella, Bree, and Olivia on my way out of my bedroom door. Bree asked, "What's going on?"

I sprinted to the front window and yelled over the alarm, "Someone is trying to break through the wards!"

I peeked out of the window, and there were two Our Lady of the Lord white vans out in front of the house. On the sidewalk stood a dozen rainbow auras outlined in purple. Lilith had found us. I returned to my room and grabbed my iPhone from beside my bed to call the cops, but I was surprised and disappointed to see I had no service. Someone in Lilith's group must have cast a spell to isolate us. I tossed the phone onto my bed in frustration.

I entered the hall and saw the ladies looking out the window. I yelled at them to get away from the glass—the wards would stop someone from physically entering the property uninvited and magic from being used against the house, but they wouldn't stop a bullet, arrow, spear, or any other inanimate object that was fired or thrown.

I stopped in front of the ladies and said, "Stay here. I'll take care of this. If things go badly, take Blue and get out of here. Remember what I told you: Find a cop and ask for Rob Quinn, and he will take care of you, understand?"

Bree obviously wasn't happy, but she nodded in agreement. I tore down the stairs and headed for the front door. I prayed the wards would hold, but I wasn't counting on it.

I thickened the air around me as a defensive measure just before I dashed out the front door. That move saved my life; it stopped five wickedly tipped arrows from turning me into a pincushion. Those arrows, suspended in the air in front of me, had sickly green liquid oozing off their razor-sharp barbed tips. The drow weren't messing around. If those five arrows somehow hadn't killed me, the poison would have.

The front door closed behind me, and the loud alarm in the house was muted. The yard was peaceful, except for the chanting of the two mages in the group trying to break my wards.

On the sidewalk in front of me were twelve well-dressed church types, but this was just their glamour hiding their true appearances. Five of them were holding longbows, which looked a little odd with the formal church outfits. Five more had swords in their hands. The last two, the mages, were making intricate gestures with their hands as they chanted.

Five more arrows joined the first five suspended in front of me. I gathered my power until blue sparks dripped from my hands.

A large Black lady looked at me; her eyes went wide at the sparks. Her exterior was an illusion, and I was willing to bet that underneath it was Lilith. I brought my hands up and unloaded a deadly strike of chain lightning, but Lilith was quicker and had leapt over and hidden behind one of the parked vans. If glamour had been powered by belief, the sight of a heavyset woman doing a Superman-like dive over the top of a van would have easily shattered its illusion.

Four of the elves screamed and collapsed lifelessly to the ground. I was pleased that one of the dead was one of the magic users. The electrical attack had also dropped two of the bowmen and one of the swordsmen. It didn't even faze the other seven, though. I had no idea if lightning would affect Lilith or not—the van had shielded her from my attack. The glamour on the four dead ones disappeared, and there was no question they were dark elves: purple skin, tall and slender forms, and pointy ears.

Elves were magical creatures; they had high immunity to elemental and magic attacks, though that immunity varied from elf to elf, as the four who had dropped aptly demonstrated.

Three more arrows joined the ten in front of me. I still had eight drow left to deal with, and these buggers could shrug off my best attack.

The pink glow of an energy bubble surrounding my property suddenly became visible. That bubble represented the wards; seeing them wasn't a good sign.

I have a bad feeling about this, echoed my inner Han Solo.

My priority became taking out the last mage before she broke my wards. My adrenaline spiked, causing me to become hyper aware of everything around me. The weight of the peace rock in my jean pocket caught my attention. I dismissed it instantly—it would be no help with this battle—but then inspiration struck me. I fished the rock out and held it in my right hand, extending my right arm out and aiming it like a rifle at the remaining mage.

More arrows joined the growing wall in front of me, but I ignored them. I called on my Air power and sent a concise but exceptionally powerful blast of wind out from my right hand. The peace rock launched out of my hand like a rocket. It shot across the front yard and slammed into the mage's left eye with a nauseating spatter of ocular fluid, blood, and brain matter. The mage was lifted clear off her feet and slammed into the van directly behind her. Her body went limp and slid down the side of the van to lie unmoving on the sidewalk.

Not even a second before the mage died, a large *boom* echoed across the yard. The pink light of the wards disappeared.

Seven left, but now there were no wards to hold them back, I thought as more arrows joined my growing collection.

Lilith and a swordsman advanced from the left, while the other two swordsmen tried to flank me on the right. The three bowmen stood where they were and shot arrow after arrow at me, which was becoming annoying. It was time to return the favor. I reversed the flow of air around the wall of arrows to flip them around. I smiled. The tips were now pointed at them instead of me. I focused and sent a severe gust of wind out directly in front of me. The arrows shot out faster than my eyes could follow and turned the three archers into porcupines. They dropped to the ground like puppets with their strings cut.

Four left, I thought as I eyed the remaining swordsmen.

I could hear sirens in the far distance; one of my neighbors must have called the cops. Help was on the way, but it would be precious minutes before they arrived. This fight would be over one way or another long before they got here.

One of the swordsmen on my right charged at me. I directed a large blast of wind at him, which lifted him from his feet and threw him tumbling back through the air. Luck was with me; his head hit the large maple tree on my property with a wet-sounding *crunch*, and he was out of this fight.

A blue flash erupted to my left. I turned and was hit by a spell of some sort. My whole body went stiff and wouldn't respond to my commands; I was completely frozen in place. Lilith lowered a magic pendant, and a dark, humorless smile appeared on her elfin face. My quick turn had left me off balance, and I fell sideways onto my lawn. The impact with the frozen ground hurt a little. I still couldn't move a muscle. Lilith and the other two swordsmen advanced, and I was completely helpless.

I strained and fought against the spell holding me in every way I could think of, but I couldn't move even a single hair on my head. I tried calling on my powers, but they wouldn't work either. I cursed to myself and felt fear begin to rise; I swore I wouldn't let them take me alive, yet here I was. I hoped the ladies had managed to get away when the wards collapsed.

The three remaining dark elves stopped about five feet from me. Lilith made her first mistake of the night: She monologued. "You have cost me many a good warrior this evening. I will add that to what you owe me. I promised you would die slowly—"

The front door of my house crashed open, interrupting her rant, and her face fell in fear. My back was to the house, so I had no idea what was happening ... until Stella's Hyde form yanked the warrior on my right off the ground by his legs and proceeded to slam the elf warrior's head into the grass. She then immediately lifted him back into the air and smashed his face on the stone tiles on the other side of her. Stella bounced the dark elf back and forth between the grass and stone until his head was mush. She let out a satisfied grunt and dropped his now-limp form to the ground.

Bree's panther-hybrid form pounced on the next-closest drow. He screamed as she tore his arm clean off. Bree rode the elf to the ground, mauling and shredding him the whole way. That elf was probably dead before he even hit the ground.

Lilith's eyes went wide as Olivia blurred in behind her and purred, "You were looking for me?" Olivia plunged her fangs into Lilith's neck and drank deeply.

The dark elf pulled a wicked-looking dagger from her belt and blindly plunged it backward toward Olivia. The curved tip didn't even get within six inches of the vampire before Olivia's lightning-fast hand appeared on Lilith's wrist. A sharp *crack* filled the air, and Lilith screamed as Olivia casually snapped her wrist like it was a dried-out twig. The dagger tumbled to the brown grass. Lilith struggled, but she couldn't escape Olivia's superior vampire strength. Olivia drained her until the life in Lilith's purple eyes was completely extinguished.

Olivia let Lilith's dead body drop to the ground. She wiped the blood at her mouth and chin, which just smeared it across her face, then proclaimed, "Elves are tasty," with a big grin.

She took a step and staggered a bit like she was drunk, and her eyes went wide. An expression of wonder danced across her face. "Oh, look at all the pretty colors," said Olivia with a happy giggle. She stared in fascinated rapture at her own hand, like she was seeing it for the first time.

Stella, now back in her familiar, dainty human form, asked, "Zack, are you okay?"

I turned my head toward her and nodded. I had been so completely occupied by watching Olivia that it hadn't dawned on me that whatever spell I had been under had broken when Lilith died. I sat up and watched Bree change back to her human form. I averted my eyes once she was human again out of respect for her modesty.

"Everyone okay?" asked Bree. She got a yes from me and Stella, but Olivia responded, "Bree, come see the pretty unicorn!"

She was staring wide-eyed at a bush at the side of the house. She swayed in the wind almost like she was dancing.

"What's the matter with Liv?" asked Bree, concern in her voice.

I laughed. "Elf blood has a narcotic effect on vampires. I believe she is tripping balls at this point."

"Bree, you're nakie! That looks fun. I will get nakie too." Olivia peeled off her Deadpool hoodie and tossed it to the ground.

The sirens were getting closer; we had less than a minute before the police arrived. I said, "Bree, take Olivia inside. Stoned vampires and cops aren't a good mix. Stella, help Bree."

Olivia was fighting with the clasp of her black bra when Bree's nude form came into my view. I quickly turned my head again.

"Let's go inside and watch a movie," Bree firmly suggested to Olivia.

"I like movies. Can we watch one that has puppies? I really like puppies," Olivia declared as Bree led her away.

Chapter 11

Sunday, February 11

The front door closed seconds before a police cruiser screeched to a halt in front of my house. I got to my feet, put my hands on my head, and tried to look as unthreatening as possible. Pro Tip: When you're standing in an area surrounded with dead bodies and the cops roll up with their sirens blaring and adrenaline pumping, don't make any sudden moves, and keep your hands up and in plain sight.

To my relief, it was Rob Quinn who jumped out of the cruiser. He looked at the chaos on my lawn as his hand rested on his holster. He was alert and keyed up until he saw me, then he relaxed a bit.

"Zack, are you okay?" he called.

I put my hands down. "I'm fine. It's all over now, except for the cleanup and paperwork."

Rob got on his radio to call in and let dispatch know what was going on. Two more cruisers pulled up. Based on the symphony of sirens in the night air, many more were on the way. Before cops got out of either of the cars, Rob put down the radio and yelled at them to set up a perimeter on either end of the street. He then went back to his call.

The police cruisers backed up in squeals of tire smoke and went their separate ways. I heard Rob mention EIRT and knew he was going to be awhile on the call, so I left him to it and went into the house to check on the girls. I also needed my iPhone to take pictures of the drow to back up my bounty claim, and my reserves were low, and I was tired—a cup of coffee sounded like heaven at that moment.

I entered the house and saw that Bree was dressed again, but Olivia was in just a pair of skimpy black-lace panties and a matching bra. I didn't see Stella; I assumed she was either checking on Blue or had gone back to bed.

"Zack!" Olivia exclaimed with a smile as I closed the front door. She blurred over to me, missed, and crashed into the cabinets by the door.

"Whoops! Whoa, I'm drunk." She clumsily extracted herself from the damaged cabinet.

It was almost impossible to get a vampire drunk on alcohol; something in their metabolism neutralized the booze. Weres were just as resistant to alcohol due to their hyper-metabolism. These two would be great to go to a party with; they would make perfect designated drivers.

Olivia saw me again and threw herself into me in a big hug. We flew back until I hit the wall behind us hard enough to dent the drywall.

"You're okay!" She was half laughing and half sobbing as she continued with the hug of death.

I felt my ribs starting to crack, and I managed to gasp out, "Olivia. Can't breathe."

"Oh," She sheepishly said. To my immense relief, she lessened the pressure.

I returned the hug and said, "I'm fine. We are all fine. Everything is okay."

Olivia just stayed glued to me. She didn't seem to be in a rush to let go. Bree was looking at us with an amused look on her face. I mouthed, "Help," to her, but Bree just smiled and shook her head at me.

Flushed with feeding, Olivia's almost nude body was warm against me. I cursed silently as my body started to react to this. To my horror, Olivia noticed the reaction too. She pressed her hips forward and laughed. "Oh, someone likes me!"

My face went a deep shade of crimson, and Bree's eyes widened. She burst out laughing. I tried to extract myself from Olivia, but she wouldn't let go.

"Olivia, there are a ton of law enforcement officers outside who I have to deal with," I pleaded.

Bree finally took mercy on me. "Liv, let's go find a movie to watch, okay?"

Olivia lifted her head from where it was snuggled against my neck and stared into my eyes with her endless green eyes. She studied me for a moment and then bit her lower lip as if pondering her options before slowly nodding in response to Bree's request. She let go of me. She didn't blur away for a change; instead, she slowly sauntered away. My eyes traveled up her long, lean legs. I almost moaned at the sight of her absolutely to-die-for ass, which was only covered by the black string-like lace thong. It seemed like she sauntered on purpose just to emphasize what I was missing.

The two of them headed for the living room to find a movie. I staggered to the kitchen to turn on the kettle.

Damn. Perky Olivia is a handful, but sultry Olivia is even scarier, I thought as I headed upstairs to get my phone.

Up to that point, I had been acutely aware that Olivia was a vampire and sometimes viewed me as food, which always kept my guard up. It finally hit me that she had been resting her head on my neck and could have fed on me easily, but I hadn't even thought about that possibility. That frightened me a bit. As that vamp got older and more comfortable with her body and powers, she would be something else to deal with.

I grabbed my phone, headed downstairs, and hastily put my jacket on. The kettle was boiling as I entered the kitchen, so I unplugged it. Rob could probably use a cup, as well, so I grabbed two mugs from the cupboard and made two black coffees.

Music blared out from the living room, and I heard Olivia exclaim, "Oh, SpongeBob," with almost childlike glee in her voice. I shook my head and laughed.

Outside, the strobing of the multiple blue and red lights danced across my front yard, lighting it up like some sort of funky disco. Rob clipped up his radio and glanced around. He saw me and smiled as I held up a mug, and we met in the center of the yard.

I handed him one of the mugs. He took a sip and said, "Thanks. What the hell happened here? Dark elves? I didn't think any existed on Earth anymore."

I answered, "You're welcome, yup, and surprise!"

He didn't reply. He just looked around at the carnage on my front lawn.

I broke the short silence. "Rob, do you mind if we walk and talk? I want to get pictures for my bounty claim … I'm sorry about the amount of paperwork this is going to leave you."

I pulled out my phone and started snapping pictures of Lilith and the two swordsmen who the ladies had taken out.

"Sure," Rob responded. "We are going to be here for a while. We have to wait for EIRT and the coroner to arrive."

I nodded and moved over to the downed archers. "Why does EIRT have to be here? There isn't anyone to take into custody." I snapped more pictures.

"They aren't sending a full team; they want someone to confirm that these are actually dark elves. There haven't been drow on Canadian soil since just after World War II, which makes this sort of a big deal. I am going to need a statement from you about all of this too."

I got the pictures of the four elves I'd fried with lightning at the beginning of the battle and then headed over to the maple tree to snap pictures of the body of the one I'd wind-tossed into it. Cops were wandering my yard, making notes and taking their own pictures, and I remembered the drow weapons.

"Rob, be careful where you step. You might want to warn your men that there are a lot of poison-covered weapons strewn about this yard."

"Oh shit, you just remembered this now?" He stopped dead, like he was in a minefield—and in some ways, he was.

I shrugged, and he yelled out, "Everyone, freeze! There are poison-covered weapons all over the place. Move carefully back to the perimeter. Someone call for a hazmat team."

I rolled my eyes. This evening—actually, now that it was coming up on 5:00 a.m., this *morning*—just got a whole lot longer, and I needed to call Walter, my nature-loving Burlington wizard, to come fix my wards. I almost phoned him right then, but I figured he wouldn't be able to get near the place until the police were done, so I let him sleep.

I eyed the female mage and the peace rock embedded in her skull. I had to hand it to Hippie Al—he had been right that the peace rock would be good at relieving stress. It had lessened mine and instantly relieved this dark elf of any stress she had too.

Rob and the rest of the cops were now on the other side of the street, waiting for Hazmat to arrive and clear the area. Rob was waving to me frantically, but I waved him off. I glanced around the yard, counting corpses, and I was pleased that I had photographed all of them.

I carefully stepped over the poison-laced sword on the ground and wandered over to join Rob and the rest of Hamilton's finest.

He shook his head at me. "While we are waiting for everyone else to join this party, you mind giving me a statement?"

"Sure, can we head over there?" I said, pointing down the road. "I'd prefer to have this just between you and me."

He nodded, and we walked down the street.

"Hey, why are you even here? I thought you were on afternoons this week," I pointed out.

"With the baby on the way, I picked up this shift when someone phoned in sick. You are lucky I did. If a rookie showed up here with those bodies all over your yard, things might have gotten a bit sticky."

I nodded and stopped midway between my house and the cruiser that was blocking the south end of the street. I took a deep breath. "I will tell you everything, but I would appreciate it if you could leave a couple things out of your official report."

Rob studied me before he said, "I can't promise, but I'll see what I can do."

I proceeded to tell him most of what had happened in the last couple of days, from the girls' failed attempt to capture McMahon to the connection between Olivia and the French vampire court. I finished by explaining about the drow searching for Olivia, which had ended in the battle this evening.

"You don't do anything half-assed, do you?" Rob shook his head as I finished. I just shrugged at that, and he inquired, "What parts do you want me to leave out of the report?"

"Leave the girls out of it; just write up that the drow attacked me for unknown reasons. Drow are evil. They do nasty shit for no reason all the time. It probably won't be looked at too closely."

Rob gave me an unsure look, and I added, "Look, if you put the girls and their connection to the French vampire court into the report, we are going to have vampire courts looking into this, media out the ass, and probable involvement from the Ministry of Foreign Affairs, the RCMP, the UN, and Odin only knows who else. You and I will be testifying in front of committees for the next year as they launch investigations and probes into this incident. You do it my way, and there will be some media buzz, but since the drow are dead and the threat is over, it will blow over in a couple of days."

The look of horror on Rob's face was enough to show me I'd made my point. He replied, "To recap, you were woken up by the alarms on your wards going off, and you were surprised to find a dozen dark elves assaulting your property. You stepped out of your house and used your power in self-defense to deal with them?"

"Yes, sergeant, that is exactly what happened," I agreed with a smile.

"And you have no idea why you were targeted by the drow?" he asked with a smile of his own.

"No idea. Maybe they took offence to the good deeds I did while acting as the Hurricane and decided to punish me for them. Dark elves are an evil race; with their warped moral code, it is difficult to fathom why they are driven to do the things they do."

Rob rolled his eyes and nodded while writing notes in his notebook.

An unmarked black SUV pulled up to us with blue and red flashing lights in its grille. The huge, unmistakable form of Bobby Knight in his EIRT tactical gear stepped out.

Rob saw him and said, "Bobby Knight! Did you get tired of getting fat on federal paychecks? Have you decided to come back to Hamilton to work for a living again?"

"Never going to happen, Rob. I love my giant expense account too much to give it up," answered Bobby with a friendly grin.

The two did the whole bro-hug thing. Bobby saw me and said, "Zack, I don't see you in five years, and now it's twice in two days. This is starting to become a habit."

"Good to see you again, Bobby," I replied.

The three of us walked back to the cluster of officers on the sidewalk across the street from my house. Rob brought Bobby up to speed, using the revised facts from my official statement.

Bobby checked out the dark elf corpses from a distance and said, "Well, this is something new; I've never seen a dark elf before. Frankly, I never expected to. This is going to create some buzz. I will call this in on a secure channel. I have a feeling this will be written up as 'Rampaging biker gang on PCP hits wrong house.' "

I laughed. It didn't shock me that the Feds would want this off the books to prevent a public panic. World War II had been a long time ago now, but parents still used drow as the boogie man to scare kids into behaving: *"Eat your vegetables, or the drow will come for you."*

Bobby left and then came back a few minutes later. With a grin, he said, "Biker attack. Rob, could you let your men know the drill?"

Rob gathered the Hamilton officers off to the side and explained the new story to them.

"Hey, Bobby. If Rob is writing this up as a biker attack, how do I get my receipt for the drow bounties?" I asked.

"I will do up a receipt and give you a link to a secure EIRT site to submit the receipt and the pictures. They will process it all and submit through back channels to the UN, which will cut a check. The paperwork will list *Twelve wanted Enhanced Individuals (Classified)* for type."

The two coroner vans showed up a few minutes before the hazmat team. Bobby briefed them, telling them that they were to bag and seal the bodies; a federal transport would be arriving later that afternoon to pick all of them up. He told the coroners that these were twelve *human* bodies.

The hazmat team arrived and suited up in their big yellow bubble suits before erecting large nylon cloth walls from the sides of my house to the street to block outside views of the yard. They got the walls into place just as the sun came up. They proceeded to sweep the area, tossing poison-covered arrows, swords, and daggers into sturdy bright-yellow containers with bold red "Toxic!" warning symbols on the sides.

An hour later, they were done. They took the crates away to be destroyed as the coroners got to work on bagging up bodies. A Hamilton Police public relations officer was briefing the press being held behind yellow police tape well away from the scene.

The news coverage on the event that night made me laugh. They reported that a Mexican biker gang had been looking to expand their drug trade into southern Ontario, so they had been trying to hit a local mob boss but had gotten the wrong address and hit the home of a local superhero instead. After the gang had fired rounds at the house, the local superhero had responded with lethal force, and none of the hit squad had survived. There were no pictures of my house, and they weren't allowed to list an address, thanks to the Secret Identity Act.

After the coroner's people left and things started winding down, I made a call to Walter to get the ball rolling on getting my wards fixed. He tried pushing me off—said that in the next couple of days, some rare bird was supposed to be flying through that he wanted to photograph—but I was tired and needed those wards redone. I offered to double his usual fee. He said I would be looking at $40,000. That was fine; the wards had worked well this evening, making them worth every penny. Walter promised to be there in under an hour. I reminded him to bring ID to get past the cops blocking my street.

I told Rob about Walter, and he let the officers know to let the wizard pass before he had me sign his report and said he was out of there. They would leave the patrol cars at the end of the street for the rest of the day to discourage gawkers. I thanked him, and he left.

Bobby handed me the receipt and the link to the EIRT secure website and said he was out of there too.

By the time Walter showed up, everyone had gone, except for the cruisers at either end of the street and the two police-contracted tow trucks that had shown up to impound the two vans for evidence.

Walter got out of his Audi carrying a large audit bag that had his tools in it. He looked at the bloodstains on the sidewalk and then walked up to me. "Zack, on the radio they are reporting this as a biker-

78

gang hit, but bikers wouldn't have broken my wards. What really happened?"

Walter and I had had a pretty good relationship over the years, and I knew I could trust him. "Drow attack."

He stopped dead in his tracks and looked at me with wide eyes. "No shit?"

"Swear to God."

"How many were mages?" he asked.

"Two."

He smiled. "My wards held up against two dark elf mages long enough for you to wake up and deal with them. Hot dog! I told you I did good work. I swear, I am going to have to start charging more."

"Yeah, too bad you can't say jack about the drow. That would make interesting advertising for you."

Walter sighed, then began pulling various crystals out of the bag and laying them out on the ground.

"Why would the drow be attacking you, anyway?" he asked as he continued.

"That is a long story that I can't go into, but your wards did good, Walter. Without them, I probably wouldn't be here now, which means I owe you a huge thank you."

He selected four good-sized crystals and put the rest back in the bag. He walked to the south corner of my property and carefully placed one on the snow and grass. He chanted something in what might have been Latin and made gestures with his hand. The crystal glowed pink and disappeared into the ground.

Walter repeated this on the other three compass points across my property. We walked up to my front porch, where he placed his right hand on my chest and chanted again, making a couple of sharp gestures with his left hand. My body tingled for a moment. A large flash of pink light covered the area for a moment, and it was over.

"All done. I'll send you the bill in a couple days."

"Really? That's it? When you installed the wards the first time, you were here for, like, three days. Fixing them only takes twenty minutes?" I asked in astonishment.

He smiled. "Installing new wards is a lot of work; you have to lay the lines down, carefully place layers of spells, and then install the power source to fuel those spells. Repairing them means only replacing the power sources and bringing the wards back up, which is much less work."

"Why does it cost $40,000, then?" I asked.

"It may be easier to repair than establish, but those spells I just casted to fix the power source and bring the wards back up are going to leave me drained for the next two or three days. That is three days that I am quite limited in what work I can do. This time, it happened to really work out for me—now I can spend the next three days birding. The fact that you are paying double is just icing on the cake." He grinned and almost skipped down my front path to his car.

Fucker, I thought to myself, but I thanked him out loud and told him to enjoy his birding.

He started up his car, gave me a playful honk and a wave, and drove off. I resisted the urge to flip him the bird and just returned the wave. I headed for my house feeling drained. It was coming up on 11:00 a.m. according to my watch.

I entered the house to the smell of bacon and other wonderful breakfast aromas, and my stomach growled in approval. I entered the kitchen and found Bree cooking up a storm. Stella sat at the table, looking half-awake and sipping her tea.

Bree glanced up from the stove top when I entered the kitchen and asked, "Hungry?"

"Starving. I might actually be able to keep up with you today food-wise."

"Doubt it, but you are welcome to try," challenged Bree.

The kettle was half full and still steaming. I made myself a coffee and joined Stella at the table. A couple of minutes later, Bree put down platters of bacon, sausages, scrambled eggs, fried tomatoes, and hash browns. The room was silent as the three of us helped ourselves. All we could hear were the sounds of us eating.

After I devoured most of my food, I said, "I thought I ordered you two to take Blue and get the hell out of here if the fight went badly for me?"

Bree finished her mouthful and answered, "You did. We had Blue downstairs and ready to go, but then I made a tactical decision. You had eliminated the magic users, the bowmen, and two of the five swordsmen. You probably would have taken the last three if Lilith hadn't hit you with that sucker-punch of a spell. I figured there were three of us and three of them, and we would have the element of surprise, so I changed the plan."

"You ignored my orders, but you saved my life. Thank you for that."

Bree smiled and nodded as she continued plowing through her second heaped plate. I helped myself to a second helping, as well, but this one was much more modest than the first—I was getting full. I knew I wouldn't be able to keep up with my boast about matching Bree's efforts.

"Now that we have beaten the drow, is the threat to Olivia finished?" asked Bree between bites.

I looked at Stella, and she glanced back at me as if asking who was going to answer this. I deferred to her.

"No, this is just a minor setback for Giselle. I don't expect her to give up this easily. She probably doesn't have any more drow to send, but the French court has over 1,000 years of accumulated financial resources behind it. I expect she will either send some of her more trusted vampires over to deal with this, or she will hire this out to other third parties."

"Which do you think is more likely?" I asked. I was appreciating Stella's keen insights on this.

"They both have pros and cons. Sending the drow, who were servants of the French court, keeps it all in-house, and sending her own vampires after us would continue that trend. The dark elves were disposable, and Giselle could deny them, even if they were caught. Sending French court vampires into Elizabeth's territory risks an all-out war with the English court, which is something Giselle will want to avoid at all costs."

Stella paused for a moment to gather her thoughts and then added, "She could ask or pay Elizabeth for access to alleviate the risk of the war, but I don't see Elizabeth granting that permission. This would also tip Giselle's hand and show how valuable she finds Olivia, which might cause Elizabeth to grab Olivia for herself to use as leverage over the French court—or make a play for the French throne.

"Losing the drow will cause her to lose face, which actually weakens her position. She is going to be even more determined to get Olivia now. I suspect she will put a large contract out on Olivia and let third parties deal with it instead."

I couldn't fault her reasoning. "I agree. Nothing will happen before tonight either way. She will be waiting to hear from Lilith, but she has played the game enough that if she sees the 'Mexican biker' report on the news, she will piece together what really happened. If she puts that contract out tonight, we should have a day or two before the real heavy hitters get involved. We might get a couple of minor locals taking a shot, but the four of us should be able to handle locals with no issue. But if Blue isn't awake by tomorrow night, we will need to consider moving somewhere else and going off the grid for a while."

Stella nodded in agreement, but Bree look worried. We finished the rest of the meal in silence.

"Bree, thank you for a great meal."

Bree smiled, and I continued. "If you'll both excuse me, I have some work upstairs in my office to take care of, and then I need to get some sleep."

I brought a coffee upstairs with me and hoped it would keep me awake for a bit longer. I logged onto the secure EIRT website and filled out the bounty form I found there. I uploaded my pictures and entered the receipt number Bobby had given me before submitting the completed form, then I shut down the computer and headed to my room.

I was out seconds after my head hit the pillow.

Chapter 12

Sunday, February 11

The insistent buzzing of my iPhone woke me; without even looking at the number, I answered the call.

The glowing red light of my digital alarm clock flashed 5:06 p.m.

"Zack Stevens?" asked a feminine and sultry voice with a cultured French accent.

"Speaking," I answered as I tried to get my brain out of its sleep-induced fog. If this was who I thought it was, I would need all my wits about me.

"Mr. Stevens, I am Giselle Dupris, master of the French court. You sound tired; I hope I didn't wake you. If I did, I apologize, but I didn't expect that you would still be sleeping at five in the afternoon. Is this a Canadian custom I am unaware of?"

I laughed. "Please, call me Zack."

I almost added "Your Majesty" on the end but remembered that the French vampire court had dropped their noble titles during the French Revolution. Most vampire courts matched the political structures of their host countries. There were a few exceptions, like the Russian vampire court using the title of *tsar* for their master and the Chinese vampire court using *emperor*, but most courts matched their human counterparts.

"Very well, Zack, and you may have the honor of calling me Giselle. Pray, continue."

"It isn't a Canadian custom to sleep till 5:00 p.m. I just had a long night that continued into the morning, as you are probably aware."

"Yes, drow attacks do tend to make a day more interesting. I apologize for that. After looking in to you, I feel that was a mistake. It probably would have been much more efficient to come to some sort of financial arrangement instead, as you are a bounty hunter and a businessman. I was hoping we might come to some sort of arrangement?"

The voice on the other end dripped with sensuality, making it difficult to remember that I was talking to a ruthless and powerful

600-year-old vampire who would kill me in a second and not lose a moment's sleep over it. I had no urge to play this glibly; this was one person I didn't want to piss off. A different approach was warranted here.

"Before we get down to offers and unsightly business proposals, can I first say that you have the loveliest voice I have ever heard? Your English is impeccable, and when delivered with that cultured French accent, it actually causes my heart to beat faster. I would happily deal with another dozen drow just to hear it again."

The line went briefly silent before she replied, "You are too kind. I was under the impression that French and Italian men vied for the title of the world's most charming men, but perhaps Canadian men should be included in that group."

I softly exhaled in relief at her reply. "Now it is you being too kind. Thank you for indulging me with this pleasant conversation. I will, with regret, lead us back to your offer."

"I find that this modern world spends too little time in cultured conversation, given their slavish devotion to the clock. This has been a refreshing change. I would like to extend an offer for you to visit me here at court after our business has concluded. You intrigue me, and I would like to know you better."

My adrenaline kicked into high gear and cleared the last of my sleep-addled mind. "It would be an honor. I, too, would enjoy getting to know you better."

"I look forward to it. Alas, to business then. I am prepared to offer you €5 million to deliver the young vampire to me intact and unharmed. I will give you my word that you and her companions will be left alone and unharmed if you comply, but if you don't accept my offer, I will have no choice but to put these terms in a contract on the open market."

I didn't know the current euro-to-Canadian-dollar exchange rate, but this would easily be in excess of six or seven million Canadian dollars, which was a staggering sum of money. I wasn't tempted— okay, I wasn't tempted *that much*—but that type of monetary reward on a contract would bring out some serious players, which would be challenging to deal with.

"Zack, are you still there?"

"Sorry. That impressive sum of money caught me off guard. It is an exceptionally generous offer, but I need to research the logistics and details of getting her out of the country and to you. I certainly wouldn't want to promise something I couldn't deliver on. Do you require my answer right now?"

"I am willing to give you twenty-four hours to decide. I will call you at this time tomorrow."

"Thank you, and I look forward to your call," I replied.

"Until then," said Giselle, and the line went dead.

I dropped my iPhone on the bed like it was a poison-covered dagger. I had bought us twenty-four hours. I wondered if that would be enough time. If Giselle had my cell number, Lilith had probably gotten in touch with her before the attack, which meant Giselle knew where I lived too.

After getting dressed and splashing some cold water on my face, I headed downstairs. The house was eerily quiet. I assumed Stella was in her room with Blue, keeping an eye on her unconscious friend, and Bree must have still been sleeping. The sun wouldn't set for another hour yet, which meant Olivia was still in her death trance in the basement.

After checking to make sure that Bree hadn't eaten the ingredients I'd bought, I used the time to make dinner. I got down to making a huge pot of spaghetti with meat sauce and a large batch of garlic bread.

I spent the next hour in the kitchen, prepping ingredients, browning meat, and simmering my sauce. I cracked open a bottle of Chianti to help me with the cooking. I loved to cook with wine; some of it even made it into the dish.

Bree wandered into the kitchen and said, "Something smells good."

"Spaghetti with meat sauce. It should be ready in ten or fifteen minutes," I said as I added the pasta to the pot.

A few minutes later, the door to the basement opened. Olivia staggered out wearing my Lions jersey and said, "Oh my aching head. I am soooooo giving up drinking dark elf from now on!"

She passed me with a groan, fished around in the fridge, pulled out one of her juice boxes, and joined Bree at the table.

The timer for my pasta beeped loudly. Olivia covered her ears and swore at the noise. I combined the pasta and meat sauce, then left it to sit for a moment as I pulled the golden-brown garlic bread out of the oven, tossed it in a basket, and put it on the table. Bree reached for a piece, but I asked her to get Stella first. She grabbed a piece anyway and then got up to fetch Stella.

I served up the spaghetti in two regular-size bowls for Stella and myself—and a huge one for Bree. Bree returned with Stella in tow as I poured myself another glass of wine. I offered them a glass, but both declined.

As we ate dinner, I told them all about my conversation with Giselle. I got wide-eyed looks and silence when I mentioned the amount of money she was offering.

"Over six million for little old me? Damn, Zack, I would have taken the money," said Olivia in awe.

"Me, too," said Bree between bites.

Olivia shot her a dirty look, and Bree laughed.

The look of deep concern on Stella's face told me she wasn't as amused. She knew, just like I did, that that amount of money would bring some talented players out of the woodwork, but neither of us vocalized our thoughts.

Bree got serious and asked, "What are we going to do?"

"We are going to sit tight for the next twenty-four hours and hope that Blue wakes up. If she doesn't, I have contacts; one of them has a place up north that he will rent to me. This time of year, the area around the place should be deserted, and we can hide out. I will contact him tomorrow if I have to, because we cannot stay here after the deadline; this place is compromised. I'll leave my phone here. We will need to avoid using the internet and credit cards, as both can be traced. I will hit the bank tomorrow and grab more cash to cover any expenses that come up. Olivia, you need a bag of blood a day to get by, right?"

She nodded, and I continued. "I will call Marion tonight and get another six bags. Add those to the four remaining, and that gives us a ten-day supply. If Blue hasn't woken up by then, we have bigger problems to worry about. Did I miss anything?"

Stella piped up. "And once Blue does wake up?"

"We'll shadow-travel to your secret lab. That seems about as off-the-grid as one can possibly get. From there, we will need to get in touch with Elizabeth. Hopefully, you can convince her to help us, to get Giselle to back off."

"What if Elizabeth won't help or doesn't want to get involved?" asked Bree with concern.

I scratched my chin as I pondered her question. "Then we have two options: hide in the lab for the rest of our days or hit the French court and eliminate the threat."

"You realize that at any time, there will be thirty to fifty vampires at court, plus their servants and human/Enhanced security teams?" interjected Stella.

I shrugged. "I didn't say either option would be easy. If we have to hit the French court, we'll do it during the day, when they are weakest. At least with Blue on our team, we don't have to go in the front door, guns blazing. She might even be able to pop us right into Giselle's daytime resting place, and then we can drive a stake through her heart, end her, and get the hell out of there. We can contact Roman after and explain that we just handed him the French court. We'll tell him to drop the bounty on Olivia, or he will meet the same fate as Giselle. If he isn't willing to play ball, we'll do the same to him and make the same offer to the next master, continuing until we find one who does."

Stella shook her head. "A 600-year-old master like Giselle can easily wake from her daytime rest. She will hear us coming! She won't lie there catatonic and let us stake her as if we were planting tomatoes."

Her pronunciation of *tomatoes* amused me. I was used to people saying *to*-may-*toes*, but with her British accent, Stella pronounced it *to*-mah-*toes*. I suppressed my amusement and said, "I didn't know about that, but there are five of us and one of her. If we hit hard and fast, the five of us should be able to take her. My other thought was to steal enough C4 to blow the French court to kingdom come and back, but that was a bit extreme, and if any of the other courts found out we'd done that, Giselle's bounty would seem like a minor problem."

"You are insane," said Stella.

"Look, it's a rough plan that we can iron out later. If we go into hiding, we will have plenty of time to figure something out," I argued.

Stella didn't comment on this, and we finished our dinner in a worried silence.

Chapter 13

Monday, February 12

When I got up the next day, there was a light dusting of snow on the front lawn. I had called Marion last night to acquire more bags of blood, and she said she would have them for me by 1:00 p.m. today.

As I made my way down to the kitchen to grab a cup of coffee, the house was quiet, which probably meant Blue was still unconscious. With Blue's status still the same, it was looking more and more likely that we would have to go on the run. If we were going off the grid, there were some preparations I needed to make.

I usually kept $10,000 of emergency money in the safe in my office, but I had raided $1,000 of that for Olivia's first blood order and shopping expenses, and I would be using another $1,000 of that for the order I was picking up this afternoon, which would leave me $8,000. I had no idea how long we would be hiding, so I decided we needed more.

I made a call to Deena at the bank and told her I needed $20,000 in cash. She said she would have the money for me by 1:00 p.m. I wrote out a business check to Walter for $40,000 plus tax for his services, and I dashed out a note saying I was going to be out of town and didn't want him to wait for his money. I also cut a check to Daryl for his tip about McMahon.

I had a quick shower and shave and then left a note for the girls that I would be back midafternoon.

My first stop was my local Best Buy. I bought two pay-as-you-go burner phones with cash and loaded both up with 500 minutes each. As I was eating lunch at Subway, I unpacked one of the phones and called Greg, my contact for a hideout, so that no record of the conversation I was going to have could be found.

Greg was a retired real estate developer who owed me one because I had saved a housing development that he owned from a wildfire. He'd been leveraged to the hilt on the properties, and the fire would have wiped him out. We had been acquaintances before the fire; after the fire, he'd had me up to that cottage up north every year for Canada Day.

He was currently wintering in Florida, which meant the cottage would probably be empty. It was winterized, so I knew it would be a good place to hang out for a week under the radar, and barely anyone knew about my friendship with Greg, so we should be safe up there.

He didn't answer my first call; it went to voicemail. I expected this, as he wouldn't know the number. I hit redial. This time, he picked up on the second ring.

We exchanged pleasantries for a few minutes, which gave me time to head outside, where fewer people could overhear.

Greg finished up the story he was telling and then said, "I am sure you aren't just calling to hear my fish-that-got-away story. What can I do for you?"

"I have a couple of people staying with me who are being hunted by some bad people. Those bad people found out my address, and I need someplace to hide out for a week or two until the authorities catch them. I was hoping your cottage was free?"

"Sure, stay there as long as you need. I won't be back in town until May, anyway. The key for the front door is under a red flowerpot in the garden shed at the side of the house. The alarm code is 5050."

"Thanks, Greg. I really appreciate this. Please don't mention it to anyone, okay?"

"Yeah, I wasn't going to say a word … Is this related to that Mexican biker attack I saw on the news yesterday?"

"It is related."

"Good luck, then, and stay safe."

We said our goodbyes. With that off the list, I headed for the bank. I had to wait a few minutes before Deena was free. She took me to her office and had me sign for the money, and then I dumped the large stacks of bills into my trusty grocery bag.

I hit Marion's next. She opened the door cautiously but welcomed me warmly once she saw it was me. I smiled at her outfit: a colorfully beaded white top, a light-brown leather vest with tassels, and a pair of faded bellbottoms.

Despite the warm hello, she still seemed nervous, so I asked, "Anyone else been sniffing around?" She shook her head in response, and I added, "Those creepy church people have been dealt with. They won't bother you again."

The tension in Marion's shoulders lessened, and she offered me a tea. Normally, I would have taken her up on this and spent some time idly chatting with her, but I wanted to get moving, and the less I was around her, the safer she would be.

I shook my head and fished out the $1,000 I had in my pocket. She took it from me and came back with the six bags of plasma, which I carefully put in the grocery bag with the money and the phones. It occurred to me that if someone found this grocery bag, they would be puzzled about what kind of person would need $20,000, two burner phones, and that much bagged blood.

"Oh, I almost forgot: When you see Al, can you ask him for another peace rock for me?"

Marion smiled and asked, "What happened to the one he gave you?"

"I gave it to someone else; it really relieved their stress," I said, not missing a beat. Technically, the drow mage was dead, so she wasn't stressing about anything anymore.

"Hold on," said Marion, and she disappeared through the glass-beaded archway to her bedroom. She returned and handed me another peace rock.

I smiled. "Are you sure? What if you get stressed?"

"I can meditate. Besides, I get the feeling you have more stress in your life than I do."

I nodded and pocketed my new peace rock, then we said our goodbyes, and I flew home. The place was quiet as I landed on the front porch and headed inside. I found Bree in the kitchen. The distinctive scent of garlic, tomatoes, and basil filled the air as she reheated the leftovers from last night.

I stocked the fridge with the additional juice boxes, grabbed a pop, and joined Bree at the table as she started in on her huge bowl of pasta.

I told Bree what I had been up to all day and asked if there was any change in Blue's status. Her mouth was full of pasta, so she just shook her head in response.

After lunch, I found two large duffel bags and gave one to Bree with the instruction to pack up all of her and Olivia's extra clothes. I took the other one and did the same with my own clothes. I put the two burner phones and $20,000 in cash from the bank and $5,000 from the safe, as well, and stuffed my jean pockets with the remaining $3,000 in case something happened to the bag.

I spent the rest of the afternoon researching information on Giselle and the French court but didn't find out anything useful.

Thirty minutes before Giselle was supposed to call, I phoned in a pizza order for our dinner and then joined Stella and Bree at the kitchen table.

"Blue hasn't woken, so we are going with Plan B," I said. "After dinner, we are bugging out to the cottage up north. It will be an hour-and-a-half flight. Make sure you dress warmly."

Stella shuddered. With a touch of desperation in her voice, she asked, "Can't we rent a car and drive there?"

"We can't. I don't have a license. Also, renting a car can't be done without a credit card. If a car rental shows up on my credit card, I guarantee that the people looking for us will see it. At that point, they'll just need to hit the rental agency and strong-arm them into giving up the location of our rental."

"Aren't you, like, in your thirties? How the hell can you not have a driver's license?" asked Bree in shock.

"Hello? I fly, remember? What do I need a car for?"

"Oh, I guess that makes sense."

Stella and Bree were discussing different options for the flight and what to bring or not bring, but I tuned them out and began thinking about my upcoming call with Giselle. I was tempted to play it tough and just tell her to go fuck herself—that if she continued coming after Olivia, I would end her. But I suspected that wouldn't deter her. In the end, I decided to go another route.

The doorbell rang at the same time my phone rang.

I looked at the display, saw the international number on it, and said, "Bree, go pay the pizza guy. I will deal with Giselle."

After handing Bree some cash, I walked into the living room to be alone and answered the phone.

"Good evening, Zack. Have you made your decision?" asked Giselle, getting directly to the point.

"Lovely to hear your voice again, Giselle. Unfortunately, that decision was taken out of my hands. When I awoke this morning, they were gone. Their shadow-traveler must have recovered from her injuries. They didn't even leave me a note. I can only guess that Olivia, with her enhanced hearing, overheard our conversation." I put as much regret into my tone as possible.

"I see. Do you have any idea where they might have gone?"

"Best guess is that they are back on English soil, but that is only a guess. I plan on looking for them around here, as I would like to collect

91

that money. They can travel anywhere in the world, so I doubt they would have hung around, but who knows? I might get lucky."

"You wouldn't be lying to me now, would you, Zack?" Giselle's voice sounded cold and deadly.

"Lying? Why would I do that? Who in their right mind would turn down €5 million? The only reason I asked for time to make my decision was to figure out a way to smuggle Olivia out of the country without attracting the attention of the authorities."

" 'Who in their right mind,' indeed. What's done is done. I will have to put the contract out on the open market now. As you say, you might get lucky and find them nearby—in which case, I will see you shortly. But even if you don't find them, the invitation to visit the French court is still open."

"You are too kind. I have always wanted to visit Paris in springtime, and now, with the added incentive of meeting you, this will be the year I fulfill that dream." I tried not to gag.

"I look forward to your visit, but now I must post that contract. Until we meet in person, then," finished Giselle, who terminated the call.

I had no idea if she had bought my story or not, but either way, Olivia—and by extension, the rest of our group—had targets on our backs.

Chapter 14

Monday, February 12

We all fueled up on pizza as we waited for Olivia to rise. I had ordered four large meat-lover's pizzas, figuring that even Bree couldn't finish that much food. I was planning on taking the leftovers with us to eat for breakfast—assuming, of course, that Bree didn't kill the leftovers as a late-night snack.

After dinner, we packed the two leftover pizzas and all but one bag of blood. Olivia woke up and had her juice box while Bree and Stella brought Blue downstairs and dressed in layers for the flight.

Olivia finished her breakfast, and we were ready to go. I hardened the air in front of us before we stepped out on the porch, just in case someone was going to take a shot at us, but nothing came flying our way. I locked my house and wondered how long it would be before I saw it again—or if I would see it again.

The girls huddled up around me, and I asked, "Everyone ready?"

I got nervous nods in response from Bree and Stella, and a "Giddyup!" from Olivia. Stella had closed her eyes and was holding on so tightly to Blue that I was surprised Blue could still breathe. We hadn't even taken off yet. I slowly increased the wind directly beneath us and lifted us up into the night sky. I flew south in case anyone was watching from a distance. They wouldn't be able to track me midair, so once we were well away from the house, I made a large loop to the west and eventually headed north.

The flight was uneventful, but I was extremely fatigued by the time we touched down in the snow-covered front yard of Greg's cottage. I'd only been here during the summers and had never seen the place in winter. It was pretty and picturesque—pristine snow covered the trees and everything. There were a total of four cottages around Greg's place. They were all dark, and it was obvious that they had been abandoned for the winter.

I took a step toward the shed containing the key and stumbled. Bree caught me before I fell. I was more exhausted than I thought.

From my place in Bree's arms, I said, "Olivia, the key is under a red flowerpot in that garden shed. Can you get it?"

"Sure," she said, and before I could blink, she had already yanked the thin metal door to the shed open.

A few moments later, she exited the shed, blurred back, and handed me the shiny silver key. I had recovered enough that my legs were steady enough to support me, so I nodded at Bree, who cautiously let go of me. I made it the few feet to the door with no issues and unlocked the door. When the door opened, we were greeted by the warning chirp of the alarm system. I punched the code into the glowing pad and turned it off.

I found the lights and got an "Oh wow" from both Olivia and Bree as they checked out the cottage. "Cottage" was technically the right term, but it felt odd to use, because this place was bigger than most peoples' houses.

The décor was rustic modern. Huge, varnished solid-oak support beams ran the length of the ceiling. Dark wood trim decorated cream-colored walls, and lots of stainless steel and glass furnished the cottage. The back wall of the cottage had floor-to-ceiling windows that overlooked the lake and offered an amazing view when the blinds weren't down, like they were now. The main level was all open-concept, except for the bathroom, laundry, and pantry areas off to the right. A staircase ran the length of the left wall to the second floor, which had the master bedroom—with its own bathroom—and two guest rooms that shared a bathroom between them. All three bedrooms had windows that viewed the lake.

The kitchen area of the main level was fully equipped with a gas range, huge stainless-steel fridge, dishwasher, microwave, and enough counter space to prep a body on. A center island countertop had chairs around it, so it could be used as a kitchen table or additional counter space. A large eight-seat dining table sat just in front of the kitchen. The oak table looked sturdy, rustic, and charming.

Bree moved into the living area and carefully placed Blue's unconscious form on one end of the U-shaped cream-colored leather couch. She plunked herself down beside Blue and sighed in pleasure as she ran her hand lightly over the luxurious leather. Stella sat down carefully by Blue's feet and rubbed herself vigorously, trying to get some heat back into herself after our long, frigid flight.

Olivia darted around the place like a hummingbird on crack, opening doors, inspecting appliances, admiring the view through the blinds, and generally making a nuisance of herself.

"This place is beautiful!" she exclaimed as she blurred by me.

"Liv, check out this couch," Bree suggested. "I have never sat on something this comfortable in my life."

Even Stella seemed impressed with her surroundings. Through chattering teeth, she said, "This truly is a place fit for a queen."

I didn't see what the big deal was. Both my house and this one had European-designed furnishings; mine just happened to be IKEA, whereas Greg's were from high-end Italian designers ... Okay, I did see the difference. Greg and his wife, Melanie, had done a stunning job with this place.

I knew that the girls would have been even more impressed with the place if it was summer. I had been. The cottage had a large and spacious deck and dock area that ran the entire length of the back of it. Sitting on that deck in the heat of summer with a slight breeze coming in from the lake was like a slice of paradise.

Stella was shivering hard, which prompted me to find the thermostat. It was currently set to sixty degrees, so I upped that to seventy. It would take a bit for it to reach seventy, so I joined the ladies in the living room and opened the mesh metal curtains on the fireplace to build a fire. I opened the flue and then sparked one of the wooden matches, lighting the newspaper I had put in place to help start the fire. A minute and a few soft breezes later, the logs caught. I carefully used my powers to push more oxygen under the logs to keep the fire going. In no time, it was going full-bore. I started to sweat standing in front of it.

Bree got up and said, "I am going to move Blue to one of the beds upstairs."

"It is only sixty degrees in the main area, and the bedrooms are going to be ten degrees cooler. Why don't you just leave her here for now?" I suggested.

Bree nodded and headed for the kitchen.

"Coffee or tea, anyone?" she asked.

"Coffee, please," I replied.

Stella looked up from warming herself by the fire and added, "Tea, please."

Olivia came back downstairs. "I put your bag in the main bedroom, Zack, in case you are looking for it."

Bree put on the kettle and stocked the empty fridge with Olivia's juice boxes and one of the two leftover pizza boxes; the other one, she left on the counter. When she was done stocking the fridge, she looked for a plate in the cupboards. I shook my head; I was still burping up pizza from two hours ago. I couldn't imagine eating another slice at the moment.

Once Bree was done in the kitchen and everyone had their beverages and snacks, we all ended up on the couch together like one big, happy family. Stella perched on the end of the U by Blue's feet, closest to the fire, and hugged her cup as if trying to leech all the warmth from it. Bree was on the other side of the U, leaning toward the fire and eating her pizza. Olivia and I were sitting farthest from the fire, as neither of us needed the heat, and vampires and fire weren't a winning combination.

The caffeine in my coffee surged through my system and perked me back up. Draining my power like I had on the flight here always hit me at first like I'd had no sleep in a couple of days, but after the initial drain period, I would physically return to normal. I probably could have headed out right then and walked five miles with no issues—even without the caffeine. I knew, though, that my powers were still running almost on empty until I got some sleep or passed enough time until the air and static around me could recharge them. A good thunderstorm rolling through would also supercharge me, bringing my power levels back up in almost no time at all.

"Are we safe here?" asked Olivia.

I shrugged. "No one knows we are here. They can't trace my phone, because it's not here. I won't be using my credit card anywhere, we are staying off the internet, and there is no car to track. Tracing us electronically is almost impossible."

Bree cocked an eyebrow. "I noticed you didn't answer the question."

I nodded. "Good catch. There are other ways of finding us, such as spells, tracker abilities, and oracles—and probably other ways I haven't accounted for." I held up my wrist and showed off the woven bracelet I was wearing. "This charm that I took from my safe should stop a spell from locating us, but I can't do anything about the other ways. Thankfully, people with tracking abilities are rare, and oracles are even rarer. Oracles tend to be reclusive, and their services are expensive. Those two options wouldn't normally be something I'd worry about, but ..."

"There is a €5 million contract out there that could bring either of those two unlikely options into play," finished Stella for me.

"Exactly. Now, the oracle option is the lesser of my worries because A) it is hard to gain quick access to an oracle, and B) oracles tend to speak in riddles that usually take time to figure out. The tracker option is the one that concerns me more. Depending on where they live and what abilities they have, a tracker could be here in as little as day. Fortunately, most trackers make enough money doing legitimate things—finding missing kids or tracking down kidnapping victims or stolen artwork—that they wouldn't touch a black-market contract with a ten-foot pole. Unfortunately, all it takes is one black-market tracker to find us."

Bree thought for a moment and then asked, "How long do you think we have until someone finds us?"

"Forty-eight hours. After that, I think we are on borrowed time."

Stella instantly said, "It is race for time between someone finding us and Blue waking up."

I nodded. "We're isolated here. There were no signs of life at the cottages on either side of us. Between Olivia's and Bree's enhanced senses, we should get some warning when whoever is looking for us gets here. With a warning, we aren't going to be an easy group to take down, even if Blue is still unconscious." I looked at Bree and Olivia. "If either you hear or smell anyone nearby, sound the alarm, okay?"

They both agreed.

I continued. "By tomorrow night, I want Olivia and Bree on different sleep schedules to monitor for intruders at all hours. Bree should be awake during the day, and Olivia will be awake at night. Stella, are you more a morning or night person?"

"Morning," said Stella.

"Okay, then after tomorrow, you will keep Bree company during her day shift. I will stay up and keep Olivia company for the night shift. Did I miss anything? Does anyone have any questions?"

"What if they do show up? What should we do, other than sound the alarm?" asked Olivia.

I thought about possible ways we could be attacked. "We all rally here after Bree or Olivia grabs Blue and brings her here. I can thicken the air around an area as large as this couch to stop any bullets, arrows, or other projectiles from hitting anyone, but I can't cover the whole house, so everyone needs to get here quick if an attack happens. Once we are huddled up here and have a clue what we are dealing with, we'll come up with a plan of attack or retreat and go from there."

We spent the next hour discussing different scenarios and different plans to deal with them, and then Stella said she was getting tired and asked Olivia to carry Blue up to their room.

When Olivia returned, we turned on the TV and watched movies together. I was going to stay up till 4:00 a.m. to start adjusting my sleep schedule; Bree was only going to stay up till 2:00 a.m. to do the same with hers. This meant Olivia would be on her own for two hours before sunrise, but she was okay with that …

Bree headed up to bed at 2:00 a.m. as planned, but came down a minute later and asked, "Where is Olivia going to sleep? All the bedrooms have floor-to-ceiling windows, and this place has no basement."

Olivia looked a little worried and then blurred from the couch to the laundry area and came back smiling. "The pantry has no windows and has a door on it. It is off the laundry room, and that only has a small window that doesn't face the pantry door. It should be safe. I'll put a 'Do Not Open until Sundown' sign on it to keep Stella from opening it by mistake."

Bree headed off to bed, and I wished I could go too. I was really starting to fade. I made another cup of coffee and sat back down with Olivia to watch my final movie of the night.

When the credits rolled on the movie, I handed the remote to Olivia. She happily looked over her choices as I left her to go to bed.

* * * * *

I rolled out of bed the next day at noon and headed downstairs to find Bree and Stella having the leftover pizza for lunch. When I looked in the fridge, I was amazed that Bree had spared two large pieces for me. I grabbed them and joined the ladies at the table.

I mentioned that I was going out shopping after I finished eating, as we certainly needed more food in the house, and asked if anyone needed anything. Both said they were fine.

The closest large city was Peterborough, so I flew there and hit a grocery store. I was pleased to find that the store was quiet and almost deserted, which I'd been expecting, since it was a Tuesday and we were months away from tourist season.

What I wasn't as pleased about was the itch between my shoulder blades. We had been on the run for less than twenty-four hours, and I already found my levels of paranoia growing by leaps and bounds.

Every time someone looked at me, I felt they were seeing a "€5 million" sign above my head.

As I stood in line at the checkout, I forced myself to be calm. It was highly unlikely that the grandma who was entering her debit card PIN like it was the launch code to the US nuclear arsenal was a top-notch contract killer. The odds that anyone in this store was actually hunting me were slim to none.

I did get a few odd looks outside the store as I loaded all the groceries from my cart into one large duffel bag. After playing grocery Tetris and arranging everything in the bag with the heavy, solid items at one end and the lighter, more breakable ones at the other, I lifted the bag up and hooked the handles over my shoulders like a knapsack. I put the cart away and wandered around back of the store. After a quick check to make sure no one was around, I put on my balaclava and flew home.

I unloaded the groceries from my large duffel bag, then took the bag back up to my room, so I could load it again with the cash and clothes I had dumped out on the bed to free it up in the first place.

I made a huge pot of chili for dinner that night and served it with a loaf of fresh Italian bread. It turned out that I was a little too crazy with the spice weasel—Stella struggled to finish her bowl. Bree and her metabolism didn't let a little thing like too much hot sauce slow her down. She finished three bowls of it.

Stella excused herself to go check on Blue and do some reading upstairs, leaving me, Olivia, and Bree to contend with the rest of the evening.

"What is the plan for tonight? More movie watching?" I asked.

The girls looked at each other and seemed to be silently communicating through eye gestures and odd facial expressions. The lack of answer about movies was telling; I wondered what was up.

Bree sighed. She must have lost whatever silent argument they were having. "Zack, you mentioned that it would be at least forty-eight hours before anyone could track us down, right?" I nodded, and she continued. "Which means that after tomorrow night, we are pretty much hunkering down here and staying put until Blue wakes up, correct?"

I bobbed my head in acknowledgement, and Bree went on. "The two of us would like to go out hunting this evening in that forest just down the road. Before we attempted the McMahon bounty, Blue was taking us out to hunt in a forest once a week. Olivia would go hunting with me in my beast form, and we never failed to catch a deer, which

Olivia drained and I ate. I know that sounds barbaric, but hunting in my true form by the moonlight in a quiet forest was amazing. After tonight, who knows when we can do this again? We are starting to go a little stir crazy already. So, can we?"

"Stir crazy" wasn't an expression I ever wanted to hear from a Were and vampire. There was little chance of someone tracking us this quickly, so it would be reasonably safe, and the odds of human hunters being out in the woods at this time of night in these frigid temperatures were remote. Even if there were hunters, with their enhanced senses, Bree and Olivia could avoid any humans out and about, which made the risk pretty low.

"One question for you, Bree: How in control of your beast are you?"

"I am in full control of it. I am aware of everything that goes on around me in that form and can understand speech, but I am unable to reply, obviously. Why? Are you worried I might attack an innocent?"

"No, it was a more selfish reason: I have never seen your true beast form before, just your hybrid one, and thought that now, when we aren't being attacked, would be a good time to see it. I will agree to your hunt on three conditions. One, I get to see your beast. Two, you avoid any humans while you are out. And three, you both need to be back by midnight. Do we have a deal?"

"Why midnight?" argued Bree.

"You are supposed to be adjusting your sleep schedule, remember? Staying out till sunrise won't help that. It is 7:20 p.m. now, which gives you four and a half hours to catch a deer. If you can't do it in that amount of time, maybe you aren't as good as you think you are."

Bree looked at Olivia, and Olivia gave her a small smile and nodded.

"Okay, Dad, we will be back by midnight," said Bree with a grin.

They both got up from the table. Bree reached for her hoodie but stopped and said, "You can get up and turn around for this part."

I got up and turned around, placing my back to them to give Bree her privacy.

Bree reminded Olivia, "You remember last time and that outfit you destroyed because we couldn't get the blood out of it? Zack probably wouldn't like the football jersey you are wearing being returned in that condition."

Olivia giggled. "Oh yeah. Getting back to nature it is, then."

I faced the fridge as they changed. I could see everything going on in the room behind me, thanks to the reflection of the highly polished stainless-steel fridge. Before I could open my mouth to warn them, though, Olivia had already stripped off the Lions jersey and was standing there, fully nude, waiting for Bree. Bree had lost her hoodie and her black sports bra by this time too.

The little angel on my shoulder was yelling at me to stop being a perv and close my eyes. The little devil on my other shoulder was going, "Dude, don't be a wuss. She asked you to turn around, and you did. Case closed." I checked out Olivia's lovely athletic form and decided that this round, it was devil, 1, and angel, 0.

My jeans were beginning to get uncomfortable as Bree peeled off the black jeans and underwear she was wearing. I glanced at Olivia's face in the reflection, and my heart beat faster. She stared directly back at me and winked at me.

Busted, I thought with a groan.

Thankfully, Bree had her back to Olivia and hadn't noticed this. I watched as Bree sprouted fur. I listened to her bones crack as they reshaped themselves in what looked to be an extremely painful process. She got lower and lower as the change continued, until finally it was over and all I could see on the surface of the fridge was two black fur-covered ears sticking up above the table.

"I'm going to wait outside. Zack, you can turn around when you hear the door close—wouldn't want you to see me naked or anything." Olivia chuckled as she turned and headed for the door. She didn't use her vampire speed to blur to the door; she just walked in a slow, lingering fashion, giving me a long look at her lovely … um … assets.

When the front door closed, I turned around. Not three feet from me was Bree in her black panther form. This startled me; I hadn't heard her move. I was shocked that something that large could move that silently. Thankfully, I managed not to jump back or flinch—displaying fear to a Were was a very bad idea.

There was a healthy amount of fear in me as I examined the lethal 300- or 400-pound killing machine in front of me. This form pretty much instantly ended the woody I had been sporting seconds ago. Bree's stunning ice-blue eyes stared at me intently. They now had cat-shaped irises. Seeing the intelligence in those eyes was both reassuring and terrifying at the same time.

When I get nervous or scared, my humor comes out. I quipped, "Damn, if I had a laser pointer right now, I could wreck this place in under a minute."

A soft growl echoed through the room. It was either a laugh or a warning, and my sphincter tightened so hard I could have crushed solid steel between my cheeks.

Maintaining eye contact with a Were was also a no-no—they took that as a dominance challenge—so I quickly lowered my gaze.

Bree turned and leisurely strolled to the front door. The grace of her muscled feline form as it moved was breathtaking. I was in total awe of her at that moment.

She stopped a few feet from the door and looked back at me as if to say, "Hey, dickhead, I have hunting to do. You want to open this thing, or should I just go through it?"

"Kitty want to go outside?" I playfully asked Bree. I got a deeper growl in response, which got me walking faster to the door.

I skirted around her, maintaining that fine balance between giving her space and not showing too much fear, then opened the door. She shot out of the house and into the night like a flash. My jaw hung open in admiration at her grace and speed. I stood in the open doorway and watched, transfixed, as her dark beast form sprinted into the night. In less than five seconds, she had disappeared into the trees and was lost from my sight.

I closed the door and spotted the pile of clothes on the floor. I picked them up, folded them neatly, and placed them in an orderly pile at the front door. It hit me then that we really hadn't discussed the logistics of how their return would work. Neither of them had a key, so I left the door unlocked. I figured Olivia could open the door, blur in, and grab the clothes. Bree would change back outside, and they could both get decent out there.

I grabbed a beer from the fridge and a seat on the couch, then turned on the TV to CNN to see what was going on in the world. Nothing earth-shattering was being reported, and I found my mind wandering. Visuals of Bree and Olivia naked popped into my head, but that led me to worry about what Olivia was going to do or say about my little peeping session earlier. I also worried a bit about the two of them being out there alone, in case my timeline for being found was off. But even a hardened professional would think twice about going after a Were and vampire in a thickly wooded area. In that environment, everything was close-range, which seriously favored the girls.

I got tired of worrying, found a movie on TV, and lost myself in it.

Chapter 15

Tuesday, February 13

Two movies later, it was coming up on midnight. I was starting to get concerned again. Remarkably, just as my watch hit midnight, the front door opened, and a bloody Olivia strolled in. I jumped off the couch in panic at the sight of the blood liberally splashed across her lower face, neck, upper chest, and hands.

Olivia waved off my concern. "Not mine! Shower time. Bye!" She then blurred up the stairs.

Bree, still in panther form, strolled in. Her muzzle was discolored with blood from the deer, or whatever animal, they had brought down. She turned and used her head to close the door. She looked down at the clothes I'd left by the door, and then her ice-blue cat eyes glared over at me.

She growled softly, and I loudly said, "Closing my eyes now. Let me know when I can open them."

The sharp *crack* of bones snapping mixed with the wet sounds of muscles tearing a few moments later. I winced in sympathy. Thankfully, they stopped after fifteen seconds or so. The room went silent enough that I could hear the continuous drone of water rushing through the pipes from Olivia's shower.

About a minute later, Bree said, "You can open your eyes now. I am decent."

I opened my eyes. Bree was fully dressed again and surprisingly blood-free. I guess whatever happened in the change took care of minor things like being covered in blood.

"Have a good time?" I asked.

"Yup, I am stuffed. I swear, fresh venison is the best thing on Earth," she said, smiling contentedly while patting her stomach.

I held up the remote and asked, "You up for a movie?"

Bree yawned and shook her head. "Nah, I am going to turn in. I need to be up at sunrise tomorrow, and that is going to be here sooner than later. Besides, fresh deer is better than Thanksgiving turkey for making you drowsy."

We exchanged good-nights, and Bree headed upstairs, leaving me to my thoughts.

I flipped the channel over to one of the late-night talk shows and got absorbed in it. I jumped in fright when a freshly washed Olivia popped up out of nowhere. I then crashed back to the couch, and that brought a smirk of amusement to her face.

"By Odin's beard, Olivia! Please don't do that!"

She giggled. "Well, that is the start of my payback. Someone was a very naughty boy this evening."

I sat up. I was about to apologize, but she sat down opposite me on the couch. She smiled at me and crossed her legs like we were acting out that scene from the movie *Basic Instinct*. I became instantly aware of the fact that she yet again had nothing on under my Lions jersey. My words died on my lips.

Olivia laughed deeply at my reaction. "I'm sensing your social life has been a little quiet recently."

I shrugged.

She continued. "Being naked has never been a big deal for me. You checking me out earlier? That doesn't bother me, but my nudity-conscious Were friend wouldn't take it so lightly. I think she seriously needs to get over it; she's a Were, so she is going to end up naked, like, all the time. I'm sure she will eventually get better with the whole thing, but for now, this gives me leverage. It will cost you to keep my silence."

"Before I hear your demands, I would like to apologize. It wasn't right of me to peep, regardless of whether you are okay with it or not."

"Apology accepted, but I still have demands," said Olivia with a grin and a mischievous twinkle in her eyes.

I took a deep breath to brace myself for whatever was coming, then nodded.

"I will give you a choice. I have spent the last year of my undead life with three women, and, like yourself, have been lacking in certain, um, benefits … Well, not totally. Bree was missing those same benefits, and there were a couple of nights this past year that we helped each other scratch that itch."

My eyes widened, and some interesting visuals popped into my head—sometimes, a vivid imagination is both a blessing and a curse. I shifted uncomfortably on the couch.

Olivia smirked, then continued. "We have roughly five hours till sunrise, and the first choice I offer is for us to find interesting and creative ways to the pass the time."

I think I whimpered a bit.

"The other option is this: Most men usually have to take me out on a date before getting to see me naked. Since you got the payoff, I want the date. I want us to go out flying tonight, as that is super awesome, and that will count as our date. Do you want to stay in or go out?"

My body was screaming, "*Stay in! Stay in!*" But the rational part of me knew that would be a bad idea. I was supposed to be protecting these girls, and sleeping with Olivia would undermine the leadership role I had assumed. Right now, though, Olivia just oozed sexuality. I struggled to find the willpower to do the right thing. Thankfully, the practical side of my brain also reminded me that sex with Olivia would involve her feeding off me, and I wasn't keen on a young, inexperienced vampire using me as a snack.

That was enough to tip the scales, and I said, "As tempting as option one is—and words can't express how tempting it is—I will go with option two. Maybe when we aren't being hunted, we can have this conversation again."

She smiled, then nodded. Part of me felt like I had just passed some sort of test. She uncrossed her legs again, but this time I made a point of looking away. She stood up.

"Okay, Zack, let's go flying," she said in a happy tone.

I nodded and got up. The Honolulu-blue jersey with the huge "90" in bright white was an issue. I said, "Go change first. A half-naked woman with glowing white numbers on her back is going to stand out like a sore thumb in the air. Find something dark to wear that will blend in better with the night, okay?"

She nodded and, to my amazement, lifted the jersey off right then and there before casually strolling to the stairs. As she walked away, she looked over her shoulder and said, "Thought I would give you something to let you think about your choice while I get changed." She gave a playful little laugh as she headed up the stairs.

I knew I had made the right choice, but damn it, it sure didn't feel like it at that moment.

Once Olivia disappeared upstairs, I headed over to the kitchen. I found a paper and pen, then wrote, "Olivia and I have gone out flying. We will be back before sunrise—Zack." I left it on the countertop.

I was wearing a white T-shirt and blue jeans. The jeans were dark enough they wouldn't stand out, and my dark-green spring jacket would cover the white T-shirt. I should be good.

Olivia returned a few minutes later. She was wearing black jeans that fit her like a second skin, a grayish-brown-colored T-shirt, and sneakers. She grabbed her black jacket off the rack and put it on.

I zipped up my own jacket, and we were good to go. I held the door for her, and she walked out into the cold, dark night. I followed.

Outside, I held out my hand toward her. Olivia stepped into me. She wrapped her arms tightly around me, and I put my arm around her. Without a word, I lifted us both straight up into the air at an aggressive speed.

I kept going up until I was a good 5,000 feet in the air, and Olivia yelled over the wind, "This is awesome! I wish I had your powers!"

I smiled, and memories of another time in my life came crashing back. The only other girl I had taken on a flight like this was Rebecca. Unlike Olivia, Rebecca had been too nervous to enjoy herself. We had only flown together once.

"Do some tricks!" yelled Olivia in an excited tone.

I nodded and shot up higher into the air. I executed a perfect Immelmann turn, followed by a barrel roll. On the downward part of the loop, I said to Olivia, "Hold on!"

I shot toward the ground like a Stuka dive-bomber, which was made even more realistic as Olivia screamed with joy. At about 500 feet, I leveled off for a moment and headed back up. I flew us farther north out into the wilderness to avoid being seen by anyone. It was a perfectly clear winter's night, and I had something in mind.

Once I got us back up to 5,000 feet, I did more rolls, twists, loops, and dips and found myself really enjoying showing off. Olivia loved every moment of it.

After doing this for a bit, I yelled, "Do you trust me?"

"Sure! Why?" she screamed back over the wind.

"Do you want to try free falling? I will catch you before you hit the ground."

Olivia smiled and let go of me. She didn't go anywhere at first, as I still had my arm around her waist and she was being held up by the same wind currents I was using. Then I removed my arm from her slender waist and used the wind to push us apart. She instantly fell away from me and started to drop.

I laughed as she screamed, "Wheeeee!" and tumbled and flew through the air. I knew that at this height, she would have about thirty seconds in free fall before hitting the ground. I flipped over midair and chased after her. I used my Air power to push myself faster, so I could catch up, closing the distance between us quickly.

About 1,000 feet from the ground, I pushed the wind under her to slow her fall and then held her suspended in the air when she reached about 500 feet. I swooped in and grabbed her up, and she hugged me tightly as I lifted us back up.

"Oh my God, that was awesome! Can I do that again?" yelled Olivia as we climbed.

We end up free falling four more times before the effort of it all started to catch up to me. I spied a high rocky ridge close by. I flew for it and set us down on top of it.

"Why are we stopping here?" asked Olivia.

"I need a rest. All of that flying is starting to drain me. Also, look up."

Olivia tilted her head to the sky, and her eyes went wide at the clear winter night sky. It was alive and full of stars at that moment. We were away from any ground-based light pollution, so the view of all those twinkling stars was like nothing you would ever see in the city.

I plunked myself down on a large boulder, and Olivia sat beside me. I glanced at my watch. It was just past 2:00 a.m.; we had plenty of time before sunrise.

"Looking at all those stars makes me feel small and insignificant," Olivia said out of the blue. "As a vampire, I could live for thousands of years, but even after I live all that time and then die, these stars will still be here."

"That can be reassuring, too—if you are still here in 1,000 years, the rest of us probably won't be. You can find a nice, dark spot like this one night in that future, and those stars will still be there. You can laugh about flying through the air and remember this night."

Olivia smiled at this. We sat quietly for a bit until she said, "Zack, I'm worried. Giselle is not going to give up, and €5 million will bring a lot of dangerous people after us. What if Bree or Stella get hurt or even killed? I'm not sure I could live with that. Maybe it would be better if you turned me in and claimed the contract reward. At least that way everyone would be safe."

"That is one solution, and I would end up sleeping on a big pile of money surrounded by many beautiful women, which would be a definite upside for me."

Olivia grinned a little but rolled her eyes.

I continued. "I doubt Bree and Stella would be happy with that option, though. Let me ask you something: If Bree had the contract on her, would you want her to give herself up to keep you safe?"

"No! Absolutely not!"

"And they would be upset at you if you turned yourself in. They know the risks. They are doing this because they love you and know you would do the same for them, so no more talk about giving yourself up, okay?"

Olivia nodded. "I understand why *they* are doing this, but why are *you* doing it?"

" 'With great power comes great responsibility.' "

Based on the blank look on Olivia's face, she didn't catch my Spidey reference. "My mother, when she was raising and training me, always drove home that we were blessed with abilities that normal people don't have. She felt it was our duty to help people in any way we could. That night in the parking lot in Toronto after the fight with McMahon, Blue and Bree were injured, Stella was freezing in the cold, and you guys had no money and no way to get home. There was no way I could I have just left you there. I'm just not wired that way. I can't explain it any better than that."

"If that is the case, why did you stop being the Hurricane and become a bounty hunter?" asked Olivia. She sounded slightly judgmental.

I told her about the night I had decided to give up being a hero and become a bounty hunter, about being hurt, broke, facing eviction, and single—and how much those ten years as a hero had cost me. "I guess I justified my move by feeling that the people on that bounty list weren't there because they were nice people and that each one I took down made things safer for everyone. I still help out in emergencies, or if I see a crime happening, I will get involved, but at the end of the day, I needed to take care of myself, you know?"

Olivia nodded. She looked disappointed, though I think she understood.

Talking and being with Olivia was odd. In some ways, she made me feel younger—I was sort of living vicariously through her and her youth, and I enjoyed how carefree she was, the way she acted, and her views of the world.

She also, at times, made me feel much older than my thirty-three years, and this was one of those times. The eighteen-year-old me, the new hero who was determined to make the world a better place out of a sense of righteousness—and to make my recently deceased mother proud—would have been disappointed in the choice I had made at twenty-eight to give up being a full-time hero. Fortunately, there was a wisdom that came with age.

As I dwelt on Olivia's disappointment in my career choice, I was glad that I had picked option number two this evening and hadn't slept with her. I was not sure that my eighteen-year-old self would have been strong enough to make that same decision though …

"Olivia, when you offered me two choices tonight, which one were you hoping I'd pick?"

She gave me a sideways glance. An amused smile crossed her face for a second before she answered, "I was pleased you picked option two. Option one would have been good too. You are great guy, and it would have been fun. I am curious about what sex would be like in this new form; all my senses have been enhanced. I see like a hawk, I can hear a whisper a mile away—right now, I can hear your heart beating in your chest—and I can track things by scent alone. With all these new and improved senses, what would sex be like? Before I was turned, I slept with three different guys, and the one thing they all had in common was that they were jerks. I think part of me was relieved when you picked option two. That probably meant you weren't a jerk."

She went quiet for a moment before she spoke again. "Maybe we can revisit option one in the future, when we aren't being hunted."

I nodded almost too eagerly at that, and she added, "I will warn you, though, that by then there might be other men in the picture—you will have competition, which means you will have to work harder at bedding me," finished Olivia with a laugh.

I smiled, and we sat quietly for a few minutes. I glance at the time on my phone but noticed the date. "By the way, Happy Valentine's Day!"

Olivia glanced at me and asked, "Really?"

"Yup, as of midnight, it is officially February 14."

She smiled, leaned in, and gave me a chaste kiss. "Happy Valentine's Day then."

I looked up at the stars again and smiled. Sure, we were being hunted, and I had no idea if we'd survive this or not, but at least I was out on a date on Valentine's Day. This made a pleasant change from being home alone or out on a job, which had been the case in recent years.

We chatted for another hour on that quiet, peaceful rock in the middle of nowhere. We exchanged stories about growing up and funny things that had happened in our lives, and Olivia asked about some of my more exciting adventures when I was the Hurricane. I shared some of the better ones.

It felt good to be out there and not worrying about being hunted or tracked; I think that time did both of our souls some good.

When I flew us back home, I once again did aerial acrobatics along the flight. Olivia laughed and whooped the whole time. Honestly, the girl was totally fearless. I wondered if that was a side effect of having died once or if that was just Olivia.

In the end, I decided it didn't matter.

Chapter 16

Wednesday, February 14

Olivia and I got home about forty-five minutes before sunrise. We hung out quietly on the couch until she left me to go sleep in the pantry.

I yawned for the fourth time in as many minutes; the long night had caught up to me, and I was having trouble keeping my eyes open. I glanced up when I heard footsteps coming down the stairs. Stella looked annoyingly chipper and alert, considering how early in the morning it was. Bree trailed behind her and looked how I felt—tired and exhausted. Her blonde hair was randomly sticking up and out, and her eyes were barely open.

I met them at the base of the stairs and wished them a good morning. Stella replied with a "Goodnight" in her crisp and way-too-perky English accent. Bree just grunted at me as we passed each other on the stairs.

* * * * *

I crawled out of bed at 1:30 in the afternoon and headed downstairs. The TV was blaring music. Bree was on the couch with her eyes closed, bopping her head around in time to the music. Stella was in the kitchen making a tea and had her back to me when I entered. I made a beeline for the fridge, trying to move around Stella, but she didn't know I was there and stepped back toward me. I held out my hand to stop her from backing up into me and touched her back without thinking about it.

She screamed and jumped away from me. Worse, before she hit the ground, she was already changing into her Hyde persona.

"Stella, it's me!" I cried as I accessed my powers to thicken the air between us.

She looked at me with her large blood-shot eye and grunted menacingly. Her body tensed, as if about to attack.

I held up my hands in a peaceful, nonthreatening way. For a moment, I thought I was about to be pounded into paste.

The music died, and Bree yelled, "Stella, no!"

The air shimmered around Stella for a moment, and then I let out a breath of relief as normal little-girl Stella was back.

"Stella, I am deeply sorry," I said as I released my power and the air changed back to normal between us.

Stella shook her head. "No, Zack, it is I who should be sorry. You have shown us nothing but kindness. My reaction just now was totally uncalled for."

"Stella, relax. No one got hurt. You were startled, and your fight-or-flight reflex kicked in."

Stella just stood there as if collecting herself. I got out the orange juice container and managed to pour myself a glass with my slightly shaking hands.

Once Stella had made herself a tea, we sat at the kitchen table.

"Did you eat lunch yet?" I asked them both.

"Yeah, we finished off the leftover chili from last night. Well, I got a little bit, but Stella hogged most of it," said Bree with a grin.

"Bree, stop telling fibs!" exclaimed Stella, shaking her head even though an amused smile was emerging from her crumbling stern visage.

"Has anyone been sniffing around?"

Stella shook her head. "Not that we are aware of, though if they came around in the last hour, I doubt we would have heard them over the racket that Bree calls 'music.' "

Bree looked a little sheepish. We talked for a bit longer, and then Stella excused herself to check on Blue. I headed upstairs, as well, and grabbed a shower, returning downstairs to make myself a light lunch after that. I was surprised to find a cold-meat sandwich waiting for me. Bree said she had made it for me while making one for herself as a snack.

After lunch, we retired to the living room and watched a movie to kill time. The rest of the afternoon wasn't much more productive. For dinner, I fried up six hamburgers in a couple of frying pans on the stove while Bree prepped a salad and the burger toppings.

When everything was done, Bree went to fetch Stella, and a sleepy Olivia popped out of the pantry. She yawned as she walked by me and softly said, "Thank you for my date last night, lover." She giggled, and I looked at the stairs in worry. Luckily, Bree was still upstairs.

Olivia opened the fridge and extracted a bag of blood from the fridge. After warming it in the microwave, she found a seat at the table.

Bree and Stella joined us a few minutes later, and we all sat down for dinner. The conversation was light and uneventful.

We were just finishing our meal when I felt a slight tingling. Bree suddenly cocked her head and said, "We have company."

"Olivia, go get Blue," I ordered.

I pointed toward the couch, and Stella and Bree followed me. The tingling sensation got stronger; someone out there was a Fire elemental. Olivia blurred to the couch and put Blue carefully down on the side of the couch, away from the front of the house. I thickened the air around us for protection.

"Bree? Olivia? Can you hear anything out there?" I asked.

They both stopped and listened for about ten seconds. Bree said, "There are at least four people heading toward the house. I heard a gun being cocked, so at least one of them is armed."

Strangely, knowing they were armed brought a bit of relief. In general, Enhanced Individuals didn't use firearms; they could do more damage with their abilities. I hoped this meant that it was just the Fire elemental and three normal humans outside.

I wanted to see with my own eyes what we were dealing with. "I am going to peek out the window. None of you move. I will keep an air shield between us and them, but remember that I can only extend it enough to cover about five feet on either side of me."

I climbed over the couch and headed to the window directly in front of the house, pulling back the blinds slightly and looking out into the night. To my right, I saw an aura in the darkness. It was solid orange with a black outline and four silver arrows at the top, bottom, and sides pointing out like a compass. I had never seen this type of aura before, but I had no doubt it belonged to someone with tracking powers.

Directly in front of the window, I could see a bright-red aura outlined in black. That was the Fire elemental. A few moments later, the red aura lifted off the ground, and then the figure in the air became completely engulfed in flames. Fire elementals, like Air elementals, could fly. I could use wind to lift me, and Fire elementals could superheat the air for lift and thrust.

The flash of a sniper's muzzle caught my eye. The shot came from about 500 feet out, in front of the house. The window in front of me suddenly blossomed into a spiderweb of jagged cracks. A loud *bang* followed that; the sound of the shot caught up to the massive round that was suspended and pressed against the cracked window. I cursed at the accuracy of the shot—if I hadn't shielded the air in front of me, that round would have blown a huge hole in the dead center of my chest. Worse, the bullet was a silver-alloyed round. I'd have been dead no matter what it was made out of, but the silver meant Bree was in danger, and silver rounds were effective against Olivia too.

Moments later, I saw flashes to the left and right of the window about 100 feet out—automatic weapons. Some of these rounds were suspended about a foot from the front window; they, too, were silver. The far windows, which I wasn't shielding, shattered. Rounds impacted the stairs and the kitchen area, then pinged off various things in the room. Glass crashed to the floor as the rounds hit the back floor-to-ceiling windows. Another high-caliber round shattered the window in front of me completely. The round and all the glass hung in the air just in front of me. I backed away toward the girls, who were all on the floor in the center of the U-shaped couch.

The nonstop gunfire tore everything apart. The noise inside the house was a hellish symphony of crashing glass and ricocheting rounds. I hopped over the couch and joined the girls on the floor behind it. Bree was almost fully nude and currently stripping off her panties in a hurry, which caught me off guard.

"Hey, Bree, you're really hot, and I'm flattered, but now is really not the time for nookie!" I yelled over the sound of the ricocheting bullets.

Olivia laughed, and Bree shot me a look that could kill. A high-powered round hit the couch, and a cloud of stuffing erupted from it, quickly bringing the seriousness of our situation home.

"Stella, is your Hyde form bulletproof?" I asked loudly.

She nodded and yelled, "I think so! I'm not sure about that larger round, though. Blue only shot me with a 9 mm."

I was a little shocked that Blue had shot Stella, and I made a note to ask her about that sometime before pushing it aside and getting down to business.

"There are six of them," I told the girls. "Two are Enhanced: The one hanging back about 300 feet from the house is a Fire elemental, and the other is a tracker. The tracker probably doesn't have any powers outside his tracking ability, but I don't know that for sure. The tracker and a human are about 100 feet to the right of the house, taking cover in the trees. There are two other humans under cover 100 feet to the left of the house. Those four are using assault rifles. Each pair is alternating fire; one is firing while the other reloads."

I paused as another cloud of stuffing exploded from the couch, then continued. "There is a human sniper who is probably using a thermal scope, given his accuracy. He is 500 feet from the house, straight across from the front window, ten feet high in a tree."

I'd been shot at before, but not like this. The sheer volume of rounds they were laying into the cottage was a new experience for me, and I wasn't a fan. Adrenaline was coursing through me now, and I was tired of being a sitting duck; it was time to take the fight to them.

"Bree and Stella, when I say, 'Go,' change forms. Once you have both changed, Olivia will grab Blue, and then all of us are going to walk to the dining room table. Stella, flip the dining table over and angle it on its side, facing the door. Bree, they are using silver-tipped rounds, so you are sitting this fight out. Stay behind the table with Blue. Once the table is flipped over, Stella, I am going to jump on your back and shield the air in front of us. Go out the front door as fast as you can and then leap toward the shooters on the right. I will fly off at the apex of your leap and deal with the Fire elemental. You land and take out the shooters. As soon as we head out the front door, we should draw their fire. Olivia, head out the back as fast as you can. Go wide around the shooters on the left and take out that sniper. Stella, once the shooters on the right are down, hit the left ones. If Olivia or me finish our targets, we will help, but I think you will probably be on your own. Questions?"

My closing question was punctuated by another cloud of stuffing as another round hit the couch.

Everyone shook their heads.

"Good. One last thing, Stella—try to take one of your targets alive. I would like to question them. Alright! Stella, Bree, change now."

Stuff crashed down all over the cottage. The front walls were becoming less and less wall-like and more like Swiss cheese. Stella's Hyde form instantly appeared, and Bree was in her hybrid form about fifteen seconds later. I got up, and Stella slowly walked forward. She effortlessly tossed one half of the couch out of the way and headed directly for the sturdy oak table. She grabbed the heavy table in her massive hands and flipped it upright with almost no effort. The rest of us followed and gathered behind the table.

Stella looked at me as if to say, "Well, what are you waiting for?"

I hopped up onto her back like I was a small child, and she edged around the table and headed directly for the front door. As she reached it, she kicked out. The door and its frame flew off into the night. Stella charged forward. She ran about five steps and angled toward the flashes of gunfire coming from our right. She made a mighty leap into the air. Fireballs rained down toward us, but I thickened the air to deflect them from hitting us.

I separated at the midpoint of her jump. The Fire elemental was about 500 feet off the ground, so I poured on the speed to get higher in the air and close the distance between us. My eyes teared up due to the high speed. I was pleased that the Fire elemental was shooting her fireballs at me and not Stella. I jinked randomly left and right, avoiding the fireballs; occasionally, I had to use my Air power to deflect a fireball that got too close. I cursed as a couple that missed me hit the cottage. It started to burn with vigor.

At 100 feet from the Fire elemental, I began gathering up the power for a potent lightning attack. Once I got close enough, I extended my hand, and a flash of deadly lightning shot from it. She tried to dodge, but I hit her in the leg. She screamed briefly, and then the flames surrounding her were instantly extinguished. She tumbled, uncontrolled, to the ground and hit it headfirst. A loud, distinct *crack* reached me as her neck snapped. If she wasn't already dead from the lightning, she certainly was now.

The strobing of blue and red lights in the far distance meant someone in the area must have called the police due to the gunfire. Help was on its way, but it would probably be at least ten minutes before anyone got there. I let my momentum carry me in the direction of the sniper. I could see Olivia's blood-red aura through the trees. As I closed in, a body fell limply from the tree. I looked into the tree to see that Olivia was fine and in one piece. She had blood dripping down her chin; I assumed she'd drained the sniper. She nimbly leapt down from the tree and blurred back toward the house.

The silence was almost deafening—the roar of gun shots had completely stopped. I turned around in the air and flew back to the shooters on the left. Stella's dotted red-and-white half-aura stood out like a beacon in the night air, and I headed straight for it. I landed in a clearing about ten feet away from her. One of the shooters was lying dead on the ground, his entire head crushed in. The other shooter, moaning in pain, was sitting against a tree with his two legs broken at odd angles in front of him. Stella was hovering over him and growling.

"Good work, Stella. Go check on Blue and Bree, okay?" I said.

She looked up at me, grunted, and lumbered quickly away toward the burning house. I walked up to the prone mercenary. He stared up at me with hate on his face. I arced a showy bit of electricity from one hand to the other, and the hateful look quickly turned to a look of concern and fear.

"The cops are going to be here in ten minutes. You are going to answer my questions before they get here."

"Fuck you," he said, then spat at me.

"Wrong answer." I shot a low dose of lightning at his crotch.

He screamed as it made contact.

I put on an intimidating smile. "Let's try this again. If you don't answer, we will see how much electric shock therapy your balls can take before they explode. Why are you here?"

"For the bounty on the vampire," he said in a panic.

"What details did the bounty contract list?" I asked.

"A yearling vampire named Olivia Johnson, captured alive for €5 million or brought in dead for €2 million. May be traveling with an Air elemental named Zack Stevens. The elemental's home address was listed as well. There was a contact number to call when the job was done."

"Anything else?" I asked as I let a few sparks fall from my fingers.

"No, man, nothing. That's it, I swear to God," he pleaded.

"How did you find us this quickly?"

"Jones is a tracker—just give him a name or a piece of clothing and he will head straight for the target. Once he saw the bounty, he called us in and we loaded up our gear. We chartered a plane from Texas and headed straight here."

"How did you get the weapons and ammo into Canada?" I asked. I was curious.

"Easy, man. About ten minutes out from Hamilton Airport, Maria, our Fire elemental, jumped out of the plane with Jones and all our gear. They used their cartel contacts to have an SUV waiting in a field for them. Once we landed and cleared customs, we had another SUV waiting for us. Then we linked up with them and headed north."

"Why didn't Jones land with you guys?"

"Jones is a wanted man; there is no way he would have cleared customs."

Interesting. I wondered if Jones had an outstanding bounty on him and what it was worth.

"Does anyone else know where you guys are? Is there anyone else coming? Before you answer, you should know that the air around you moves differently when you lie. I'd suggest you think carefully on your answer," I warned. This was bullshit, but I figured he wouldn't know that.

"No, and no one else is coming. Jones wouldn't risk sharing that bounty with anyone else. We are a tight crew; it was just the six of us."

Olivia blurred up at that moment and looked down at the prone man. "Oh, look—another yummy snack." She still had blood covering her chin and neck, and her fangs were fully extended.

The guy took one look at her, pissed himself, and fainted.

Olivia laughed and retracted her fangs.

I sighed. "I guess I'm not getting any more out of him. No, you can't eat him. You, young lady, are on a strict one-bad-guy-a-day diet."

A series of loud *snaps* and *cracks* filled the air behind me. I turned and saw the entire flame-engulfed cottage crash down on itself. Bree and Blue came to mind in a panic, but I calmed down when I spotted their auras off to the side of the house with Stella's.

"Don't worry—everyone is fine," said Olivia. "Bree also managed to grab the two intact bags of blood from the fridge; the rest were shot up."

"I'm assuming the duffel bag full of cash didn't make out either?"

Olivia's sad expression told me the answer before she even shook her head.

Between the destroyed blood and cash, the resources we needed to stay off the grid were rapidly running out. Olivia had fed well this evening on the sniper, but only two bags left meant we only had two days' worth of food for her. We were now down to the $2,500 I had in my pants pocket and the burner phone in my coat pocket. But I was more concerned with the lack of blood than the lack of cash. The money was more than enough to cover a week's worth of motel rooms and food, but the lack of blood was an issue. We could stretch things out with some deer blood and letting her feed off me and Bree, but that would only buy us a couple more days.

The sirens were getting much closer. I turned to Olivia and said, "Go wash your face in the lake. Tell Bree and Stella to change back and look as nonthreatening as possible. I will deal with authorities, okay?"

118

She nodded, and then, with a slight breeze, she was gone.

I glanced over at the wreckage, concerned that the fire might spread. Thankfully, there was enough snow on the clearing around it that the fire would stay contained. I dreaded the call I would have to make to Greg to tell him about his cottage, but on the upside, we were all alive and relatively unharmed. The cottage could be replaced; people couldn't.

Chapter 17

Wednesday, February 14

Ifished my hero ID out of my wallet and held it out in front of me as the police pulled up. The ID was hideous and sported a big neon-green cross on it, but it did allow law enforcement to quickly notice it. A black-and-white Ontario Provincial Police SUV rolled up and stopped about ten feet from where I was standing. The echoes of more sirens in the distance meant this cruiser was the first of many.

The officer got out of the SUV and looked warily at me. I was pleased that he hadn't drawn a weapon, though his holster was snapped open and his right hand was firmly resting on the butt of the gun.

He closed the distance between us quickly. I slowly lowered the hand with the ID in it and held it out to him. I spotted *O'Connor* on his nameplate and wasn't overly shocked that a natural redhead had a common Irish surname.

"There were reports of gunshots. Are there any active shooters on the property, Mr. Stevens?" he asked, handing me back the ID.

"Call me Zack. There are no active shooters on the property; all hostiles have been dealt with. There are five dead and one injured hostile who will need an ambulance. Two of the hostiles were Enhanced, so you should probably put a call in to EIRT. The cottage we were staying in is burning, so a fire truck would be good too. The cottage is isolated, so there is little chance of the fire spreading, but the house did have a gas line. There are four female Enhanced Individuals to the right of the house. They are with me, and I would suggest not approaching them—they are all a little keyed up right now."

He nodded, "I'm Sean. If you'll excuse for a moment, I need to call this in."

He picked up the radio handset on the front of his uniform and talked to dispatch. I put my wallet back in my pocket and waited for him to finish. Another OPP cruiser pulled up as he was on the radio. This one was a Crown Victoria, rather than an SUV, and the officer tucked it neatly behind O'Connor's vehicle.

Sean asked dispatch to have a perimeter set at the junction of the mile-long access road and the main road. The two officers had me lead them to the lone survivor, who was still slumped over against the tree, unconscious. Sean checked him for a pulse and nodded. He stood back up and whistled at the pile of used brass casings around the area. Then he spotted the couple of assault rifles on the ground.

Olivia instantly materialized beside me, causing both officers to jump and reach for their weapons.

"Stella and Bree are freezing," said Olivia.

I was relieved that neither officer had drawn their guns. Both seemed to relax a bit as they assessed that Olivia wasn't an active threat. It was a benefit that both were relatively younger officers and tended to view vampires as Enhanced Individuals; some older officers would have viewed Olivia as a monster and would have been quicker to draw weapons.

Before I could answer, Sean said, "They are welcome to sit in my cruiser to warm up. We will need to get statements from them anyway."

I nodded, but Olivia had already disappeared. I spotted her a moment later beside the smoldering cottage with Stella and Bree beside her. I watched as she hoisted Blue up onto her shoulders, and then all of them headed toward the cruiser.

A fire truck drove by us, heading straight for the cottage. An ambulance came in right on the fire truck's tail, and Sean waved the ambulance over. The ambulance stopped, and a couple of EMTs got out and started dealing with the lone survivor.

Sean told the other officer to accompany the ambulance when it left and to take the survivor into custody once he was cleared from hospital.

The ladies walked by us, making a beeline for the SUV. Stella and Bree were shivering. Bree's shirt was covered in blood. I was concerned about this for a moment, but then I spotted the two bags of blood clutched in her hand. I assumed she must have dumped all the bags from the fridge into her discarded shirt to carry them out of the cottage. She was also barefoot; I winced in sympathy.

Sean must have noticed the same thing, because he said, "There are blankets in the back of the cruiser. Help yourselves."

Bree nodded. She and Stella moaned in relief as they opened the door to the warm SUV a few moments later and jumped into the backseat. Olivia passed Blue's unconscious form to them and then went around back, opened the tailgate of the SUV, and grabbed two heavy gray blankets. She joined the rest of the team in the back of the SUV a few moments later.

"Does the blue female require medical assistance?" Sean asked me.

"No, she is in a self-induced healing coma. There is nothing anyone can do for her."

"In that case, can I get a statement from you about what happened here?"

I nodded and spent the next thirty minutes answering most of his questions about what had happened.

Near the end of his questioning, we walked toward the cottage. The fire department had extinguished the fire. They were in the process of wrapping up. I felt terrible at the sight of the blackened and charred remains of Greg's beautiful cottage. I was going to call him but wanted to wait for EIRT. A Fire elemental had torched this place, so the damage and rebuilding cost should be covered under the Federal Enhanced Individuals Emergency Fund. Once I got the details of what was and wasn't covered, I would call Greg and break the bad news to him.

As the fire truck was heading out, two black unmarked SUVs came rolling in with flashing red and blue lights going in their grilles. They came to stop about twenty feet from where the one shooter had died and the other had been injured. All of them got out in tactical gear, though they hadn't bothered with helmets, and their weapons were slung.

There were six of them, and two of them had auras. One aura was orange with pale green, which told me that the man was a telepath, but there was thick black outline around the aura, and that usually indicated evil—not something I expected from an EIRT member. The other aura was vivid purple with a brown-and-silver outline, which meant Werewolf. The outline of the aura on the Werewolf was large enough that he'd probably been a were for at least thirty years.

The four human members of the team consisted of three men of different shapes and sizes and a powerfully built woman whose blonde braided ponytail hung out from the back of her knitted black hat.

Sean left me and headed for the EIRT team. He approached the Were; based on his positive body language, it was obvious they had worked together before and got along well.

After a minute, Sean pointed at me. The Were nodded and headed my way, the rest of his team on his heels. The posture of the team was relaxed but alert as they approached, so I slowly retrieved my wallet and fished out my ID again.

The dark-haired Were stopped a few feet from me. He studied me with his serious gray eyes for a few moments and said, "I'm Sargent Ray Dunham. Do you mind if I examine your ID?"

I shook my head and handed him my ID. He took it from me, and I explained, "Usually, I work south of here, so we haven't met before, but if you call Bobby Knight, Frank Greenfield, Dana Schoen, Mike Tavush, or Hector Garcia, any of them will vouch for me."

He nodded. "All of them are good people, but I am always surprised Bobby was able to get into EIRT with his small size."

I laughed. "Nice test there. No one who has met Bobby would ever call him 'small' unless they were being ironic."

He nodded, smiled, and handed back my ID. "Do you mind explaining what the hell happened out here? It looks like you were hit by a team of pros, judging by the quality of their weapons and the amount of ammo they expended."

I started to explain what happened, but then it felt like someone was trying to drive an icepick into my brain. I glanced around, and my eyes stopped on the EIRT member who had the telepath aura. He stared intently at me with an amused smile on his face, but a bit of confusion showed as well. He was probing me, hence the major headache I was getting. I flicked a bolt of lightning at him—not enough to seriously injure him, but enough to knock him on his ass and wipe the smug look off his face. The pain instantly went away.

The four human members of the team all pointed their MP5 submachine guns at me. Ray's eyes flashed for a moment, but he didn't shift. I automatically thickened the air in front of me and began gathering my power to access at a moment's notice if this went any further downhill.

"You just assaulted an EIRT officer. You will stand down. You are under arrest," said Ray in a cool tone.

"Sure, but Officer Probes-a-Lot there better be in fucking cuffs, as well; mentality probing someone with a valid hero registration is a felony," I replied, not dropping my defenses in the slightest.

Ray's head snapped around. He shot the telepath an angry glare and asked, "Benny, is this true?"

Benny ignored Ray's question. The telepath's face darkened in rage, and he was clenching his fists as he stared at me. Another stab of pain flashed deep into my brain.

I began charging up a blast that would do more than just knock him on his ass and said, "He has three seconds to stop his assault, or I'm frying him where he stands, and he won't be fucking getting up again."

"Officer Sidana, stand down!" yelled Ray.

The throbbing pain in my head stopped.

"Simmons, Randall, relieve Benny of his weapons, attach a power-blocking collar, and put him in the truck in cuffs."

The blonde woman and the largest man on the team turned and pointed their weapons at Benny. I briefly thought he was going to resist, but he slumped his shoulders and allowed the man to take his weapons. The female officer attached a silver power-blocking collar to him, cuffed him, and led him away. I knew the human EIRT officers wore a variant of the power-blocking collars, so I didn't worry about him mentally attacking them. These collars were designed to block mental and magical attacks against them, so if Benny hadn't wanted to go quietly, he would have had to physically fight them, rather than using his powers.

"Sorry about that. Benny is a good guy—"

"No, he isn't. Look, Ray, can we talk by ourselves for a moment?" There was something I had liked about Ray Dunham right from the start, and that was why I wanted to trust him with my aura secret. Ray struck me as professional but flexible. Both were great traits to have when dealing with things that go bump in the night. Too many EIRT officers were rigid, my-way-or-the-highway types.

He looked annoyed, but turned to the two remaining officers and said, "You guys start going over the crime scene."

"Sorry, Ray, one other thing—the one guy who survived mentioned that Jones, the tracker, was wanted. Can you have your guys do a search on that? He was based out of Texas. I have a feeling if you find out who that guy is, it will make all our lives easier."

"Desmond, you catch that?" asked Ray, and the shorter officer nodded.

Ray turned back to me and added, "Anything else?" in a tone that said there better not be.

I shook my head.

The two other officers wandered off, leaving me and Ray alone to talk.

"Okay, Mr. Stevens, we are alone. This better be good."

"Please, call me Zack. I am about to tell you something that only a couple of people know. I will do this if you leave it out of your report and keep it strictly to yourself, okay?" He nodded, and I added, "I'm going to need your word as a Were on this."

His eyes widened, but after a moment, he said, "I swear as a Were this will just be between us. How did you know I was a Were?"

"I can see the auras of any Enhanced Individual. Your aura tells me you are a Werewolf, and even though you look like you are in your late twenties, I'm going to guess your real age is fifty- or maybe sixty-something."

"I will be fifty-seven in March. You got that just from my aura?" he asked.

"Yeah, the colors of the aura tell me the type of power, and the size tells me the strength."

He pondered this for a moment and said, "That is a handy trait to have, but I don't see why you are telling me."

"The reason I am telling you is Benny. Benny's aura is orange with pale blue, which tells me he is a telepath, but it is bordered in a thick black outline. That black outline means one of two things: either he has a demon possessing him, or he has done some exceptionally evil things. Either way, there is no way he should be in an EIRT uniform."

Ray rubbed his temples—his life had just gotten a lot more complicated. "Benny has only been on my team for three months. Before that, he was working the EIRT counterterrorism division. Before he joined EIRT, he had been working on the UN counterterrorism group for a couple of years in some extremely dark places. He came highly recommended, but due to the sensitive nature of his work, a lot of his personnel file was classified. He has been solid, but there have been a couple of incidents—like today—when he overstepped. I assumed it was due to the highly dangerous environment he'd been in, and I hoped that, in time, he would adjust and fall in line. If what you are saying is true, that won't be the case."

Ray went quiet, as if pondering what I had told him. In the silence, another thought popped into my mind. "On a completely unrelated note, if you don't mind me asking, are you part of a pack?"

"Yeah, I am the enforcer for the Barrie pack. Why?"

"Is the pack strong and stable?" I asked, ignoring his question for a bit.

"Shawn, our alpha, has been alpha for about fifty years now. He takes his role seriously and looks out for all our members. We, of course, have the odd rogue, but we deal with that quickly. There are dominance squabbles at the lower tiers, but there are rules in place to deal with that too. Once a dominance match is done, it is settled for good. Thanks to Shawn's leadership, ours is probably one of the better packs in the country."

I was pleased at his answer; that type of pack was exactly what I was looking for.

"I'm sure Sean told you there were four Enhanced Individuals who were with me." He nodded, and I continued. "One of them is a Werepanther who was spawned by an alpha; the alpha died that same night. She has been a Were for just over a year. She is powerful for her age; she can do hybrid and partial transformations." I paused as his eyes widened at the last part, and then I added, "She is remarkably controlled for her age, but since the night of her turning, she has never been around another Were."

"Jesus, so she doesn't have a pack, then?"

I shook my head. "She looks at the other three girls as her pack."

"She sounds impressive. If she was a wolf, I doubt she would have made the year without going rogue; wolves feel the pack urge harder than cat-type Weres, but even cat-types strongly feel the urge to join a pack. I'm guessing you are asking if she can come visit and get some exposure to her own kind?"

I nodded. "Are you just a wolf pack?"

"We have a female Weretiger in our pack, seven Werebears, nine Wererats, and just over forty Werewolves. We are open to all Weres. A Werepanther is odd, though; I didn't think there were any in Canada. I know most are out of South America, and there are some in Asia and Africa. She would be welcome to visit, though."

"I wouldn't have thought Weretigers were common in Canada either."

"Sabina, our Weretiger, emigrated from India about seven years ago. Now, I thank you for the information on Benny, and I hope in the future I can help your Were friend, but I have five dead bodies and one seriously injured one. Do you want to tell me how all this happened?"

I took a deep breath and started my explanation with the girls' failed attempt to capture McMahon, moving on to their injuries and them being stuck in the freezing cold with no money and no way to

126

get home. I told him about getting them healed and offering them a place to stay until their shadow-traveler was back on her feet. I moved on to Olivia being a threat to the current master of the French vampire court's claim to the throne, the drow/Mexican biker gang story, and the €5 million bounty that had gotten put on Olivia's head. I explained that I had called a friend in Florida who had agreed to let me use his place. I finished with the attack after dinner and our response to it.

"Damn, you really did step in it, didn't you?" Ray said when I had finished.

I nodded and asked, "As a Fire elemental torched the house, I'm assuming damages will be covered under the Enhanced Individuals Emergency Fund?"

"Yeah. I will write out a claim receipt for your friend when we wrap this up, but it should all be covered."

I glanced at my watch. It was just past 10:00 p.m., so I asked, "Do you mind if I call Greg, the owner, and let him know the bad news?"

"Sure. I need to talk to him anyway to confirm you were given permission to be here."

I picked up my burner phone, found Greg's number, and hit "Dial." The phone rang three times before Greg picked up. "Zack, I was just about to turn in for the night. Everything okay?" said Greg.

"Hey, Greg. There is no easy way for me to say this: We were attacked earlier, and the cottage was completely destroyed. I can't tell you how sorry I am about this. I am standing here with an EIRT sergeant who assures me all the damages will be covered by the Federal Enhanced Individuals Emergency Fund. If there are any shortfalls, I will make up the difference."

"Are you and the people you are protecting okay?" he asked as I finished.

"Yeah, we are all fine."

"That is all that is important. Zack, that housing complex you saved for me years ago ... I made a killing off that. You could burn down three cottages, and I would still owe you. This will make Martha super happy; she has been itching to renovate that cottage for the last couple of years, and now she can."

I was floored by how well Greg was taking this. I'd known he was good people, but I'd just burned down his summer home, and he didn't seem the slightest bit concerned.

"Thanks, Greg. I really appreciate how well you are taking this. Sergeant Dunham from the EIRT would like to have a word with you, if you don't mind."

"Sure. Put him on."

I handed the phone to Ray. He asked for Greg's full name and confirmed both that Greg was the owner of the property and that he had given me permission to use the place. There was a pause after this and then Ray replied, "It is my understanding that the adjustor will assess the values of the surrounding properties and use the average value of the properties to establish the compensation you will receive."

Ray handed the phone back to me, and Greg said, "Zack, this is awesome! All the properties around me were bigger and worth more than mine. I am probably going to actually come out ahead—again."

We chatted for another minute and then said our good-nights to each other. I hung up.

"Now I need to talk to the girls to confirm what happened this evening," said Ray.

"Can I ask a favor on that?"

Ray nodded, and I continued. "Can your female office do the interview, rather than you? Bree, the Were, has never met another Were, and I'm not sure now would be a good time for her first introduction to one. My bigger concern is Stella, though, whose Hyde persona can crush any of us like we are bugs. She … isn't comfortable around men."

Ray looked puzzled for a brief moment, then a flare of anger appeared in his eyes as he understood what I'd meant. His hands curled into fists and then the flare of anger was gone. "I have no issue with Jane Simmons taking their statements; she hates the cold, anyway, and will be overjoyed to be in a nice, warm SUV."

"I appreciate you working around their issues."

He nodded, got on his walkie-talkie, and called Simmons over.

While we were waiting, Officer Desmond came back and said, "Sarge, this night just got a whole lot more interesting. The search came back on the dead tracker. He is wanted in connection with a whole bunch of crimes, including the deaths of four DEA agents, multiple cartel witnesses, and eight Mexican police officers. The Fire elemental is probably Maria Martinez, who is also wanted in connection with those same crimes, as well as a string of arsons in Texas and Mexico."

"Well, Zack, it looks like you took down two dangerous individuals," said Ray.

"Did either of them have bounties on them?" I asked.

Officer Desmond smiled. "Yup, Jones had a $1 million bounty on his head, and Maria had $1.2 million bounty on hers."

I think I actually might have staggered a bit as those numbers hit home. Even with splitting that with the three girls in the fight tonight, the bounties still put over a half-million US dollars in my pocket. The girls were like my bounty good-luck charms; after McMahon, the drow, and this, I had made some serious coin in the last few days. On the other hand, I would still need to be alive in the near future to spend it—we were still being hunted by some serious heavy hitters.

"Shit, I am in the wrong business." Ray laughed.

Jane Simmons showed up. Ray brought her up to speed about why she needed to get the statements from Stella and Bree. She nodded and headed off to the OPP cruiser the ladies were warming up in.

"Zack, can you join Desmond and me while we process the crime scene and paperwork?" asked Ray.

I nodded and followed them as they walked toward the yellow tape.

Chapter 18

Thursday, February 15

It was past midnight before Ray and his team were done with us. At the end of it, Ray handed me three receipts—two for the bounties on the tracker and the Fire elemental and one for Greg's damage claim—and said, "We are going to stop at a nearby church and see what happens with Benny. I hope you are wrong about him, but if it is demon possession or Benny has been doing illegal things, both need to stop. I have your number, so I will call you and let you know what happens."

Ray shook my hand and headed for the lead SUV. I carefully folded the receipts and put them in my pocket. Between the bounties and the cottage replacement costs, I had just put better than $3 million in my pocket.

The snow started falling as I walked over to the SUV in which the ladies were all keeping warm. Sean was talking to another officer nearby. He saw me heading over, and by the time I had reached his cruiser, he had joined me.

Sean volunteered to give us a lift to a motel in nearby Peterborough that fit our needs—cheap and clean—and in minutes we were on the road. The red neon Highway 7 Motel sign shone out of the darkness as we got closer; the large "M" in "Motel" had burnt out. Sean pulled into the lot of the two-story building. The reception area was in front of a row of rooms, and judging by the nearly empty parking lot, we weren't going to have an issue getting a room for the night.

Sean said, "It doesn't look like much, but I know the family that owns it. They take good care of the place."

Once the cruiser came to a stop, I told Olivia to come in with me, then got out of the car. We went in and secured two adjoining rooms for the night. I had Olivia put a mental whammy on the attendant so we didn't have to give ID or a credit card. We registered as "John Smith and family."

We headed back out into the cold night and got the rest of our party from the SUV. I thanked Sean for the lift.

"Try not to burn this one down, eh?" he grinned.

I rolled my eyes in response.

He put the cruiser in reverse and disappeared into the night, and we hurried up to our rooms.

I unlocked the door, and Bree and Stella pushed me out of the way in their haste to get into the warm room. There were two queen-sized beds that took up the bulk of the room, and there was an older-model flat-screen TV on the wall. The room was plain but clean.

The door at the back of the room led to a bathroom with a shower/tub combo. There was another door between the two beds that connected this room to the second one we had rented. Bree made a beeline to the small fridge in the corner of the room.

Olivia dumped Blue on the first bed, and Stella immediately lifted the covers to that bed and jumped in, trying to get warm again. Bree closed the door to the small bar fridge after stuffing Olivia's juice boxes into it.

My burner phone buzzed in my pocket, surprising me—other than the people in this room, only Gary and Ray knew the number. I hadn't expected either of them to call me so soon after the cottage incident. I fished out the phone, and "R. Dunham" flashed on the display. I answered it.

"Zack, it was a demon. Benny fought and struggled as we approached the church, but with the cuffs and the power-blocking collar on, he was limited in what he could do. As soon as we entered the church, thick black smoke poured out of every orifice on his body and disappeared into the ground."

I never thought I'd be relieved to hear of a demon possession, but in this case, I was. The other option—Benny being an exceptionally evil human—would have been much more difficult to deal with. My gut suddenly went cold when I remembered that many people who got possessed didn't survive the exorcism. "How is Benny now?"

"He is dazed. He didn't even know who we were! The last thing he can remember is heading into a building in Iraq on a recon mission for the UN counterterrorism squad he was on."

"At least he is still alive, and the exorcism didn't kill him."

The idea that a demon had been in control while Benny had been part of a deep-cover UN task force and working three months for EIRT did not make me happy. Odin only knew what information the demon had found, and usually, when one demon knows something, it isn't long until they all know. It was also odd that a demon would have gone to the trouble of keeping up Benny's persona. Demons thrived on chaos, blood, and destruction. For one to be this restrained, a higher-level demon had to be pulling its chain. That type of control and vision didn't bode well—I wondered what was brewing.

Ray snorted. "Yeah, being alive is better than being dead. This is going to create a huge shitstorm, though. Headquarters is going to want to know everything the demon learned and see every file the demon handled while pretending to be Benny. The UN is going to need to know too. They are also going to have to try and recreate his steps."

"Where is Benny now?" I asked.

"He is asleep in an SUV. We are heading back to headquarters, and we'll check him into the infirmary there and have a doctor look at him. Why?"

"Once someone has been possessed, they are extremely vulnerable to possession again. If any of you have any religious items like a crucifix or a Star of David, put them on Benny now and don't let him take them off. I'd suggest grabbing a case of water and having a priest, rabbi, or some other religious figure bless it too. Make sure he drinks a bottle of it per day; that should keep him safe until he regains his strength."

"We already have a crucifix on him, but the water is a good idea. Anything else?"

I remembered everything I could about demon possession and then said, "I would strongly suggest that you install a nondenominational chapel at headquarters. Have religious leaders come by, give sermons, and bless the chapel. Make it a requirement that all EIRT officers have to walk through that area at least once a month to prevent something like this from happening again. The idea of a demon having access to EIRT resources scares the shit out of me."

EIRT was part of the RCMP, but all government Enhanced Individual response squads shared information. The demon had had access to just about every government-sponsored Enhanced Individual response squad in the world. Whatever was coming next might not be directed at Canada, but someplace else in the world. If demons were planning something long-term and taking this much care in executing the plan, whatever was coming was something dangerous and new.

"You and me both, my friend," Ray agreed. "I'll bring your suggestion up with my captain as soon as I see her, but once the fallout hits HQ, I'd be surprised if something like that didn't happen even without the suggestion. We are almost back at base, and the building blocks cellphone signals, so thanks for your help. When your Were friend is up for it, she has an open invitation to meet the Barrie pack—it is the least I can do to repay you for this."

"Thanks, Ray. We'll take you up on that offer once our current issue is dealt with. Take care, and I will talk to you later."

Ray either hung up or was cut off after that. I ended the call and put the phone back in my pocket. I had no doubt that Olivia and Bree, with their enhanced hearing, had heard both sides of the conversation, but I could tell Stella was curious, so I told them all about Ray, Benny, and the possession.

The ladies seemed horrified about the idea of another creature taking over someone's body. I couldn't fault them—something like that would certainly be up there on my nightmare-scenario scale.

Bree spoke and pulled me out of my musings. "So, I can go meet the Barrie pack once we deal with this whole contract-on-Olivia thing?"

I nodded and asked, "How would you feel about that?"

Bree went quiet for a moment, and a clear expression of concern appeared as she thought about it. "Not sure. It would be nice to talk to others who get furry once a month like I do, and they may have tips on how to deal with it better and how to stay calmer, but I'm guessing Were politics are probably as complicated as vampire ones, and I'm not sure I want to get involved in that."

"The politics only come into play if you join the pack. This would be nothing more than a visit. Besides, we still have to take down a master vampire and survive and stay safe from people looking to collect €5 million on Olivia's pretty head, which means you have time to think about it. Let's focus on one problem at a time." Bree nodded at that and I added, "I rented us two rooms, but I think it would be a good idea if we all slept in this room."

Bree looked at Stella and Blue on the first bed and then at the one I was now sitting on. She frowned, and I realized that she thought we'd be sharing a bed.

"Relax. You are going to be up with Olivia until sunrise tomorrow, right?"

She bobbed her head in agreement, and I continued. "Good. The two of you can watch TV in the other room, but keep the sound down and the door between the rooms slightly ajar—and stay alert. If you hear anything odd, wake us immediately. Just before sunrise, Olivia can rest in the bathtub in this bathroom, and we will use the bathroom in the other room during the day. Wake Stella and me in the morning, and we will take the daytime watch while you get some sleep."

Bree seemed relieved about this plan. I continued. "If we get hit tonight, Olivia grabs Blue, gets to the bathroom, and stays there. Bree, Stella, and I will deal with whoever is attacking. If we get attacked tomorrow during the day, Bree grabs Blue and gets into the bathroom and changes. Stella and I will deal with whoever or whatever is attacking us. Any questions?"

Everyone shook their heads.

Bree and Olivia unlocked the door between the two rooms and left. I killed the lights and wished Stella good night before I stripped off my jeans. I fell asleep almost as soon as my head hit the pillow.

* * * * *

I woke up to Bree gently shaking me and saying my name. The room was semi-dark, and it took a second for me to remember where I was. I got up and put my jeans on while Bree woke Stella.

I reeked of sweat and smoke; dealing with that was mission one. "Stella, do you mind taking the first watch at the window? I want to grab a shower. Once I'm done, I'll take the next watch, and you can freshen up."

Stella nodded and headed for the front window. Bree was already in the bed I had just gotten out of. She contorted in odd ways under the covers, and then a pair of jeans were flung out from under the blankets and hit the floor. At first, I didn't understand why she had hidden under the covers to take her pants off, but then I figured out that she probably hadn't had time to rescue her undergarments from the cottage. I left her to it and slipped into the other bathroom.

Twenty minutes later, I was showered and dressed again. It sucked getting back into the same clothes, but at least the shower had made me feel human again.

I slipped into the sleeping room through the connecting door, and Bree's soft snores to my left brought an amused smile to my lips. Stella stepped away from the window when I entered the room. Neither of us had taken two steps farther when something heavy shattered the window. A grenade rolled out from under the blackout curtains.

I called my powers to me, but before I could act, Stella transformed instantly into her Hyde form and smothered the grenade. A deafening explosion rang out a second later. The floor under Stella collapsed, and her large form tumbled through the newly created hole in the floor.

My ears rang. Smoke, dust, and debris filled the room. Even though Stella had taken the brunt of the blast, the air pressure change in the room had been immense. I was slightly stunned and disoriented, and I had no idea whether Stella was alive or dead, but I had no time to worry about that. I yanked Blue's prone form off the bed and handed her to a confused and naked Bree, who had just leapt out of bed.

I yelled and pointed toward the bathroom. She coughed, but nodded, and carried Blue to the bathroom. I turned back to the window and thickened the air around me. The front doorknob disappeared in a cloud of splinters, and a large tattooed man carrying a sawed-off shotgun kicked the door open. He saw me and fired instantly. I returned the favor, sending a powerful arc of lightning at him. The silver pellets of buckshot caught in the thickened air, hanging suspended in a one-foot cloud in front of me at about chest height. Whoever these assholes were, they were playing for keeps. That blast would have killed me if I hadn't thickened the air as a shield.

My burly opponent wasn't so lucky. My lightning blast lifted him clean off his feet and blew him out the door and over the railing. He didn't even scream as his body tumbled over the edge. I cursed at myself—not for killing him but for using enough juice in that blast to fry an elephant. In my defense, I was still a touch dazed from the grenade explosion earlier.

Two large holes appeared in the curtains, and another bunch of shiny BBs joined the first group in my cloud. Another large biker-looking guy appeared in the doorway, this one carrying a pistol. He fired off a couple of rounds at me, but they were stopped by my air shield. Two more quick shotgun blasts created more holes in the curtains.

I was tired of this shit; I sent a powerful blast of wind out in front of me. The biker with the pistol was lifted off his feet. His head slammed viciously off the doorframe, leaving a bloody stain. He joined his buddy over the railing. The curtains ripped from the rods and vanished out into the parking lot below. Two leather-clad bodies went with them.

The wind blast also did a great job of clearing the dust and smoke from the room. The bed in front of me shot forward and fell into the hole that Stella had gone through earlier. I hoped I hadn't just dropped a heavy bed on Stella.

None of the attackers had had auras, which meant they had been human. That threw me for a loop; what the hell kind of dumb human was stupid enough to attack a room full of Enhanced Individuals? I groaned as I realized that €5 million would be enough to bring out tons of stupid.

I smiled at the now-familiar pissed-off grunt coming from the parking lot. A moment later, Stella landed on the walkway outside the room, her large, ugly mug peering in at me through the window. Bullets and buckshot hit her from both sides, and she roared in anger. She turned to her right and charged after whomever had shot from that direction.

Stella had the right idea; I was tired of playing defense. I gathered the air around me and flew out of the room. Someone fired at me from the left as I exited. I looped around in the air and saw three bikers firing weapons at me. I was about to hit them with lightning when a scream of terror to my right caught my attention. I dove lower to avoid the skinny biker as he tumbled through the air I had just been occupying. I winced as he crashed into the neon sign. The sign exploded in a shower of sparks and glass. The idle thought of *At least they don't have to worry about the burnt-out "M" anymore* brought a grin to my lips.

The bikers on the left opened fire in my direction. My mirth vanished as bullets hung suspended in front of me. I gathered my power. A split second before I was going to lash out with a fatal arc of electricity, I remembered there might be innocent civilians cowering in their rooms. I toned the power down to a "stun" level.

An arc of chain lightning shot out from my hand and hit all three bikers. They spasmed for a few moments and then collapsed like puppets with cut strings. They twitched on the ground and then went still. They were all out of the fight for at least the next ten minutes.

I inhaled deeply and couldn't resist thinking, *I love the smell of ozone in the morning.*

A gruff, panicked voice below me yelled, "Mac! Start the car! Start the car!"

I turned and spotted three more bikers running for their lives down the far staircase, with Stella's lumbering form in hot pursuit. The drivers of two white vans at the end of the lot were frantically trying to turn over the ignitions. The air was filled with the sound of sirens closing in from all over the city, so at least the cavalry was on the way—not that it was really needed now.

The bikers made it to the bottom of the staircase as Stella reached the top. She leapt off the stairs in one huge leap and landed squarely on the trailing biker. There was a brief scream; the lot echoed with the sounds of bones cracking and other gruesome wet noises as that biker was flattened under Stella's huge feet. The two remaining bikers ran even faster for the nearest van. Stella jumped again, flew over the two panicked bikers, and landed in a shower of metal and glass on the hood of the driver's side of the closest van.

The remaining van peeled out of its spot, squealing its tires just as the bikers reached it. The lead guy yanked on the side door handle, tossed it open, and dove in. The van floored it and left the remaining biker behind in its dust.

I sent a large blast of wind directly under the driver's side of the van, and it flipped over onto its side. It skidded and sparked down the lot for about ten feet before coming to a dead stop.

An angry roar came from within the other van as Stella tore herself free of her metal-and-plastic prison. The remaining biker looked back in absolute fear and ran toward me in a blind panic. I casually sent a bolt of lightning at him. He yelped in pain as it hit him and collapsed in a twitching mess onto the ice-cold pavement before going still.

Stella's bulbous large eye looked around the lot, searching for more threats. It landed on me floating in the air, and I said, "Everyone is down; we're good."

Chapter 19

Thursday, February 15

The sirens were getting louder with every passing second. In her Hyde form, Stella would create tension with the locals that we didn't need, so I told her to get back to the room and change back.

I flew back through the window frame and yelled, "Bree, we are clear! All threats are down. The cops will be here in moments, so change back to your human form."

A growl of approval came from the closed bathroom. I found my spring jacket and headed for the front door, grabbing my hero ID from my wallet as I exited the room. Stella's smaller human form darted past me a moment later and disappeared into the room.

Two white-and-blue cruisers came screaming into the parking lot. They stopped hard, brakes squealing, just in front of the van I'd tipped over earlier. Going to either end to use the staircases would have taken too much time, so I hopped over the railing and took the more direct route down. I held up my hero ID one hand and slowly raised the other into the air to look as nonthreatening as possible. This pose had been way too common for me recently. I kicked around the idea of just getting the ID tattooed on my hand to save time in the future.

An officer got out of each cruiser with their weapons drawn. They scanned the lot, looking for threats. Two more police cruisers pulled into the lot, and the sound of multiple sirens closing meant more were on the way. The dark-haired officer in the nearest cruiser spotted me and yelled, "Are there any active shooters?"

I said no and shook my head at the same time. He seemed to relax a bit. I wondered why he had to ask—if there were any shooters still around, I wouldn't be standing out in the open like I was.

He stood up and holstered his gun but kept his right hand firmly on the butt of it. The officer cautiously approached me and took my ID. I raised that hand into the air as well.

The officer studied my ID for a few long moments and said, "Can you tell me what happened here, Mr. Stevens?"

"Can I put my arms down?" I asked. He nodded, and I explained. "My companions and I were resting when one of the attackers threw a grenade through the window. This was followed up with them opening up on the room with shotguns and pistols—"

The officer interrupted, asking, "Any idea why they would attack you and your companions?"

"Yeah, one of my friends has a rather large contract on her head. I'm guessing they were trying to cash in on that."

"Your ID lists you as an Air elemental. Are your companions Enhanced as well?"

"Yup—vampire, Were, Tank, and blue-skinned alien who can teleport."

He made a "One moment" gesture with his hand and yelled at one of the other officers, "Pierre, get EIRT on the line; this is one of theirs." Then he handed me back my ID. He pointed at the four leather-clad bodies lying in various unnatural positions behind me and asked, "Are they all deceased like these?"

"No, there are three lying up in the causeway above us and to the left who are just stunned and will probably be coming to shortly. The dude lying in the middle of the lot is also stunned ..." I paused as more police cars came into the lot with sirens blaring. Once the noise died down, I continued. "There are two in the tipped-over van who probably are alive as well."

The officer held up his finger at me again and waved over a couple of fellow officers. He explained that some of the assailants were stunned and told them about the ones in the van, and they left us to go deal with them.

"Are there any others who might be alive?" he asked.

I looked at the four behind me and shook my head, then turned my attention back to him. "Those four are definitely dead. The guy pancaked at the end of the far staircase is totally dead, as is the guy in the first van, so nope, just the ones I mentioned. Oh wait! I forgot about Mr. Signpost over there, but if he is alive, it would be miracle."

"You are being very flippant, considering you and your companions just killed six people."

His statement pissed me off. I knew he was deliberately provoking me to get a reaction, which meant he viewed us as suspects and not victims. I was not a morning person at the best of times, and the explosive start to this morning already had me in a bad mood. This just made it worse, which is why I simply replied, "Seven."

"Excuse me?" The officer looked confused.

"We killed seven people—the four behind me, pancake guy, van guy, and Mr. Signpost … If you want to be super accurate, the total is actually twelve, as we killed five more last night after we were attacked in a cottage that burned down east of here, but that was dealt with by OPP and EIRT. Oh crap, I forgot the twelve bikers that we killed in Hamilton three days ago. That was also self-defense, and Hamilton Police and EIRT can confirm that, so that brings the grand total to twenty-four in the last seventy-two hours."

The officer just gaped at me, wide-eyed and speechless.

"Look, it has been a long week. I'm sorry if I'm not broken up about a bunch of assholes who started my day by lobbing a grenade through my window and trying their best to aerate me and my companions. I am ending this interview. I will wait for EIRT to arrive."

His face darkened with anger, and I smiled. I'd scored a point with that last comment. I decided to pour some salt on that wound. "In the meantime, there are two things you can do for me. The first is to send someone for a crapload of food; my Were companion is working on no sleep and no food and has changed twice in the past hour. She is probably hungry enough to actually eat anything that moves. The second thing is to make sure no one goes into the room missing the door and windows above us—or the room to the left of it. The sun is up, my vampire friend is lying prone in a death trance, and my blue alien friend is in a healing coma and unable to defend herself, which means the Were and the Tank are both feeling overly protective at this moment."

"Now see here, Mr. Stevens. It is not our job to provide food to suspects—" His eyes widened again, and he kept opening and closing his mouth, but no sound came out. I had messed with the air around him to silence him.

"Let me try this again: I can fly out of here right now, and there is nothing you can do to stop me, so either you send someone for food, or I will go get it myself. I am not joking about the Were upstairs—if she gets hungry enough, she won't care if something is in a wrapper or a polyester uniform, understand? Nod yes or shake your head no."

The officer went an even deeper shade of red as he tried again to yell at me, but no sound came out. After a few seconds, his shoulders slumped, and he nodded yes.

I stopped messing with the air around him and said, "So, do I leave the crime scene and get food, or can you send someone to get some food?"

"We"—he paused for a moment, as if surprised that he could talk again, then said—"will send someone to get some food."

"Thank you."

"I should arrest you for assaulting an officer with that sound trick you just did."

I smiled. "I dampened the sound around you, so technically I didn't lay a finger on you or 'assault' you in any definition of the word. This has been a fun chat, but I am going to head back up to my room. Please have someone yell up when the food or EIRT arrives."

I didn't wait for his reply. I lifted myself off the ground using my Air powers and flew into the room in seconds. Stella was sitting on the remaining bed with the covers wrapped around her, trying to keep warm. Bree was pacing back and forth between the bed and the closed bathroom door.

She stopped her pacing when she saw me and said, "Is everything okay? I really need food."

"Everything is fine. EIRT is on the way. We will have a bunch of questions to answer when they arrive, but this was clearly self-defense. The local police are sending someone to get food. It should be here shortly. As this room is a touch drafty now, why don't you and Stella move to the other room and warm up? I will stay here and make sure nobody goes into the bathroom."

Stella nodded and grabbed the blankets around her, awkwardly getting off the bed. She headed for the other room with Bree just behind her. They closed the connecting door, and I sat on the bed Stella had just vacated. I propped a pillow up against the headboard and got comfortable.

A good twenty minutes later, a female voice just outside the door said, "Mr. Stevens, I have the food you requested!"

I smiled at the deep, hungry growl that echoed from the room beside me and quickly got out of bed. Just outside the room, there were two cardboard drink trays. Four coffees sat on the bottom tray, and four orange juices sat on the top tray. Four large McDonald's bags sat beside them. A female and a male officer were both making a hasty retreat toward the nearest staircase. I picked up the trays of drinks and used my Air powers to levitate the bags of food as I headed back inside.

The connecting door opened as soon as I entered the room. Bree grabbed all four bags out of the air and disappeared back into the other room. It probably only took me seconds to follow her, but by the time I entered, she was already halfway through a good-sized Danish and moaning in contentment. I put the drinks down on the side table between the beds and grabbed a coffee for myself. My own stomach rumbled, so I decided to risk life and limb by reaching for one of the closed bags.

Bree was working on the second Danish now and growled as I went for one of the bags.

"Bree," admonished Stella in a no-nonsense tone, "there are four huge bags of food there. Zack just risked his life for us; the least you can do is share a little of that."

"Sorry," mumbled Bree with a mouthful of Danish. She gave me a small, reluctant nod.

I grabbed a McMuffin and a Danish for myself and left the room. I sat back on the bed again and wolfed down the McMuffin in no time flat. The Danish met its demise in about the same amount of time. I kicked around going back into the other room to get more, but wisely thought it wasn't worth getting between the hungry Were and her food again.

The food made me feel better, but the caffeine was really what I needed. I was just finishing my coffee when, to my astonishment, Bree opened the connecting door and said, "I have an Egg McMuffin and a Sausage and Egg McMuffin left. I'm willing to give you one of them."

"Did Stella get some food too?"

She nodded, and I said, "I'll take the sausage one, please."

She tossed it to me and closed the door. I stared at the breakfast sandwich for just a moment like Bree had just given up her firstborn child. Then I smiled and dug in.

After finishing the Sausage and Egg McMuffin and my coffee, I went to go grab another coffee. Stella looked up from the bed and smiled as I entered the room. Bree was in the other bed, already sound asleep. The wastebasket in the corner was overflowing with McDonald's bags and packaging. One coffee and one orange juice remained on the table. I grabbed the coffee and offered it to Stella, but she made a face at me and waved me off. I smiled and headed back to the other room.

I had just sat back down on the bed when someone yelled up that EIRT had arrived. Coffee in hand, I headed for the missing door. In the parking lot, I spotted two unmarked black SUVs with flashing lights in the grilles, which confirmed for me that EIRT was, in fact, here. The heavily armed federal team was gathered around the officer I'd razzed earlier and two plain-clothed men who I assumed were Peterborough police detectives.

I was stunned for a moment at the sight of a dwarf in EIRT gear with sergeant stripes on his sleeve. I had never met a dwarf before; they seldom left the fae realm. His aura, though, was what I would have expected. It was rainbow, which meant fae, with a ring of earth-brown and silver surrounding it. The aura was a good six inches wide, which meant he was quite strong.

The other Enhanced Individual was also an oddity. I had never seen his type of aura before, so I didn't know exactly what he was. The core color was orange, so he was a member of the Super class. The secondary color was a pale-green ring, which meant he was a telepath or had some sort of mental ability. What threw me was the third ring, which was pink and outlined in a black-and-white checkered ring. I had never seen that combination before. He was decently powerful but not amazing, if the three-inch width of his aura was any indication.

He also stood out physically in contrast to the dwarf. He was easily over six feet, probably closer to six-and-a-half feet, which gave him a good two feet of height over the dwarf. He was rail thin, even in the bulky uniform and flak jacket. He looked as if a good wind could knock him over. He had the palest skin I had ever seen not belonging to a vampire, which was the total opposite of the dwarf's ruddy skin tone. The jet-black hair peeking out from under the helmet and his dark eyes made him look creepy.

The taller of the two detectives briefed the dwarf. The officer I'd argued with earlier bobbed his head in agreement every so often, which brought a frown to my face. I guessed the locals weren't giving me a stellar recommendation due to my earlier behavior with that officer.

One day, my mouth and attitude would get me into trouble, but I knew it wouldn't be today; the grenade blast in the room and the number of illegal weapons scattered around made it obvious this had been self-defense. I was also willing to bet that when the cops ran the IDs on the bikers, they would all have criminal records.

The conference wrapped up, and the shorter detective pointed at me up on the walkway. It was time to make my entrance. I leapt up and used my Air power to lift me over the safety railing, then flew toward the group. I landed in a classic superhero landing about six feet in front of the group.

The dwarf rolled his eyes at me but waved me over. When I got closer, he held out his hand and said, "Sergeant Gregor Redrock."

I was disappointed that Gregor sounded like your typical Canadian. I'd been hoping for a deep Scottish burr—too many stereotypical books and movies, I suppose. I introduced myself and handed him my hero ID as a courtesy. He glanced at it long enough to confirm my name, then handed it back.

Given his gruff demeanor, I figured I'd try and get off on the right foot with him. "I met Sergeant Ray Dunham last night. Can I ask how Benny is doing?"

He nodded. "I heard he is doing well. He seems to be recovering. Bad business, that. Benny is lucky to be alive after being ridden by a demon for six months. I don't mean to be abrupt, Mr. Stevens, but can you tell us in your own words what happened here?"

I took a deep breath and covered everything that had happened in the attack. Sergeant Redrock was keeping one eye on me and the other on the EIRT officer with the mysterious aura. After each detail I covered, mystery guy would give a small nod to Sergeant Redrock. I knew his power was something mental and figured part of it was to tell if someone was lying or not. I was tempted to tell a small lie in my statement to test my theory but didn't want to annoy them, and so stayed truthful.

The EIRT officer being a walking lie detector really had my curiosity piqued. It was a useful power for interrogating suspects, but EIRT's main purpose was to fulfill a SWAT roll. It made no sense risking him on the front lines if this was his only power. The lie detection must only have been part of his power. Elementals were highly mental-resistant, which got me wondering how his lie-detector power worked. If he was probing my thoughts, I should have been able to feel it, but I wasn't even getting a whiff of a mental probe.

I finished, and Sergeant Redrock said, "Thank you for giving us your statement. It seems this was a clear case of self-defense. We have gotten some of the IDs of the attackers, and all of them have extensive criminal records. You are free to go."

I was a bit surprised—usually, this part took a lot longer—but I guess when you know if someone is telling the truth or not, it makes things much simpler. Judging by the expressions on the faces of the detectives and the officer I'd pissed off, I wasn't the only one surprised at this.

I flew back up to the second floor, but I was stopped dead in my tracks by red warning tape now blocking the missing door and windows. I shrugged and walked over to the door to the adjacent unit where Stella and Bree were, and to my surprise it, too, was covered in red warning tape.

"Excuse me. Where do you think you are going?" said a strong, authoritative feminine voice.

I turned to see a dark-haired middle-age woman marching toward me like she was on a mission. She wore an open parka with a gray business suit underneath. The suit was being sorely taxed by her larger size.

Once she came to a stop in front of me, I said, "To my room?"

The lady had a lanyard around her neck that read "M. Hernandez, City of Peterborough, City Engineer." The picture on it had to be ten years out of date. "I cannot let you do that. The blast has compromised the structural integrity of the center unit, the two adjacent ones, and the ones below it. All of them could collapse at any time."

"Sure. Where did you put my companions?" I asked.

She gave me a look like I was on crack. "We were told that all the units were unoccupied."

"Someone got their facts wrong. I have two companions in this unit and two in the one next door with the hole in the floor."

"They can't be in there. It isn't safe."

"Great, I will go get them—"

"I can't let you go in there."

I rolled my eyes and said, "How about I knock on the door?"

She nodded, and I rapped hard on the door. We waited for a few moments before Stella opened the door.

"Oh, my dear God! There is a child in there!" Mrs. Hernandez exclaimed. She immediately began tearing the red tape off the door like it was on fire. Once the tape was off, she motioned to Stella to come out.

Stella shivered and said, "I am not dressed for the weather out there." She promptly slammed the door in the city engineer's face.

The city engineer began pounding on the door in a panic to "rescue" Stella. I called her name a couple of times, but Mrs. Hernandez ignored me. She screamed as I used my Air powers to lift her off the ground by a couple of feet. I moved her a few feet from the door and stepped forward so I was between her and the door. I lowered her back to the ground. "Now that I have your attention—"

She hastily crossed herself.

I continued. "That 'child' is over 100 years old and can transform herself instantly into a much larger and almost indestructible form. She is in no danger. Take a deep breath and relax."

She looked at me for a moment, then closed her eyes and muttered something in Spanish. Her earlier screams had caused five more suits to coming running toward us, and all five of the newcomers started speaking at once when they arrived. I couldn't get a word in edge-wise. I dampened the air around all of them, and it went silent. They all gaped at each other like fish out of water before finally turning their attention to me.

"Now, here is what we are going to do …," I began.

Ten minutes later, one of the city workers arrived with room keys to two new rooms three doors down from where we were. I knocked on the door to the unit Stella was in and yelled to her that it was me. A moment later, the door opened. I explained that we were moving to units down the way because our current ones weren't safe. I told her to wake Bree because I would need Bree to carry Blue, and that I would move Olivia. She didn't like that I was moving Olivia during daylight. Truth be told, I wasn't happy about it either. But if the room did collapse, Olivia would be totally exposed. If I covered her in enough blankets for the short trip, she should be fine.

Mrs. Hernandez objected to the fact that I would be entering the damaged unit. We argued about it, but I told her I could enter it without touching the floor and demonstrated this by floating in front of her. I explained that both of my other companions were incapacitated, and she agreed.

I floated into the room and opened the connecting door while Stella got Bree up. I flew to the bathroom and used my Air power to lift Blue from the floor, floating us into the main room. Bree grabbed Blue from me, and she and Stella headed to our new rooms. I grabbed all the blankets from the beds and floated back to the bathroom, where I found Olivia in her death trance in the bathtub. I had never seen her in this state before. I found it rather unsettling; she wasn't breathing, had no pulse, and was cold to the touch. In other words, she was dead.

146

I floated her body into the air and tossed blankets over her. I put two of them around her head, arms, and torso, and one over her legs and feet.

I flew us both out of the room and into the daylight. I took the corner too fast, though, and to my horror, the blanket covering her legs lifted, exposing her bare feet. They immediately began smoking. I frantically covered them again and hastily beat out the flames. After a few long moments, the smoke stopped. I continued at a slower pace and started whistling innocently as I walked.

I breathed a sigh of relief as I entered the room. I spotted the still-comatose Blue lying on the nearest bed. Stella closed the door behind us.

"Hey, do I smell barbeque?" said Bree in an excited tone.

I groaned and said, "No, that is just Olivia."

"What?!" exclaimed Bree, obviously angry. She rushed over and snatched the bundled Olivia out of the air and away from me.

"She's fine. I put the fire—" I said, but Bree interrupted.

"*Fire*? My best friend in the whole world was on fire, and you think this is 'fine'?"

Bree's eyes started to glow; she finished her last sentence with a growl. I didn't want to provoke her, so I quickly lowered my eyes.

Thankfully, Stella came to my rescue. "Bree, find your happy place!"

Bree turned to Stella and growled again, but immediately lowered her head in shame. She hauled the still-bundled Olivia off to the bathroom. I went to follow, but Stella stepped in front of me and shook her head. "Let her deal with Olivia; give her some space."

Olivia would be fine. She'd wake up and have some blood, and—*Oh shit!* I ran out of the room and back to our old rooms. Mrs. Hernandez was putting the tape back up on the door. She saw me coming and said, "Let me guess: There is a baby in the room you forgot to mention."

I think my sarcasm detector damn near exploded at her tone. "I need to go back in."

She closed her eyes, muttered something under her breath in Spanish, and said, "Fine, but flying only, okay?"

I nodded, lifted off the ground, and coasted into the room without the big hole in the floor. I went through the connecting door into the damaged room and made a beeline for the fridge, pulling out the two bags of blood, then leaving. Mrs. Hernandez's eyes widened at the sight of the bags of plasma, but she wisely just ignored them and went back to taping up the door.

I entered the room again and put the bags carefully in the fridge. Bree exited the bathroom looking much calmer.

I asked, "How is she?"

"Her feet are badly sunburned, but that seems to be the extent of the damage. She isn't going to be happy with you when she wakes up, but after getting some blood, she should be fine. Sorry about overreacting earlier; I get grumpy when I'm tired."

"No problem. I should have been more careful when moving her. You get some sleep. Stella and I will keep watch from the other room."

Bree nodded and slipped into the empty bed beside the one with Blue on it. Stella and I went to the other room via the connecting door.

"Do you want me to keep watch?" she asked.

I shook my head. "No one will hit us for the next few hours with the amount of police outside."

"How did the bikers find us? You paid cash and used a fake name."

I had been thinking the same thing earlier and figured that either someone had spotted us when we had arrived here—or the OPP had a leak. I told Stella my guesses.

She shrugged in response. Stella turned on the TV and watched CNN, leaving me to my thoughts. It dawned on me that I still had close to $3 million in bounties and damage claims in my pocket. I was horrified when I realized that a stray shot or whatever could have destroyed them. I pulled out my phone and logged onto the motel's free Wi-Fi. I entered the bounty website and filled out the two bounty forms electronically. It was a pain in the ass doing it from my phone, and I missed my laptop, which had been destroyed in the fire. I took a picture of the damage receipt and e-mailed it to Greg with a link to the website he would need to put his claim into. I felt better getting that off my list.

With that done, I thought about the latest attack. This one really bothered me. Last night's attack had been carried out by pros, but the fact that norms had attacked us in broad daylight today really drove home the fact that we had a bull's-eye on our backs with this contract. We needed to find another place to hide. Once the sun went down tonight, I would take Olivia out and see if we could find an empty cottage in the middle of nowhere that we could "borrow" for a bit. I hated the idea of breaking into someone's summer place, but motels had a lot of innocent people. There was no way we could stay at another motel after what had happened this morning. This time of year, there should be a ton of empty cottages; we just needed to find one that didn't have an alarm on it and still had heat and power.

It wasn't a great plan, but it was all I could think of. With two bags of blood left, we had four days. If Blue didn't wake up by then, we were in real trouble.

Chapter 20

Thursday, February 15

The rest of the afternoon was uneventful. Bree slept, Olivia was in a death trance, and Blue remained in her healing coma. Stella and I spent the time quietly watching TV and keeping an eye out for threats. The police presence in the lot remained heavy all afternoon. They took pictures, bagged bodies, taped off areas, towed the two vans, and handled the other details that were involved in dealing with a crime scene.

Around 5:00 p.m., Bree opened the connecting door and simply said, "Food," as she wandered past us to the bathroom.

I looked at Stella. "Pizza?"

Before Stella could even answer, Bree yelled from the bathroom, "Pizza's good! Get extra cheese on mine."

I was shocked that she could hear me over the constant loud drone of the fan in the bathroom; Were hearing was truly impressive at times.

"Will the pizza place have tea?" Stella asked with a look of longing.

I shook my head. "I'll make a Timmy's run, though; I could use a coffee."

Stella seemed pleased at that, and I called in an order for four extra-large pizzas, all with extra cheese and various toppings. I hung up, peeled off $120, and handed it to Stella. She looked puzzled at this, so I said, "In case the pizza guy arrives before I get back. Give him all of it; that will cover the pizza and his tip."

I grabbed my jacket and headed out. I didn't know Peterborough that well, but the nice thing about any city in Canada was that if you went out a few blocks, you would usually stumble upon a Tim Hortons.

I was back at the room ten minutes later with two large coffees and one large tea. I handed the tea to Stella, and she gave me back the money I had given her for pizza. The fan got louder as the bathroom door opened, and I turned to see Bree wrapped in a large white towel. Her blonde hair was wet enough from the shower that it looked brown. My eyes were pulled down to the impressive cleavage peeking

150

out from the top of the towel. I stood there, open-mouthed, as she walked toward me.

Bree grabbed one of the coffees I was holding. "Eyes up here, mister! And thanks for the coffee." Then she promptly turned and headed back to the bathroom. Normally, I hate undersized motel towels, but seeing Bree's legs fully exposed and her ass barely covered in her towel, I was starting to think they had been too generous with the size.

A happy sigh behind me pulled my attention away from Bree's charms. Stella was smiling with contentment as she sipped her tea. It amused me that the large tea looked like a bucket in Stella's small hands.

I sat on the opposite bed from Stella and Blue and watched TV while we waited for the pizza to arrive.

Fifteen minutes later, Bree emerged from the bathroom wearing the same black sweatshirt and blue jeans she had been wearing since the cottage fire. I made a mental note to hit a Walmart tonight; all of us could use a change of clothes—in Bree and Olivia's case, a change of clothes and some shoes. I was down to less than $2,000 in cash now, but the blood supply would run out before the money, so blowing some of it on clothes wouldn't hurt us too badly. I could have used the money to buy some blood, but all my contacts were in Hamilton, and visiting them would be too risky. Buying black-market blood was out, as $2,000 wouldn't buy much. There also were a lot of scammers in those markets that passed off animal blood as human. Animal blood would be better than nothing, but it was only about a quarter as effective as human blood.

Bree joined me on the bed, sipping her coffee and watching TV.

She perked up five minutes later. "Pizza's here, unless we are being attacked by someone driving a crappy four cylinder that is misfiring and burning oil."

I looked at her oddly, and she said, "What? I used to help my dad fix our cars, okay?"

"That's cool," I said. It was impressive that she was mechanically inclined; God knows I wasn't. I didn't even know how to fill a car with gas.

There was a knock at the door a few minutes later. I glanced over to Bree to confirm it was safe, and she said, "I can smell the cheesy goodness from here, so it's the pizza guy."

My paranoia kicked in, and I thickened the air in front of me just in case the pizza guy had a weapon. I answered the door and almost immediately dropped the air shield; there was no way this kid was a hardened killer. I paid him and grabbed the stack of pizzas and the cans of pop.

Bree was staring at the pizzas like they were Brad Pitt. I swear she was almost drooling.

"Eyes up here, missy," I said to her as I walked back into the room.

Stella giggled. Bree was puzzled for a moment, but then she laughed as she got the joke. I handed her the top box as I went by. She promptly ignored everything as she dug in.

I had just taken my first bite when a loud "Ouch! What the fuck happened to my feet?" came from Olivia in the other room. The string of curses got louder as she got closer. She tossed open the door between the two rooms and said, "Does someone want to explain to me why my feet are well-done?"

Bree pointed at me while stuffing another slice of pizza into her mouth.

Olivia angrily turned toward me, her fangs fully extended.

I got a bit nervous. "Yeah, we were attacked while you were, um, sleeping. The room got destroyed, and the city engineers wouldn't let us stay, so we had to move to these rooms. I covered you in blankets, but the one covering your feet slipped off when I moved you. Sorry. Your juice boxes are in the fridge."

Thankfully, the last line caught her attention. Her gaze lifted from me and toward the fridge. I winced as she made painful sounds and let loose another colorful array of curse words as she gingerly danced to the fridge. She grabbed a bag of blood and drained half of it in one long gulp.

"Aaahhh," she sighed as the blood did its usual magic. She casually walked over and plunked herself down on the edge of the bed with Bree and me.

I checked out her feet. They were back to their usual vampire-pale color, like nothing had even happened.

While we ate, Stella and I filled in Olivia about the biker attack. Bree grunted in agreement or support—talking would have involved her having to pause her eating, and that wasn't going to happen. At the end of it, I told Olivia my idea about finding an empty cottage to hide out in.

"Why do you need me to come along?" asked Olivia.

"You'll be able to tell if anyone is home quicker than I can."

She nodded. "Once you're done eating, we'll head out."

Not two seconds after she had finished speaking, an unfamiliar voice said, "Where am I?"

"Blue!" cried all three of the ladies in unison. Blue sat up and rubbed her eyes.

Stella hugged Blue with tears in her eyes, and Bree and Olivia quickly joined them. The hug broke up and Blue looked over at me, studying me quietly with her deep-purple eyes.

Stella noticed where Blue was looking and said, "Blue, this is Zack Stevens. He took us in after we lost the battle against the Earth elemental."

I waved at Blue, and she gave a small nod of acknowledgement.

"How long have I been out?" Blue asked.

"Six days," answered Stella.

"Can someone explain to me what I have missed?"

Stella nodded and went over everything that had happened since the battle with James McMahon, while Bree and I ate our pizza and Olivia finished her bag of blood.

At the end of it, Blue simply said, "It seems prudent that we leave here as soon as possible for the lab."

We cleaned up and packed up our meager belongings. Ten minutes later, Blue turned off the bathroom lights so the area just outside of it was in darkness. She focused for a brief second and opened a portal in the shadows.

Bree and Olivia stepped through and were gone. I was next. I was a bit nervous, but I took a deep breath and stepped through.

I don't know what I had been expecting while shadow-traveling, but the process was boring and remarkably uneventful. One moment I was standing in a motel room in Canada, and not even a second later, I was standing in an underground mad scientist's lab in London. There was no dizziness, no big flash of streaking light, no body parts materializing before my eyes—nothing.

Stella and Blue appeared behind me, and the portal closed. Bree and Olivia disappeared down the corridor to the left. Stella and Blue walked around me and sat down on stools around one of the four large, sturdy wooden workbenches in the center of the room.

I just stood and took in the wonder that was Sir Reginald's secret laboratory. It was like stepping into the pages of a Mary Shelley novel. The polished wood and brass and the lack of modern appliances really made it feel like I had stepped back 100 years in time.

Two large Tesla coils gave off blue sparks and arced lightning back and forth over to my left. I used my Air power and lifted myself between them, letting the jagged lightning roll over my body. My body tingled as my powers quickly recharged to full levels. This was almost as good as being in a real thunderstorm; I may have moaned in pleasure for a moment.

Stella and Blue were both staring at me with open mouths. I guess someone purposely placing themselves in between two Tesla coils isn't something you see every day.

Topped up and feeling a little giddy from the recharge, I lowered myself to the floor again and turned my full attention to the place. The four sturdy wooden worktables were the centerpieces of the room. Stella and Blue were sitting at the closest one to me on my left. The one to its right was empty except for the leftover pizza boxes. The two tables directly behind them were a different story. One was covered in test tubes, glass vials, copper line, and brightly colored liquids; the other had brass gears, metal plates, wires, and various other mechanical bits strewn on it.

Two brass-and-wood automations mechanically shuffled around the lab; the motion caught my eye. The taller of the two was dusting and polishing brass, and the shorter one was dutifully sweeping the stone floors. Sir Reginald might have been a total scumbag of a human being, but the fact that these two things were still functioning after this much time was a testament to both his genius and the quality of his work.

Mad scientists were an oddity. Under the laws of physics, most of their inventions shouldn't work. I believed that magic played a large part in their creations. Mad scientists would deny this, but magic was really the only explanation for how some of their creations worked. It would also explain why pretty much all their creations couldn't be duplicated by anyone else.

The constant hum of the Tesla coils behind me had me wondering how this place still had power after this long. Sir Reginald had died in 1903; electricity wouldn't have been commonplace in London at that time. He had to have a power source here in the lab. What type of power source could run for 100 years with no one even touching it?

There were three corridors leading off the main chamber, one each to the left and right of the tables and one directly behind the tables. An ornate wooden door stood on the wall behind the left rear table.

What was more intriguing were the two large metal hatches in the wall behind the right rear table. The hatches resembled the watertight doors that warships sported on their bulkheads.

At the far side of the corridor to my left was this huge contraption with gleaming brass and levers all over it. I guessed this must be the Food-O-Tron the girls had told me about. Whatever it was, it certainly looked impressive.

Bree returned wearing comfortable-looking gray sweats, and Olivia entered behind her. She was wearing this long, flowing black-lace dress that looked like a black wedding dress. She had put on dark-purple lipstick and dark eye shadow, and she was looking quite goth in the get-up, except for the plastic silver and sparkly tiara and matching wand she was carrying. She greeted us with "Bow, minions, for you are in the presence of the Mistress of Darkness, Princess Olivia, ruler of this royal court!"

Bree rolled her eyes, and Stella laughed when she saw Olivia enter the room. Blue didn't bother glancing up to see what Olivia was wearing or going on about, but her tail was doing leisurely figure-eight motions.

It was nice seeing Blue up and around, and I could tell that being back home again took a ton of stress off the other three as well. I had to admit that being in a secret lab buried deep underground certainly felt safer than sitting in a cottage or a motel, like we had been. Unfortunately, while this security was nice, it didn't change the fact that there was still a huge contract on Olivia. I didn't want to spend the rest of my life looking over my shoulder, which meant we needed to figure out how to get the contracted lifted.

Chapter 21

Thursday, February 15

We gathered around the table to discuss our current plight. I cleared my throat and said, "While it is great that Blue is back with us and we are safe here for the moment, that doesn't change the fact that there is still a contract on Olivia and we only have one bag of blood—"

"Two," Olivia interrupted me. "There's a bag still in the fridge from before we left."

"Okay, two bags of blood, and I have just under $2,000 in my pocket—"

This time, Stella cut me off. "We have £500 in cash tucked away here at the lab."

I nodded and continued. "The money helps, but the blood is the real issue. We have a two-day supply; after that, things get interesting. We need to deal with the French court to end this contract. I think our first step is to talk with Elizabeth and see if she can help us out of this mess. Has there been any contact from her, Stella?"

Stella held up a smartphone I hadn't seen before and said, "I checked as soon as we got back here. Elizabeth has left several texts and one voicemail asking where we are and demanding we contact her soon. I'm holding off calling her back until we discuss what we want to do next."

"My first question is, how secure is this place? Where are the entrances and exits? How many people know where it is?"

Stella said, "There are three exits, but all three are locked and no one knows the codes, including me. Sir Reginald's old townhouse is gone. There is a large apartment building on its old location, which means that even if we knew the codes, that entrance is probably blocked. The main entrance, which he used to the get his huge robot to the surface, exited to a warehouse, and that is gone too. There is now a supermarket over the top of that exit. The last exit is an emergency escape, and I never found out where it came out. I would guess that is probably blocked, but unless we open the door, we won't know."

Stella paused for a moment before she continued. "As to how many people know about this place, the entire English court knows it exists. I'm sure they have spies or informants from other vampire courts in their midst, so those courts might know about it as well. They know it exists, and they know it is underground in London somewhere, but I doubt any of them know the exact location. They may be able to find out by looking up Sir Reginald's old townhouse records, but then they still have to figure out a way to get down here."

"How far underground are we?"

Stella shrugged. "I am not sure of the exact depth, but it is probably at least 500 feet down from street level."

"How do you get a cell signal this far down?"

Stella smiled. "After Elizabeth gave me the phone, she tried calling, and it didn't get through. I researched this, and we got a signal booster installed in the electrical closet in the apartment building's basement directly above us. This is the only room that gets coverage. I barely get a bar, but it works."

I was impressed that she was able to get a signal—even with a signal booster. "Clever. I noticed runes on the upper walls and ceilings. I'm assuming Sir Reginald put those in to block spells or magic from locating or penetrating this place? Some Earth elementals can travel through the ground, which means they might be able to get in here. There are some Enhanced Individuals who can phase through matter—they would possibly be able to get in here, too, but normally, people with a phase ability only go short distances, like through a wall or a door. Our depth might prevent that. We seem to be pretty secure here, but we need blood for Olivia and food for the rest of us, which means we can't stay hidden down here forever."

Bree said, "If the Food-O-Tron was working again, that would eliminate the need for us to get food."

"I will look at it. If the Food-O-Tron works off electricity, I might be able to use my power to trace the power inputs in case there is a short or a loose wire somewhere."

Bree shook her head. "I looked at it with Stella when it broke, but we couldn't find what the issue was. Who knows, though—maybe you'll get lucky."

That didn't bode well. Bree was mechanically inclined, and Stella was a genius and an amateur inventor. If the two of them couldn't fix it, we were probably out of luck. "I'll still give it a shot; it isn't working, so it's not like I can make it worse. Worst case, we can buy food anywhere now, thanks to Blue. We can shop in different locations all over the world to minimize the chance of getting caught. The blood supply is a little trickier, but that might be something Elizabeth can help us with."

Stella frowned. "The English court feeds directly off donors and not from medical plasma. Elizabeth is traditional in that aspect."

"She might be traditional, but she isn't stupid. I am willing to bet she has bags stashed in a fridge somewhere on her estate in case of emergency—or she has contacts who can get it for her."

Stella frowned. "That assumes she is willing to help us. She has to know about Olivia now, and she is not going to be amused that I kept Olivia hidden from her. Elizabeth may insist that Olivia swear fealty to her."

My confusion must have shown, because Stella then explained, "There are two types of vampires: free and sworn. Younger free vampires may enter a master's territory without permission. Vampires over 100 years old must ask for permission, but not doing that can be overlooked if the vampire in question doesn't draw attention to itself. Free vampires do not receive any protection from the vampire courts, and they are considered second-class citizens in the vampire world. Sworn vampires are members of a vampire court. They are protected by the court, and there are other benefits as well. The downside to being sworn is that the master or one of their lieutenants can order them around. A sworn vampire may not enter the territory of another master without first getting prior permission."

This seemed to be a possible solution, but Stella didn't seem to think so. I asked, "Why would Olivia being sworn to Elizabeth be a bad thing? It would probably stop Giselle, as she wouldn't want to piss off Elizabeth."

"That is true," said Stella, "but once Olivia is sworn, Elizabeth could order Olivia to do things she wouldn't want to do, and Olivia would have no choice but to obey. For instance, Elizabeth could order Olivia to attend her court for the next decade or two. It is also customary for a master to provide entertainment to another visiting master or a master's lieutenant. Being sworn is like being a slave; this is not something I want for Olivia—"

Olivia interrupted Stella. "If you are going to contact Elizabeth, you might want to do it soon. The sun will be up in a couple of hours."

Stella reached for her phone, and I said, "Hold on, Stella. Arrange a meeting for tomorrow night for all of us. If Elizabeth is unhappy, I don't want you and Blue facing her alone. We should all be there."

"I don't think that is wise," argued Stella.

"If she detains you and Blue, we are as good as dead. We would be trapped down here with no food, no way out, and only a two-day supply of blood for Olivia. Elizabeth could hold you and Blue for any amount of time."

Stella's eyes widened as that scenario hit home. She made the call. We only got one side of the conversation, but through Stella's answers and body language, I could tell Elizabeth wasn't happy. Stella hung up and said that we were to be there thirty minutes after sunset tomorrow.

I nodded. "I don't think there is anything more we can do to improve our situation until we find out if Elizabeth will help us or not."

Everyone went quiet at that. My nose twitched as I caught a whiff of my clothes; they reeked of smoke. With everything on hold until our meeting with Elizabeth, it was time to do something about my lack of attire.

I turned my attention to Blue. "Blue, are you able to do some more shadow-traveling now?"

Blue looked surprised at this request. "I am able to, but may I ask why?"

"I need to buy a change of clothes."

"I can take you wherever you need to go. Do you wish to go your home to retrieve these items?"

I shook my head. "Too risky—there may be people watching my house. If I could get a lift to a Walmart in Winnipeg, I will pick up what I need there."

"Why Winnipeg?" asked Stella.

"Because the Walmarts in Ontario closed five minutes ago. Winnipeg is an hour behind, so they will still be open ... I could also use a Timmie's coffee as well."

Bree perked up and exclaimed, "Donuts!"

"Sure, no problem. Blue, can you drop me off and pick me up, say, forty minutes later?"

Blue nodded, and we got up and headed over to the darkened corner we'd arrived through earlier. She made a small motion with her hand and opened a portal.

As Blue and I stepped into the shadows, Bree yelled, "Bring back donuts, or don't come back!"

The world changed, and in less than a blink of an eye, we stood behind a Walmart. It was cold, and snow blew around us. I clenched my fists at the Humans First graffiti sprayed in bold neon-green letters on the wall in front of me. I was relieved that Bree wasn't here to see this. She'd been frothing mad when the TV news station we had been watching covered a Humans First protest march in Washington, DC.

Humans First were a radical anti-monster organization that believed all individuals with powers were a threat to humanity. They believed that all Enhanced Individuals should be killed or sent off to live on reservations. These groups had been popular after World War II and up through the early sixties, before they seemed to fade into the background.

They had made a comeback in recent years after governments around the world passed the bills and legislation banning the term "monster" as derogatory and replacing it with "Enhanced Individual." In some ways, Humans First and organizations like it were a natural reaction to those laws; when monsters were in the shadows, they were easier to ignore. Since the passing of the new pro-Enhanced-Individuals laws, though, many were getting more airtime.

Blue pulled me from my musings. "I will return here in forty minutes."

She shuddered from the extreme cold and disappeared. I couldn't blame her; even with my resistance to cold, I felt a slight chill due to the brutal temperatures.

I walked around to the front of the store and grabbed a cart. Twenty minutes later, I exited the store with my purchases in a large shopping bag. I slipped around back again and looked around. Then, seeing it was clear, I took to the air. I had never been to Winnipeg before, but I figured a Tim Hortons would be close by. I spotted one and flew toward it, landing in a darkened alley about a half block away from the store.

I walked out of the alley onto a quiet, deserted street and made it to the Tim's in short order. A bored middle-age lady in the familiar brown uniform looked at me warily as I entered, so I removed the balaclava and approached the cash register, ordering two-dozen donuts, two large black coffees, and two large teas before I paid her for them.

She held up the box. "Any preference on which kind?"

"No. A nice mix of different ones is good," I replied.

She nodded and began randomly grabbing donuts from each of the different trays for both boxes I ordered.

A couple minutes later, I had my tickets home and beverages. I grabbed a table in the corner, since I had ten minutes to kill before I needed to meet Blue. The Wi-Fi password was printed on the receipt, and I risked using my burner phone.

I checked my e-mail. A reply from Greg was waiting for me. He'd gotten my e-mail and had already filed his claim for the damage to the cottage. There were a couple of other e-mails from other people, but I didn't bother answering them—they could wait.

On a whim, I logged onto the secure EIRT site and checked the status of the drow claim. It was still being processed, but they had assigned values to each of the drow. The total for all twelve came to $201,976 dollars. I smiled at total. The bounty on a drow normally ranged from $10,000 to $20,000 apiece. For twelve, the range could be $120,000 to $240,000—at over $200,000, the final number was closer to the higher end. I owed the girls for the three drow they had taken down, so they would get $50,494 as their share once I was paid.

With two minutes to go, I locked my phone and began gathering up all my stuff. The restaurant door opened, and a guy in a blue balaclava and a big black coat that had seen better days came in. He made a beeline for the cash register and then reached into his jacket and pulled out a large knife.

"Give me all the money in the cash register and no one gets hurt," he said in a grizzled voice.

I sighed as the lady hit a button on the register to open the cash drawer. I arced a shot of electricity at him, and he cried out for a brief second. The lady screamed in surprise, and he dropped to the floor. The would-be robber was twitching and drooling on the floor, no longer a threat. I got up and wandered over, picking up his knife and putting it on the counter, out of his reach.

"Call the cops," I said.

The shaken attendant grabbed the phone and started to dial.

I grabbed my Walmart bag, donuts, and beverages, and disappeared out the door. I entered the empty alley and took to the air, landing behind the Walmart. Blue appeared a minute later. Sirens had started up in the distance, but as I entered the shadows, the noise was gone.

Chapter 22

Thursday, February 15

When I returned to the lab, I was greeted by the ladies. Bree looked at the two boxes of donuts like they were water and she had been in the Sahara for a week. I held out one of the two boxes to her, and she smiled as she took it from me, then walked away while protecting her treasure.

I opened the remaining box and helped myself to a glazed donut before I offered them to Stella and Blue. They stared at the selection for a moment, and then Blue picked a chocolate glazed donut, and Stella went with a powder-coated jelly donut. I handed the extra coffee to Bree and was pleased that I'd guessed right that Blue was a tea person.

Olivia looked at us all happily eating donuts and said, "You all suck."

"I have some good news," I said. "While I was out, I used my phone to check the status of the drow bounties from the attack outside of my house. They are still processing the claim, but it looks like your share will be just over $50,000, which you can split among yourselves. Stella, do you have a bank account?"

She finished her mouthful of donut and said, "Yes. Elizabeth got me a passport, ID, and bank account to help with bringing me into this time. She did this for Blue as well."

"Good. Before going after McMahon, did you register with the UN as bounty hunters?"

Stella looked confused and shook her head. "Why would I need to register? Aren't the bounties open to everyone?"

I took a deep breath and went into the tax advantages of being registered with the UN as a bounty hunter. If you weren't registered, you had to pay resident-country taxes on the bounties you collected anywhere in the world. Registration also helped payments get processed more quickly by the banks; a bank would put a hold on bounties larger than $10,000 to make sure the money wasn't the profit of crime, drugs, or terrorism. The final perk of registering was that the UN provided an ID that was both helpful when dealing with law enforcement and could be used to speed up the process of a claim.

Stella had questions about what was involved in the process of applying, and then she asked a question that didn't seem to be connected to anything we had just been talking about: "Zack, are you staying with us until we have resolved this issue with Olivia and the French court?"

"I was planning on crashing here for the night, but I hadn't thought much past that. You guys are safe here, so I guess I could go home ... But the contract on Olivia mentions me, which means that they will come after me while looking for a lead on Olivia. With the wards on my house and my contacts in Hamilton, I'd probably be pretty safe, and I can take certainly care of myself. That means I can stay or go, depending on what you prefer."

"Stay here, at least until this is resolved. After the contract has been taken care of, I was wondering if you would be interested in expanding your business?"

Even though Stella's tone had been casual, all four of them were looking at me intently. Even Bree had paused in her quest to eliminate every donut in the room to watch me.

Taking them all on as partners was an interesting idea. They were all Enhanced, and their abilities would be an asset. Blue's travel abilities would be worth her weight in gold—they would allow me to take a much wider selection of bounties. Since meeting them, it had been a banner time for collecting bounties: McMahon, the drow, and the tracker, and the Fire elemental were by far the biggest ones I'd ever gotten. I also found myself enjoying the ladies' company and would miss them once this ended.

On the other hand, joining up subjected them to more risk. The individuals on the bounty list were dangerous—otherwise, they wouldn't be on the list. What if I got one of the ladies killed because I had teamed up with them? Could I live with that? But if I turned them down, would they just do it on their own anyway?

I suspected that Blue made decent money working as transportation for Elizabeth and the English court, but they'd gone after the McMahon bounty, so Blue's wages probably weren't enough to cover living expenses for the four of them. Just keeping Olivia in plasma and Bree fed would be large expenses.

All these questions would be moot, though, if we didn't figure out how to deal with Giselle and the contract on Olivia first. I laughed at myself for worrying about the risks of bringing them on board when we would be lucky to survive the next couple of weeks.

"Would you be interested in joining me, then?" I asked.

They all nodded except for Blue, but Blue would go where Stella went. Blue had not left Stella's side since we had returned.

I was tempted to take them up on the offer right then, but I had been working solo for so long that I wasn't sure how I'd work as part of a team. This was a big decision, and I wanted more time to think about. I said, "Look, let's deal with the French court first. Once that's out of the way, we can revisit this conversation. That gives us all time to think about it some more, okay?"

Stella said, "Fair enough," and did her best to suppress a yawn.

The sun was about to rise, so Olivia said she was done for the night. Stella and Bree both announced they were turning in too.

I said, "The coffee has perked me up a bit. I'll look at the Food-O-Tron and see if I can fix it."

Stella looked at Blue, and Blue said, "I have been in a coma for almost a week, so I am going to stay up for a bit too. I will assist Zack with his work."

Stella nodded. "Blue, show Zack where the spare rooms are and let him pick one. It probably wouldn't hurt for you to give him a tour of the place too."

The room cleared out, leaving Blue and me alone. The only noises were the sounds of the movement of the automations as they continued cleaning the lab, and the constant hum and crackle of the Tesla coils at the back of the lab.

"Care to give me that tour?" I asked.

Blue pointed at my Walmart bag of clothes and countered with, "Do you want to wash those first?"

I nodded, and Blue led me to the laundry room in the east corridor. The washer and dryer weren't anything like their modern equivalents. The washer was made of brass and looked like a refrigerator that was lying on its side. The dryer was made of brass and iron and looked like a giant cauldron with a lid.

Blue help me remove the various tags and stickers on the clothes and showed me how to load the washing machine. She closed the doors, turned a dial, and then pulled a lever, and the machine hummed to life.

We headed back to the main lab, and Blue began my tour. She opened an ornate door that I'd spotted earlier in the back right of the lab. On the other side of the door was a richly decorated library/study. Floor-to-ceiling bookshelves surrounded the entire room. The books on the shelves were old, with faded brown-leather covers and precise gold lettering on their spines. After reading a couple of the titles, I realized they were all reference manuals and science books. I wondered how much the books must be worth. They were all over 100 years old, and it wouldn't surprise me if many them were first editions.

There was a plush and intricately designed throw rug in the center of the room with two comfy-looking leather easy chairs on it. A side table beside each chair held a lamp.

"This is Stella's favorite room," said Blue.

We went back into the main work area, and she closed the door behind us. We moved over to the two large steel hatches on the right side of the room. Blue turned the wheel in the center of the right one and opened it. The cool air that escaped as she opened the sturdy six-inch-thick hatch clued me in that this was a large walk-in fridge.

"Cleaning out this fridge after the contents had been sitting in there for over 100 years was one of more unpleasant things I've ever done," said Blue.

The fridge was spotless inside and mostly empty. Only one shelf near the door had a selection of condiments and salad dressings. The unit was huge; it was a good six feet wide and probably ten feet deep.

Blue closed the hatch and then reached for the left hatch. "I should warn you that there's a cadaver in this one."

It wasn't every day that someone told you they had a body stashed away. I was about to ask a question when Blue said, "It will make sense when you see it."

She turned the wheel and opened the door. Frigid air blasted out—this was the freezer. It was empty except for a large container of ice cream on the shelf next to the freezer door and the large headless corpse resting against the far wall of the freezer.

The body was huge. It was easily six feet tall, even without the head, and had to weigh a good 280 pounds. It wore only a dull-gray pair of shorts. The skin was an odd sickly green color, and there were scars and stitches all over it, like someone had sewn the body together.

Oh my God ... Sir Reginald had made himself a Frankenstein's monster.

Blue smirked at my reaction. "His name was George. Sir Reginald did indeed construct the body from pieces of other dead bodies, and he managed to bring it to life. He was so proud of his creation that he brought Stella down to the lab to see it. Stella was both amazed and horrified at George. She said George would just mindlessly obey, doing whatever Sir Reginald ordered him to do. Stella also said that she felt bad for George. His face had a look of such profound sadness on it, and it was as if he knew he had once been more than just a collection of parts—and not just a mindless slave of Sir Reginald."

"What happened to the head?"

Blue shrugged. "I asked Stella the same question, and she didn't know. She recalled Sir Reginald being in a foul mood a couple of days after she met George, and she never saw George again—until we found him like this when we were exploring the lab."

Blue closed the door, and we headed down the north corridor between the study and freezer. As we walked down the corridor, Blue pointed out the spare rooms and said I could use any of them. She showed me the spare bathroom, and then we exited the corridor and entered a massive empty chamber that reminded me of a hangar. Hoists and empty chains hung from the ceiling.

Blue was silent as I took in the huge open area. Then she said, "This is the chamber in which Sir Reginald made the giant robot that led to his demise. The main entrance to the lab is on the far right side of the northern wall."

The northern wall had two enormous, intimidating steel doors that were closed. There was a device at the bottom of the wall to the right of them that looked like a round typewriter. The round-typewriter thing was built into the wall. I asked Blue about it, and she said that was where the access code for the doors was entered. Our steps echoed off the metal floor and around the cavernous chamber as we wandered over to the access panel. The odd interface of the panel had letter keys in the center area, with number and symbol keys around the outside.

When Stella had mentioned access codes for the doors earlier, I'd assumed a ten-digit keypad, like a lot of modern doors had. This thing had forty to fifty keys. Who knew how long the access code was? I could understand now why they hadn't figured it out …

We left the hangar room and proceeded down the far west corridor. Blue pointed out the rooms belonging to the four of them and the bathrooms at each end of the corridor.

I asked about the water supply, and Blue said Sir Reginald had tapped an underground spring. This made sense. If he had connected into the city water lines, someone would have noticed the water loss or the connection by now and shut it down.

Midway down the corridor was a solid-looking steel door with another round typewriter keypad attached to the wall beside it.

"This is the escape access. We don't know where it leads," said Blue.

"Can you use your shadow-traveling abilities to jump to the other side of the door and see where it leads?"

"I could if there were any shadows in there. I suspect the passage is either pitch black—and therefore has no shadows—or it is fully lit and has no shadows. In either case, I can't find a path to it."

We continued past Olivia's and Bree's rooms and the bathroom on the opposite side and then made a left. After a short walk, we came back into the main chamber of the lab. The south wall had the Tesla coils in the corner to our right. In the far corner of that wall was the exit that used to lead to Sir Reginald's townhouse, and another access pad that matched the earlier ones.

We crossed the lab and entered the east corridor again. On the north wall was the broken Food-O-Tron; it was a good ten feet across.

On the south wall, there were two doors. Blue opened the closest one, and the room it opened to was bare except for a large cylindrical device tipped over on its side. Blue explained this was the stasis chamber that Stella had spent over 100 years in.

She opened the next door, which led to a room that was just storage. The boxes were modern; this room was used as a dumping ground for their stuff. I looked back down the hall, and my interest was pulled to the first door on the east wall, which was marked "Power Room."

"Blue, can we take a look at this room?" I asked, itching with curiosity about the power source for this place.

"Not much to see in there, but sure."

The door wasn't locked, and it opened into a sparse, small room. In the center, there was a black box that stood about three feet high and was two feet wide and a foot long. Two massive, thick cables extended out of either side. Both cables ran down the sides of the box and along the floor before disappearing into the wall. There was a small brass plaque on the top of the box.

I moved in closer to the machine, and my powers easily sensed the massive amount of electrical power coming off the thing. I leaned in to read the neat script etched into the plaque: "Interdimensional Power Tap. Do Not Open."

My knees trembled as I backed out of the room. Blue looked at me with concern.

"Sir Reginald was insane," I pronounced. "He opened a portal to somewhere in space and time, which takes an immense amount of power to do, but once the portal is open, it is self-sustaining and harnesses an immense amount of power. He is tapping that to run this place. I'm guessing one of those feeds is connected to the Tesla coils, allowing them to burn off any excess power or surges. If the portal loses integrity, it will unleash a catastrophic burst of energy."

"How bad would that be?" asked Blue. She sounded worried.

"It all depends on the size of the portal and what it is connected to. It would probably vaporize this lab, but it might do the same thing to the city above, all of Britain, or even the whole planet." I shuddered.

Blue's purple eyes went wide, and she quickly closed the door. That actually made me laugh—as if closing the door would make a lick of difference if that thing went up.

Her tail, which had been just hanging loosely behind her, went straight down, emphasizing her fear. Blue gave me an odd look, and I told her what I was thinking. She smiled.

"It is a concern, but it has been running fine for over 100 years. What are the odds it is going to break down now?" I tried to reassure Blue—and myself, if I was being totally honest.

I winced about having asked, *What are the odds it is going to break down now?* It reminded me of a sports announcer saying, "He hasn't missed a field goal from this range in thirty-three consecutive tries," and you just know the kicker is going to shank it and miss after that …

Thankfully, Blue didn't catch my wince of self-doubt, and she seemed to relax. Her tail rose back up closer to its original position, then she nodded, and we continued the tour.

We passed the laundry room, and Blue stopped at the next room, which was marked "Supplies." She opened the door, and I glanced inside. It was a large room lined with shelves that were packed with wires, gears, lightbulbs, chemicals, and just about anything else a mad scientist could conceivably need. There were a ton of fascinating things in this room, but I didn't have the urge at that moment to do a full inventory of what was there.

Blue took us out of the room and deeper down the corridor. There was only one more door on the left, and it was at the end of the hall, which didn't surprise me—that supply room had been huge.

The first room on the right was labeled "Disposal." Blue opened the door. The room was about four feet deep, and the entire opposite wall was made of steel. A large hatch sat in the center of it. To the right of the hatch was a big red button.

"Garbage disposal," Blue said. "Open the hatch, dump whatever you want to get rid of inside, close the hatch, and hit the button. Open the hatch a second later, and not a single speck of whatever you put in there remains. Stella thinks Sir Reginald built a disintegration ray inside of it."

My first thought was *At least if I ever need to get rid of a body, I am all set.* I put that dark thought aside and followed Blue to the next stop on our tour.

The last door on the right of the corridor was a heavy-duty steel job with a small shuttered viewing hatch in it. I slid the hatch open and peeked inside. The room was small and empty with solid steel walls. There were marks all over the walls. It took me a moment to figure out what they were—scratches.

"Is this the room you used to lock up Bree during a full moon?"

Blue nodded reluctantly.

Bree had told me that it had taken her only three full moons to master the beast. The amount of damage Bree's beast had done to the walls in only three nights was both impressive and horrifying. I'd thought the fact that Bree had managed to control her beast after only three full moons was extraordinary, but I was even more impressed now that I saw the handiwork of her beast's rage etched into the walls like that.

I closed the hatch again. We walked a short distance until we came to the large hangar, but we didn't enter.

As we wrapped up the tour, I found myself conflicted. The accomplishments of Sir Reginald were impressive, almost awe-inspiring. The lab itself was amazing—the engineering involved in building something this large so far underground in complete secrecy in the nineteenth century was a feat that few people would have been able to accomplish. Add in the power source, bringing George to life, a walk-in fridge and freezer, and a washer and dryer before these were commonplace—not to mention the automations that were still working after 100 years, the Food-O-Tron, a giant steam-powered robot, and a means of providing clean water and air to this place—and he started to make Edison look like a slacker. It was hard not to be impressed.

Then I thought about the hell he had put Stella through: the sexual abuse, injecting her with the Hyde potion, creating and using the stasis chamber on her, and Odin only knew what else ... I didn't want to admire someone who deserved to be loathed for his crimes. How did someone who was capable of all this wonder also do things so unspeakably terrible?

Blue stayed quiet as we walked, leaving me alone with my thoughts. She led us down the east corridor and stopped when we reached the Food-O-Tron. Even if this thing didn't replicate food, just the immense size of it would have been impressive. It had to be ten feet wide and a good seven feet tall. Looking at the cast-iron hatches, gleaming brass, switches, and levers, I wasn't feeling confident about getting it fixed.

I turned to Blue. "Any idea on how we can access the inside of this thing?"

She pushed a knob near the top right side of the machine that opened a narrow passageway at the side.

I went into the passage and got behind the Food-O-Tron. As I looked over all the wires, gears, and pulleys inside of the thing, I wondered what I was even doing here. This thing was incredibly complex. I had said I would try, though, so I closed my eyes and focused on the electricity running to the machine. I sensed the electricity in the main feed, and it came to a junction box that had five feeds running off it into the machine. I traced each of the feeds and smiled as I sensed an electrical fault in the fourth one. The connector looked fine externally, but when I pulled it off, underneath was blackened and charred. No wonder Bree and Stella had missed this.

I showed Blue, and she said there were spare connectors in the supply room. Ten minutes later, we'd replaced the connector.

On the way out, I found a manual tucked into a pouch just inside the access hatch. It was the user manual to the Food-O-Tron. We close the access hatch, and Blue pulled main lever on the Food-O-Tron. It began to whirl, hum, and come to life.

Two minutes later, Blue and I were enjoying some fresh-baked oatmeal raisin cookies in the main lab area. I sat, reading the manual. I found it was easy to add new items to the Food-O-Tron. I also decided I needed something to drink to go with the cookies. I went through the recipe book attached to the machine and was disappointed in the beverage choices, which consisted of tea, milk, Guinness, and an India pale ale. I had been hoping for coffee or Coke.

Since neither was on the list, I had Blue use the shadows to take me to Calgary. I picked up a large Timmie's coffee, two-dozen mixed donuts, and a half-liter bottle of Coke.

Fifteen minutes later, I had all of them added to the Food-O-Tron. The only issue I had was the coffee. For the Coke, I poured it into the one of the machine's pint glasses, but coffee in a pint glass wouldn't work, so I used the teacups instead. The problem was the teacups were dainty, and one barely held a quarter of my large coffee. In the end, I used two teacups and replicated those.

Buoyed by my success at adding items to the Food-O-Tron, I joined Blue back at the table and said, "Since we can add items to the Food-O-Tron and it can replicate any organic item, what if we added one of Olivia's bags of blood?"

Blue's purple eyes widened, and she smiled, showing off her pointy white teeth. "If it can duplicate blood, then we would have unlimited supplies and could hide out here indefinitely."

I nodded but added, "The problem is, if it doesn't work, we will have wasted half of Olivia's remaining supply."

We decided it was worth the risk and poured out a bag into one of the pint mugs, then added it to the Food-O-Tron. The machine dinged once it had finished, and I removed the empty pint mug from the beverage hatch and dumped it into the cleaning compartment on the machine.

Blue looked at me. "Did it work?"

I shrugged. The empty glass was a good sign, but there was only one way to find out, so I reached up and pulled the lever. The machine came to life again, and after a minute or so, a bell chimed, and it went silent again. I opened the hatch and smiled at the sight of a full pint mug of blood sitting there.

Blue took out the glass, gave it a sniff, and said, "Smells like human blood."

We dumped out the glass in the sink and put the glass back in the Food-O-Tron to be cleaned. We'd have to wait until Olivia got up that evening to test it for sure, but I felt pretty good that it had worked.

The long day, though, had caught up with me, and I wished Blue a good night and turned in.

Chapter 23

Friday, February 16

The next day, I got up at what would have been noon Eastern time but was 5:00 p.m. London time. I hit the bathroom and was grateful the toilet wasn't too hard to figure out. It was pretty similar to the modern version, other than the water tank on the back was about four feet higher than normal.

The shower, however, took me a moment to figure out. There was a main dial that was marked both "Hot" and "Cold." I turned it to "Hot," but there was no tap to turn on. There was a chain hanging from the ceiling. I pulled on that and almost screamed as it dumped a shit-ton of cold water on me. I let go of the chain, and the water stopped. I stood back, reached in, grabbed the chain, and pulled it again.

It took about a minute for the water to warm up. It was nowhere near as hot as I'd have liked, but at least it was warm. I had to keep pulling on the chain for the water, which made it tricky to shower, but I got clean. I shaved, brushed my teeth, threw on some deodorant, and combed my short hair.

I entered my room and got dressed in my new khakis and collared golf shirt. I broke out the new brown-suede casual dress shoes that completed my outfit. Somehow, I didn't think jeans and a T-shirt would cut it at the English court. I checked myself out in the mirror and felt pretty good about how I looked for the meeting. That feeling lasted until I stepped into the main lab and saw how the ladies were dressed.

Bree was in an elegant black cocktail dress with black three-inch heels. Stella had changed from her usual plain white dress to a more formal-looking green silk-and-lace dress. Blue was in her usual blue-scaled armor, at least. I knew by the look I got from Bree that I was underdressed.

"Don't say a word. I know I screwed up and am underdressed for tonight, but this is the most formal thing I have here. We have less than a half an hour before the meeting, and I need food, which means this will have to do," I said as I walked by them and headed for the Food-O-Tron.

I flipped the dials for coffee first and perused the recipe book. I was familiar with many of the dishes in the book, as my mother had been English and had made many of the traditional English dishes listed here when I was growing up. I hit a winner at entry #87: Cornish pasties. I was delighted, as they were a personal favorite.

As I sat down, Bree said, "Thank you for fixing the Food-O-Tron."

"I thought you were going to have to fix it again by how much Bree used it this afternoon," teased Stella.

"Shush, you. I was just making sure everything worked," answered Bree defensively.

"Yes, by ordering every item in the recipe book," replied Stella with a laugh.

"It wasn't 'everything'! Anyway, Zack, thank you for adding coffee, Coke, and donuts to the choices. Do you think the blood will work for Olivia?"

I looked at my watch and said, "We will see in a few minutes when she gets up, but I don't see why it wouldn't. The machine is design to replicate any organic item, and human blood certainly qualifies as organic."

I cut into the pasty and examined it. It was different than my mother's recipe in that it used cubed beef, as opposed the ground beef that Mom had used. But it had carrots and potatoes and seemed pretty close to her recipe. I took a bite and instantly decided there was nothing wrong with this version.

The pan had two good-sized pasties. I had just finished the first one when a sleepy-looking Olivia—wearing an oversized, worn-but-comfy-looking T-shirt—entered the room and made a beeline for the fridge.

"Olivia, stop," I said, getting to my feet.

She gave me a look that said, "Whatever you want, it can wait until after I have eaten."

Despite the hungry vampire, I continued. "Come over to the Food-O-Tron. I have a surprise for you."

She reluctantly joined me at the machine. "This had better be good, or I am feeding off you right now." She stepped closer, sniffed me, and said, "Actually, you smell really good, so I might just feed off you anyway."

I took that as her making a joke and explained that I had learned how to program the Food-O-Tron and had used one of her juice boxes to add it to the machine. She seemed to perk up at that, and I showed her the entry, how to set the switches, and then pushed the main lever to the right. The machine came to life and start clacking away.

"You mean this machine can produce as much blood as I want?" she asked with growing excitement in her voice.

I nodded, and she added, "I am no longer rationed to one bag a day?"

"Nope—that is, assuming this works. My Tim Horton's coffee worked, and if it can do that nectar of the gods, human blood should be easy."

Olivia smiled at that but never stopped watching the machine intently. It dinged, and she opened the hatch to the beverage dispenser.

"Try a small sip to make sure it is okay first," I warned.

She sniffed the pint-mug of blood. "It smells right, but let me give it a try." She took a tiny sip and smiled. "It tastes right, but more importantly, I can already feel my body responding like this is the real thing."

With that, she brought the glass to her lips and gulped down about half of it. As excited as I was that it had worked, watching Olivia suck back that much blood had me worrying I was going to "enjoy" my Cornish pastie again real soon, and I made myself look away.

"Zack, I'm done. If I want another one, how do I do that?" she asked.

I showed her where to put her empty glass to get it cleaned and explained that the switches were still set from before, which meant all she had to do was push the main lever right to start the process again.

"When you're finished," I said, "you need to get changed, as we are meeting with Elizabeth in twenty minutes."

"Not a problem. I have my stuff laid out and ready to go."

I joined Stella, Bree, and Blue at the table, and they were already discussing tonight's meeting.

"With the Food-O-Tron working and it being able to provide Olivia with blood, don't be too anxious to make a deal with Elizabeth now. We can hide out here for the long haul if we need to," I said as I cut into my second pastie.

Stella nodded. "It puts us in better position, but we are still going to be looking over our shoulders at every turn. Elizabeth, with the strength of the English vampire court, could force Giselle to end this. The downside, of course, is that Olivia would have to swear fealty to her and become her slave."

"She offered you and Blue protection. Can we leverage that? There is a risk of you both either being injured or killed if someone comes after Olivia for the contract money," I said.

Stella pondered this for a second. "Elizabeth wouldn't go for that—the contract is on Olivia. If Blue or I were harmed, then she would avenge us, but it is not enough to get her to force Giselle to stop."

"Would she be willing to use her spies in the French court to make Roman an offer on our behalf?" I asked after finishing my mouthful of food.

"What offer would that be?" replied Stella.

"Giselle has forced us into a situation where it is either us or her. If we take her out, can Elizabeth talk Roman into rescinding the contract and leaving us alone?"

"Interesting. He gets the French throne, at no risk to him, and only has to agree to drop the French court's interest in Olivia. That is an option. The problem is, we'd still have to kill a master in her own lair, which won't be easy. If we can get Roman on board, and we can pull this off, it ends the threat to us. Elizabeth would probably be willing to make that deal at no cost to us; removing Giselle as the master of the French court would make it less of a threat, which is an upside for her."

We kicked around the different ideas until Olivia appeared before us, dressed and ready to go. She was in the formal black wedding dress she had been wearing last night, with black high heels, and had her hair up and her makeup done. She wasn't wearing the tiara and had left the plastic wand behind this time.

We all got up from the table and headed with Blue to the shadows in the corner. We all took each other's hands and stepped through …

We stepped out of the shadows into a dimly lit sitting room. Around the room, there were deep-brown mahogany shelves that contained hundreds of leather-bound books that looked older than I was. I could probably bet some of them were even older than Stella.

The Persian rug we were standing on was intricately designed; it was more like a piece of art than something my feet should have been stepping on. There were two comfortable and expensive-looking leather chairs beside me with a gorgeous, obviously antique table between them. The room was roughly the same size as my master bedroom, but the value of its contents easily surpassed the value of my entire home.

A distinguished older gentleman in a butler's uniform stepped forward and said, "Mistresses Stella and Blue, lovely to see you again."

Stella smiled. "Hargraves, always a pleasure to see you. These are my companions, Zack, Bree, and Olivia."

"I am charmed to meet all of you. I would offer you refreshments, but alas, I have strict instructions from Her Majesty to bring you to the main chamber immediately. Hopefully, you will overlook my poor hospitality on this occasion," said Hargraves with an almost profound sadness to his tone.

"I understand. One mustn't keep Her Majesty waiting. Perhaps we will visit again soon when time isn't as pressing," said Stella.

Hargraves smiled. "That would be delightful, and I shall look forward to it. For now, however, allow me to direct you to the main chamber."

We followed Hargraves out of the sitting room and into an elegantly decorated hallway. There were large portrait paintings on the wall of somber-looking individuals, who, by their clothing, had not walked on this Earth in hundreds of years. On the other hand, we were at the English vampire court, so a few of them might still be kicking around here somewhere.

The hallway made all sorts of left and right turns, which quickly gave me a rough idea of how massive this place must be. We passed closed doors and the occasional open ones. I got quick glimpses of the rooms behind the open doors. Some looked like small offices with cubicles, desks, modern computers, and phones. Others were simple living quarters that looked unoccupied, with the odd bathroom thrown into the mix.

We stepped out into what must have been the main hallway, and I admired the seemingly endless expanse of rich, dark hardwood laid in an ornamental thatch pattern. The wood was so highly polished that I almost expected to see my reflection in it. The walls were done in an off-white color that had this subtle marbling pattern to it. I was far from an art aficionado, but even I recognized some of the paintings on the walls; I had no doubt that any of them were worth more than I had ever made in my life, even with the recent bounties included!

The high-vaulted ceilings were just as impressive. The cream-marble archways ran not only horizontally across the ceiling but interconnected with the other arches in an X-shape pattern that ran down the length of the extensive hallway.

The hallway had a timeless quality to it, but there were some modern touches too. LED lighting had been worked flawlessly into the seams of the arches and provided soft, diffused lighting. There were small, dark Plexiglas bubbles mounted in the ceilings, which probably had CCTV cameras in them. We were probably being monitored closer than a whale at a Vegas casino.

At the end of the hallway were two large, imposing wood-and-iron doors and two equally imposing guards standing beside them. Their auras told me they were vampires—and probably had been for fifty years or so. Both heavily muscled men were in dark suits. They were wearing ear-pieces and dark aviator sunglasses. They reminded me of presidential Secret Service agents I'd seen on TV, but larger, scarier versions.

The bald and ebony-skinned guard stepped forward and smiled warmly as Stella walked up to him. "Stella, it has been too long. I am going soft without your sharp wit to keep me on my toes." His grin lit up his face, and there was a warmth to it that lessened his imposing appearance. His voice was a deep, resonating baritone; I suspected he would be a heck of a singer if he had a mind to be.

"Devon, it has been too long. And there is nothing soft about you," said Stella as she reached up and playfully grasped his thick bicep.

My eyes widened at Stella's comfortableness around Devon, and I upgraded him in my mind from just "hired muscle" to something more. I was curious about how he'd managed to earn Stella's trust. Of course, Stella and Blue had been working around the English vampire court for five years, so maybe it was just time that had done it.

Devon nodded, but then his smile faded. "It is wonderful to see you, Stella, but Her Majesty is quite anxious for your presence. Our scanners are only showing Blue's sword as a possible threat, but does anyone else have weapons on them?"

Blue pulled out a silk ribbon from a pouch on her belt and tied off her sword in a peace bond. I had wondered why she had removed her six daggers and the various other instruments of death she usually carried and put them on the table back at the lab …

Devon eyed the rest of us critically as each of us shook our heads.

"You may proceed." And with that, he turned and opened the nearest solid-looking door and made a motion for us to enter.

Stella entered first, and the rest of us followed. The throne room was as impressive as Stella had described it, but my eyes were instantly pulled to the lady on the throne. The aura she had around her was, by far, one of the largest I had ever seen. It radiated out in a blood-red glow three feet in every direction around her. My knees weakened slightly at the pure power this woman projected.

Elizabeth's physical self was a total contrast to the immense presence of her power—she was small and almost dainty. She probably would struggle to be called five feet tall, and her thin, waif-like form was easily less than 100 pounds. It was almost amusing that something that small and harmless-looking was probably in the top 5 percent of Enhanced Individuals in terms of power and probably in the top 1 percent in terms of influence, as master of the English court.

Her piercing green eyes gazed down upon us like she was a hawk and we were lowly mice cowering in the field. Elizabeth was breathtakingly beautiful. Her long auburn hair flowed in tiny ringlets down her neck and shoulders like a waterfall. Her porcelain-white skin was flawless and accentuated her emerald-green eyes and blood-red lips.

The long, graceful green silk grown, with its silver embroidery and elaborate stitching, was truly spectacular. It was only surpassed by the huge emerald that hung from the platinum necklace and rested against her chest.

It rocked me to my core that I had barely noticed the two vampires standing at the base of her throne. The female on her left had an aura that extended out almost a foot from her, and I guessed she was probably over 250 years old. The male on the left had a smaller aura and was probably around 150 years old. The male vampire's aura concerned me a bit, as the black outline was thicker than the other two vampires combined. It wasn't quite as bad as the outline Benny, the telepath from EIRT, had had, but this was someone I certainly wouldn't be quick to turn my back on.

The female vampire was a study in contrasts, as her long dark hair and blue eyes stood out against the paleness of her skin. The formfitting black bodysuit she was wearing outlined her unmistakably feminine curves, but the tall black-leather boots with a dagger hilt protruding from the tops of each one—and the hilt of the sword that was strapped to her back—meant she wasn't just there as eye candy. It was next to impossible to miss the large scar that ran from the top of her right eye and down her cheek to her jawline. She stood deadly still and expressionless, but her sharp blue eyes were carefully studying our every move.

The male vampire had a small, roguish smile on his face, as if he found this entire scene either amusing or beneath him. The amused smile, however, stopped at his grey eyes; those eyes told a different story, as they were cold and dead and, judging from the black outline of his aura, were probably a better representation of the person behind them.

I didn't notice any visible weapons or the telltale bulge of a shoulder holster under his expensive tailored black suit, and figured he was unarmed. I wasn't sure if that scared me more or less than the intimidating female vampire he was mirroring at the base of the throne.

Stella reached the foot of the raised dais. She had angled away from the male vampire and closer to the female one. She knelt before Elizabeth, and the rest of us followed suit.

The room was deathly silent, and we stayed kneeling in this position for what felt like forever, but it was probably only a few minutes. I was assuming Elizabeth kept us this way to let Stella know that Her Majesty was clearly unhappy with her. My nervousness gave way to anger, as I hated games like this.

Elizabeth's powerful yet sultry voice said, "You may rise."

We stood, and Stella remained quiet as Elizabeth studied us.

"It seems, my young friend, a lot has happened since we last met. You have new companions. It would please us if you would introduce them to this court."

Stella answered, "Of course, Your Majesty. This is Bree, a Werepanther."

Bree stepped forward and curtsied with her eyes lowered.

When Bree moved back, Stella continued, "And this is Olivia, free vampire, spawn of the late Henri of the French court."

Olivia stepped forward and performed a curtsey of her own.

Stella turned to me. "This is Zack Stevens, Air elemental."

I stepped forward and bowed.

" 'Air elemental'? I had assumed by his dress that you were perhaps golfing after this, and he was your caddy," said Elizabeth in a snide tone.

Without even thinking about it, I said, "I would be honored to go golfing with Your Majesty, preferably on a bright and sunny day."

Stella gasped beside me, and before I could blink, the female vampire had drawn her sword, and its razor-sharp edge was resting directly against my neck. I readied my Air and Electrical powers on instinct but doubted I could do anything to stop that blade from removing my head from my shoulders. I cursed myself for being so stupid; when I got nervous or angry, my mouth had a bad habit of becoming unfiltered. I hoped this time it wouldn't cost me my life.

To my amazement, a soft, refined laugh came from the throne above me. I wanted to raise my eyes but didn't dare.

Elizabeth cleared her throat. "I have occupied this throne for centuries, and I cannot recall the last time someone was so bold in my presence. Your comment amused me—for that, I will let it go this one time."

Before I even drew my next breath, the female vampire had retracted the blade, sheathed it, and resumed her original position. I trembled slightly at that display of prowess.

"I assume that there is a reason, then, for your casual attire?" asked Elizabeth.

I took that as permission to speak. I lifted my head and said, "My deepest apologies for my attire. It is entirely out of ignorance and necessity. I was not aware of court etiquette, and by the time I realized I was underdressed, there was no time to correct the issue. I cannot return to my home due to the contract on Olivia, and currently have a very limited wardrobe from which to choose. It will not happen again."

"Yes, my network of informants said that you and your companions have had a trying few days. Due to this, I will overlook this slight—this time."

I bowed deeply and gratefully stepped back, and Elizabeth turned her full attention back to Stella. "I am pleased that Blue has recovered from her injuries, for we have missed her and her services during this time. I am, however, displeased to find that you are keeping secrets from me, secrets that are a potential threat to this court and the French court. Would you care to explain why you felt this was necessary?"

Stella spent the next few minutes explaining how she and Blue had found Olivia and Bree … "After months of helping them, they became more than just strangers we had rescued. The four of us became a family, and I felt a deep bond toward them. They became the daughters I knew I would never have. I thought about bringing Olivia to you, but I knew she wouldn't be suitable for court life.

"You have been nothing but kind to Blue and I in these last five years, and your subjects, for the most part, have been good to us as well. I consider many of the vampires here my friends. I am astute enough to realize that not being a vampire permits me to be relatively isolated from court politics, as no one here views me as a threat to their position.

"Olivia is sweet, fun, and courageous, but she is young and naïve and nowhere near ready to handle life at this court. If she lasted a week before getting herself killed, I would be surprised. That is why I kept everything from you, as I wasn't ready to send someone I view as my adopted daughter to her death. If there is to be fallout from this, then I beg of you, my queen, please punish me, not Olivia," finished Stella, who then knelt before Elizabeth again.

"Oh, get up, my little one. I am upset with you, but I cannot stay mad at you, as you well know. It is totally in your nature to take in strays. How can I be mad at you for something you cannot help doing? Besides, you have wormed your way into the hearts of too many of my loyal subjects, and I fear a coup if tried to punish you," laughed Elizabeth.

Stella got to her feet, and Elizabeth added in a serious tone, "That said, do not make a habit of this, understood?"

"Yes, Your Majesty," answered Stella somberly.

Elizabeth turned her attention to the male vampire at the base of her throne. "Charles, the Romanian ambassador has arrived and is in the parlor. Please attend to him, and I will be there when I am finished here."

"Very well, Your Majesty," he answered with a crisp English accent and headed for the door.

Elizabeth was silent until Charles left. As the heavy door closed, she said, "My time is short. How do you plan on dealing with the French court?"

"My first choice would be for you to offer Olivia and Bree your protection," answered Stella without hesitating.

"This cannot be done, unless Olivia is willing to swear fealty to me and come to court. As you have already said, she would be unsuited for that. I assume you have another proposal for us?"

"I know you have spies in the French court. Would you be willing to use one of them to reach out to Roman and make a deal on our behalf?"

"What do you have in mind?" asked Elizabeth.

"We plan on taking out Giselle. If we do this, it hands the throne to Roman. The deal we want is that, if we secure the throne for him, will he rescind the contract and leave us alone."

Elizabeth smiled. "Oh, little one, what a perfect solution. You have learned much in your five years of visiting us. Roman would be only too happy to make that deal, as he has no love for Giselle—and I get a troublesome and ambitious master off the French throne. I will arrange this and contact you when it is done. I must point out, though, that if you fail at this attempt, I will have to deny knowing anything about this, and you will be on your own. A war between the French and English courts is not something I can afford to start at this time."

"I understand, Your Majesty," said Stella.

"Is there anything else? I must get to the ambassador shortly."

"One small thing: Bree and Olivia need new IDs," added Stella with a sheepish smile.

"Very well. Sarah can arrange that. I will leave you now. Please do be careful; I would miss not having your company."

"I will try my best, Your Majesty, and thank you, Your Majesty," answered Stella.

Elizabeth smiled and nodded, then, to my absolute amazement, misted completely away. I had heard rumors that high-level vampires could do that, but I had always assumed it was people just mistaking the vampires' blinding speed for that ability. But Elizabeth actually transformed herself into mist ...

Chapter 24

Friday, February 16

Sarah's stoic and unsmiling face, with her deep, intimidating facial scar, suddenly blossomed into a joyous smile. She dashed forward, picked up Stella in a hug, and twirled her around.

Sarah leaned her mouth closer to Stella's ear and said, "Stella, I was beside myself with worry about you when you didn't answer Elizabeth's texts and phone calls."

"I survived that. Now, whether I survive your embrace is another matter," teased Stella.

"Oh sorry," said Sarah, who gently put Stella back on firm ground.

I have to add that between Elizabeth's unexpected warmth, lack of punishment for Stella and myself, and now with her top lieutenant hugging and fawning over Stella, my whole "serious and somber" vampire image was being shattered pretty hard.

Stella introduced Olivia and Bree to Sarah. Stella then turned toward me and said, "And this is Zack. He is the reason we are still alive. He saved us from our botched bounty attempt and paid for Bree and Olivia's healing. He opened his home to us to hide out in while Blue recovered, and he fended off a drow attack aimed at capturing Olivia. He saved us from Fire elemental and her team of assassins, who were after Olivia. We owe him a great debt."

Sarah nodded in approval. She leaned in, hugged me, and softly said, "Thank you for saving Stella and her friends." She stepped back and gave me another look, which was hungrier and more predatory. In a sultry tone, she asked, "You can control electricity with your powers, correct?"

I nodded, and she almost purred as she said, "I knew it; I could smell that ability on you when we hugged. I had relationship with a French Air elemental named Pierre back in the 1800s. Sex and feeding off him were amazing. My body would tingle for days afterward. If you have some time later, maybe I could thank you properly for saving my Stella?"

I was speechless—and torn. Sarah, in her black-leather form-fitting suit, was a dead ringer for that actress in those vampires vs. Werewolves movies who was just about every geek's wet dream. She was smoking hot, and I could feel my body reacting to her. On the other hand, the look she was giving me made me feel like I was the last piece of sushi at a sumo wrestler's convention, and that scared the crap out of me.

Olivia blurred between us. She put her hands on her hips, faced Sarah, and said, "Hey, grandma, if anyone is feeding off Zack, it is me. I called dibs on him first."

Sarah laughed at this. She licked her lips and said in a tone that dripped with sexuality, "We could share. Together, I'm sure we could both thank Zack properly that way ..."

An enticing image of Sarah and Olivia popped into my head, and I almost moaned.

Stella's small form stepped between them and said, "Sarah! Olivia! Knock it off!"

They both stared hard at each other for a few seconds. Sarah smiled and backed up a couple of steps, and Olivia moved closer to Bree again. Sarah gave me a playful wink and turned her attention to Stella again.

"Sarah, maybe we can get started on those IDs for Olivia and Bree?" said Stella, trying to redirect her vampire friend.

Sarah nodded. "Let's go to my office. I will take their pictures to get the process started."

Sarah led us from the chamber and questioned Blue, "Tell me, Blue: How did you get yourself injured? It's not like you to let someone get the drop on you."

"I underestimated my opponent's speed. The Earth elemental, in that rocky form, looked slow and ponderous. He caught me off guard with a quick right hook. I barely had time to lean back, so I didn't take the full brunt of it. Even that half-delivered punch was enough to knock me out of the fight. I won't ever make that mistake again."

It dawned on me that I knew only the bare basics about Blue's abilities. I decided to correct that oversight and asked, "Blue, I know you can shadow-travel, and that sword of yours is magically enhanced— or at least has some properties to it that are beyond a normal sword. Do you have any other abilities?"

"May I ask why you are asking?" replied Blue, giving me a wary look.

"We will probably be going into combat together. I already know Bree, Olivia, and Stella's abilities, but want to make sure that I am not missing any of yours in my planning."

184

Blue gave me a firm nod of approval. "I am faster and stronger than a normal human of my size would be, but not much better than a human athlete in their prime. I have better healing abilities than a human, and if I go into a healing trance, the process is even more effective. I can see equally well in the dark as I can in the light. My armor is like your Kevlar vests in that it will stop a projectile penetration but not the kinetic force behind it—though my armor is superior to Kevlar, as it can hold up against blades as well. I have trained in the art of the blade and unarmed combat my entire life. That training allows most moves to be muscle memory."

Sarah laughed and said, "Blue is being much too modest. She has beaten me a number of times when we have sparred, and I have trained for 400 years and have more speed and strength than she does."

I stumbled a bit when Sarah mentioned "400 years." By her aura, I'd estimated her age to be 250 years. My aura ability was always accurate, and it bothered me that I'd missed by that much.

Blue snorted and said, "Sarah is being too kind in her assessment. She only loses when playing the role of the aggressor and if she allows me to pick my terrain. In the open, and with me as the attacker, I would lose every time."

Sarah shrugged, and I took that moment to interject. "You have been a vampire for 400 years?"

Sarah smiled. "You know it is impolite to ask a lady her age? But since you asked, the number is closer to just over 500 years, actually. In my first century as a vampire, I played a much more subdued feminine roll than the current champion-of-the-court role I hold now."

Shit. My initial estimates of her age had been even more off than I had first thought. I knew Elizabeth's age was around 800 years old and her aura was, like, three feet. Therefore, if Sarah's aura radiated out a foot, then 250 years old should have been a pretty accurate guess. I knew that the power of a vampire's sire played into a vampire's power, and I speculated that maybe Elizabeth's sire had been exceptionally powerful, and Sarah's sire had been a weak vampire. But something felt off here.

"You seemed surprised at this. Can I ask why?" asked Sarah as she studied me.

"Without going into too much detail, one of my lessor abilities gives me information on an Enhanced Individual's power. I know Her Majesty's age is around 800 years old, and the reading I got off you put your power at just less than a third of that. Therefore, I estimated you at 250 years old. My ability is usually unerringly accurate. I have never been that far off before, and that has me concerned."

Sarah seemed amused at my dilemma as we entered her large, spacious office. The office was impressive; there was a grand wooden desk in the center of it that wouldn't have looked out of place at the White House. The desk had three large-screen monitors set up in a row on it. Tucked under the monitors were various turtle-themed items: a mug, painted shells, a small plushy, two small jade turtles, a small potted plant with turtle designs on the pot, and just about every turtle knickknack you could imagine. The was a large fish tank behind the desk, but it wasn't filled with water and instead had plants, sand, and two live turtles that were each about six inches in length.

"This is an impressive collection," I said, nodding to the swords, knives, daggers, axes, maces, spears, and polearms mounted to the walls. Judging by the quality of the pieces, there had been a lot of money spent.

Despite the instruments of death lining the walls, the office had a warm feel to it, and it was obvious that Sarah spent a good amount of time here.

Stella took one of the two chairs in front of the desk, and Blue made a gesture that I should take the other one, but I shook my head. She shrugged and took the other seat.

"Zack, since you were kind to my Stella, I will answer why your estimate was off. Be warned, though, that the next time I give information to you it won't be for free."

I nodded, and Sarah continued. "The 'master' title isn't just ceremonial; there is power connected to it too. Elizabeth, as master of the English court, pulls power from every vampire in her territory. She gets more from those who are sworn to her, of course, but any free vampire in her territory unknowingly gives her power as well. The amount of power Elizabeth gets is tiny, but when you take some from every vampire in Britain, Canada, and Australia, that adds up quickly."

"Shit." This would apply to Giselle as well. The French court covered all of France, Spain, Portugal, and Belgium, which meant that she would have a pretty good base of power to pull from.

Sarah took a digital camera from her desk. She walked over to the far wall, pulled down a plain white screen from the ceiling, and extended the screen to the floor. "Bree," she said, "if you could step over here in front of the screen, I will get your ID picture. Please hold still and don't smile."

Sarah snapped about five pictures. She studied the digital screen on the camera and made a satisfied nod. She called Olivia up next. Sarah repeated the process with Olivia; she frowned at first when viewing the pictures, but then nodded to herself, as one must have passed her requirements.

She placed the camera on the desk. "Stella, I do worry about you taking on Giselle. It won't be easy taking out a master. I would fight beside you, but I am sworn to the English court, so I can't get involved—for political reasons."

"I understand, Sarah. This is our fight, but I appreciate the sentiment. Any suggestions on how best to do this?" asked Stella.

"A high-explosive antitank rocket fired from a distance during the day—or, better yet, a nuclear bomb," laughed Sarah. She got somber after a few seconds and said, "Hit her at noon; that is when our kind is at their weakest. Please don't misunderstand that she will be easy to take out at noon, but it *will* be easier. Blue should be able to transport you all directly into her sleeping chamber, where she should be alone. Have Olivia try to enthrall each of you. If she can do that to any of you, leave that person at home. If *she* can enthrall you, then Giselle will be able to do it with ease, and you don't want to end up fighting one of your own. Bree, in her Were form, is safe from enthrallment, but if she reverts to human, Giselle will roll her mind. Zack, hit her with your electrical attack; that will prevent her from turning to mist and fleeing the room. If she escapes the room, get out of there. You have no chance beating her and her daytime forces combined."

The room was quiet for a few moments as we all considered the daunting task ahead. Stella changed the subject. She asked about Romeo and Juliet, which I soon realized were Sarah's two turtles in the tank behind her.

A few minutes later, we said our goodbyes to Sarah. As we were about to leave, she said she should have the new IDs ready for Bree and Olivia in the next couple of days. I was surprised that the IDs would take a couple of days, considering the resources of the English court, and I asked about it.

Sarah said, "The IDs will be done in a few hours; it is the decade's worth of background that takes the time. Posting and backdating things on social media, setting up fake-but-bulletproof references, ten years of tax returns, etc. The IDs are easy. It is the history that takes time."

I nodded, and Stella thanked her for her time. Blue opened a shadow portal in the corner of Sarah's office, and we all stepped through and return to the lab.

Chapter 25

Friday, February 16

I dashed from the shadows and managed to reach the Food-O-Tron seconds before Bree. She glared at me as I adjusted the switches to order a Coke. I smiled at her and pulled the lever.

She growled and said, "Thought you'd be smarter than to get between a hungry Were and her food."

"I'll risk it. I'm just grabbing a Coke, and then it is all yours."

The machine dinged. I grabbed my hard-won Coke and left Bree to it. I joined the rest of the crew at the table. We talked for a bit about how well the visit had gone with Elizabeth and kicked around a few strategies for how to take on Giselle. We came up with a short list of supplies that would be helpful in the upcoming battle, and Blue said she would procure the items on the list tomorrow.

In the end, we were in a holding pattern: Until Elizabeth got Roman's agreement to the deal, we couldn't go after Giselle.

Bree joined us at the table a good ten minutes later. She was carrying a Coke and two cast-iron pans that each had a dozen donuts. She graciously put the first pan between Stella, Blue, and myself, but kept the second one for herself. A dozen donuts was much less food than usual for Bree; she had probably finished a meal while waiting for all this stuff to replicate. Olivia blurred over to the machine to order herself a glass of blood.

Sir Reginald's mad-scientist laboratory was an incredible feat of engineering, but it lacked things to do: no internet, no TV, and no computers. The problem was there were no modern outlets to plug anything into. I found out that Stella had three lithium-ion batteries for her cellphone. She left one recharging at the English court and kept a spare one here at the lab.

The interdimensional portal certainly didn't lack for power. I wondered if we could add a couple of invertors to the power here—converting DC to AC—and get some regular power outlets installed. Then it dawned on me that by wanting to make changes to this lab, I was already thinking we would be a team going forward. I looked around the table. Stella and Blue were conversing deeply, no doubt discussing strategies and ideas for our upcoming fight. Bree was happily munching down donuts, and Olivia was pacing back and forth anxiously, waiting for the Food-O-Tron to spit out her drink. I had to admit that I enjoyed being in their company, and I had truly begun to deeply care for this wonderful group.

I had been on my own for sixteen years and never thought it would be anyone but me. My deepest desire was to start a family. I'd pictured myself with a wife, a couple of kids, and maybe a cat or a dog—but it would have still been just me going out to take on bounties. Here, I had an opportunity to take on four more capable partners and gain a family. Sure, this family wasn't how I'd imagined it would be, but in this day and age of families with two moms or two dads, did it really matter? The four of them loved and looked out for each other; any of them would willingly lay down their lives to protect the others. As far as any of them were concerned, they were family, and that is just what you did for family. I longed for those types of connections, and I would be honored to be a part of their family.

I decided to keep my decision to partner up with them to myself. There was still the small matter of taking on the master of the French vampire court in her lair, and if we survived, there was still the other small matter of Roman lifting the contract to deal with.

Olivia pulled me from my musings as she returned to the table with her half-empty glass of sustenance.

"Cards?" she asked the table.

Bree and Stella nodded. Olivia was gone and returned in less than five seconds, holding two full decks of cards in her hand. I swore that I would never get used to that vampire speed of hers.

I found out that playing cards was the main way the ladies relaxed and killed time around here. We ended up playing cards until about 2:00 a.m. London time, and then Stella, Blue, and I needed sleep and turned in for the night. Bree stayed up to keep Olivia company.

The next morning after brunch, Blue went out to grab the list of supplies we would need.

She returned carrying a large army-green-colored case and put it on the table. The case had, stenciled in yellow letters, the words "M67 Grenades." She opened the case, and there were twelve green tennis-ball-sized grenades neatly laid out.

"Are these what you wanted?" asked Blue

I nodded, and she closed the case. Blue then transported me to a gas station so I could fill a red plastic jerry can with gas, then we popped back to the lab. The gas was to make a Molotov cocktail; the rest of the ingredients and items we needed for that, I could scrounge up around the lab.

Blue, using the shadows, had spied on the French court and had found Giselle's daytime resting place. Our basic strategy was that Blue would open a portal to Giselle's lair. In the center of the sparely furnished room, there was a stone sarcophagus. We would toss in the grenades, which would hopefully be enough to destroy or damage it and stun Giselle, and then toss the Molotov cocktail. If we got lucky, she would be trapped under the debris from the sarcophagus and burn to death. Worst-case scenario was that the burning fire in the center of the room would be an obstacle she would have to maneuver around and not come straight at us as we entered. I don't care who you are—a bunch of grenades and a Molotov cocktail being tossed on you is going to be a crappy start to your day.

"Zack?" prompted Stella. "Blue and I were discussing Giselle. Blue suggested that after dinner, we get Olivia to try and mind-roll each of us, like Sarah suggested. Once we have determined who is resistant, we can start training on taking down Giselle. As we are attacking her at noon and Olivia won't be available, we will get Olivia to play Giselle during the training. Thoughts?"

The training suggestion brought an idea to mind. "I think both ideas are worth exploring. Blue, is Giselle's resting chamber smaller than the hangar out back?"

"Yes, it is probably double, if not triple, the size of her chamber. Why?"

"I was thinking that on the floor of the hangar, we could spray-paint the outline of the chamber, mark out where the access door and the stone sarcophagus are, and use that as our training area."

Blue nodded in approval. "Good idea—get us all used to fighting in a more enclosed space and how to deal with a vampire a small, confined area. I do not believe we have any spray paint in the lab, though."

"Not a problem. Just transport me to a Canadian Tire, and I will pick up a few cans."

"I will clean out of the center of the hangar while you two are gone," added Stella, who headed to the north corridor.

Blue took me to a Canadian Tire in Whitby. She warped us in around back of the store. I hadn't been to Whitby before, but it was odd how many Canadian cities looked the same. The corporate chain stores just seemed to dominate the landscape. The order might change—the Subway before the Staples, or a Ford dealership on the opposite side of the street—but it felt sometimes like they just cloned a main street in one city and dumped those same stores everywhere else.

The plus side to this was that even when you were in a new city, it was easy to find what you were looking for. Want a burger? Just find where the Harvey's, McDonald's, or Wendy's was on the main drag, and you were good to go. Or in my case, need spray paint? Just find a Canadian Tire or a Home Depot, and presto! Shopping adventure done. The downside, of course, was that cities and towns lost their character and charm, as they all looked the same.

I did light up when I saw there was Popeye's Chicken right beside the Canadian Tire. I loved their spicy breaded-chicken sandwich. I hurried into Canadian Tire and grabbed my spray paint, as Blue would be returning in twenty minutes …

It took twenty-two minutes for me to get the paint and my chicken sandwich and fries, but thankfully, Blue was kind enough to wait for me.

She cocked an eyebrow at me. "I thought you were just getting paint?"

"I couldn't resist adding another meal to the Food-O-Tron. Trust me: You will thank me for this later. Speaking of which, let's get going. My wonderful bag of chicken goodness isn't getting any hotter."

She sighed but grabbed my hand, and moments later, we were back in the lab. I handed off the paint to her and dashed for the Food-O-Tron. I grabbed a cast-iron pan and started the process of programming the machine.

Blue was finishing off marking the corners of the outline of Giselle's lair with the spray paint by the time I joined them. The door was marked, as were the four corners of the sarcophagus.

Stella and I just stood there and watched Blue paint her lines to connect her marks together. She did the door and sarcophagus sections in neon green to make them stand out from the wall. The air filled with a chemical paint smell that was a bit overwhelming. I converted the air directly around me to get rid of the smell. I wondered how good the lab's ventilation was. It occurred to me then that with the exits to the surface blocked, any ventilation pipes should have been blocked as well. Obviously, that wasn't the case, as we were all still breathing, but it got me wondering. The only explanation was that somewhere around the lab was some sort of oxygen-reclaiming machine.

An oxygen machine made sense, as I was sure the ventilation pipes would have been blocked by now. The problem I had now was that if the machine malfunctioned, I would be spending a good chunk of my day using my powers to convert carbon dioxide into oxygen so we didn't suffocate to death. I made a mental note to find an air-monitoring device that would set off an alarm if oxygen levels dropped below a certain amount. As amazing as this lab was, it was quickly dawning on me that there were several unpleasant ways to die down here.

Stella rubbed her temples and said, "The paint needs to dry, and those fumes are giving me a headache. Shall we retire to the main chamber?"

I nodded, but truth be told, I didn't think moving to another room would make that much difference.

We entered the north corridor and headed for the main chamber. To my amazement, midway down the corridor, the paint smell was gone. The ramifications of this really blew my mind; it meant that Sir Reginald had set up different ventilation systems for different parts of the lab. It actually made more sense this way—multiple smaller machines versus one big one. The multiple machines gave the whole system built-in redundancy.

As I said before, Sir Reginald was a scumbag of a human being, but I couldn't fault his scientific genius.

We sat at one of the tables and chatted about training for a bit, but until Olivia and Bree were up, we really didn't have much to do. I had no idea how long it would take Elizabeth to get Roman to agree to our terms and figured I'd have a lot of free time on my hands. I would have loved to use this lull period to build a couple of model planes. I kicked around getting Blue to shadow-travel us to my basement so I could grab my modelling supplies, but it was too risky.

In the end, I asked Blue to portal me to a mall in Ottawa, so I could grab some books to help kill time. I picked a bunch of books, but then my nose caught the aromas coming from the food court, and I checked it out, figuring I might find a few new items to add to the Food-O-Tron. There was a cheesesteak place, and I couldn't resist. Five minutes later, I was standing in a remote area outside the mall with a steaming cheesesteak and freshly made lemonade in hand, praying Blue would show up soon while the sandwich was still hot.

A minute later she arrived, and I was soon back at the lab adding both the cheesesteak and the lemonade to the Food-O-Tron. I managed to convince Blue to take me back and forth to the mall four more times. On the first three trips, I grabbed a cheeseburger with BBQ sauce and grilled onions, a shrimp Pad Thai, and an Arby's roast beef sandwich with curly fries. On the fourth trip, Blue told me to make it count, as she was done dropping me off and picking me up, so on that last trip, I went with half a dozen large cinnamon buns.

Bree was up when we returned and was sitting at one of the four tables eating something from a cast-iron pan. She was wearing comfy grey sweat pants with a matching grey top. She must have showered just before joining us, because her short blondish hair was still damp.

Her head shot up, and she turned around. "Do I smell cinnamon buns?"

It had taken less than five seconds from when we'd exited the shadows for her Were nose to pick up the scent; a part of me couldn't help but be amazed.

"Yup, just going to add them to Food-O-Tron." I then asked, "What are you eating?"

"Shepard's pie. Once you have added the cinnamon buns, it would be a good idea for you to test that they were added correctly and make a batch."

I smiled and headed for Food-O-Tron. I scooped the still-warm Cinnabons from the box and placed them in a cast-iron pan, then put the pan in the main food hatch. I adjusted the switches to a new number and pulled the main lever up to add them. The machine chugged to life.

It would take a couple of minutes, so I stepped back into the lab and told Bree about the other items I had added.

Her face lit up like a kid on Christmas Day, and she said, "Oh God, the Food-O-Tron has dishes with *fries*! Thank you, thank you, thank you! How many babies do I owe you now? Two, I think? Hold off on the cinnamon buns for now. I'll take the cheeseburger with fries first ..."

Chapter 26

Saturday, February 17

When the sun went down that evening, our resident creature of the night rose from her deathly slumber and graced us with her presence. And by "graced," I mean Olivia grunted at us as she walked by the table and headed directly for the Food-O-Tron to order a pint of wake-up juice.

Her outfit for the evening had more than caught my attention. Gone was the long, gothic-looking black wedding dress, and in its place was a white cotton crop top with no bra and pair of black yoga pants that looked almost painted on. If those pants had been on a guy, I could probably have made an excellent guess at what religion he practiced.

Bree cleared her throat and said, "Zack, close your mouth and stop staring at the underdressed vampire."

"Hey, you had your dessert tonight; let me enjoy mine, okay?"

"Pig," sighed Bree.

I reluctantly turned my attention back to the table. "No, if I was being a pig, I would suggest we adopt her outfit as our official company uniform," I said with a leering grin.

Bree smiled at this, which surprised me. I figured I would get another "Pig" comment—or at least a punch.

"I'm not sure a halter top and yoga pants would be a good look for you, Zack," said Bree, eying me as if picturing me in that outfit.

"I'm pretty sure if you saw the pasty white skin of my expanding belly hanging out, it might be the one thing on this planet that could actually suppress that voracious Were appetite of yours."

Stella giggled at that. She laughed even harder when Olivia said, "If you like, Zack, I could take them off right now, and you could put them on to test that theory of yours."

I'd forgotten about her enhanced vampire hearing and realized that she had caught my entire conversation with Bree. I felt a bit of heat come to my cheeks at this.

Olivia walked around the table and sat across from me. She straightened her shoulders, which pulled my attention to her nipples outlined clearly in the thin white material. She winked at me while taking an amused sip from her glass. This brought even more heat to my cheeks, and I quickly looked away.

Bree and Stella were amused at my discomfort, but they lost it when a slightly confused Blue asked, "Do all human males go that shade of red when they are aroused?"

Olivia almost spit out the mouthful of blood, but thankfully managed to swallow it before she burst out laughing with Bree and Stella.

I covered my eyes with my hand, rubbed my temples, and said, "It is a common trait that all humans have when they are embarrassed."

"Oh. My apologies. I just assumed with your obvious sexual interest in Olivia—"

"Blue, please stop. It is possible that someone can faint from embarrassment, too, and if you continue, I might demonstrate that."

Blue shrugged. "Very well, Zack, I shall let the matter drop in concern for your physical safety."

It took another long minute for the three ladies to compose themselves and for a sense of decorum to return to the table. I swear, at one point Bree was laughing so hard I thought she was going to pee herself.

As awkward as it was being the center of their amusement, it was good to see and hear them enjoying themselves. In the upcoming battle with Giselle, I honestly wasn't sure if we would survive or not. Better they laugh and live a bit, than brood about it.

After Olivia finished her breakfast, Stella brought up the mind-testing idea to her. Olivia seemed reluctant at first, but in the end agreed to do it. I volunteered to go first.

I stared into Olivia's piercing green eyes, and a look of intense concentration fell across her features. I swear her eyes glowed for a moment, and she said, "Zack, you are under my thrall and will cluck like a chicken."

I smiled at this request, but the smile faded as the pain in my head increased. Thankfully, it was more a dull ache then the icepick-like pain that Benny from EIRT had brought on.

"You will cluck for me," said Olivia in a firm tone.

"Go cluck yourself; that is not happening."

The pressure went away, and Olivia shook her head. "I hit him with everything I had, and he was immune to it."

"Zack, did you have any urge to follow her command?" asked Stella.

I shook my head. "None, but there was a dull pain in my head, and I am not sure, if Giselle did the same thing, how much the pain would increase."

Stella seemed to consider this. "Well, the important thing is she won't be able to control you and use your powers against us. If you avoid eye contact, then you should be fine. Bree, do you want to go next?"

Bree nodded and turned in her seat beside me to face Olivia directly.

Olivia smiled at Bree. "You will cluck for me, minion!"

Bree almost instantly began making chicken noises. I found this both amusing and frightening at the same time. It was scary how quickly Olivia had dropped Bree under her control. I could imagine Giselle doing the same thing, except changing it to "You will kill your friends." That realization made the humor of the situation vanish instantly.

Olivia turned her gaze away from Bree. Bree shook her head like she was trying to clear her mind and said, "I don't remember what just happened. I assume I was clucking around?"

Olivia had a look of sadness and shame on her face. "I'm sorry, Bree. I would never use that power on you ..."

"I know, Liv. You did good. We needed to test this, okay?"

Olivia nodded, and Stella spoke up. "We will have Olivia test you again when you are in Were form, but as we are training for the assault on Giselle after this and you'll need to be in Were form for that, we will wait until she has tested Blue and myself."

Blue volunteered to go next and turned her seat to face Olivia. I cursed to myself as Blue shortly began clucking. I had been hoping that her alien nature would mean she was immune. Olivia released Blue from her mental thrall.

"That is unfortunate. It seems I will not be able to directly participate in the upcoming battle. All is not lost, however. I may be able to strike from the shadows without actually entering the room."

The idea that she could strike with her sword if Giselle got close enough to a shadow in the room cheered me up; it might be enough of a surprise that it could turn the battle in our favor. Blue not being in the chamber also relieved another concern I had: She was our only way in or out of the place, and if she got hurt or killed in the fight, we had no escape. Under that scenario, even if we defeated Giselle, we would probably be killed by her daytime security force.

It was Stella's turn next. Olivia rolled Stella almost instantly. Hearing Stella clucking in her proper English accent was hysterically funny. Bree and I ended up losing it in a fit of laughter. Olivia lost her concentration, too, as she too began chuckling. Stella stopped clucking and looked at the three of us like we had lost our minds.

She asked what we were laughing at, and Bree managed to calm down enough to tell her.

"It is not my fault you philistines have butchered the language so badly you find the Queen's English amusing," said Stella with indignation, but the corners of her mouth tugged up in amusement.

When we all recovered, Stella added, "Well, it seems I am susceptible to Olivia's mental suggestions. Shall we try it again when I am in my Hyde form? I would suggest that you ask me to do something other than clucking. I doubt my Hyde form can make that noise."

Olivia nodded, and in less than second, Stella had switched into her monstrous alter ego. Hyde looked at Olivia and made a low grunt.

"You are in my thrall. Flap your arms like a chicken," ordered Olivia with a slight glow to her eyes.

Nothing happened for a few seconds, and then Stella shook her head side to side in a distinct "no" gesture.

Stella's Hyde form being immune to vampire mind-rolling was a huge relief to me. If it was just Bree and I going in to attack Giselle, I doubted our chances. Adding the insane strength and durability of Stella's Hyde form gave us a much better chance.

"Should I try again?" asked Olivia, looking for direction.

Stella's Hyde form just shrugged, as if to say, "Why not?"

Olivia did her Jedi mind trick again on Stella, but this time directed her to dance. Thankfully, the same result happened, and Stella didn't do as directed.

I blinked, and Stella was back in her harmless-looking ten-year-old body with her dated white dress and polished black shoes.

"I clearly heard Olivia's command, and there was a slight tingling feeling at the edges of my mind, but at no point did my Hyde persona have any urge to follow those directions. Whether Giselle is powerful enough to override that protection or not, we will have to see. I suspect that she won't be able to. Bree, can you change into your hybrid form now? I want to confirm that you are immune, as Sarah suggested. You can remain in that form. After this, we will proceed to the hangar and begin our training."

Out of the corner of my eye, Bree nodded and began lifting the grey hoodie over her head.

"Do you want me to wait in the hangar?" I asked as Bree lost the sweatshirt and exposed the black sports bra she was wearing underneath it.

She shook her head. "We will be fighting together, and I need to get naked to change—and end up naked when I change back. I need to get over this. You have already seen me naked, which means this is nothing you haven't seen before anyway. Now, that said, this isn't easy for me, so try not to be a dick about it, okay?"

I nodded in response. Bree took a deep breath and yanked down the sweatpants and her underwear in one quick motion. I turned my head to give her privacy out of reflex.

"Look at me, Zack. Let's get this out of the way, okay?" insisted Bree.

I turned back as she was lifting the sports bra over her head, and in a few moments, she was standing completely nude in front of me. She gave me a tentative smile, and I gave her a small supportive nod in return. This felt really awkward. This was a big deal to her, and I was trying to behave myself and not be a total pervert about it, but despite that, my body was reacting to the sight in front of me. Thankfully, Bree stepped away from the table, and moments later, her body began to tremble slightly as she underwent her change. Her limbs and fingers extended, and the dark fur began to sprout across her pale skin. I cringed as I heard bones popping and snapping as she continued.

In less than fifteen seconds, Bree's human form was gone, and in its place stood a lethal feline killing machine. She moved closer to the table, and her blue cat's eyes stared at Olivia in challenge.

Olivia wasted no time. "You are under my command. Dance for me!"

A low, menacing growl erupted from Bree's Werepanther form just after that, but she didn't move or dance. It seemed that Sarah had been correct: Bree in Were form was immune from Olivia's mind-control powers.

"I think that confirms what we were told," said Blue. "Stella, please change again, and we will head to the hangar to practice."

Stella nodded, and in an instant, she switched forms. With Bree's well-muscled six-and-a-half-foot-tall deadly form on one side of me and Stella's giant seven-foot-plus Hyde form on the other, I was feeling quite small and vulnerable at that moment.

Blue turned and headed for the north corridor, and Stella's large, ponderous frame lurched after her. Olivia fell in beside Stella, which made an odd contrast between her vampire grace and Stella's stomping gait as they walked. I followed them and felt Bree's hot breath on my neck as she followed closely behind me.

There was only a faint trace of the overwhelming paint smell that had been here earlier.

Blue wasted no time and gathered us over to the southeast corner of the painted outline of Giselle's chamber. "Zack, your plan was to toss in a number of grenades through the shadow portal to hopefully kill, disable, or stun Giselle. I will close the portal for three seconds, preventing us from getting caught in the blast. You, at that point, light the Molotov cocktail, and when I open the portal again, you toss it through. Once again, I will close the portal for a couple of seconds to stop any of the blast or flames from reaching us."

Blue paused to let that sink in. "The lights in the chamber are located on the center of each of the four walls; this puts the shadowed areas in the corners. The flames will probably remove the shadows in the southwest corner where we have been tossing things through. I will open a portal to the southeast corner. At this point, we will send Stella through, followed by Bree, and then you last. Stella, when you go in, move to your right and head for Giselle. Bree, you go left but hang back and protect Zack. Zack, step through, and as soon as you see Giselle, hit her with lightning to disrupt her mist ability. Stella, at this point you close in on Giselle and hit her with everything you have."

The three of us nodded in understanding, and Blue continued. "Olivia, for these exercises, you will be playing Giselle. Go inside the room and stand near the coffin in the center. Zack, use your lowest setting on the lightning, and for these exercises, a touch will be considered a full knockout hit. We don't need anyone seriously hurt, so Olivia, Bree, and Stella, remember to pull your punches. Any questions or concerns?"

I kicked around what she had outlined. "One question: If there is a full-fledge fire burning in the room, that will change the visibility and how we are able to get around the room. Should we put something in there to represent this?"

Blue agreed, and she had Stella's Hyde form follow her out of the room. They returned a minute later carrying 3 four-foot-wide floor-to-ceiling wooden bookcases. Blue arranged them in the southwest area of the room in a roughly triangular shape and said the area inside the shelves was the fire.

With everything in place, we ran our first training drill and tried to take Olivia down.

The first thing I learned was that my electrical attacks messed with Olivia's superhuman speed; while she was being hit, she could only run as fast as a normal person. As Stella moved towards her, Olivia ran to the left, and I was able to keep hitting her with the electricity until she slipped behind one of the bookshelves. A moment later, she blurred away and appeared beside me, and said, "Bang! You're dead," as she placed her hand on the back of my neck.

Blue called an end to the exercise, and we discussed how to do things differently. We decided that there was no point in Bree hanging back to protect me, as Olivia's speed was too great to intercept before she killed me. I suggested that I could thicken the air around me, like I had done at the cabin and the motel to stop the bullets. That should be enough that I could move away from Olivia before she killed me. I could then hit her with electricity again, slowing her down, which would allow Bree and Stella to attack her again.

Before restarting the fight, Blue moved the bookshelves more apart so they took up more room. Once she was done, she said, "I am going to change these each time, so they are never the same way twice. We are throwing in liquid fire, which makes the shape hard to predict, and this will be a good way to make everyone adjust on the fly."

The second mock attack went better, as Olivia didn't kill me right away, and Stella actually managed to grab her. That counted as a kill.

Olivia whined at this and argued, "There is no way Stella could kill me in one shot. We have sparred and trained together, and I have taken hits from her before and shrugged them off. Unless you stake or decapitate Giselle, she is not going down in one shot."

Olivia had a good point, and I realized that we should all have wooden stakes. We made a note to make some for tomorrow, but in the meantime, Blue warped the two of us out to a Canadian Tire. I bought a couple of foam pool noodles. We brought them back and cut them down. The new rule was that if we stabbed Olivia in the chest with one of our "stakes," that counted as a kill.

The next round went terribly for us. Olivia tagged all of us without us hitting her with a stake. Blue broke the round down, showing where each of us had made mistakes. She adjusted the bookshelves representing the fire in the chamber and simply said, "Again."

The next round went a little better, as Stella and I were taken out by Olivia, but Bree managed to stab Olivia with her foam stake.

After Blue had reviewed the round and adjusted the "fire" again, I said, "Blue, before we go again, can I try a small experiment with Olivia?"

She nodded, and I asked, "Olivia, does the electrical attack hurt you at all?"

Olivia shook her head. "It tingles and messes with my speed, but it doesn't hurt."

"Do you mind if I try upping the power a bit and see what happens?"

Olivia shrugged, and Blue said, "You are trying to determine if the electrical attack can do more than just disrupt the mist and speed abilities of a vampire?"

I nodded. "I am barely using a hundredth of what I can do. I want to up it to 10 percent of my power and see how that works."

Olivia agreed and stood in the center of the room. I zapped her with a more powerful burst.

I hit her for a few seconds and then stopped. "Well?"

"There was a little discomfort, and the tingling sensation was much stronger, but other than that, I was fine."

"Can I try again with a higher amount?"

Olivia agreed, and this time I hit her with about 20 percent of a full charge for a few seconds. This got her gritting her teeth, and she visibly showed a bit of discomfort.

"Okay, that hurt a bit—not overwhelming pain but certainly not a pleasant feeling. It really stung where you made contact," said Olivia, idly rubbing her stomach.

"How much did you hit her with?" asked Blue.

"About 20 percent of a full charge."

"Olivia, can he try again with a higher blast?" asked Blue.

Olivia sighed but nodded and braced herself. This time, I spent a moment gathering some power and hit her with about 40 percent of what I could do.

"FUCK!" screamed Olivia. She twitched as the shimmering light-blue arc of electricity sparked into her.

I stopped after a few seconds, and Olivia glared at me with murder in her eyes. This time, there was a noticeable black mark on her tummy where I had hit her. My concern grew due to her fangs being fully descended, and I was pretty sure she was more than just a touch pissed off at this moment.

"Olivia, hit the Food-O-Tron and get some refreshment, okay?" said Blue.

Olivia stayed focused on me for a few long seconds, but then dropped her intense gaze a moment later and nodded. She blurred out and was gone from the room a second later.

"Thoughts?" asked Blue.

"That certainly had an effect on her, but not as much I'd hoped. If Olivia can take that and still be standing, I suspect that would be the same effect as if I hit Giselle with 100 percent. The problem is, if I use the full power, I cannot shield myself at the same time. If I try that and Giselle breaks free, she will kill me in less than a second. The other problem is that I can't keep up that level of power for too long, and anyone touching Giselle is going to get shocked too."

"You were hoping that hitting her with a full blast would knock her out, and then we could just stake her and finish her off?" asked Blue.

I nodded, and we discussed some different ideas and strategies until Olivia returned. I was pleased that she was back to her usual perky self and the mark on her stomach was gone. She took her place back in the center of the fake chamber, and we tried again.

Over the next three hours, I lost count of how many times we ran the drill, but it was a bunch, and I was bone-tired by the time Blue said we had done enough for the night. Bree and Stella changed back to their human forms, and as a group, we headed for the main chamber. I was surprised upon entering the chamber that Bree didn't head for her clothes, but instead walked her naked ass directly to the Food-O-Tron. I probably shouldn't have been shocked that she chose food over modesty.

About thirty seconds later, she came back to the room. "My food is being prepared. No one even think about poaching it," she warned in a deadly serious tone. She grabbed her clothes off the table and started getting dressed. Just as she put on the last piece of clothing, the Food-O-Tron dinged, and she was gone. Bree returned with a familiar cast-iron pan, and inside was a Philly cheesesteak and fries.

Stella and Blue excused themselves and said they were going to bed. We wished them good night as they left the main chamber.

"Now that the machine is free, I am going to make myself a pick-me-up," announced Olivia.

"It is currently making me a lemonade to go with my sandwich," said Bree after happily swallowing a huge bit of cheesesteak.

"Okay. Zack, can I get you anything?" asked Olivia.

"A lemonade would be nice, thank you, Liv ... I mean *Olivia*," I corrected, as I remembered that Olivia only let Bree call her Liv.

Olivia smiled. "You can call me Liv if you want."

The Food-O-Tron dinged, and before I could reply to Olivia, she had blurred off. I was touched that she was okay with me calling her Liv.

"So, what did you think?" asked Bree between bites.

"I think you have nothing to worry about. You look amazing naked," I said with a smile.

I heard Olivia laugh at that from out in the corridor. Bree sighed and said, "Not that, you dick. I was talking about the training exercises."

"Honestly, I think we are screwed. Out of all the times we ran the scenario this evening, only once did we pull off a complete victory where we took out Giselle and nobody got tagged. On the other hand, we might get lucky, as we aren't simulating what damage the grenades do, and we're only outlining where the fire is but not what damage it could do as well. We might come through the shadow portal and find Giselle incapacitated; we might just be able to walk directly up to her and drive a stake through her black heart without an issue."

Bree was about to reply, but Olivia was suddenly there and put a tall glass of lemonade in front of each of us. Before either of us could thank her, she was gone again.

"I'm never going to get used to that vampire speed," I mumbled under my breath as I took a sip from my glass.

Bree raised her glass at me in agreement and took her own sip. She swallowed and said, "Don't forget that in these scenarios, Olivia knows we are coming and is ready for us. Giselle won't be expecting to be attacked in her own chamber. That element of surprise could make a huge difference."

"I agree, but it probably offsets the fact that Olivia isn't as powerful as Giselle. I think scenarios are pretty fair as they stand."

Olivia joined us at the table with a half-empty pint mug of blood. "At least you guys get to fight; the contract is my fault, and I can't even help in the attack."

I could tell she was bothered by this. I tried to cheer her up. "Liv, you are helping with these training scenarios. You even let me fry you with lightning just to test a theory. I'd love to have you there, but we have to attack during the day, when Giselle is at her weakest. You would fight for Bree or any of the others, so let them do this for you, okay?"

"Still sucks," said Liv with a frown.

Bree reached out, put her arm around Olivia, and gave her a supportive hug. I really did feel for Olivia; I knew it would drive me insane to have my friends risk their lives on my behalf. If we failed, Olivia would still be wanted and would have lost her best friends in the process.

To distract Olivia, I said, "Hey, I'm too tired to think about anything else, but too keyed up to sleep. Anyone up for some cards?"

Olivia perked right up at this and blurred out to grab the playing cards from her room. Bree glanced over to me and gave me an approving nod, as she knew exactly what I had done. Olivia was a bright girl, but thankfully, she was easily distracted. There were times I could almost hear her mind going "Ooooh, shiny" as her attention was pulled away to something new.

Liv returned, dealt out three hands, and we lost ourselves in cards for the next couple of hours. After that, I called it a night and went to bed.

Chapter 27

Sunday, February 18

The next morning, I was up at about 10:00 a.m. and hit the Food-O-Tron for breakfast. The lack of breakfast items on the menu was a bit annoying. There was only one breakfast listed: bacon, sausages, eggs, toast, hash browns, and fried tomatoes. Don't get me wrong, it was good, but if I ate it for breakfast every day, it was going to take a lot more wind power to lift my fat ass through the air going forward.

I punched in the code for Sir Reginald's jumbo breakfast. While I waited for the Food-O-Tron, I pondered the different options I could add: cereal and a yogurt/granola bowl were the first two ideas. An A&W Bacon-and-Egger sandwich popped into my head, and I immediately thought, *Oh yeah, I have to add that*. Granted, it wasn't exactly low-calorie, either, but it was less calories than what I was currently making.

The machine dinged, and I floated my ginormous breakfast over to the table to join Blue and Stella. Stella was currently having tea, and Blue was finishing one of the same super breakfasts.

After breakfast, Blue reminded me that we needed to go get supplies for making wooden stakes.

"Actually, speaking of traveling, I do have a favor to ask?" I said with a hopeful smile.

"By your demeanor, I am guessing you wish to travel somewhere for another food item to add to the machine?" she answered in a slightly disapproving tone.

"Hey, don't be like that. You enjoyed the spicy chicken I added yesterday."

"True. It was enjoyable to have a spicy dish on the recipe list to choose from. What are you adding today?" asked Blue.

I mentioned the A&W's Bacon and Egger and got blank stares in return. I said, "It is a poached egg with bacon and cheese on a bun."

Stella rolled her eyes. "What is it with Americans and their need to turn everything into a hamburger-style meal?"

Part of me bristled at being called "American." I was Canadian; Americans were our gun-toting neighbors to the south. On the other hand, A&W had probably started as an American chain first. It might have been an American who had invented the warm, melty joy that was the Bacon and Egger.

"Americans—and Canadians—are slaves to the clock and, on average, work more than anyone else in the Western world. As a consequence of this, we are always pressed for time. I believe the quest to turn everything into a hamburger isn't an entirely accurate description. What we want is the ability to eat any food one-handed while driving or walking. This breakfast, for instance, would not be a good meal to eat in a moving vehicle, whereas the Bacon and Egger can easily be consumed with one hand."

"Ah yes, far be it for you heathens to do something civilized like sit down and enjoy the pleasures of leisurely meal. This, of course, explains your ungodly preference for coffee"—Stella shuddered and continued on her rant—"over the far superior beverage of tea!"

I laughed. "Ah yes, the English: masters of the dining experience, with such delightful dishes as toad-in-the-hole, bangers and mash, bacon roly-poly, bubble and squeak, and blood pudding. The same culture that believes beef should only be cooked one way: well-done until it resembles shoe leather. I think the only reason England took over India was to add some real food dishes to their boring and bland menus."

Stella giggled and conveniently changed the topic. "When you are out buying stakes today, try and find something bigger and larger for my Hyde form. I'm afraid if you buy a normal-size one, I will snap it like a toothpick."

We chatted about more mundane things, and after breakfast, I hit the shower. Sir Reginald's gravity-fed shower was okay, but I really missed the water pressure and almost-scalding-hot showers at my own house. After shaving, brushing my teeth, and the rest of my usual morning bathroom routine, I got dressed and went and found Blue.

I managed to convince her to take me to a twenty-four-hour A&W in Woodstock, Ontario, where I bought two Bacon and Eggers and a large orange juice. Blue had me back to the lab in short order, and I added my two Bacon and Eggers to the Food-O-Tron. With Bree being the main user of the Food-O-Tron, I went with two versus one to save her some time. I poured the orange juice into a pint mug and added it to the Food-O-Tron as well.

A short time later, we emerged from the shadows in Newfoundland into a gusty grey winter's day. It wasn't currently snowing, but the wind was fierce, and judging by the dark clouds on the horizon, the snow was coming soon.

Blue shivered. "How much time did you need?"

"Thirty minutes," I said, and an instant later, she was gone.

I was really getting the feeling that Blue, like Stella, wasn't a fan of Canadian winter weather—for some unknown reason.

I entered the orange-themed store. It took me no time to find a couple of nice five-foot-long-by-inch-and-a-half-diameter wooden dowels that would be perfect for making stakes. It took me a while longer to find something suitable for Stella's Hyde form. I ended up going with a pine table leg that was four inches in diameter and thirty-four inches long. I grabbed a handsaw and two utility knives and made my way to the register.

I stepped out from the store, and the snow began falling. By the time I made it to the back of the store, there was a whiteout. The fierce storm cut visibility down to less than ten feet, which meant there was less chance of anyone noticing Blue or myself. I found the spot I'd arrived at and just enjoyed the storm while I waited for Blue to arrive.

Blue popped in and barely stepped out of the shadows before grabbing me and yanking me back to the lab. I brushed the snow out of my hair and made my way over to the table where Stella was sitting. I laid out my purchases for her inspection. She picked up the heavy table leg in her small hands and nodded approvingly.

I had started taking the cardboard labeling off the handsaw when Blue said, "Why did you bother with the saw and the knives?"

"To cut the wood and sharpen points on them?" I said in a sarcastic tone, thinking the purpose was obvious.

Blue shook her head and picked up the two dowels and the table leg. She moved over to the far table with all the discarded gears and metal parts on it. She picked up one of the dowels and secured it in the sturdy hand clamp that was bolted to the edge of the table.

She turned to me. "So, about one and half feet long?"

I nodded, and she drew her sword. She studied the dowel for a moment and, in less than the blink of an eye, swung the blade. At first, I thought she had missed, as the dowel was perfectly intact, but she sheathed the sword, casually reached over, and lifted off the top section of dowel.

"Holy shit."

Blue's strike had been so precise and the blade had been so sharp that it had cut all the way through without disturbing the wood.

Blue unclamped the wood, raised it a foot and half, and re-clamped it. I watched in awe as she did the same thing again.

In no time, she had both dowels cut up into 6 one-and-half-foot pieces. She clamped the table leg down with the narrow end pointing up, then drew the sword again and made two quick diagonal strikes at the tip. She moved over ninety degrees and made two more fast strikes, then sheathed the sword again, unclamped the table leg, and handed it to me.

"Is that enough of a point?" she asked with an amused smile dancing across her face.

I admired the precise way in which she had cut the four sides equally at about a thirty-degree angle. Now the table leg had a wicked-looking point on it.

I just nodded, as words failed me at that point.

"There are some people in my old world who would have been appalled at me for using the Keetiyatomi blade in such a fashion. I, however, see the blade as a tool. It will never break and never dull. Why would you not use it this way?"

"Does the blade's name mean something?" I asked.

"Yes, the closest translation for its name in English would be 'Bright Death.' "

Blue clamped down one of the dowel pieces and, in short order, added a nice pointy tip to it. She did the same with the other five pieces. As she finished each one, she put them on the table standing up on the blunt end. Each one stood perfectly straight up, and there was less than a millimeter in height difference between all six. Looking at the six almost identical stakes, I would have sworn they had been machine made, and yet, Blue had done it freehand, just by eyeballing them.

"Remind me never to get on your bad side," I said in total awe of her abilities.

She laughed.

We carried the stakes over to the far table and placed them with the crate of grenades and the components for the Molotov cocktail.

A sleepy-looking Bree walked into the main chamber and made a beeline for the Food-O-Tron.

"New breakfast recipe in the Food-O-Tron for you," I said.

"Coffee first, food second" was her mumbled reply.

About a minute later, Bree yelled from the Food-O-Tron, "What the hell is a 'Bacon and Egger'?"

I turned on the stool until I was facing her. "You've never had an A&W Bacon and Egger?" She shook her head, and I added, "Trust me—food of the gods. Order it. You won't be disappointed."

I turned back and asked Blue, "How long have you been training with swords?"

She scratched her chin. "About fifty Earth years. It is hard to be exact, as time and calendars on my world are different from Earth's."

I wondered how old Blue was. She looked healthy and fit and in the prime of her life—much better than any fifty-plus human I had ever seen. If she was human, I would have guessed her age to be midtwenties.

I was about to ask about her race's life expectancy when Bree sat down beside me at the table. She grabbed one of the Bacon and Eggers, looked it at critically for a moment, shrugged, and took a bite. She swallowed, smiled, and said, "This might be the ticket to the third baby I owe you now!"

Bree got up with the first Bacon and Egger in her hand and headed for the Food-O-Tron. She pulled the lever down to make another pair of them. The first Bacon and Egger was gone by the time she returned. In the end, she went through six of them, and I honestly think she considered getting another two but held off.

With lunch out of the way, we talked a bit more about training, the supplies, and the plan for taking on Giselle again, but the conversation ended quickly. We knew we what we had to do; we just needed Elizabeth to secure the deal with Roman.

Blue left us to go do sword drills in the hangar. Stella left us to putter around with some of the stuff on the workbench that had all the mechanical pieces on it. She was building something, but I had no idea what.

The afternoon dragged on, but eventually, Olivia was up, and we all had dinner together. After dinner we all ended up in the hangar, running through practice drills again. Blue was just as relentless in making us do drill after drill as she had been the first night.

The next three days followed the same pattern: lazy afternoons with intense drills at night.

That fourth night of training got a little heated. Everyone was tired of the waiting, and the stress of it was starting to get to all of us.

"Bullshit!" yelled Olivia at Blue. "I tagged Bree earlier in the round, so she was out of the fight!"

Bree, in her hybrid Were form, growled in disagreement at Liv's words. It was odd—Bree could only growl in her Were form, but she would change her tone, volume, and body language so that each of the growls meant something different. What worried me was that I was becoming fluent in Growl.

Blue calmly argued, "I didn't see you make the tag. Therefore, Bree was still alive and in play. You lost this round."

"Whatever. I know I tagged her but give them their fake win. Either way, you all need to get better. Giselle is a master, and there won't be any questions about if she hits you or not …," said Olivia.

Liv's Giselle shot was unfair; the three of us had been making good progress since we had started the training. I was beginning to instinctively know what Bree and Stella were going to do before they did it. That helped us work better as a team. I was also very much aware of where our strengths and weaknesses were as a team and played to them. We were now winning more than we were losing.

"Enough!" said Blue. "Everyone take your positions, and let's run this again."

We lined up, and Olivia took her spot back in the center of the room.

Blue said, "Go," and Bree, Stella, and I jumped into the pretend chamber. Liv had blurred away before we even entered, which was technically cheating. A moment later, she slammed into me, and I fell hard enough on my ass that I was winded and saw stars.

"Was that a tag?" Olivia sarcastically asked in Blue's direction.

In anger, I lashed out with my Air power. I lifted Liv off the ground and slammed her into the far wall of the hangar.

"Oops, sorry, death reflex," I said with a false smile.

Liv got to her feet. "I'll show you death reflex, asshole!"

She disappeared in a blur, and my only thought was *Oh shit*. I barely managed to thicken the air above me in time. Liv ended up suspended motionless in the air less than two feet away from me. Her mouth was open in an angry grimace, and her fangs were fully extended.

Stella's crisp English accent cut through the air. "Olivia! Zack! Knock it off before someone gets hurt!"

Liv retracted her fangs, and I used the air to lift her a couple of feet away from me and gently put her down on her feet.

"Olivia, go get yourself a drink," said Stella in a firm tone.

Olivia looked at me and lowered her eyes in embarrassment before she nodded and blurred out of the room. I got to my feet, and Stella was standing in front of me with a decidedly unhappy look on her face. I held up my hand to cut off whatever she was going to say. "I know: That was uncalled for, and I screwed up. I will apologize to Liv when she returns, okay?"

Stella gave me a curt nod. "Bree, change back. We've had had enough training this evening."

I couldn't help but agree with Stella. I went to find Liv and get my apology out of the way sooner than later.

I found her sitting at the table in the main room, half-heartedly drinking her glass of blood. She looked as I entered the room.

"Liv, I'm—" I started to say.

But she cut me off. "I know. I'm sorry too."

I sat down beside her. "You want to talk about it?"

"No." She paused for a moment, then said, "Maybe … I don't know. This waiting is driving me insane. Yet, at the same time, it means I don't have to risk seeing all the people I love go into a battle that I can't be a part of. I like this place—it makes me feel safe—but it also feels like a prison, too, you know?"

I couldn't imagine what Liv was going through at that moment. I'd hate the idea of people risking their lives for me. The problem was, there wasn't anything we could do to change it. We had to hit Giselle during the day when she was at her weakest. I wondered, if this mission went badly and Bree, Stella, and myself were killed, how much of Liv would die too. I knew she and Blue would survive, but I also knew that Liv wouldn't be the same after it.

A hot, sweaty, and naked Bree walked by us and pulled me from my thoughts. She made a beeline for the Food-O-Tron. Blue and Stella came in a moment later. Stella eyed Liv and me warily but seemed to relax as she noticed we were sitting calmly and not trying to kill each other.

Stella headed for us and was about to say something when her phone rang. Everyone in the room stopped dead and just looked at her. She fished the phone out and answered it. She didn't say much, other than the occasional yes or no, but Bree exclaimed a happy "Yes," and Liv stiffened beside me. I guessed that it was Elizabeth calling, and Roman had agreed to the deal.

"Thank you for calling, Your Majesty," said Stella as she ended the call. She smiled and said, "The deal is in place, and we are a go."

A feeling of relief and dread hit me at the same time. I was relieved that the waiting was finally over; the problem was, now we had to take out a vampire master in her den, and that was no small task.

We all sat around the table and started going over details. We decided to attack tomorrow at 11:00 a.m. London time, which would make it noon in Paris.

We just about had everything ironed out when a thought hit me. "What if Roman is playing both sides? He agrees to the deal but warns Giselle what we are up to? Tomorrow, we could be walking into a trap."

Blue pondered my concerns for a few moments. "It is possible. That would be in line with vampire politics. I have been monitoring the French court from the shadows, and I will check to see if anything in their procedures has changed."

I felt better at this. Blue could listen in or watch anywhere there was a shadow. That would make it difficult for the French court to pull off a trap without her finding out about it.

We discussed a few more minor details, and Stella said, "I'm going to get some sleep. Tomorrow is a big day, and I'd suggest you all do the same."

Blue nodded. "I, too, am going to retire to my room. I will check on the French court first and then call it a night."

I figured that would be a good idea, too, and wished Bree and Liv a good night. I wasn't surprised to see that Bree elected to stay up longer. She would keep Liv company, and I'm sure the two of them wanted to talk. If things didn't go well tomorrow, this would be the last time Liv would see Bree alive.

Chapter 28

Friday, February 23

The ringing of the windup alarm clock caused me to bolt upright in surprise from a deep sleep. I reached over and silenced it while my sleep-fogged brain tried to figure out what the hell was going on. I eventually remembered the secret lab, the girls, and that today was the day we were taking on Giselle.

I threw on some clothes and went to find some sorely needed coffee. As I entered the main chamber, Stella and Blue abruptly stopped whatever they were doing at the table. They had strangely guilty expressions. I moved closer to the table, and there were two empty cast-iron pans sitting between them. Oddly enough, their hands were below the table as if hiding something.

My nose gave me the final clue I needed to solve the mystery. I smiled to myself. "What are you two up to?"

"Nothing," they answered in unison.

"I see. Hey, Stella, you have a little bit of cheese—or maybe that is egg—just below your lower lip," I pointed out in a gleeful tone of voice.

Her hand came up automatically, and it was holding the last third of a Bacon and Egger. She sighed in resignation and with a defeated look said, "Alright, we tried your breakfast sandwich …"

"By the *two* cast-iron pans, that would 'sandwich*es*'—plural. I do believe someone went on a superiority rant about Americans turning all foods into a hamburger or something like that. Now, I will be gracious in my victory. I am just pleased you enjoyed them."

Stella nodded sheepishly and tucked into the remaining part of her sandwich. Blue did the same.

I adjusted the switches on the Food-O-Tron to order my two tiny teacups of coffee. I joined them at the table while I waited.

"Are either of you planning on making sure Bree is up soon, or are we going to send her into battle today hungry to make her extra fierce?"

Stella smiled at my humor. "I was going to wake her soon, but figured I'd wait until you got your breakfast first. She does tend to monopolize the machine."

The machine dinged at that moment, and I said, "That would be the rest of my coffee, and I will order my breakfast now. Please wake Bree in a few minutes."

I had just sat back down at the table with my food when Bree walked by and mumbled, "Good morning," under her breath.

She joined us at the table a few minutes later, and after a little light conversation, the table went quiet, as everyone just seemed to want to be alone with their thoughts. You could almost feel the tension in the air due to the enormity of the task ahead of us.

I finished my food and excused myself. After putting my dirty dishes back in the Food-O-Tron to be cleaned, I headed for the bathroom to grab a shower.

After I finished up my morning bathroom ritual, I disappeared to my room to get dressed. Putting on tighty-whities, blue jeans, a T-shirt, socks, and running shoes felt a bit odd for an upcoming battle. I didn't have chainmail, platemail, or a Kevlar vest handy—and doubted any of those things would help in the slightest against Giselle—so I decided I might as well be comfortable. I guess I could have risked Blue transporting me back to the house to grab my old hero uniform, but honestly, me in spandex at thirty-three years old didn't look as good as it had when I'd been in my prime.

I returned to the main chamber and began making a Molotov cocktail. We still had an hour to go before everything kicked off, but this gave me something to do, other than dwell on things.

The timing between tossing the grenades and the Molotov cocktail was going to be tight. Me fumbling with a lighter would be a bad idea, and I found a candle. I figured I'd light the candle and set it behind us; this would allow me to just turn and light the Molotov.

Blue joined me, and we moved the pile of supplies we were going to use over into a corner near the shadows. The two of us spent the next twenty minutes going over the timing on pulling the pins and releasing the spoon on the grenades, throwing them, and closing the portal. We also reviewed me lighting the Molotov, Blue opening the portal again, me tossing it through, and Blue closing the portal again.

We were both satisfied that we had the timing down pat. A quick glance at my watch told me that we still had thirty minutes to go.

Blue pulled Stella from the room and disappeared down the east corridor, whether to go back to their rooms or have a private conversation, I couldn't say. I sat down beside Bree, who was sitting quietly on her own. She was just staring blankly off into the distance, lost in her own thoughts.

She gave me a tight smile and said, "It seems odd that Olivia isn't here. I know she isn't supposed to be joining us and isn't able to be awake at this time, but I have always fought beside her. Even in the training, she was there. Okay, she was on the opposite side, but she was still there."

"I know, but we'll be fine. We have trained and drilled at this, and the three of us make a pretty good team. This will be over soon, and without that contract on Olivia's head, you guys can actually get on with your lives."

I was impressed that my voice sounded much more confident than I felt at that moment. I kind of felt like an old English sea captain: Doesn't matter if you are scared; do your duty and project your authority to inspire the men.

Bree smiled a little at that and then got serious again. "Thank you for all that you have done for us—and for risking your life today as well."

"You're welcome. It hasn't been so terrible for me either. Since meeting you guys, I have taken down some of the biggest bounties in my career, enjoyed all of your company, gotten to see this amazing lab and the Food-O-Tron ... I have also gotten to travel all over Canada and visit the English vampire court. To top all of that off, I have to admit that you and Olivia are easy on the eyes, and one of you owes me—what is it up to now?—three babies, I believe?"

Stella and Blue entered the room again at that moment, and Blue took control. "We have fifteen minutes before we are a go. Let's huddle up and make sure everyone has their roles down one last time."

She systematically went over everything, one detail at a time, and then ordered Bree and Stella to change.

Blue handed me my two grenades. While we waited for Bree to finish changing, I stared intently and nervously at the two explosives in my hand. They were supposed to have a four-second fuse on them, and we were throwing on the count of two, so we should be fine. The problem was, I suddenly remembered that the lowest bidder won military contracts, and I wondered how good the quality control was on these two deadly little beauties.

As the seconds ticked by, my heart rate picked up and my adrenaline started to surge. I regretted the two Bacon and Eggers, which felt like they were rocks in my knotted-up stomach. I closed my eyes and gave a silent prayer to whatever deity might be listening, on the theory it wouldn't hurt.

Bree stepped up to my right in her powerful hybrid form and gave a soft growl. Stella, in her Hyde form, was directly behind Bree and ready for action.

"One minute," said Blue to my left.

I carefully put the grenades down and lit the candle behind me. I was pleased to see my hands didn't shake too badly doing this. I turned back, picked up the grenades, and got ready.

"Ten seconds," said Blue in a calm, steady voice.

"For Olivia!" I said in a firm voice.

"For Olivia," repeated Blue with a determined grin as Bree roared loudly in approval and Stella grunted.

"Time," announced Blue as she opened the portal.

I pulled the pins on my two grenades. I kept the spoons firmly held down as I held one in each hand.

"Four," started Blue.

At "Three," I released the spoons.

"Two."

On "One," Blue and I tossed the grenades into the shadows. My heart stopped for a second as I overcompensated for my weaker left arm and the one grenade tumbled much higher through the air than I had intended. It just cleared under the top of the shadow portal, and I exhaled in relief.

I bent over and grabbed the Molotov cocktail. I turned toward the candle, and the rag stuffed in the top of the bottle lit with a satisfying *whoosh*.

Blue nodded at me as she opened the portal again. I heaved it through with a throw that any minor-league pitcher would have been envious of. Blue shut the portal as soon as it went through.

Two seconds later, Blue opened another shadow portal and yelled, "Bree! Go!"

Bree jumped into the shadows a moment later. Stella was hot on her heels, and as soon as she disappeared through, I followed. I pulled the wooden stake from my back pocket as I stepped through.

Entering Giselle's chamber was like entering a small piece of Hell. I choked on the dust and smoke in the air. To my left, the fire was raging and had consumed that whole corner of the room. The heat of

217

the flames had me sweating profusely almost instantly. My instincts kicked in, and I used my powers to filter the air, allowing me to breathe freely again.

Other than the *hiss* and *snap* of the fire beside me—and the constant muted drone of an alarm going on outside the chamber—it was strangely quiet. Through the smoke and the haze, I could make out a large pile of rubble in the center of the room, which I assumed was the remains of Giselle's stone sarcophagus. I strained to make out the heavy black-iron door in the far corner of the room. To my relief, it was still there; we'd been concerned that the pressure from the grenades would blow it clear of its mounts. That door was the only barrier between us and the French court's daytime security forces.

Between the door and the destroyed sarcophagus, part of me was starting to feel optimistic. So far, everything was going according to plan.

Bree cautiously approached the heap of rocks in the center, which hopefully was now Giselle's final resting place. She held the stake defensively out in front as she kept moving closer.

She reached the edge of the remains of the sarcophagus, and a rage-and-pain-filled scream filled the room. Like a phoenix rising from the ashes, Giselle exploded from the pile of rocks and landed on her feet. The damage she had sustained was horrific; her entire lower half had been burned away to the bone. Staring at the blackened charred bones of her legs, it defied logic that she was still able to stand. Giselle's upper body wasn't much better; her left side was a mess of burnt, dripping flesh. Her upper right side, however, was barely marred. The contrast of the perfect, beautiful features of her right side versus the disfiguring damage to her left made it hard to look at her.

Despite the damage, she stood rock solid and didn't seem weakened in the slightest. I got the feeling we had just kicked over a hornet's nest.

Her eyes glowed red as she surveyed the room. They stopped on me and widened in recognition; I assumed she must have seen a picture of me in her files.

She hissed. "You will die for this!"

It felt like an icepick was being driven into my brain as she attempted to mind-roll me. I tore my gaze from her eyes and focused on her midsection instead, and the pain receded.

An angry, animalistic roar drowned out everything in the room. To my surprise, it was Bree who had made the noise. Her ice-blue cat's eyes flashed like lasers in the haze of the room. She tossed aside the wooden stake she had been carrying, roared again, and leaped for Giselle. Three hundred pounds of enraged Werepanther slammed into the master vampire, and Giselle barely budged. Instead, she jammed her ruined left forearm into the snapping jaws that had been on target for her throat. Bree raked Giselle with her front and rear claws. Chunks of charred flesh were torn away from Giselle, and jagged lines of black blood appeared on her previously undamaged skin as Bree continued her mindless assault. The shear savagery of Bree's attack seemed to be keeping Giselle off balance.

I wanted to help by tossing some lightning, but Bree's frantic attack made it impossible for me to assist her. Stella's Hyde form stood back, looking confused; she, too, wanted to help but was also blocked by Bree.

My mind raced as I tried to figure out what the hell Bree thought she was doing. This hadn't been in the plan. Why had she just dropped her stake? In our training, I'd never seen Bree act like this. It was like she was in some sort of mindless berserker rage.

My heart sped up as it dawned on me what was going on. It wasn't Bree attacking Giselle; it was her beast. Bree had lost control. I cursed, as I should have seen this coming. Bree would be angry that Giselle had threated her friend. The beast had used that anger to rip control away from her. The beast would be furious that someone intended to harm a member of its pack.

The implications of this were bad. The beast wouldn't care about friend or foe—only pack mattered. Stella would be fine; the beast would consider her part of the pack. Even if it didn't, I didn't think the Were's claws or fangs could penetrate her Hyde's toughened skin. The big question was, did the beast consider *me* part of its pack? For my own safety, I'd have to assume the answer was no and make sure she didn't get close to me.

Giselle hammered a hard-right punch directly into the Were's snout. It barely made the beast pause. Giselle's whole front area was now a total shredded mess. The master vampire's right hand became blurred as it drove a flurry of savage punches into the beast's head. With each passing second, the beast's attacks became slower and slower as Giselle continued laying into her.

Giselle was hitting the Were so hard and so fast that the left side of the Were's face was turning into a puffy mess of hamburger. Despite the relentless pounding, the beast never stopped attacking. A loud *crunch* filled the room, and Giselle's left hand went limp. The beast had snapped Giselle's forearm in its powerful jaws.

The small victory was short-lived. Moments later, the glow in the beast's blue eyes went out as another brutal barrage of punches landed. Its eyes rolled up in its head, and 300 pounds of Werepanther dropped to the stone floor like a sack of potatoes. Giselle reached down and grabbed one of the Were's black fur-covered legs. In a blink, she tossed the unconscious Were across the chamber like a ragdoll.

Bree hit the north wall hard enough that a cloud of stone dust came up from the impact, and I almost cried out at the heart-wrenching sounds of wet tissue and shattered bones. She fell to the stone floor in an unmoving heap.

Oh shit! I thought. Giselle had just tossed a 300-pound Were across the chamber like it was nothing. *Good thing we are attacking her when she is weak ...* I almost giggled in hysterical fear at that random thought.

Stella grunted and charged at Giselle, which pulled my attention back to the fight. Giselle was starting to fade and about to mist out of here. I brought up my right hand and arced lightning at her. As soon as the electricity touched her, she instantly became solid again.

Stella roared in, with the large wooden table leg leading the way. Giselle struck like a snake and grabbed the wooden stake clean out of Stella's massive hand. She snapped it in half with ease. In a blur of motion, she whipped the broken pointy end at me, and it stopped point-first a mere six inches from my head, thanks to my air shield.

Stella swung a massive left hook that made contact with Giselle's chest. I was pretty sure I heard ribs crack and had no doubt that a similar blow would have easily killed me. Giselle flew back toward the north wall, but that hit disrupted the flow of electricity I had been hitting her with. She flipped in the air and sprang off the back wall like a spider monkey, then was gone.

Fuck, I hate vampire speed! Before that thought even finished, Giselle—in all her angry glory—was less than a foot and half away from me.

She inched closer through the thickened air, and I frantically poured on the wind power, trying to keep her at bay. I was hitting her with what would have been equivalent to Category 5 hurricane-force winds, and she was still inching closer. Her clawed feet were embedded deeply into the solid stone floor like it was soft clay.

She bared her elongated fangs at me as she pushed closer. In desperation, I swung the stake in my left hand forward with everything I had. Unfortunately, it wasn't enough. She easily intercepted my arm like I was a small, weak child. I gathered my power and was planning on hitting her with every bit of electricity I could throw at her in an attempt to throw her off me.

Just before I was about to release it, she crushed my forearm like it was paper. The pain hit home, and I screamed in agony. All control I had over my powers disappeared, and my air shield was gone.

In my haze I saw her bring her head back and knew that in a second, she would tear through my exposed neck like a hot knife through butter.

The ground shook as Stella growled and stomped toward us. This caught Giselle's attention. She spun around, yanking me by my shattered arm. My shoulder popped out of its socket as she flung me as she turned. I was suddenly flying across the chamber.

I was careening head-first toward the solid-looking stone wall. If I hit it head-first at this speed, I was dead. I barely managed to push enough wind to turn my body before hitting the wall with my right shoulder, which made an ear-splitting *crack* as the bones of the socket shattered like glass. My side hit next and knocked the wind out of me, just as the blinding-white flash of pain from my shoulder hit home.

I hit the floor hard a few seconds later, but it barely registered over the pain of my broken and battered body, and I might have blacked out for moment ... I ended up flat on my back on the stone floor. My right arm felt like dead weight—from the shoulder down was numb. I prayed the shoulder would go numb, too, but every couple of seconds, a fiery-hot poker of pain emanated from it. My left arm throbbed as the crushed forearm and dislocated shoulder joint tried their best to keep up with the agony of my right shoulder.

A huge, rhythmic pounding against the iron door pulled my attention that way. The heavy iron door shuddered with each bang, and I wondered just what the hell was on the other side of that door, trying to force its way in.

Bree's black, furry clawed feet lying motionless against the north wall caught my attention. I willed the feet to move, but they remained depressingly still. I prayed she was just unconscious and not dead, but didn't hold out much hope. Even if she wasn't dead, with the way the iron door shuddered under each massive blow, it wouldn't be long before Giselle's daytime forces would be joining this fight. Two of the three of us were down, and things didn't look promising at this point.

My own helplessness at this moment began to fuel the cold rage that was building from within me. I reached deep and began gathering every scrap of power I had left. I was going to try something I never had done before. My mother, in my training, had warned me it was possible for an elemental to pull more power than they were capable of, but it came at a great cost. At a minimum, it would leave the caster powerless for weeks or months—or even burn out their power completely, if they were lucky. If they weren't lucky, it would use up their life force completely and kill them.

I was going to hit Giselle with every ounce of electricity I could muster and fry the bitch.

Giselle was laughing. "Keep squeezing, you dumb brute. It won't get you anywhere, and when you get tired, I will break free, drain your friends, and kill you slowly."

Stella's Hyde form had Giselle pinned in a bear hug and was slowly walking along the south wall in my direction. I kept gathering more and more power as I watched the struggle between them. If Giselle broke free, she would come for me first, and when she went to feed off me, I was going to give her a shocking surprise.

Stella reached the corner and turned her back to me. A flash of light streaked through the darkness of the shadows. For a moment, I thought that, in my pain-induced haze, I'd imagined it. Then a thin black line appeared across Giselle's neck. Black blood slowly began to ooze from it.

Blue had managed to strike from the shadows and, even without entering the room, managed to play a key role in this battle.

Giselle's head tumbled from her body, hit the floor, and rolled over toward me. It stopped, facing me about three feet away. To my astonishment, the eyes blinked in almost disbelief. Giselle's mouth moved, but no sounds came out, as there was no body attached to it to push air through her vocal cords.

Just as I started to believe that even this wouldn't be enough to kill her, the life faded from her eyes, and they remained locked in a final distant, accusing stare.

With relief, I released the power I'd been gathering. The pain I had been denying with my anger came flaring back with a vengeance. Moments later, I mercifully blacked out.

Chapter 29

Friday, February 23

I awoke in a strange bed covered by a thin sheet. My right arm was strapped down, immobilized against the side of my body, and my left arm was in a sling across my bare chest. I could feel the denim against my right hand, which meant I was still wearing my jeans. By the plain tiles on the ceiling, the ugly institutional-green color on the walls, and the overwhelming smell of antiseptic in the air, I guessed I was in an infirmary somewhere.

My right shoulder had a dull but bearable pain, unlike earlier in Giselle's lair. My left forearm wasn't a bundle of joy, either, but that pain, too, was at least manageable. My back was sore and so was my right leg, which was odd, as I didn't remember anything hitting it.

I was a little concerned, to say the least, about where I was. With both my arms out of commission, I was feeling as vulnerable as a newborn babe at that moment. It would be just my luck that this infirmary belonged to the French court, and they were healing me just to be able to torture me longer.

I turned my head left, and there was an empty bed about eight feet away, which didn't tell me anything. I craned my neck to the other side, and Olivia was sitting on the side of another bed. To my relief, Bree's blonde-haired head was resting on a pillow. The fact that Olivia was sitting there unrestrained made it highly unlikely that we were being held prisoner here.

Olivia must have heard my movements or sensed my stare. A moment later, she instantly appeared in front of my bed and said, "Zack, you are awake. How are you feeling?"

I tried speaking, but nothing but a raspy whisper came out. My mouth and throat were parched, due to the smoke I had inhaled.

"Hold on. Let me get you some water," said Olivia as if reading my mind.

About a minute later, she was back with a glass of water and a flexible straw. She lowered the glass and gently placed the straw against my lips. I awkwardly sucked some of the water up through the straw and almost moaned at how good it tasted.

After I had finished most of the glass, she pulled the straw away and looked at me expectantly.

"Thanks," I said. "I'm okay. How is Bree?"

"She is going to be okay. She woke up a couple of hours ago, but her head was killing her. They gave her some painkillers for the pain, and she went back to sleep. How about you? Are you in any discomfort?"

I started to shrug, but with a messed-up shoulder, decided that would be a very bad idea. "I feel like I was hit by a truck, but I'll live. Where are we?"

"The infirmary at the English court. After the battle, Stella had Blue take you and Bree here for healing. They have a full-time healer on staff. He healed Bree first, due to her head wound being more life-threatening than your injuries. He healed the bones in your shoulder and your arm but then ran out of juice. He'll be back later after eating and resting to recharge his power, then he will fix the muscles that were damaged and the rest of your injuries."

I idly wondered what this healing was going to cost Stella, but figured I'd discuss that with her later.

If Olivia was here and awake, it had to be past 6:00 p.m. The infirmary had no windows and no clocks; I couldn't guess what the actual time was. Olivia informed me, when I asked, that it was just after 10:00 p.m. London time.

"Where are Stella and Blue?" I asked.

"Blue was doing some transport jobs for the court, and Stella was in a private audience with Elizabeth. It seems Elizabeth was overjoyed with the gift Stella brought her."

I gave her a look as if to ask, "What gift?"

Olivia smiled. "Giselle's head, of course!"

"Of course! Who doesn't like a little head?"

Olivia snorted and shook her head at me. She gently sat down on the edge of my bed. "I still can't believe you guys pulled this off. Thank you, Zack. Knowing that contract is going to be lifted is a huge weight off my shoulders. I feel like I can actually plan a life now."

I nodded in response.

We chatted about more mundane things like movies, books, and music for a bit, which, as far as the movies and music, made me feel old by what things she liked. I was shocked at the number of movies I considered must-see classics that she hadn't seen, and I made a mental note to correct that oversight as soon as possible.

After about an hour, Olivia said, "You are starting to smell really yummy. I am going to search this place for a juice box."

As she walked away, I realized that she still made me a little nervous at times; not being the highest member on the food chain was an uncomfortable feeling. I was acutely aware that in my present condition, I was in no shape to defend myself. Being in this condition in the middle of the freaking English vampire court didn't soothe my nerves in the slightest.

As if on cue, I caught the distinct sound of heels echoing down the hall, and they were heading toward the infirmary. Sarah appeared at the doorway, and I had to smile at her outfit. She was wearing what could only be described as a naughty nurse costume: a little one-piece number that was much too short and showed way too much of her red-bra-clad cleavage. She had a little white hat with a Red Cross symbol on the front, and the outfit was completed by black fishnets and four-inch heels. She had a large plain-brown envelope in her right hand.

"Someone told me a tasty Air elemental was in need of some TLC," she purred in a sultry voice.

"Evening, Sarah. Lovely to see you again."

"Ah, there is my favorite patient," exclaimed Sarah with delight.

She strutted into the infirmary like she owned the place and headed directly for me with a lustful look in her eyes. Strangely enough, though, she didn't make nervous. I wasn't sure why that was—whether it was something I sensed about her personality or control, or whether I knew that we were under Elizabeth's protection and no one would be stupid enough to defy her, I wasn't sure.

Sarah reached the edge of the bed and looked me over with an expression that was part concern and part amusement. "The lack of useable hands could make this interesting. I don't mind doing the all work, and I'm sure I can make you feel much better ..."

I laughed at her boldness. "Sarah, if I was going to spend quality time with you, I would want to be 100 percent; even then, I'm not sure I would be able to keep up with you."

She let loose a soft peel of delighted laughter at my reply and was about to say something when Olivia returned.

"Back off, grandma!" snarled Olivia as she approached with a bag of plasma in her hand.

"Oh, the yearling returns," said Sarah, and she got a gleam in her eye as she noticed Liv's snack bag. "Can I get you a sippy cup for that?"

"Only if I can make you one with prune juice. I hear that is good for seniors," answered Olivia, taking a long pull off the bag.

Sarah tilted her head slightly to acknowledge that Olivia scored a point. "You will be happy to know that the €5 million contract has been rescinded, so you are back to being worthless again."

Olivia smiled for a moment but frowned as she caught on to the "worthless" part.

"Thank you for delivering that news to me in person. I know it takes much more effort to get around in your golden years, and I appreciate the effort on your part. Also, that costume is impressive. Was it challenging getting it on over the Depends?" asked Olivia with a smile.

"Okay, ladies, let's all play nice, alright?" I said, trying to take things down a notch.

"Of course, Zack. I just stopped by to make sure you were okay and to see if you needed anything. I also brought gifts for Olivia and Bree," said Sarah as she placed the large brown envelope on the bed. "Their IDs are set up and ready to go: passports, drivers' licenses, birth certificates, SIN numbers, ten years of completed and filed tax returns, background stories—the works. So, little one, you and Bree can walk in the daylight, so to speak, with no worries."

Olivia gritted her teeth and reluctantly said, "Thank you."

Sarah gave a small nod. "Now, as you seem to be in somewhat capable hands, Zack, I will leave you to her care."

She turned and slowly walked out of the room. I had to admit, my eyes followed her steps until she was gone from sight.

Olivia put her half-empty bag down the bedside table, reached across me, and snatched up the package. She pulled out two new Canadian passports and opened the first one.

" 'Bree Cattrall.' Hey, that's kind of cool. Bree has a last name with 'cat' in it; she'll love that. I wonder what my new last name is?" Olivia grabbed the other passport and said, "That bitch!"

"What did she do?"

" 'Olivia Dick.' She gave me the last name of 'Dick'!" growled Olivia.

I chuckled quietly. I thought about consoling her, but she was strong enough to handle a funny last name and, in time, would be fine.

As Olivia sulked and finished her juice box, I figured, with how bad this day could have gone, this minor injustice wasn't the end of the world. We were all alive and relatively in one piece. Olivia didn't have a death threat hanging over her, and in the next few hours, the healer would return, and I'd be back to normal.

I was tired, which was surprising, considering how long I'd slept already, but my body had a lot of healing to do, and I drifted off back to sleep.

* * * * *

I felt a pair of unfamiliar hands on me, and my eyes shot open. There was a dark-haired man in a white lab coat standing over me with his hands on my right shoulder. He was outlined in a pale blue-and-silver aura, which my sleep-fogged mind somehow managed to translate to *healer*.

"Just relax, Zack. I'm Karl, the English court's healer. I'm just about done fixing you up," he said in a culture European accent.

I nodded as everything started coming back to me. I suddenly noticed that everyone was here and standing around the bed, watching Karl work. Bree was standing and awake. She was wearing a pair of green hospital scrubs, and her blonde hair had a massive case of bedhead, but I was overjoyed to see her up and around. Liv looked bored but concerned, and her eyes kept flicking between me and Bree as if making sure we were both okay. She smiled at me when our eyes met. Stella and Blue were here too. Stella's young face was truly beautiful at this moment; gone were the worries that had been there since this whole adventure had started, and in their place was an almost carefree smile. Blue stood stoically behind Stella with a neutral expression on her face, but her tail was happily dancing around behind her in slow circles.

I felt an intense tingling in my shoulder, and then the feeling faded. Karl removed his hands, produced a pair of surgical scissors, and cut away the bandages that had kept my arm restrained.

"Well, how do you feel?" he asked.

I tentatively tested my formerly shattered shoulder and smiled. I tested my left forearm, flexed my back, lifted my right leg, and said, "Some of the areas tingle a bit and are a little stiff, but everything seems to be working. Thanks, Doc."

"That is to be expected. You had several serious injuries. They are fixed, but you will need a few more days until you are fully recovered. Take it easy, get plenty of rest and food, and you'll be fine."

With that said, Karl packed up his black-leather medical bag and left. I carefully sat up in the bed, and Liv and Bree sat down on the edge of it. Stella sat down on the opposite side of the girls. I was a bit surprised that not only did Stella sit but she was less than inch from my leg. She looked at me and gave me a small smile and a nod. I was touched at this gesture of trust. Blue was the only one not on the bed at this moment, and she just stood protectively behind Stella.

Stella said, "So, Giselle is dead, Liv is safe, and we are no longer being hunted. Any thoughts on what you are doing next?"

"Well, for the next couple of days," I said, "I'll be following the doctor's orders and taking it easy. After that, I expect I will get back to bounty hunting. I'm thinking of expanding my business; I recently had an offer from a group of talented and capable Enhanced Individuals who wished to partner up with me. Hopefully, they are still interested?"

Liv blurted out, "Yes." Bree nodded, and Stella immediately looked over her shoulder to Blue. Blue gave the slightest nod, and Stella said, "We are in."

"Hold on! Not so fast!" said Bree, and we all looked at her in concern. She added, "We are in, but Zack isn't allowed to design the team uniforms. Or, if he does, then me and Liv get to design his."

We all laughed.

"Bree, I think you are being too hasty here. You and Liv in white crop tops with no bras would make catching male perpetrators super easy—while they are distracted, Stella could just Hyde-up, walk up behind them, and bop them on the head without any issues."

"No deal. I'm sure the five of us can take down anyone without me having to use, um, the 'girls' like that."

I laughed and nodded in response. I turned to Stella. "I glad you all want to join me, but the paperwork on this is going to be a nightmare. We have to get all of you bounty IDs, come up with a partnership agreement, figure out where we are going to work from, set up a company bank account, and Odin knows what else. You might wish that Giselle had won by the time we are done."

Stella shrugged. "I'm sure we can work it out."

Liv jumped in and said, "Oh! We are going to need a company name ... How about 'Liv and Her Minions'?"

Bree eye-rolled so hard in response that I was worried that she might have damaged her ocular muscles. "Nope. Not happening."

Olivia immediate tossed out another Liv-centric name, and Bree shot that one down as well. Liv got on a roll, and I tuned her out. My currently company name was a seven-digit numbered Ontario company, and I reckoned we'd just use that. All the bounties I took on were from the UN Bounty website, so a catchy name wasn't required. I didn't have the heart to break that to Olivia, though, and just let her have her fun.

Blue looked at me. "I will modify the training program so that it has all five of us working together, rather than just you, Bree, and Stella. I also think a physical training program would be useful to make sure everyone is in peak form going forward."

I nodded slowly in agreement at that last point. The ladies were all in good shape, so I had a feeling this was directed mostly at me. I hated exercising, but I could have stood to lose a few pounds. I also had a feeling that to keep up with this bunch, I would need to be in better shape.

Stella turned to Blue, and the two of them began discussing different ideas on how to do a partnership agreement and how the command structure would work both in combat and out of it.

It had been a crazy twelve days. We'd survived drow assassins, a Fire elemental, and way too many people with guns—and had taken down a master vampire. I had gone from being a lone wolf to being part of team. More importantly, I'd gained a family, albeit an odd and weird one—but a family nevertheless.

After being on my own for so long, it was a nice feeling to know that I had a group of people around me who cared and who I cared deeply for. I had no idea what the future might bring, but I knew that it would be interesting.

Epilogue

Monday, February 26

It had been three days since our battle with Giselle. The team decided that going forward, we'd use my house in Hamilton as our main base and living quarters. The last couple of days, we'd been making nonstop trips via the shadows, moving their stuff from the lab to the house. We'd still use the secret lab, as it would be stupid not to. The Food-O-Tron kept Liv supplied with blood and Bree supplied with food, which was no small feat; Stella liked tinkering around in the lab, making inventions; and we'd continue to use the main hangar to do training. We also would use it as a fallback position in case anything like the Liv contract situation came up again.

The moving stuff was mostly one way, but I moved a ton of books from my room to the lab as well. If we ended up hiding there again, I would have something to read. I'd also ordered a power convertor online to convert the DC power to AC, which would allow us to install modern power outlets. I had a buddy who was an electrician who I'd get to install it when it came in. Once that was in place, I planned on putting in a flat-screen TV and a Blu-ray player, then dumping a ton of movies there as well.

The ladies had all applied for UN bounty hunting IDs. We were in a holding pattern until those were approved and came in. We were still waiting for the payout on outstanding bounties to clear from our time on the run. Stella and I were working on changing my numbered company, so everyone was a partner in it. We were also in the process of working out a partnership agreement that everyone would be happy with. Tomorrow, Blue was starting us all on a training regimen that I was dreading, but I needed to do something about my expanding waistline.

For tonight, though, I was on my own. There was one thing I had left to do, and that was why I was standing on the rooftop of a certain thirty-story condo building, waiting for Dr. Chapman to exit the building. Darryl, my street contact, had been watching the building for the last couple of days. It seemed Dr. Chapman liked to hit a trendy bar around 11:00 p.m. each night to pick up ladies. I was hoping he would repeat that pattern tonight, as I wanted to have a word with him.

The good doctor's night wasn't going to go as he had planned. To start with, his shiny yellow Porsche 911 Turbo S seemed to have developed some electrical problems. Funny that you send a few thousand random volts of electricity through a car, and it tends to short everything out. They just don't make cars like they used to. I was willing to bet it was going to be a pretty penny to fix.

It was a beautiful night for February in Toronto. The temperature was just above freezing, which, compared to the double-digit negative temperatures we'd been having, seemed almost balmy. The sky was perfectly clear, making the stars pop out in the night sky.

I glanced at my watch, and it was just coming up on eleven o'clock. Right on schedule, Dr. Chapman wandered out of the building. I did so appreciate punctuality.

He raised his key fob, then frowned as nothing happened. I gathered my powers and sent a large gust of wind down under him, lifting him straight into the air like a rocket. I also dampened the sound around him, preventing his screams from waking the whole building.

Once he reached my level up on the roof, I tapered down on the wind and held him suspended in the air. I expanded the sound-dampening around both of us, and his screams reached my ears. His eyes widened as he saw me.

I couldn't resist using the line "What's up, Doc?"

"You … Oh God … Please … Let me down."

"You may want to be more specific—unless you have an ability to fly that I'm not aware of."

"Please put me down *slowly*," he pleaded.

"In a minute. We are going to have a little chat first. Your answers will determine how quickly you return to the ground, understand?"

He nodded frantically. "Please, anything! Please don't kill me!"

"After we visited your office, we were attacked by dark elves, followed by a Fire elemental who brought along some men armed with automatic weapons, and then a biker gang decided to start our day off by throwing a grenade through our window. This all happened due to a €5 million bounty that was put on the head of my young vampire friend, compliments of the French vampire court. Any ideas how that might have happened? And before you answer, this is one of those questions that will determine the velocity by which you return to the ground."

Dr. Chapman went even paler. "I didn't want to, but I had no choice. I work for the French vampire court. I am required to pass along any interesting information I come across to Giselle, or she will end me."

"Explain the hold she has over you."

"I did part of my medical studies in Paris and had a gambling problem. I got into debt with some bad people; Giselle bought up the debt. She had me act as the healer for the French court for a couple of years. After that, I asked to return to Toronto. She agreed, but I was to report anything I came across regarding Enhanced Individuals—or anything else that would be of interest to the French vampire court— to her."

This puzzled me, as a healer on staff in Paris surely would have been more use than an informant in Toronto, so I asked him about that.

"Giselle rules a part of Quebec, due to its historical ties to France. Giselle, and Henri before her, were always interested in ways to destabilize Canada to move it out from under Elizabeth's control and into theirs. They pumped money into the Quebec separatist movement and have spies and agents throughout Canada."

Interesting. If the French vampire court could pick up Canada, that would be a nice shift in power. It would strengthen them and weaken the English vampire court at the same time. I wondered how much Elizabeth knew about this.

"You said Giselle specifically bought up your debt and not the French vampire court?"

Chapman nodded. "Giselle ran the intelligence arm of the court under Henri. Even when she became the master of the French vampire court, she continued running the spy network. My debt is to her directly."

I hated that I had indirectly helped this worm, but maybe it was for the best. I said, "Well, congratulations, Doc. It seems like you are now a free man."

"What do you mean?"

"Giselle is dead. My companions and I killed her four days ago. It was the only way to get the contract off Olivia. Roman is now the master of the French vampire court. I get the impression than Giselle wasn't the 'sharing is caring' type of girl, and I would assume your debt died with her."

Chapman's eyes just about bugged out of his head at this, and I continued. "Going forward, you are going to respect patient confidentiality, and what is said in your office *stays* in your office. I will email you my contact information. On the off chance that someone from the French vampire court does contact you, you are to get ahold of me immediately. If this happens, I will arrange protection for you by the English vampire court. If I catch even the slightest whiff of you selling or spilling patient information, I will return and give you one short flying lesson you won't like, understand?"

"Yes, thank you. All I ever wanted to do was just be a healer. I won't mess up this second chance!" gushed Chapman.

"See that you don't. I took out my anger at you on your car's electrical system. I don't think you will be driving anywhere for the next couple of days. Be thankful—cars can be fixed."

I didn't wait for his reply and let the air holding him up go. He screamed as he plunged in free fall to the parking lot below. I waited until he was about twenty feet from the ground before I used the air to slow his descent, then placed him gently on his feet on the ground. I smiled as he dropped to his knees and kissed the concrete.

I called Blue and asked her to come pick me up. I could have flown home, but this was quicker, and she could take me to the lab first, as I had a craving for a Bacon and Egger ...

The End.